death wave

TOR BOOKS BY
Ben Bova

death wave

wave

Ben Bova

A TOM DOHERTY ASSOCIATES BOOK

New York

DEATH WAVE

Copyright © 2015 by Ben Bova

A Tor Book
Published by Tom Doherty Associates, LLC
175 Fifth Avenue
New York, NY 10010

www.tor-forge.com

Tor® is a registered trademark of Tom Doherty Associates, LLC.

Library of Congress Cataloging-in-Publication Data

Bova, Ben,
  Death wave / Ben Bova. — First edition.
      p.   cm.
  "A Tor Book."
  ISBN 978-0-7653-7950-4 (hardcover)
  ISBN 978-1-4668-6874-8 (e-book)
  I. Title.
  PS3552.O84D43 2015
  813'.54—dc23

                              2015023075

Our books may be purchased in bulk for promotional, educational, or business use. Please contact your local bookseller or the Macmillan Corporate and Premium Sales Department at (800) 221-7945, extension 5442, or by e-mail at MacmillanSpecial Markets@macmillan.com.

First Edition: November 2015

Printed in the United States of America

0   9   8   7   6   5   4   3   2   1

To Alan Macrae, who builds homes and
befriends writers

Everybody knows they are going to die, but no one really believes it.

—*Spalding Gray*

death
wave

RIO GRANDE GORGE

It was a bright, hot morning, a typical New Mexico high desert summer day with a stiff breeze blowing in from the mountains. But there was trouble in the air.

Acting Sergeant Hamilton Cree, New Mexico Highway Patrol, sat in his air-conditioned cruiser and watched the traffic piling up on U.S. 67. As ordered by the World Council security team, he had swung his cruiser to block the lane that entered the bridge over the Rio Grande Gorge and turned on his BRIDGE TEMPORARILY CLOSED sign. The words hung in midair over the roof of his cruiser, big enough to see twenty car lengths down the road.

Another cruiser was blocking access on the other side of the bridge.

Cree was nearing the age of twenty-three, the year in which his required public service would be ended and he could leave the Highway Patrol with a reasonably healthy pension. The big question in his mind was whether he should be content to live off the pension or try to find a job that brought in more income. If he did get a job, he knew, his pension would be cut off; if he ever lost the job, he'd be up the creek.

It was illegal to get married while working off his public service obligation. But would the pension be enough to support a wife and start a family?

One of the truck drivers sitting in the growing line of traffic was leaning out the window of his rig and hollering, his face getting red. With an unhappy sigh, Cree opened the door of his cruiser and stepped out into the baking heat. He had never been able to accustom himself to this high desert and its bone-dry climate. Even the wind felt like it was coming out of an oven.

Cree had been born in Louisiana, where the air was as soft and moist as a wet towel. Even in Nashville, where the family had moved to escape the greenhouse floods, summers were milder, gentler. Coming to New Mexico wasn't his idea; he'd been assigned there.

He was exactly six feet tall, or 1.828 meters in the government's files, lean as a fishing rod, with a longish face and sad brown eyes. His hair, trimmed to an official Highway Patrol buzz, was a light, sandy color.

"What the hell you idiots holding up traffic for?" the truck driver was hollering to no one in particular: just venting his anger at being delayed.

Walking slowly toward the truck, Cree mentally counted the few days remaining until he could take off the Highway Patrol uniform for the final time.

"What's your problem?" he called to the irate driver.

"Problem? I got a delivery to make and a schedule to keep and you pissants are blocking traffic. I don't see no accident or construction or nothing. What the hell's the big idea?"

Frowning to show he didn't like what was going on any more than the trucker did, Cree said, "It's the star traveler. He wants to show off the gorge to the woman he brought back to Earth with him."

"Star traveler?"

"Yeah. The guy who went to what's-its-name . . . New Earth, they call it."

"And he came back here to block traffic? That shits!"

With a shrug Cree said, "Just hang in there, buddy. Nothing you or I can do about it. Orders from 'way high above."

"It still shits!"

"Cool down, buddy. You can tell your bosses that you were delayed by an official government order."

"I ain't got no bosses. I'm not a fuckin' public service time-server, like you. I *own* this truck."

His brow wrinkling, Cree asked, "Then what're you doin' driving the rig? Ain't it automatic?"

"Yeah, it runs by itself. But the friggin' law says a human has to be present in the cab at all times, in case there's an emergency. Don't they teach you guys the law of the land?"

As a matter of fact, Cree remembered something about the so-called safety redundancy law; he had just never paid much attention to it. He'd never had to.

"So you just sit there while the truck drives itself?"

"That's right."

"Weird. Whattaya do with all that time?"

"Play computer games. Take new orders. Watch vids. Whatever."

"Porn?"

The trucker scowled at Cree. "Look, buster, I don't deliver on time, it comes outta my profits. Can'tcha let me through?"

"Nothing I can do about it," Cree said. "Sorry."

He turned and started walking back to his cruiser, leaving the trucker to boil in his own angry juices.

And he realized that there really was nothing he could do about it. Nothing he could do about almost anything. He'd been assigned to the public service program as soon as he'd finished high school. The psych people sitting behind their desks gave him a battery of tests, then sent him to a training center where he was taught how to be a police officer.

The public service program was for guys like him, Cree understood. Women too. Youngsters who had no prospects for a real job, not with robots doing most of the labor. You went into a clothing store or a food market or even a bar and there were robots politely and efficiently doing the work.

So they assigned you to public service, and you took what they gave you. Or else you went into the labor pool and sat around doing nothing, at minimum wage. Cree figured being a cop was better than being a bum.

But not for much longer.

He ducked back into the cool comfort of his cruiser and slammed its door shut. Out on the bridge he could see this guy and a gal walking slowly across the pavement. From this distance she looked like a regular woman, even though she was an alien from New Earth. Not a care in the world, either of them. The bridge had been cleared for them. Traffic stopped. Not even pedestrians allowed on the bridge. Nearly a dozen World Council security spooks standing around at both ends of the bridge, as if we can't handle the job by ourselves. Just so they can see the gorge without being bothered by traffic or other people.

Then a new thought struck him. Maybe the World Council people are afraid he's brought back some kind of virus from New Earth. Or his woman's carrying a bug and they don't want anybody to catch it.

Naw, he told himself. They would never have let them out of quarantine if they were worried about that. Would they?

From somewhere far back in the line of waiting traffic somebody honked his horn.

Yeah, Cree thought. That's gonna do you a lot of good.

A star traveler. He gets all kinds of special treatment, and what do we get? Five years of mandatory public service and then you're out on your own, sink or swim. Live on the pension they give you or find a job someplace that a robot hasn't already taken. Try to find a wife and have some kids.

Must be nice to be a star traveler.

Jordan Kell

+++

Jordan Kell felt uneasy as the world council security team quietly, politely, efficiently moved all the tourists and sightseers off the bridge. At either end of the span, New Mexico Highway Patrol cars were blocking access to the bridge. Cars, buses, and big, lumbering cargo trailers were piling up on the roadway in lengthening, simmering lines.

Above the Highway Patrol cruisers giant holographic signs warned:

BRIDGE TEMPORARILY CLOSED

Jordan could see one of the truckers leaning out of his cab, arguing unhappily with one of the troopers. More cars and other trucks were coming up the road and stopping beneath the bright New Mexico sun.

Squinting up at the cloudless turquoise sky, Jordan thought, Our Sun isn't as hot as Sirius, but it's still scorching enough to start tempers boiling.

He turned to Aditi, his wife, whom he had brought back from Sirius. With an unhappy sigh, he told her, "We'd better cut this visit short."

Jordan Kell was a lean welterweight of a man, handsome in a distinguished way with strong cheekbones, thick silver hair carefully groomed, his equally silver mustache trim and graceful, his

steel-gray eyes still capable of sparkling humor, despite everything.
He wore a short-sleeved white shirt with dark slacks and comfortable suede shoes.

Aditi was from New Earth, the solitary planet circling the star
Sirius. Fully human, she was slightly taller than Jordan's shoulder,
slim and youthful, with a pert nose, short-clipped hair as red as au-
tumn leaves, and alert, intelligent brown eyes. She wore a simple
sleeveless short-skirted dress of pale green.

She was a trifle more than thirty years old. He was nearing his
two hundred and twentieth birthday. One hundred and sixty of
those years he had spent in cryonic suspension, aboard the spacecraft that had carried him and eleven other men and women across
eight light-years to the star Sirius and its one planet, and then back
to Earth again. Physically, somatically, Jordan Kell was not yet
sixty. He still had the strength and skill to play tennis, sail a racing yacht, compete in a fencing tournament—if he had the time or
the inclination.

Aditi asked, "Cut our visit short?"

Forcing a smile, he said to her, "They're giving us a private view-
ing, keeping everybody else away from us."

Aditi smiled back. "You are an important person, Jordan."

He cocked his head slightly to one side. "It seems . . . unfair,
somehow."

"You are displeased?"

"They're treating us like royalty, keeping us separated from the
crowd, the common people."

"We've seen plenty of people," Aditi countered. "The interviews,
the news broadcasts . . ."

"All carefully controlled by the World Council's managers. I
wanted to show you our world, our people, but they're keeping us
in a cocoon."

"It's a very pleasant cocoon," she said, a smile dimpling her
cheeks. "Very comfortable."

"Yes, I suppose so." Still, he felt dissatisfied.

Aditi said, "You promised to show me the gorge."

"Yes, I did, didn't I?" He took Aditi by the hand and together they walked out onto the bridge.

It was just as Jordan Kell remembered it—almost.

Leaning against the bridge's anti-suicide fence, he looked down. Far below, the river still cut its way through the cliffs as it had for millions of years. The faithful sun still beamed its warmth across the desert scrubland that stretched to the horizon in every direction.

But where once sagebrush had perfumed the summer air, and at dusk elk would amble through, browsing, while prairie dogs would pop out of their snug burrows to forage among their antlered neighbors, now the land was covered with the white domes of prefabricated homes and bare concrete streets that formed a grid among them. A new city was growing on land that had once been held in trust by the Bureau of Land Management.

Suddenly a hawk plunged down from behind him and dove deep into the gorge before swooping up again and heading for the sky. Jordan felt his heart sing.

Turning to Aditi, Jordan said, "This is one of my favorite places on Earth."

The glare-blocking contact lenses she wore had turned dark, yet he saw the question in her eyes. Pointing down into the gorge, Aditi said, "There's certainly nothing like this on New Earth."

"Your Predecessors built New Earth," Jordan replied. "This old Earth has been shaped by natural forces, over billions of years."

She arched a brow at him. "It seems to me that you humans have done your share of changing your planet."

"True enough," Jordan admitted ruefully. "True enough."

He looked out at the growing city of gleaming white solar-powered homes. They were being built for the tide of refugees displaced by the global climate shift. To Jordan they looked like an invading alien army that had come to claim the once-inviolate emptiness.

Leaning over the bridge's rail again, he stared down into the gorge and at the river glittering far below. Nearly two hundred years had passed since he'd last been at this spot, Jordan told himself. So much had happened. So much was changing.

Jordan smiled down at the river. Sadly. Despite the climate shifts that had drowned seacoasts and flooded cities all over the world, despite the new towns built for the refugees, the Rio Grande still flowed its age-old course from the mountains to the distant Gulf of Mexico—which had grown into an inland sea that was threatening to split North America in two.

Age cannot wither her, Jordan quoted to himself, nor custom stale her infinite variety. Not so, he realized. Even the Rio Grande would soon be changed to suit the needs of the people driven from their homes, their lives, by the greenhouse floods. They're going to divert the river to provide aqueducts and drinking water for the newly built cities, so that the newcomers can water the lawns they were going to plant and flush their toilets.

With a shake of his head, Jordan straightened and turned to his wife.

"Seen enough?" he asked.

"I suppose so."

"Let's go, then." Eyeing the growing line of stopped traffic, he added, "Before things turn ugly."

As if in answer, a car horn bleated angrily from down the line.

With Aditi at his side he started walking back to his car—and his responsibilities. He had traveled to a planet circling another star to find her and rebuild his life. Now he had returned to Earth to tell the people of his birthworld that there were other intelligent creatures scattered among the stars. And that they all faced an implacable wave of death sweeping through the stars toward them.

Jordan turned to one of the security agents that walked a respectful few meters from him and Aditi. "Let's get to the airport; we've caused enough bad feelings here."

The young man—trim, athletic, wearing an off-white summer-weight jacket and tan chinos—glanced at the line of waiting vehicles. "You're an important person, Mr. Kell. They can wait until you're ready to go."

"I'm sure each one of them feels that he's important, too."

The security officer shrugged and said, "Yeah, maybe so." Then he sprinted ahead and opened the door of the unmarked sedan they were approaching.

Jordan stopped at the parked car and looked up into the bright, cloudless sky. He knew that death was racing toward planet Earth at the speed of light.

How did it come to this? he asked himself. How can I save them all?

barcelona

Anita Halleck watched Jordan Kell's impulsive visit to the Rio Grande Gorge from her office in the palatial headquarters of the world government.

Alone in the imposing office, she leaned back in her sculpted desk chair and stared intently at the three-dimensional viewer built into the opposite wall.

The satellite cameras showed the man and his alien woman clearly enough, and the smoothly competent team of security men and women escorting them.

Why did Kell want to see this particular place? she asked herself. Not merely view it holographically, but actually, physically go there. With the woman. What's he up to?

Halleck had taken pains to ensure that Jordan Kell and his alien wife were insulated from the world's news media. Everything about the returning interstellar explorers was carefully controlled. They were guarded night and day, protected from the prying eyes and excitable voices of the news media. And the ignorant public. Already there were fanatics babbling their fears of an alien invasion.

And there was Kell, strolling like a stupid tourist through the rough semi-desert country baking under the cloudless sunshine of New Mexico. He seemed to be searching for something as he peered down from the bridge into the river, which glinted in the sun as it surged between the rock walls of the gorge it had carved.

What's he after? Halleck asked herself again. He's scheduled to report to the Council here tomorrow, and he's off daydreaming in some miserable scrubland. He certainly doesn't appear to be troubled by this message of death he claims to be bringing back from Sirius.

And the woman, this alien from Sirius. She definitely looks human. He claims she's as human as any one of us. But how can that be true? She's from another world, circling a different star. He's fallen in love with her, and love can make the most intelligent man behave like a fool.

Like Jordan Kell, Anita Halleck had been born more than two centuries earlier. Unlike Kell, she had spent all her years awake and active—except for the few months she had been dead.

Killed in the crash of a rocket hopper craft on the Moon, Halleck had been saved and restored to life by the medical miracle of nanotherapy. Her body was filled with virus-sized nanomachines that repaired her mangled organs, knitted her broken bones, and guarded her against infections like an almost-intelligent immune system.

Nanotechnology was totally banned on Earth. While lunar communities such as Selene depended on nanotechnology for their very survival on the airless Moon, the people of Earth—some twenty billion of them—feared the possibility of nanomachines gone wild, devouring everything in their path like an unstoppable wave of mindless destruction.

Truth to tell, there were plenty of criminals and fanatics and out-and-out lunatics among those twenty billion who would unleash a nanomachine plague for profit or passion or merely the insane notoriety of slaughtering millions. When Anita Halleck recovered from her temporary death, she learned that the nanotech ban meant she could never return to the world of her birth.

It was Douglas Stavenger, the founder and mastermind of the lunar nation Selene, who convinced Halleck to use her brains and drive in politics. Earth had been hit by a second wave of greenhouse warming, the Greenland and Antarctic ice caps were melting down, coastal cities all across the globe were being flooded, millions of refugees sought shelter, food, hope.

Bright and determined (some said to the point of ruthlessness), Halleck became a force in Earth's tempestuous politics. From Selene, on the Moon, she fought her way to the top of the world government.

And on the day she was installed as chairperson of the governing council, she pushed through a special exemption to the antinanotech laws. Anita Halleck would be allowed to live and work on Earth. No one dared gainsay her return to the world of her birth.

Tall and youthful despite her years, thanks to the nanomachines teeming inside her, Halleck was as slim-waisted and smooth-skinned as a thirty-year-old. She presided over Earth's painful recovery from the greenhouse flooding. As Greenland and Antarctica melted away, as climate patterns across the world changed drastically and sea levels rose catastrophically, Anita Halleck harnessed Earth's resources and technologies to feed, house, educate, and build new lives for the hundreds of millions driven from their homes by the relentless floods.

One of her achievements was a global engineering program to save as many cities as possible from the rising sea level. Dams and weir systems rose like medieval fortifications to protect major cities, the world capital of Barcelona among them.

Earth's geography changed, but the people of Earth—helped by their own skills and resources, plus the generous aid from human communities spread halfway across the solar system—managed to stabilize their civilization and survive the worst crisis in human history.

Then came the realization that Greenland's melting ice cap was pouring torrents of cold fresh water into the North Atlantic Ocean, threatening to cut off the Gulf Stream that warmed Western Europe. Soon the climate of the British Isles and much of Europe would be plunged into Siberian cold and desolation. Every effort must be made to dam up the melting waters, including their under-ground flow.

The World Council faced another global challenge of frighten-ing proportions. Halleck led the massive geoengineering project to meet this new challenge.

And on top of that Jordan Kell and his companions returned from New Earth, with this alien woman and a warning of a still-deadlier catastrophe rushing through interstellar space to destroy everything.

albuquerque

slouching back on the sofa of his basement studio apartment, Hamilton Cree sipped on an energy drink as he watched a rerun of last year's world cup finals on his wall screen.

It had been a long, frustrating day. First the traffic detail up north of Taos, then a raid on a drug house in Española, and finally the long drive home to Albuquerque.

The drug raid had been a farce: a half-dozen pimply kids cooking up some recreational junk in the kitchen of one of the new prefabs that had been set up for the flood refugees. City kids, from back east, snotty and yelling about their constitutional rights. Thought they'd masked all the surveillance sensors in their miserable little government-furnished house.

The robots burst into their hangout and tranked them while Cree and the other live officers waited outside and watched on the remote cameras. Drones circling overhead, the whole nine yards, just to bust some teenagers who had nothing better to do.

His phone buzzed. Almost glad of the interruption, Cree saw on the ID screen that it was his brother, from Nashville. He told the phone to put the call on the wall screen. He'd thought about getting a 3-D viewer, but decided to save the money and stick with the flat screen.

Brother Jefferson was eleven years older than Hamilton, but he still looked like a kid: he could afford rejuve treatments.

"What's happening, Hambone?" asked Jeff, with his vid-star smile.

Hamilton hated his childhood nickname. Wearily he replied, "Same old shit."

Jeff was the oldest of the family's four boys and he had a real job as a bank supervisor in Nashville. Plus a wife and two kids of his own, a girl and a boy.

"Got a promotion," Jeff said brightly.

"Yeah?"

"Yeah. I'm gonna be manager of our branch office in Hendersonville."

"Good for you, Jeff."

For the next half hour Hamilton listened with a growing mixture of envy and resentment as Jeff bragged about his latest step toward a happy retirement.

At last Jeff asked, "So what about you? Still guarding the highways of New Mexico?"

"Not for much longer," Hamilton said, feeling the way he had when the school year was nearing its end.

"Anything interesting?" Jeff prodded.

So Hamilton told him about the star traveler. "Held up traffic for more'n half an hour, just so he and his alien gal could see the gorge."

Jeff seemed impressed. "He's been to another star. He's met aliens."

"She looks pretty human."

"They claim the New Earth people are just as human as we are," Jeff said. "But I don't see how. They're aliens. Aliens aren't human."

"I guess."

"You know, Hank's working in Chicago now, for the firm that sells those energy screens."

"He is?"

"Yep. He's going to send me one to put in my car. Like an airbag, only it's stronger and protects the whole insides of the car, even if it's totaled."

"The energy screens are alien technology."

"That's right. One of the star travelers opened his own company to sell 'em. He's rich!"

"From alien technology," Hamilton muttered.

The brothers chatted for a few minutes more, then Jefferson said, "Gotta go now. Dinner bell's ringing."

"Okay. Say hello to Gina for me."

"Sure. Whyn't you come over here sometime and see us? The kids'd love to see their Uncle Hambone."

Hamilton forced a grin. "Sure. Soon's I get the chance. Got a three-day weekend coming up; maybe then."

"Good. See ya then."

"Yeah."

Hamilton cut the connection and the wall screen went back to the World Cup. He leaned back on the sofa once more, thinking, Those damned star travelers. They get rich, they get to block traffic, they make us feel like little insects.

But he didn't really feel like an insect. He felt like a man, a man who had somehow been left behind. A man who was filled with a growing, simmering resentment.

Once-sleepy Taos was booming, thanks to the government housing construction that was changing the face of the desert. The city's airport was expanding to accommodate the loads of materials and construction workers being ferried in daily from all across the country. Jumpjet cargo carriers lowered themselves on roaring streams of hot exhaust gases along the airfield's perimeter aprons, while bigger jetliners bored in to land on the newly extended runways, then raised their hinged noses to allow trucks full of men and materials to trundle out.

Rocketplanes were still fairly rare at the Taos airport, but the security people who escorted Jordan Kell and his wife had requisitioned one for them. Local workers and travelers gaped at the sleek, swept-wing craft as it took off like an ordinary airplane, then fired its rocket engines to arrow it high above the atmosphere. In little more than a half hour the plane was gliding in for a landing at Chicago's sprawling Banks Aerospaceport.

A blank-faced team of World Council security agents guided them to an unmarked door. Outside, a sleek, low-slung limousine was waiting for Jordan and Aditi, with still more security people positioned around it. The two of them ducked inside, and the limo pulled away from the curb.

It was an air-cushion vehicle, and Jordan felt some alarm when the driver accelerated past the teeming highway traffic in a special lane reserved for government and emergency vehicles.

The security woman driving for them seemed as happy as a fighter jock as she blasted past the wheeled cars at blurring speed. Jordan saw that there were separate lanes for private automobiles, and still others for trucks and buses.

"We don't touch the roadway," their driver was bragging. "Wheels up, jets blasting, and away we go straight downtown, past all these dawdlers!"

Jordan wondered what would happen if a private car tried to cut into the restricted government lane. Can't happen, he told himself. Those private vehicles are controlled by the traffic management system: everything kept safe and orderly. Humans don't drive their own vehicles anymore—except for this speed-happy would-be jet jockey.

There were no safety belts. The driver assured them that they weren't needed. "This car's equipped with energy screens that'll protect you from anything," she assured her passengers.

"Really?" asked Jordan. He pushed both hands into the seemingly empty air in front of him and, sure enough, felt a slightly spongy resistance.

"Even a full-speed head-on collision!" the driver enthused.

Trying to put the picture of a high-speed crash out of his mind, Jordan turned to Aditi, who was sitting beside him, looking equally tense.

"It'll be good to see Mitch again."

"Yes," she agreed, her eyes flicking at the cars they were passing. "And Paul."

Mitchell Thornberry and Paul Longyear were the only others who had returned from New Earth with Jordan and Aditi. Jordan's brother, Brandon, and the rest of the eleven scientists had elected to remain and continue their studies of the world that had been constructed by aliens to resemble Earth almost exactly, and peopled with humanlike beings.

Thornberry was a thoroughly Irish robotics engineer, Long-year a Native American biologist. Both had been staggered by what they'd found and learned on the alien-built planet circling the star Sirius. Back on Earth, though, Thornberry had accepted his round-the-clock security detail as a status symbol he had earned; Longyear found it oppressive and fled to the reservation in North Dakota where he'd been born, as far from cities and prying eyes as he could get.

A pair of security agents, wearing dark jackets over white turtleneck shirts, were waiting for them when they pulled up the driveway of the New Ritz Carlton Hotel. Though the hotel was more than two centuries old, its façade looked unchanged to Jordan. The lobby was still an elegant, understated work of art, with a completely automated registration desk, together with a smaller desk manned by human receptionists, for the old-fashioned. Human-form robot bellmen stood in a silent row, ready to carry luggage without expecting a tip.

Still more World Council security agents smoothly whisked Jordan and Aditi up to the hotel suite reserved for them, where they changed for dinner: from the travel bags waiting for them. Jordan pulled on a light blue suit, with a silver and turquoise bolo tie at his throat; Aditi chose a softly flowing dress of coral that complemented her auburn hair nicely.

The security team waiting in the hallway led Jordan and Aditi to a private dining room that the World Council had reserved for this little reunion, then stayed discreetly outside. The walls of the room were comfortably decorated with three-dimensional digital viewers that were programmed to show picturesque scenes from many spots on Earth, plus views from the Moon and planets, as well as art displays from the world's most prestigious museums, public and private.

Thornberry himself was standing by the side table laden with bottles and finger foods as Jordan and Aditi stepped in. He was a solidly built man, just about Jordan's own height but thicker, heavier in the torso and limbs. The quizzical little smile that had once lit his face was gone now, replaced by a more sober, almost puzzled expression.

"Ah, there you are!" Thornberry said heartily as he turned to greet them.

Jordan blinked at the man. On New Earth, Mitch had always worn comfortable, casual clothes—almost to the point of sloppiness. Now he was wearing a perfectly fitted plum-colored velour jacket, precisely pressed white slacks, and a crisp pale blue long-sleeved shirt.

As he grasped Thornberry's extended hand, Jordan said, "Mitch, you're a fashion plate."

"It's these adaptable fabrics, don't ya know. They adjust to fit you. Make anybody look good."

"Well, you look like a million international dollars."

"Make it a hundred million," Thornberry said, his beefy face smiling broadly. "More like three hundred million, in fact."

"You are a wealthy man?" asked Aditi.

"Thanks to you, m'dear. And your technology. Those grand and lovely energy screens your people invented. I filed a patent application for 'em as soon as we started back for Earth, don't you know. By the time we got home I was *rich*! No more academic life for me. B'god, university presidents are coming to *me* to beg for money!"

Jordan laughed.

"You know, they're using energy screens to dome over whole cities to protect 'em from the weather," Thornberry nattered on. "And reinforcing dams and levees. We're even working on developing 'em for propulsion!"

Jordan said, "I had no idea."

"It's been a busy three weeks, let me tell you," said Thornberry. "Imagine me, a wealthy nob."

"Has it been only three weeks since we returned?" Jordan mused. "It seems much longer."

"Three weeks tomorrow," Thornberry confirmed.

Nodding, Jordan said, "The World Council meeting is tomorrow morning."

"That it is," said Thornberry, sobering. He gestured toward the dining table. "Come on now, let's eat. Or would you rather have a drink first?"

"A little sherry. Amontillado, if they have it." Turning to Aditi, Jordan joked, "I haven't had a sip of amontillado in more than a hundred and fifty years."

"Paul's not here yet," Aditi pointed out.

"He can't make it," said Thornberry. "Some sort of family commitment. It'll be just the three of us."

Jordan felt his brows knit. With his Native American heritage, Paul Longyear had been especially sensitive about meeting an alien race. Despite all that Aditi's people could do, the biologist remained suspicious of their motives. And once he had returned to Earth, the constant security bodyguards of the World Council had unnerved him.

"Too bad. I was looking forward to seeing him again," Jordan said.

"You'll have to settle for just me."

"Good enough," said Jordan.

Dinner was exceptionally delicious, Jordan thought. Fine wine and excellent food. Robot waiters catered to their every whim. Yet the world beyond their dining room weighed on Jordan.

"The entire planet's geography has changed," he commented between bites of roast lamb.

"That it has," said Thornberry. "Sea level's still rising."

Shaking his head, Jordan murmured, "I thought they had stabilized the global climate."

"So did everybody. Fusion energy finally replaced fossil fuels." Thornberry's beefy face darkened into a scowl. "But it was already too late. The Greenland and Antarctic ice caps are melting down. Nothing we can do to stop 'em. Too much heat stored in the oceans."

Aditi glanced back and forth at their somber expressions. Trying to brighten things, she suggested, "Perhaps we should go to North Dakota to visit Paul."

"Perhaps," Jordan conceded.

"I'm not sure he'd want to be visited," said Thornberry. "All this security the World Council has attached to us has upset him."

"It is rather unnerving," said Jordan, "having these security people surrounding us wherever we go."

Thornberry's beefy face broke into a smile. "It's not that bad." Gesturing to the room around them, he said, "This is a lot grander than sitting in the public dining room, don't you think?"

"You're getting spoiled," Jordan half-joked.

"We're important people, Jordan, m'lad. And you, Aditi, you're an alien from another star. Of course they're guarding us, protecting us."

Jordan nodded. But he said, "It's still rather unsettling."

As dessert was being served, their conversation finally turned to the next day's meeting.

His face utterly serious, Thornberry asked, "You're going to tell them about the death wave?"

"They already know. It's all in the report I submitted to the Council."

Waving a thick-fingered hand, Thornberry warned, "Ahh, they're politicians. They don't read, they have aides do their reading for them."

Jordan looked into his friend's sky-blue eyes and saw a great sadness there. "You don't think they'll act?"

"On a threat that's two thousand years away? Get real, Jordan. They'll put it off, sweep it under the rug, kick the can down the road and hope it gets lost."

Aditi spoke up. "But there are other intelligent species much closer to the death wave. We've got to help them."

Thornberry huffed. "Don't count on it, m'dear. Don't count on politicians rising to the challenge."

World Council Headquarters

Twenty-one men and women sat around the council table, representing every power group on Earth and beyond. They made a colorful lot, some wearing western suits and dresses, others in Eastern saris and robes, kimonos, caftans, even one woman in a flowered sarong. Hardly a gray hair among them; they were all youthful and vigorous, no matter what their ages, thanks to rejuvenation therapies.

Three of the members were not physically present, but joined the meeting as holographic images. Douglas Stavenger, of the lunar nation of Selene, was the more prominent of them. He had served two ten-year terms as chairman of the Council. Seated beside him, also in holographic representation, was George Ambrose, the oversized, red-thatched leader of the rock rats—that loose coalition of miners and explorers scattered through the Asteroid Belt. On Stavenger's other side sat the representative from the habitat in orbit around the planet Saturn.

Like Stavenger, Ambrose and the delegate from Saturn were on the Moon. It took nearly three seconds for electronic signals to go from Earth to the Moon and back again. That was awkward, but bearable. It took upwards of a full hour for signals to reach the Belt and return, and more than twice as long to span the distance to Saturn. That made real-time conversations impossible, so Ambrose and the woman from Saturn traveled to the Moon for Council meetings.

Anita Halleck sat at the head of the long, polished table and watched her fellow World Council members chatting and gesticulating among themselves. Like monkeys, she thought. Jabbering monkeys.

The digital clock on the screen built into the tabletop before her showed exactly three P.M. Halleck tapped her manicured fingernail on the gleaming surface only once; their talking stopped immediately. All heads turned to her.

"I'm glad that you all could attend this meeting," she began, her voice a warm contralto. "We have before us only one agenda item: the report from the head of our expedition to Sirius C."

"New Earth," added the representative from Sub-Saharan Africa, in a deep-chested rumble.

"Yes," said Halleck, without smiling. "The so-called New Earth."

Pressing a pad on the keyboard beneath her tabletop screen, Halleck looked toward the double doors at the head of the room as she said, "Please welcome the leader of our Sirius expedition, Mr. Jordan Kell."

Everyone around the table turned as the double doors swung silently open and Jordan stepped through. He was wearing a collarless navy blue blazer and light gray slacks. And holding the hand of his slim, lovely, red-haired young wife, who wore a simple knee-length frock of golden yellow.

The entire Council rose to its feet as Jordan and Aditi walked the length of the table and stopped at the two empty chairs on Halleck's right. No applause, not a word from any Council member, but their hushed respect for Jordan Kell—and their curiosity about his wife—was palpable.

Everyone sat down except Kell, Aditi, and Halleck.

"Mr. Kell," said Halleck, "we have all read your report, of course, but the entire World Council is eager to hear what you have to say."

Jordan made a stiff little bow. Halleck sat down, but Jordan clutched Aditi's hand and kept her standing beside him. He scanned the long table. They know the facts, he told himself. Now to make them understand the realities.

"To begin with, I would like to introduce to you my wife, Aditi. She is a native of New Earth."

That caused a stir up and down the table.

Aditi smiled politely and Jordan released her hand. She took her seat.

Jordan hesitated a moment, then went on, "Aditi is as human as you and I. She—and the other people of New Earth—were created from DNA samples taken from people of Earth."

"Then it's true!" snapped a middle-aged Asian from halfway down the table. "We *have* been visited by aliens."

Almost apologetically, Jordan replied, "Oh yes, the basis for all those UFO stories over the years is indeed true, although some of the stories have been exaggerated rather wildly. But the fact is that aliens have been visiting Earth for centuries and have taken tissue samples from humans, plants, and animals. That's how they created the biosphere of New Earth."

"These aliens were machines, not people?"

With a nod, Jordan said, "The people of New Earth call them their Predecessors: machine intelligences that are millions of years old."

"And they constructed the planet we call New Earth?"

"Yes. They have been studying Earth for ages, and decided to construct a world that was almost exactly like our own. Their reasoning was that once we attained spaceflight technology, we'd be curious enough to go to Sirius to see what the planet was all about."

"Fantastic."

"Unbelievable."

"Incredible."

Halleck cut through their astonished comments. "The question is: *Why* did they go to such trouble? Why not merely come to Earth and show themselves to us?"

With a glance at Aditi, Jordan answered, "As I said, they have studied us for centuries. They realized that we are rather paranoid and xenophobic, prone to violence."

"That was all in the past," said a woman in the saffron robes of a Buddhist monk. "We have learned to overcome such instincts."

"Have we? Within our own lifetimes we've seen nuclear conflicts and biowars nearly depopulate whole continents. To say nothing of the fighting in the Asteroid Belt."

"But that was more than two hundred years ago," the woman argued. "We have found the way to peace."

"And the World Council enforces it," said Halleck.

"Yet those instincts for violence—especially against strangers—are still inside us," said one of the Europeans. "Two centuries of relative peace have not changed us into angels."

"That's why the inhabitants of New Earth were frightened of us," said Jordan.

"*They* were frightened of *us*? That's hard to believe."

"Believe it," Jordan said. "They wanted to contact us—they felt they *had* to contact us. But they were very worried that our reaction to contact would be violent."

Halleck objected. "With their superior technology, they feared we'd be violent? Why, they could wipe this planet clean of all life, if they chose to, couldn't they?"

"Perhaps," Jordan conceded. "But their mission—their very reason for existence—is to save intelligent life wherever they find it, not to destroy it."

"That's what they told you. But suppose it isn't true?" asked the woman in the sarong. "What if they've come here to conquer us? To overwhelm us?"

Jordan smiled sadly. "If they have, they're going about it in a strange way. They've given us new technology: the energy screens, biomedical advances beyond anything we have been able to do for ourselves—"

Halleck interrupted. "But they haven't told you how they can travel faster than light, have they?"

the death wave

Jordan stared down at Halleck, seated beside him.

"Faster than light? That's impossible. Nothing in the universe can travel faster than light."

One of the Europeans, short, stocky, swarthy, with a thick shock of jet-black hair, wearing a dark, slightly rumpled business suit, lumbered to his feet.

"I am an astrophysicist . . . or, at least, I was an astrophysicist before I was appointed to membership in this council."

A wave of rueful chuckles spread around the table. Most of the Council members had stepped away from careers in business or science or academia to take on the responsibilities of the World Council. While it was possible to run for Council membership in an open election, most Council members were selected by a computer-directed lottery; to refuse the honor was not permitted, except under the most exigent circumstances. Hardly any of the Council members had been professional politicians, although that is what they had inevitably become. And their staffs had plenty of lifetime politicians working behind the scenes.

Halleck said, "Professor Rudaki. Your daughter is still on New Earth, isn't she?"

With a blunt nod, Rudaki answered, "Yes. My Elyse is studying the white dwarf star, Sirius B."

"The Pup," Halleck murmured. Jordan thought she did it to show that she was not entirely ignorant of astronomical jargon.

Rudaki ignored it. To Jordan, he said, "While Einstein showed that no body containing mass can exceed the velocity of light, there is no such restriction for information."

Jordan knew where he was heading.

Jabbing a stubby finger in Jordan's direction, the astrophysicist continued, "You tell us that these aliens of New Earth have warned that a wave of intense gamma radiation is heading toward us."

"Yes, the result of a massive gamma burst in the core of the Milky Way nearly thirty thousand years ago."

"The front of this wave is two thousand light-years away, from us."

"And heading toward us at the speed of light."

"How do the aliens know of this?"

"They've observed it," Jordan replied. "From planets closer to the core of the galaxy, where the explosion occurred."

"Exactly. And if this wave destroys all life, who would be left alive to report on it?"

"The death wave destroys all *organic* life. But the aliens who observed it were not organic. They were intelligent machines."

"Intelligent machines," Halleck muttered.

Aditi spoke up. "Our Predecessors. They created New Earth and my people. They have visited your Earth many times."

"I find that hard to believe," one of the other Council members challenged. "Our best robots are hardly what I would call intelligent. They have no self-awareness, no . . . no divine spark."

"We're not here to debate philosophy," snapped the woman sitting beside him.

Aditi explained, "Organic life is finite. All organic species become extinct, sooner or later. But some intelligent organic species develop inorganic intelligence. Machine intelligence can be virtually immortal."

Silence fell around the table.

"Machine intelligence has superseded organic intelligence in many parts of the universe," Jordan explained. "One day, I suppose, intelligent, self-maintaining machines will become our descendants."

For long moments no one spoke a word. Then Rudaki shook his head and said, "You don't understand. I don't care if they were intelligent machines or intellectual rocks."

"Then what—"

Rudaki asked, "How can their observations of the gamma wave get here before the wave itself does? How can the *information* travel faster than the wave itself?"

Jordan saw perplexed looks on the faces of most of the Council members.

His brow furrowing, the astrophysicist explained, "Observers ten thousand light-years closer to the core of the Milky Way observe the gamma wave, yes? Their information of that phenomenon should take ten thousand years to reach us here, if their communications are limited to the speed of light, as ours are."

Halleck understood. "You're saying that the aliens must have some form of communication that moves information faster than light."

"Yes," Rudaki said emphatically. Looking at Jordan, he asked, "What have they told you about their communications technology?"

"Not very much," Jordan admitted.

"Not much?"

Feeling embarrassed, little short of dim-witted, Jordan said, "The question barely came up. Even your daughter didn't delve into it very deeply. There was so much else to do, to discover . . ."

Halleck looked at Aditi. "What can you tell us about your communications technology?"

Aditi shrugged. "Very little, I'm afraid. I'm not trained in that area. But I can ask our leaders back on New Earth about it."

"And wait sixteen years to get their answer," grumbled one of the councilmen from down the table.

"Oh no," Aditi said. "It should only take an hour or so."

That sent a shock wave through the conference room.

"Then you *do* have access to faster-than-light communications!" Halleck snapped.

Her facial expression somewhere between surprised and wounded, Aditi replied, "Yes, of course."

"You can communicate with Adri, back on New Earth?" Jordan asked.

Nodding slowly, Aditi said, "When I have to."

The holographic image of George Ambrose ran a hand through his shaggy red mane. "That means I can attend these bloody meetings from Ceres, 'stead of riding clear to the Moon for 'em."

"We could link the entire solar system into a single human community!" marveled one of the Council members.

With a thin smile, Halleck mused, "We can turn this council into a truly effective government for the whole solar system."

"Now wait," warned Stavenger's hologram. "Selene is a free nation. We attend these Council meetings as an independent entity."

Jordan saw the dreams of power and control in the eyes of most of the men and women around the table, especially Halleck's. And he realized that Aditi saw it, too. She looked shocked, crestfallen.

"Virtually instantaneous communications," Halleck purred. "This could open an entirely new era for the human race."

"Wait," Jordan said, raising his voice to silence the buzz going around the table. "We still have to decide what to do about the death wave."

"That's not going to be a problem for two thousand years, Jordan," said Halleck. "We have more immediate priorities to deal with."

"Damming up the meltwater flow from Greenland is our first priority," said one of the councilmen.

"But there are planets that will be engulfed in the death wave much sooner," Jordan urged. "We've got to help them. If we don't, whole civilizations will be annihilated."

"All in good time," Halleck said. "First things first."

FiRSt thiNGS FiRSt

Jordan felt terribly weary by the time he and Aditi returned to their hotel suite, across the public square from Barcelona's fourteenth-century Gothic cathedral.

"I hadn't expected that," he admitted as he dropped onto the handsomely striped sofa in their sitting room.

Aditi stood uncertainly in the middle of the big, carpeted room. Late-afternoon sunshine was pouring through the windows, although the noise from the busy streets below was completely blocked by the acoustical oscillators mounted on every window in the hotel.

"Did I do the wrong thing?" she asked. "Should I have kept silent about our communications capability?"

Jordan smiled up at her and patted the cushion next to him. "No, you were perfectly correct," he said as she sat down beside him. "Never lie or try to hide the truth. Rudaki had it figured out already. If you hadn't been completely open and honest it would have raised a lot of suspicions among the Council."

"Chairwoman Halleck seemed to pounce on the idea."

Jordan sighed. "She sees power in it."

"How shortsighted," said Aditi. "How sad."

Jordan looked into her troubled eyes. "Can you really communicate with Adri in real time?"

"Almost real time."

"The equipment . . . ?"

Aditi tapped her curly auburn hair. "It's in here. Installed when I . . ." She hesitated. "Installed before birth."

Jordan nodded. He understood what she meant. Aditi and the others of New Earth had been gestated in artificial wombs, like the biovats human agro-engineers used to cultivate meat.

"Have you been in contact with Adri?"

"Now and then."

"Could you contact him now?"

"Yes, of course. It might take a few hours, though."

He smiled wanly. "That's better than eight years, one way."

Aditi smiled back at him, then sat primly on the sofa beside Jordan and closed her eyes. After a few moments, she opened them again and said, "I've sent Adri our entire meeting with the World Council."

"Just like that?" he marveled.

A little apologetically, Aditi replied, "It's given me something of a headache, I'm afraid."

Jordan reached for her hand. "Perhaps a little fresh air is what you need."

They went for a stroll on Las Ramblas, a collection of streets lined with shops and restaurants and theaters where all of Barcelona seemed to be parading every hour of the day and long into the night. Along the broad median separating the two sides of the streets were stalls that vended everything from holographic digital dancers to ice-cream cups. Half the city seemed to be walking along, shopping, eyeing one another, the women in colorful sweaters or dresses, the men in smart jackets and slacks. Everyone was talking, laughing, even singing.

Walking silently, unsmilingly, near them were half a dozen security agents of the World Council. Bodyguards, Jordan thought. But he wondered how far they would allow him and Aditi to go from the hotel.

Holographic salesmen dotted the sidewalk. And women. People

walked right through their images, the ultimate in ignoring a sales pitch. Sleek open-topped cars glided by almost silently on the streets, their occupants protected from the weather by invisible energy shields. More money in Mitch's pocket, Jordan thought with a wry smile.

He marveled at the sheer exuberance of these Catalonians. Over the centuries they had built a magnificent, vibrant city for themselves, a city that pulsated with the pure joy of life, and had protected it against the floods that had swamped so many other cities. Yet Barcelona and its people were doomed, Jordan knew. *The entire Earth is under a death sentence, unless I can get them to act. Unless I can make them understand what's in their future.*

As he and Aditi nibbled at *tapas* at a sidewalk bistro, under the watchful eyes of their security detail, she noticed his abstracted mood.

"You're not happy, Jordan."

"How can I be? Knowing what we know, how can we be anything but depressed."

She nodded and reached for her glass of carbonated water. "It will take time to convince them. You knew that when we left New Earth."

"But there are other worlds that don't have time," he insisted. "Worlds that need our help. We've got to—"

"Jordan," Aditi said, quite seriously, "we will do what we can. We will do what we must."

"But will it be enough?"

Cocking her head slightly to one side, Aditi smiled as she replied, "We'll find out, sooner or later. For now, let's return to our hotel and see what Adri has to say."

"You've established contact?"

"Yes, of course."

Of course, Jordan echoed in his mind. *Nearly instantaneous communication, faster than light. She takes it for granted.*

They hurried back to their hotel.

Jordan sank onto the sofa once again and Aditi sat beside him. She pointed to the holowall, which showed a three-dimensional image of the nearby Pyrenees Mountains. They looked raw and sharp to Jordan; they'd been bare of snow since the first greenhouse warming had struck.

The mountains faded away and Adri's kindly, smiling face appeared. Jordan felt startled, despite himself.

"Friend Jordan," the old man began. "It is good to speak with you again."

Adri was the leader of the small community of humanlike people on New Earth. He appeared to be wearing a bluish robe, filigreed with delicate tracings. His face had a slightly Asian cast to it, completely bald, spiderwebbed with age. His eyes were almond-shaped, pale blue; his skin a soft brownish yellow, almost gray. He was smiling slightly in a kindly, nearly fatherly way.

Jordan saw that Adri was in his office—if that was the proper word for it: a spacious, airy room on the top floor of the main building in the city that the aliens had built for themselves. Windows on every wall let in abundant sunlight; through them Jordan could see the city that he had lived in during his stay on New Earth.

"I'm afraid," Adri began in his thin, almost whispering voice, "that a true conversation between us will be terribly awkward. Even though our communications travel faster than the speed of light, there is still a lag of almost an hour between us and you."

"Eight point six light-years, traveled in less than an hour," Jordan murmured. "Not bad at all."

But Adri kept on talking, without pause. "I apologize for not discussing our communications capability with you earlier. As you recall, our policy has always been to answer your questions completely and honestly, but not to bring up new information until you show you are ready to deal with it by asking questions about it.

"The astronomer among your group, Dr. Rudaki, has become very interested in communicating faster than light. But of course, she would be, with her interest in showing her observations to you."

Elyse Rudaki, Jordan knew. Our team's astrophysicist. Just like her father. He recalled that Elyse and his brother Brandon had coupled on New Earth. He hoped their romance was flourishing.

Adri plowed ahead. "As you know, friend Jordan, Aditi has sent me the meeting of your World Council. As we expected, they are not terribly upset by the news you have brought them. Two thousand years must seem like an impossibly long time to them. Far too long for them to worry about."

But the other worlds, Jordan thought, the intelligent creatures who will be destroyed by the death wave in the next century or two . . .

As if he could read Jordan's mind, Adri continued, "However, there are at least six other planets bearing intelligent species that are in imminent danger from the death wave. It is our hope that your people can save them. Intelligence is very rare in the universe. We cannot sit idly and allow an intelligent species to be destroyed. That would be tantamount to genocide.

"This is a heavy responsibility for you, I know. But I also know that you will strive your best to accomplish it. Most intelligent species destroy themselves before they reach true adulthood. You people of Earth are on the cusp. You are beginning to understand how precious intelligence is. You have the power to help other intelligent creatures to survive, to reach adulthood. But do you have the will to undertake this task?"

Holding up a lean, warning finger, Adri continued, "You are also dangerously near your own destruction. Already the climate shifts you have inadvertently triggered have devastated much of your world."

"What can we do?" Jordan blurted, even though he knew his words would not reach Adri for nearly an hour.

As if he anticipated the agonized question, Adri went on, "You are alone in this quest, friend Jordan. You and Aditi. I can counsel you and offer an old man's advice. But it is you who must convince your fellow humans that they must reach out to the creatures who are in danger of succumbing to the death wave. The responsibility is on your shoulders. Yours, and Aditi's."

Jordan turned toward his wife, sitting beside him. She looked just as awestruck as he himself felt.

San Francisco

Nick Motrenko admired Rachel Amber's nicely rounded butt as he boosted her over the sagging chain-link fence that ran along the perimeter of the old, abandoned fort.

Like Nick, Rachel was young and energetic. And really good-looking, with a lithe, supple body, long dark hair sweeping halfway down her back, and cool blue eyes that sparkled like sapphires. Besides, the word was that she was really good in bed.

As soon as they both got over the fence, Rachel asked, "Won't we set off some alarms or something?"

"Naw," said Nick. "This place has been abandoned for so long, nobody gives a damn about it."

Which is why Nick liked the ancient fort. Beyond its gray, weathered stones he could see the glittering bay and the graceful Golden Gate Bridge. Best of all, there were no sensors or cameras or microphones planted to spy on people. Not like in town, where you couldn't hiccup anywhere without half a dozen government sensors taking it down, not even in church.

Nick was athletically lean and tall, but seemed physically incapable of smiling. His high-cheeked face was almost always set in a dour, doleful grimace. Some of his buddies called him a sourpuss, although more than a few young women thought him soulful.

Rachel slowly turned a full circle, taking in the ankle-high grass waving in the wind coming off the bay, the gnarled and bowed trees, the scruffy clumps of thick bushes sprouting here and there.

"You'd think somebody would've developed this land. Y'know, built houses on it or something."

"The government owns the land. This used to be an anti-missile base, back in the old days."

"Still, they could put a lot of housing here."

Nick shrugged. "The government doesn't give a damn about making money, just spending it."

"I guess," she said, stepping carefully through the overgrown grass and weeds, looking out for broken glass or other junk. "It's sorta like a park. Kind of wild."

"Good place to be alone together," Nick said, as he took her hand and led her toward the edge of the bluff that overlooked the bay. The sun was hot, the wind off the water cool, and there was nobody else around to bother them.

The two of them were in skintight jeans. Rachel wore a self-powered sleeveless top that shifted hues as she walked, like a shimmering rainbow. Nick had on the latest-mod wraparound hiker's blouse, hanging shapelessly to his hips.

"Let's get out of the sun," Nick suggested. He started toward a small stand of stunted trees off to their left. The wind made their branches rustle.

Once they stretched out side by side in the shade of the trees, Rachel said, "It's like we've got a whole world just to ourselves, isn't it?"

"Sort of."

"Like New Earth."

Propping himself on one elbow, Nick asked, "What do you know about New Earth?"

"All the chat rooms are full of the images that the star travelers brought back. It looks like the Garden of Eden, sort of."

Nick's normal scowl deepened. "The star travelers. And that alien woman they brought back with them."

"She looks just like a human being."

"She's an alien."

"You haven't shown much of their stuff on your blog," said Rachel.

"I don't just run what everybody else is showing. I want original material for my blog."

"I saw your piece about 'beware of Greeks bearing gifts,'" Rachel said. "Why are you so suspicious?"

She was smiling at him, teasing him, really, but Nick didn't catch it. Quite seriously, he replied, "Because I want to interview this Jordan Kell character and the government won't let me do it. They won't let *anybody* get near him."

She shrugged deliciously. "He's an important man. He's been to another star."

"That's what I want to be," Nick said.

"A star traveler?"

"An important man. I want to *be* somebody. Not just another nobody living on a government subsidy."

"How are you going to do that?" she asked.

"I dunno. Interviewing the star traveler for my blog would be a good start."

"Gee, yes."

"But they won't let me near him. They've got him all buttoned up."

"They're protecting him."

"From what?"

"From nut cases and weirdos, I guess."

"You think I'm a nut case or a weirdo?" he asked, almost belligerently.

"No," Rachel said softly. "I think you're very intense, very dedicated."

Nick cupped his hands behind his head and gazed through the trees' leafage into the cloud-flecked sky.

"I want to *be* somebody," he repeated in a whisper.

Rachel turned to him. "Y'know, there's a guy down in Mountain View that I saw a couple of times. You ought to go see him."

"A guy? Who?"

"He's a guru or something. You know, like a holy man. Very wise. Maybe he could help you."

"A holy man?" Disdain was clear in Nick's voice.

"Not holy like a priest. Not religious. But he helps people. Helps them to find their way."

"Sounds like a nut case."

Very seriously, Rachel said, "He helped me. I wouldn't have found you if he hadn't helped me."

"Really?"

"Really."

For the first time that day, Nick Motrenko smiled. Later, he smiled even more. The word he had heard about Rachel was right. Better than right. And they hadn't even needed a bed.

PLANS

+++ ++++++++++ +++++++++++++++++++++++++++++++++++++++

+++++ ++++++++++++ ++++ +++++++++++++++++++++++++++++++

Anita Halleck leaned back in the therapy chair and waited for its heat and vibrating massage to ease the tension in her back.

The arrogance of the man, she said to herself, thinking of Jordan Kell's appearance at the Council meeting earlier in the day. What does he know of how we've struggled while he was off on his star voyage?

We've fought our way through two bouts of greenhouse flooding. We're working to prevent the Greenland meltdown from turning Europe into another Siberia. We've survived climate changes that have altered the map of the planet, we've rebuilt entire cities and shifted whole populations across continents, we've learned how to handle a world population of twenty billion, keep them at peace, keep them secure, and now Jordan Kell expects us to send missions to the stars.

He's a dreamer, she told herself. Or worse, an idealist. What does he know about the realities of politics? Of the forces that motivate people?

On the other hand, she thought as her taut muscles slowly began to relax, he holds the secret of faster-than-light communication. Or at least, his alien wife does. That's the key to real power. The rock rats scattered among the asteroids can live independently of our control because it takes so long to communicate over those distances. I can give an order to administrators out in the Belt, but it won't reach them for more than an hour. And their response will take just as long to get back to me.

I could bring those dissidents out at the colony orbiting Saturn back into our grasp. And the Jupiter habitats. Even Stavenger and his precious Selene could be brought under our control, if we play our cards right.

Instantaneous communications! I could weave a system of command and control across the entire solar system! And out to the stars!

The communicator in the armrest of her chair chimed softly.

"Answer," Halleck snapped, irritated by the interruption of her thoughts.

"Signore Castiglione is here," said the bland synthesized voice of her automated system.

Halleck sat up straight, the pain in her back forgotten. "Send him in!" she said as she got to her feet and swiftly walked to her desk.

Her office door swung open and Rudolfo Castiglione stepped in, smiling handsomely at her.

"Rudy," said Halleck, extending her arms to him. "Good of you to come on such short notice."

Castiglione was only slightly taller than Halleck, but his broad shoulders and slim waist gave the illusion of an imposing figure. His face was finely sculptured, and his green eyes sparkled with merriment. Rumor had it that he'd used stem cell therapy rather than plastic surgery to remodel his once-prominent nose.

He was wearing a golden brown leather jacket over a deeper brown open-necked shirt, dark form-fitting slacks, and highly polished midcalf boots.

Looking him over, Halleck realized all over again that he was a handsome devil. And she knew from personal experience that he was a lighthearted rogue, capable of doing deeds others would blanch at with an unscrupulous smile on his face.

"Sorry for the attire, Anita. I was skiing when your call came through." As he bussed her on both cheeks he added, "Damnably hard to find decent snow these days. The artificial stuff just isn't the same."

Halleck disengaged from him and slipped behind her desk while Castiglione casually dropped onto one of the burgundy leather armchairs in front of it. He leaned back and crossed his legs, completely at ease.

"I need your advice," she said, without preamble.

"Something to do with this fellow who's come back from Sirius?"

"How prescient you are."

He made a self-deprecating little smile. "You met with him this afternoon, I know."

"The whole Council met with him."

"And?"

"He could be troublesome."

"Oh? In what way?"

Halleck outlined the results of the morning's meeting.

"Instantaneous communications?" Castiglione whistled. "That could be worth several fortunes."

"It could help to weld all the human settlements throughout the solar system into one united community."

"With you at its head."

Halleck shot him a mock frown. "With the World Council directing it."

"Of course," said Castiglione.

"But it won't be easy getting the details of their technology, Rudy. Kell is obsessed with this so-called death wave. He wants us to build starships and go out to save other worlds."

"Sounds expensive."

"Extravagant."

"The man's an idealist."

"Exactly."

With a sardonic grin, Castiglione said, "I understand you've been working hard to keep him away from the news flaks."

Halleck nodded minimally. "Oh, he's been cooperative enough, so far. He doesn't want that alien wife of his to be the object of their attention."

"Smart fellow. They'd hound her to death." Castiglione arched a brow. "She's a pretty little thing. I wonder if she's really as human as he claims she is. Might be fun to find out."

"Curb your enthusiasm, Rudy," Halleck mock-growled.

"So why'd you call me?"

"I'm trying to plan ahead. Kell is all worked up over this idea of a death wave sweeping toward us."

"Not for another two thousand years, from what I understand." With a knowing smirk, he added, "Why, you might be retired by then."

Halleck was not amused. "Be serious, Rudy. Kell wants us to send missions to other worlds, planets that are much closer to the death wave. He wants to save the alien civilizations he claims are in danger."

"Very noble of him."

"Very expensive—a half-dozen starships. Or more."

"We can't afford it, is that it?"

"It would throw our budget seriously out of kilter."

With a disapproving shake of his head, Castiglione muttered, "We can't have that."

Leaning forward in her desk chair, Halleck said, "I know Kell. If we refuse to mount these star missions he'll go to the news media. He'll turn his pretty little alien wife into an interplanetary celebrity and try to work up the public to force us to build the ships and send them out to the stars."

"A holy crusade, eh?"

"An extravagance we can't afford."

"So you don't want him arguing with you in public, is that it? Are you afraid he might end up replacing you as head of the Council?"

Castiglione smiled charmingly as he said it, but Halleck flinched almost as though he'd slapped her in the face.

Recovering almost instantly, she said, "That's why I need your help, Rudy. I can't have this madman running wild and upsetting all our plans for the next hundred years. He'll ruin everything!"

"So he's got to be muzzled."

"One way or another."

Castiglione steepled his long fingers and brought them to his lips, almost as if he were praying. "I see," he murmured.

"Can you do it?"

"What's in it for me?"

"The gratitude of the World Council and its chairwoman."

He looked unimpressed. "Couldn't you make it something more, er . . . tangible?"

Halleck said nothing for a long moment. Then, with a completely straight face, she replied, "I understand you're having some unpleasantness over unpaid taxes."

He shrugged. "A tax prosecutor who hasn't stayed bribed."

"With what you owe and the penalties attached, it comes to a considerable sum."

"More than I can pay."

"I could make the tax department settle for ten percent of what you owe."

"You could make them drop the prosecution altogether."

She sighed dramatically. "I suppose I could."

"And I suppose I could make Jordan Kell disappear. Him, and his pretty little wife."

Halleck nodded agreement.

decision

Jordan hardly glanced at the squat, four-armed robot valet as it carefully packed his clothes into his one travel bag. Another robot, equally efficient and silent except for a barely audible buzzing, was packing for Aditi.

It was midmorning, the day after the World Council's meeting. After finishing their packing, Jordan intended to have a quick lunch and then leave Barcelona, heading for his home in Cornwall.

The world has changed so much, he thought: almost-human robots, whole continents reshaped by the greenhouse floods, the World Council acting as a benevolent authority that muzzles the news media and tries to keep the public from being alarmed about the death wave. But Cornwall will be the same as ever; the rocky beaches and the eternal sea won't have changed. At least, the sea level rise apparently hasn't swamped the cliffs altogether.

And from Cornwall I can reach the news media. I can make my case to the public about the death wave and the worlds that need to be saved from it.

Looking around the bedroom, he realized that Aditi was nowhere in sight. Where is she? He stepped into their sitting room and saw her standing by the soundproofed windows, staring across the plaza at the ornately carved façade of the cathedral. The high sun cast vivid shadows across the figures of saints and angels, frozen in stone.

He stepped up behind her and clasped her shoulders gently.

"It's magnificent, isn't it?" Aditi murmured.

Staring at the intricately carved stonework, Jordan replied, "Nearly a thousand years old."

"We have nothing like that on New Earth."

"The cathedral was built when religion offered the only explanation for life's mysteries."

"They built it by hand, without power tools or computers or robots."

"Human sweat."

"But someone planned it. Someone had a vision of what it should look like when it was finished."

"I suppose so," Jordan said, "although it took several generations to finish it. You know, across the city, the new Cathedral of the Holy Family was only finished a hundred-some years ago. It took more than two centuries to complete it—even with computers and power tools."

"Religion is a powerful force among your people."

Jordan nodded as he turned Aditi to face him.

"I'm afraid I have to change the subject, dearest."

"Oh?"

Walking her to the colorful sofa, Jordan said, "Halleck and the World Council are not going to build the starships we need."

She sat primly beside him, but there was steel in her voice as she said, "Then we must withhold the energy screen that can shield this world from the death wave."

Jordan shook his head slowly. "I'm afraid that tactic won't work."

"Why not?"

Raising a finger, Jordan explained, "First, they know that they have two thousand years before the gamma wave arrives here. For them, that's an infinity. They're in no hurry to face the problem."

"But they've got to, sooner or later."

"They'll choose later. Second, they don't really need our help. Thanks to Mitch, the people of Earth know how to build energy screens."

"But a system that can protect the whole planet—and the other human habitations in your solar system—that's a different order of magnitude from the baby screens Mitch has been dealing with."

"Same physics," Jordan countered. "The real secret of the energy screens is that it's possible to make them. When the time comes, human scientists and engineers will figure out how to shield our worlds."

Before Aditi could reply, Jordan went on, "Besides, they'll know that we couldn't withhold the information if they needed it. We couldn't consign the human race to extinction. I know I couldn't. Could you? Could Adri?"

She hesitated a heartbeat, then slowly answered, "No, of course not."

"Any threat we make to withhold the information they'd need to save themselves would be hollow, and Halleck and her ilk would understand that."

"Then what can we do?"

"That depends more on you, dear, than it does on me."

"What do you mean?"

Jordan took a deep breath, then plunged in. "I've been cooperating with Halleck to avoid publicity. I haven't wanted the news media to turn you into a center of their attention, an object of curiosity. And that's what they'll do, if I try to make a public issue of the death wave."

"An object of curiosity?"

Grimly, Jordan explained, "They'll want to know everything about you. You won't have a moment to yourself. Once you allow yourself to become the focus of their attention, your life won't be your own. They'll be at you every minute of the night and day."

"But the Council's security guards . . ."

Shaking his head, Jordan warned, "You have no idea how frenzied the news media can become. Public figures have been literally hounded to death by paparazzi and their ilk. Once you open yourself to their attention, the security people won't be able to protect you. I doubt that they'll even try."

Aditi thought that over for a moment. Then, "That seems a small price to pay for saving the planet."

"Easy enough to say now, dearest, but once those wolves begin hounding you, you won't have any privacy at all. Not a moment's worth."

Aditi shrugged her slim shoulders. "I'm willing to face that, if it's necessary."

Jordan looked into her warm brown eyes and saw that she was completely serious.

"I don't think you understand what you'll be letting yourself in for."

She gazed back at him, unwavering. "If that is what it takes to save your people . . ."

He hesitated. Jordan knew that she was right. Yet he knew that he was also right: her life would be torn apart once they opened themselves to the news media. My life, too, he realized.

"Perhaps you should ask Adri about this," he suggested.

Nodding, Aditi said, "I will."

He got to his feet, thinking, We could stay in Cornwall and live quietly. Sooner or later Halleck and her successors will realize that they'll have to protect the human race from the death wave.

But what about those other worlds, those other races who'll be wiped out if we don't help them? Can we stay quietly in Cornwall and allow whole intelligent races to be extinguished?

He knew they couldn't.

action

+++
++

The door buzzer sounded. Jordan turned and looked at the video screen that showed who was outside their door. A pair of security guards, from the stern, youthful looks of them: one man and one woman. The man was fiddling with his wrist communicator.

Jordan looked down at his own wrist. It's too early to start for the airport, he saw. What do they want?

He opened the door.

"We're not finished packing yet. Give us a few minutes more—"

The two security agents pushed past him, into the sitting room. "We've had a warning of an attack on you," the woman said, her voice flat and tense.

"An attack?" Aditi echoed.

"Get away from that window, ma'am," said the male agent, pulling a slim pistol from beneath his jacket.

The woman also had a gun in her hand, Jordan saw.

"Who's going to attack us?" he demanded. "Why?"

As if in answer, the window blasted inward, blowing shards of plasticized glass across the room. Aditi was knocked to the carpet, covered with bits of glass. Jordan dived toward her.

A pair of black-clad men swung through the open window on cables suspended from above, shouting, "Kill the aliens! Kill the invaders!"

The female security guard dropped to one knee and shot the nearer of the two attackers, who toppled over backward and slumped to the floor beside Aditi. As Jordan covered Aditi with his body, the guard's partner shot the other one.

Aditi's eyes were wide with shock, but as far as Jordan could see, she was unharmed. Strangely, although she was covered with slivers of glass, Jordan could not see any cuts on her bare arms or legs.

The male security guard pulled Jordan to his feet, then they both bent down to help Aditi stand up.

"Are you all right?" he asked her.

"Yes, I think so," Aditi gasped. Looking down at the attackers, she breathed shakily, "They . . . they wanted to kill us."

Jordan felt glacially calm inside. He realized this was frequently his reaction to physical danger: cool, deliberate self-control. The anger, the rage, came later.

Gesturing to the two black-clad bodies, he asked, "Are they dead?"

The woman answered, "No, sir. We use electric tranquilizer charges. Shocks their nervous system. They'll be able to face interrogation in an hour or so."

"If the darts didn't overshock them," her partner said, with a grim smile.

The woman started speaking into her wrist communicator. Calling for backup, Jordan figured. Through the open doorway to the bedroom he saw the two robots. They had frozen, as if someone had removed their power supply. They're not programmed to handle assassination attempts, Jordan told himself.

Turning back to the young man, he asked, "What do we do now?"

Still gripping his pistol, the guard said, "We sit tight, right here. Our people are going through the hotel, from roof to basement. Drones are scanning the whole area outside and an evac jumpjet is on its way here for you."

With a single brusque nod, Jordan turned to Aditi. She looked pale, shaken. "You'd better sit down, dear."

He led her to the sofa and sat beside her.

"You're sure you're all right?"

"Yes . . . I just need a few moments . . ."

The door swung open and another pair of security people stepped through, nodding wordlessly at the two already there as they went to the inert bodies of the would-be assassins and knelt beside them.

"Medical team," the young man told Jordan.

"How long do we have to wait—"

A slightly older man came into the sitting room. He was wearing a cream-colored jacket that fitted him exactly and tight slacks of pearl gray. Smiling handsomely, he made a polite little bow before Jordan and Aditi.

"How do you do? I am Rudolfo Castiglione, special assistant to Anita Halleck, chairwoman of the World Council."

He was a handsome devil, Jordan saw, but his smile looked somehow less than sincere, his green eyes almost amused.

Jordan got to his feet and extended his hand. "You got here very quickly."

Castiglione shrugged nonchalantly. "You have never been out of our sight since you arrived on Earth three weeks ago. When we got wind of this plot to assassinate you, naturally we increased your security screen. Chairwoman Halleck herself told me to go to you, to make certain you'd be safe."

The two medics had reactivated the robots, which rolled into the sitting room, lifted the still-unconscious bodies of the would-be assassins, and carried them out.

Jordan watched it all, unconsciously grasping his own wrist to feel his pulse. Strong and steady. To Castiglione he said, "Well, your team arrived just in time to save us. We appreciate your prompt action."

Castiglione's smile became even brighter. "It was a rather narrow scrape, wasn't it?" Looking down at Aditi, he asked solicitously, "You weren't harmed, were you?"

"No," she said, with something of her normal tone returning. "I'm fine."

"Very good. Excellent!" Hiking a thumb toward the shattered window, he went on, "These windows are made with special glass. When they are broken, they shatter into a million particles, but none of them are sharp enough to break one's skin."

"Very safe," Jordan said.

"Yes," said Castiglione. "Now we must whisk you away to a place where you'll be perfectly safe."

"My cottage in Cornwall—"

"No, no. Impossible, I'm afraid. They know of your cottage. They'll try to get to you there."

His brows knitting, Jordan asked, "And who might *they* be?"

"Fanatics," Castiglione replied without an eyeblink's hesitation. "Lunatics who believe that we are about to be invaded by alien monsters."

"I'm not a monster!" Aditi objected.

"Of course not," said Castiglione. "But there are those who believe that the aliens who, er . . . constructed you are preparing to invade our planet and wipe out the human race."

"Poppycock!" Jordan snapped.

"Yes, certainly. But that is what they believe. And they are ready to kill for their beliefs, as you just saw."

Jordan glanced down at Aditi. She seemed recovered now, her firm little chin set determinedly.

"The best way to combat such fears," he said to Castiglione, "is to show the world that Aditi is as human as you or I. We have to turn to the news media to—"

"No!" Castiglione yelped. "You can't go out in public. You can't become an object of the media's feeding frenzy. We're not even allowing a public disclosure of this assassination attempt. It would lead to copycat attacks, for certain."

"I don't agree," said Jordan.

Looking disappointed, almost hurt, Castiglione said, "You will have to discuss that with Anita Halleck, then."

"Very well. The sooner the better."

Castiglione's smile returned. "Good. The first thing is to get you to a place of safety."

The female security guard stepped into their conversation. "Jumpjet is landing on the hotel roof."

"Fine," said Castiglione. Extending his hand to Aditi, he said, "Come with me, please, lovely one."

"Where are we going?" she asked.

"To a place where you'll be completely safe," said Castiglione.

tarragona air force base

once he and Aditi reached the roof, with castiglione and a half-dozen security guards around them, Jordan saw that the hotel had a helipad up there, complete with a small control booth and still more security people standing around, gripping deadly looking black guns, looking on guard, steely-eyed.

A jumpjet sat on the pad, its swept-back wings drooping slightly, the nozzles of its jet engines swiveled downward for vertical flight. The plane seemed sparkling new, the blue and white insignia of the World Council emblazoned on its silvery side and tail.

Castiglione extended his hand and helped Aditi up the metal ladder and into the jumpjet. He followed her inside, between her and Jordan.

The passenger compartment of the plane was small but plushly comfortable, with cushioned couches on either end of it. Jordan and Aditi sat side by side on one couch, Castiglione facing them. Through the glassed partition behind his handsomely smiling face Jordan could see the two helmeted pilots. Once the three passengers clicked their safety harnesses on, the machine hauled vertically off the roof, pirouetted once in midair, then headed out toward the glittering sea.

Jordan could see the statue of Christopher Columbus at harborside, pointing vaguely in the direction of America. Plenty of ships at the piers, mostly cruise liners, with freighters and container ships moored in the deeper water. Farther out was the seawall built to protect the city from the sea level rise caused by the first wave of greenhouse warming. It extended out to the edges of the city. Like the wall of a medieval castle, Jordan thought. Construction cranes and barges dotted its length: building it higher, stronger, against the rising sea caused by the new meltdowns of the Greenland and Antarctic ice caps.

It was smoothly quiet inside the jumpjet. Good acoustical insulation, Jordan thought.

Leaning toward Castiglione, he asked, "Where are we going?"

"To a safe place," the man answered, his eyes on Aditi.

Jordan felt uneasy. He didn't quite trust this smiling, good-looking stranger who seemed focused on his wife. He knew that Halleck had detailed security people to shield him and Aditi from the news media's unwanted attention, but a whole team of guards, including medics and a jumpjet?

Be grateful they were there, he told himself. Otherwise you and Aditi would be dead.

Aditi asked, "Where is this safe place?"

Castiglione's smile widened as he laid a single slender finger across his lips.

The jumpjet flew down the Catalan coastline for almost half an hour, then landed at a smallish airfield. As they approached the ground, Jordan could not see any commercial planes: only military jets, in blotches of brown camouflage paint and, farther off, what looked like rocketplanes, sleek and bright in the Mediterranean sun.

"This is the Tarragona Air Force Base," Castiglione said. "Very safe, very secure. You will stay here for the time being."

"And how long will that be?" Jordan asked.

Castiglione shrugged elaborately. "Until we have dug out all the fanatics who want you dead."

Aditi spoke up. "That could be quite a while, I suppose."

"Yes, quite a long while. But you'll be very comfortable here. You'll see. The military don't live like Spartans, you know. They like their creature comforts, just as you and I do."

"Once we're on the ground," Jordan said, "I'd like to contact Mitchell Thornberry and let him know what's happened."

Castiglione frowned. "I'm afraid that communications beyond the perimeter of the base will be impossible. We don't want anyone to know where you are."

Jordan didn't feel the slightest surprise. But he said, "Thornberry will be worried if we simply disappear. He and Dr. Longyear—"

"We will contact them and let them know you are under protective custody."

"Can I talk with Ms. Halleck, at least?"

"At least?" Castiglione laughed. "The head of the World Council, and you say 'at least'?"

Jordan was finding it easy to dislike the man. "At least," he repeated.

Nodding, Castiglione said, "Yes, of course you will be able to speak with her. She is very concerned about your safety."

"I'm sure," said Jordan.

Jordan had to admit that their accommodations were indeed quite comfortable. Not as posh as the hotel, but the quarters Castiglione showed them, on the top floor of a barrackslike cinderblock building, included a king-sized bedroom, a small but neat sitting room, a kitchen, and a modern lavatory.

"Your home away from home," Castiglione said expansively.

"Very nice," Jordan replied. Thinly.

A single robot painted army brown carried a double armful of bags and boxes into the kitchen.

"Stocking your refrigerator," Castiglione explained. "Your clothes and things from the hotel will be arriving soon."

Jordan nodded complacently and waited for Castiglione—and the robot—to leave. Once the door shut behind them, he turned to Aditi.

"It's been quite a day."

She was looking doubtfully up at the ceiling beams. The rooms looked immaculately clean to Jordan, but he wondered if there were microphones or pin-sized cameras hidden here and there.

As if she understood his anxiety, Aditi said, "I've blocked the bugs."

Jordan felt his brows hike upward. "You have?"

Tapping her left temple, Aditi smiled impishly. "They won't be able to spy on us."

"Well," he said, sliding his arms around her waist, "that's something, I suppose."

assessment

+++
++

Jordan looked into Aditi's eyes. "Are you truly all right?"

"Yes," she said, running a hand along her bare arm. "Not even bruised."

"When that window burst, you didn't even scream," he marveled.

"There was no time. Before I could draw in a breath you were on top of me, protecting me."

He shrugged. "It seemed like the right thing to do."

Her face grew somber. "They wanted to kill us. To kill me."

"They knew where we were," Jordan murmured. "In that enormous hotel, they knew exactly which window was ours. And they were able to rig cables from the roof, where the helipad is, to get to our window."

"What are you saying, Jordan?"

Leading her to the cushioned bench that served as a sofa, he said, "They had excellent intelligence. They knew where we were and how to get to us. The helipad workers must have seen them setting up the cables."

"They must have thought they were window washers or maintenance people."

"In black jumpsuits?"

Frowning, Aditi repeated, "What are you saying, Jordan?"

He didn't answer. Instead, he sat on the less-than-comfortable bench and pulled Aditi down beside him.

"Well?" she demanded.

Jordan could feel himself frowning. He didn't like the scenario playing out in his mind.

Trying to make his expression more relaxed, he replied, "Would we have agreed to be shut away in this military base if we hadn't been attacked?"

"No, of course not."

"I'm just wondering . . ."

"Wondering?"

"What if the attack was all a fake, a stunt to frighten us into allowing Halleck and her people to hide us away, out of the public's sight."

Her eyes widening, Aditi asked, "Why would she do that?"

He shook his head. "Perhaps I'm just a touch paranoid."

Aditi got to her feet and headed for the kitchen. "I think you're just hungry. We haven't had anything to eat since breakfast, and that was *hours* ago."

As she started rummaging through the cupboard and refrigerator, Jordan went to the tiny counter that separated the kitchen from the sitting room and perched on one of the stools there.

"Halleck has kept us away from the news media almost entirely," he said. "We haven't talked to a reporter or commentator since the day we landed on Earth."

"That's not entirely true," Aditi said as she pulled a pair of prepackaged meals from the freezer. "We've conducted several interviews."

"Not live. Not in person. The questions were handed to us by a World Council public relations official and we responded to them remotely."

"Still . . ." She peeled off the covers and the meals instantly heated.

Jordan continued, "Then we go to the World Council meeting

and it's quite clear that they have no intention of dealing with the death wave—"

"It's too far in the future for them to consider it a real threat."

"Or to build the starships we need to help other worlds in danger."

Aditi placed the steaming packages on the bar, and then started searching the kitchen drawers for silverware. "That was wrong of them," she agreed.

"And what can we do about it?" he asked.

She picked a pair of forks and knives from a drawer and came around the counter to sit on the stool beside him.

"Try to convince them that it's our moral obligation to help those worlds that are in danger," she said.

"Yes, but part of the convincing would be to go to the news media and tell the public the full story."

As she cautiously tasted a forkful of the prepackaged food, Aditi said, "But you didn't want to do that. You said that would make me an object of intense media attention."

He grinned ruefully. "That's putting it mildly. Yet Halleck must have realized that would be our next move, and she staged this assassination attempt to get us to come quietly to this comfortable little prison, so she could keep us out of the public's eye."

Aditi stared at him. "You think so?"

"Yes, I do."

Aditi chewed thoughtfully for several silent moments. At last she put her fork down and said, "Jordan, I agree with you. I think you are right."

"You agree?"

"Yes. I agree that you are a little paranoid."

Jordan's shoulders slumped. But he muttered, "Even paranoids have enemies."

*   *   *

Shortly after their impromptu lunch, a young, somber-looking Spanish soldier knocked at their door, with a stoic robot holding their travel bags from the hotel.

"With Señor Castiglione's compliments," the soldier said in almost accentless English.

"*Muchisimas gracias,*" said Jordan.

The young man's face broke into a warm smile. "*De nada,*" he said. He stayed at the door as the robot trundled into the bedroom and, at Aditi's direction, left the bags on the king-sized bed. Then both the soldier and the robot left their quarters.

Once they finished unpacking, Jordan looked through the bedroom window and suggested, "Let's take a walk. It seems to be a pleasant afternoon outside."

The same soldier was sitting on the steps of the barracks' front door when they got downstairs. He said nothing to them, but Jordan saw that he got to his feet and followed them at a distance of a few meters.

They strolled down a paved sidewalk, then hesitated at the corner of an intersecting street. Jordan turned to the young soldier. In Spanish he asked if he could show them around the base. The youngster smilingly agreed and led them up and down the well-ordered gridwork of streets, and out to the edge of the airfield.

Pointing, he showed Jordan and Aditi where the mess hall was, then said in English, "Since you are guests here, it has been decided that you may take your meals in the Officers' Club."

"That's very gracious," said Jordan.

"Señor Castiglione insisted on it," the soldier replied. "I am told that he wants you to be completely comfortable here."

"How very thoughtful of him," Jordan said, with a cold smile.

mountain view

"This is where your wise man lives?" Nick Motrenko asked, puffing with exertion.

He and Rachel Amber were struggling up a steep embankment along the side of Highway 101. Traffic was buzzing in orderly fashion along the old road, every car, truck, and bus moving at precisely the speed limit, neatly spaced by their automatic guidance systems.

Rachel had borrowed a coupé from the library where she worked and parked it on the shoulder of the highway. Nick hoped the police drones patrolling the road wouldn't send an impoundment team before they got back to it.

Gulping for air, Rachel said, "This is where he told me to meet him."

Nick frowned unhappily. The area was hardly the kind of place he'd expected. Looking around, he could see in the distance the old space museum and amusement park down by the water's edge and, farther off, the clustered buildings of venerable Stanford University. Rolling green hills were studded with row after row of government-built housing, identical as if they'd been stamped out of a cookie cutter.

He'd been skeptical of Rachel's description of this wise man, this guru whom she idolized. But she was so enthusiastic, so determined to get Nick to meet the guy, that Nick gave in and made the trip down to Mountain View with her. "The things a guy will do to get laid," he muttered to himself.

They reached the top of the embankment and there was nothing to see. No buildings within a kilometer or so, not even a tent.

"There he is!" Rachel said, pointing excitedly.

A dozen or so people were squatting on the grass a few dozen meters away, in a sort of glade that was shaded by stately old trees. She started running toward the group, her face alight with anticipation. Nick hurried after her.

A tall, gangling black man was standing before the little group, pacing up and down as he talked and gestured with both his long arms. He was wearing what looked to Nick like a bathrobe, grayish white. As the two of them got closer, Nick saw that the robe badly needed a washing, and the man's face was stubbled with several days' worth of heavy dark beard.

". . . I was like you," the man was saying, in a deeply sonorous voice, "lost, adrift in a world not of my making, accepting the pittance that the government doled out in exchange for remaining idle, useless, impotent."

Despite himself, Nick felt the words hit home. That's what I am, he told himself: idle, useless, impotent.

The man nodded once at Nick and Rachel as they sat down at the rear of the little group. He was really tall, like a basketball pro, but gaunt, just skin and bones. Rachel was staring at him in wide-eyed awe; Nick felt jealous.

Raising his voice slightly, the man continued, "But then I had a life-changing experience. I killed a man."

The group gasped.

"He was a child molester. He had been convicted by the courts and released by the psychologists. But then he struck again and was arrested again. He was evil personified, and he had learned how to cheat the penal system. I was in jail with him. I had been arrested for hacking into the scoring program for the year's high school examinations. I was fourteen years old."

The man paused. Every eye was riveted upon him. Every breath abated, waiting for his next words.

"He raped me. In my prison cell he beat me nearly unconscious and sodomized me. I thought my life had ended. I felt pain, and humiliation, and deep, deep shame."

Again he paused. Then, "It took me years to realize that *I* was not responsible for his foul deed, *he* was. It took me years to track him down. But I did it. I found him." Holding both his hands in front of him like claws, he said, "I killed him. With these two hands, I destroyed the foul beast."

Nick stared at the man, just as every other man and woman in the little group was doing.

"Ever since, I have lived outside of society. Ever since, I have been an outcast. But let me tell you, it is better to be an outcast than a nothing. It is better to do what you must, to rid the world of evil, than to sit by comfortably and pretend that eradicating evil is someone else's responsibility.

"You must take the responsibility on yourselves. You must rise and strike!"

AS THE SHADOWS OF DUSK LENGTHENED ACROSS THE TARRAGONA AIR BASE, JORDAN AND ADITI STROLLED TO THE OFFICERS' CLUB FOR DINNER, WITH THEIR AIRMAN "ESCORT" walking along beside them. He stopped at the steps to the club, though.

Almost blushing, he said in a low voice, "I am not an officer."

"I'm sorry," Jordan said in Spanish. "Thank you very much for guiding us."

"*De nada*," the young man said, smiling shyly.

Inside the Officers' Club, Castiglione was standing at the bar chatting with a pair of men in crisp, well-fitted uniforms. One was gray haired, with a chest full of ribbons. The other was obviously younger, probably the older officer's aide, Jordan thought.

The club occupied the entire ground floor of one of the smaller buildings on the base. It was far from plush, with wooden tables scattered across the plank floor and plain undecorated lightbulbs dangling from the ceiling rafters. Jordan almost expected to see the floor covered with sawdust. There was a stage at the far end of the room, with acoustical equipment and microphones stashed to one side of it.

Jordan smiled at the lone bartender, a squared-off robot with four extensible arms, its metal body anodized army brown and a serial number stenciled across its chest. No gossiping with that bartender, he thought. No soulful philosophic conversations long after midnight.

Smiling brightly, Castiglione introduced Aditi and Jordan to the two officers, a captain and a colonel in the Spanish Air Force. Jordan got the impression that they were both in the intelligence service.

"You are comfortable here?" the colonel asked in English as the bartender stood mutely awaiting their orders.

"Quite comfortable, thank you," Aditi replied.

Jordan asked the bartender for amontillado for both himself and Aditi.

"Not for me," she said.

With a knowing smile, Jordan said, "That's all right. I'll drink both of them."

Castiglione guffawed.

Dinner was pleasant enough. Both the officers knew of Jordan's old reputation as a diplomat, and both were curious about Aditi and her fellow natives of New Earth.

"The entire planet was built by your people?" asked the colonel.

"By our Predecessors," Aditi responded.

"Predecessors?"

"Intelligent machines," Jordan explained. "Millennia old."

"Incredible."

Jordan explained, "It was their Predecessors—the intelligent machines—that discovered the death wave that's approaching us."

"Death wave?" the captain asked.

As Jordan described the deadly wave of gamma radiation expanding through the Milky Way galaxy at the speed of light, Castiglione said lightly, "It won't reach our vicinity for another two thousand years. We have plenty of time to prepare for it."

"But there are other intelligent species," Aditi countered, "on other worlds much closer to the wave front. We must help them, or they will all die."

"I suppose we should, sooner or later," said the captain.

"Sooner," Aditi said. "Those creatures will die if we don't reach them soon enough."

"And it will take years, centuries even, for us to reach them," said Jordan.

With a wave of his hand, Castiglione said, "That's a matter for the World Council to consider. For the present, why don't we order our dessert?"

After dinner, Castiglione walked them back to their quarters, chatting amiably about nothing of consequence.

At their door, he smiled at Aditi and said, "I hope you have a pleasant sleep."

"And the same to you," said Jordan. But he thought unhappily that Castiglione would dream of Aditi.

Once they went to their bedroom Jordan sat on a corner of the bed and began to slowly take off his shoes.

"You look . . . pensive," Aditi said.

He looked up at her. "Ever since we returned from New Earth, something has been bothering me. Tonight I finally realized what it is."

She sat beside him, a questioning look in her eyes.

"Nothing's changed," Jordan said.

Aditi blinked at him.

"I've been away from Earth for nearly two hundred years, and this world is pretty much the same as I left it."

"But the flooding has changed the shapes of the continents, hasn't it?"

"Yes, but that's not what I'm talking about. The *people* haven't changed. They're pretty much the same as they were when I left for New Earth, nearly two centuries ago."

"Are they?"

"Oh, the technology has advanced a bit," Jordan conceded.

"Even without Mitch's energy screens, they've made progress in transport and energy. I understand they've learned how to use green plants to generate electrical energy. And I suppose there've been new breakthroughs in biomedicine and elsewhere, as well. But . . .'"

"But?"

"The *people* haven't changed," he repeated. "Their attitudes haven't changed. We've brought back irrefutable evidence that there are other intelligent species scattered among the stars and they shrug off the news as if it's nothing important."

Aditi pondered that for a moment. "Perhaps it will simply take more time for the importance of the news to sink in."

With a shake of his head Jordan responded, "I don't think so. I think the people of Earth are locked in outmoded ways of thinking, and they're not going to change."

"We've only been here three weeks, Jordan. Give them time to adjust their attitudes."

"No. They're not going to adjust. The World Council doesn't want them to adjust. And the Council holds the keys to power, controls the news media, controls their lives. They're burying their heads in the sand, just as they did with climate change."

"You think so?"

"Twenty billion human beings, living cheek by jowl on this planet. They're locked into a mind-set that can't accept change. And Halleck's World Council is happy to keep things that way.

"It's a side effect of longevity," Jordan continued. "When people can live for centuries, their attitudes, their prejudices, their worldviews live for centuries with them. The world's birth rate has sunk almost as low as the death rate. New generations are too small to have much effect on society. People like Anita Halleck—even Douglas Stavenger—can remain in power for centuries. Society doesn't change. It can't! Not with the same people in charge, with the same ideas and attitudes they've carried around with them for two, three hundred years."

Looking truly distressed, Aditi asked, "What can we do?"

"I'm not sure," Jordan replied. "But the first thing is to get out of this prison. We can't do anything while we're bottled up in here."

castiglione flew back through the darkening night to barcelona. It was nearly midnight when he finally arrived at Anita Halleck's villa in the hills on the outskirts of the city.

She was in her study, a high-ceilinged room paneled with old-fashioned bookshelves filled with old-fashioned paper books that had never been opened.

Halleck was sitting in a regal-looking armchair, a snifter of cognac in one beringed hand.

As soon as Castiglione stepped into the room she said, "I've just had a report from the head of the surveillance team. All the devices in their quarters went dead within seconds of their entering the rooms. Cameras, microphones, everything."

"Too bad," said Castiglione, heading for the bar built into the other side of the room. "It would have been interesting to watch that pretty little woman."

Frowning, Halleck went on, "They replaced the devices while she and Kell were with you at dinner, and as soon as the two of them got back from the Officers' Club the devices went dead again."

Castiglione reached for a decanter of port. "She must be disabling them," he said.

"Obviously."

Crossing the lush Persian carpet to sit in the wing chair facing

Halleck, Castiglione shrugged nonchalantly. "We suspected she had certain . . . eh, capabilities. Now she's proven it."

Frostily, Halleck demanded, "What other *capabilities* might she have?"

"Faster-than-light communications."

"Exactly. We have to get that from her."

Castiglione took a sip of port, then said, "Perhaps she'll tell us about it voluntarily."

"And if she refuses?"

He waggled his free hand in the air. "There are ways."

"Do you think they'd work on her? An alien?"

"They'd work on Kell. She loves him, she doesn't want to see him hurt."

Halleck stared at him for a few moments. Then, "I wonder."

"It would be interesting to find out," said Castiglione.

"Must your mind always be in the gutter, Rudy?"

He smiled thinly. "You never seemed to mind it before."

Her eyes narrowing, Halleck said, "Suppose we make a deal with Kell. We offer to build the starships he wants, in return for her telling us how to build a faster-than-light communications system."

Castiglione's smile widened. "And once you have that knowledge, you don't have to go through with building the ships."

"We can run into unexpected difficulties with the program," Halleck agreed. "After all, building half a dozen starships is no small project."

"Kell would scream his head off to the news media. He'd make a powerful stink about your going back on your word."

"Not if he's safely contained. Someplace where he can't reach the media. Or anyone else, for that matter."

Castiglione pursed his lips momentarily, then said, "I don't think that airbase is tight enough to contain him."

"It's under a full security guard, isn't it?"

"Yes, but they're all Spanish Air Force people. I'd feel better if we had him stored away somewhere under our own security."

Halleck nodded slowly. "Somewhere off-Earth, perhaps?"

"Someplace where they'd be totally dependent on us. Even for the air they breathe."

Once they were in bed together, with all the lights out, Jordan asked Aditi, "Are you certain that all the cameras and microphones have been disabled?"

"Why? What do you have in mind?" In the darkness, he could hear the impish tone in her voice.

"Can you contact Adri?"

More soberly Aditi replied, "Oh. Yes, of course."

"I think he can help us to get out of this prison."

"From eight light-years away?"

"I think so."

It took more than an hour, but at last Adri's aged, seamed face appeared in the bedroom's three-dimensional viewer, casting a ghostly light through the room.

"Friend Jordan," Adri said in his soft whispery voice. "And Aditi, my dearest."

As usual, Adri was wearing a floor-length robe. This time it was a pale yellow, embellished with twining traceries. He appeared to be standing in a moonlit garden. Jordan remembered that New Earth had no moon; the pale light must be coming from the dwarf star companion of Sirius, he realized.

Knowing that a two-way conversation was impossible with a time lag of more than an hour, Jordan began, "Adri, we need your help. The people controlling Earth's government are indifferent to the death wave. They feel a danger that's two thousand years away isn't real; at least, it's not close enough to rouse them to action.

"What's worse, they probably won't move to help the other intelligent species who are in danger from the death wave . . ."

On and on Jordan spoke, explaining in detail what he and Aditi had experienced since returning to Earth. His throat grew hoarse, and Aditi slipped out of bed to get him a glass of water.

"I'll wait for your reply," Jordan croaked. While I try to recover, he added silently. I haven't spoken nonstop for this long since I tried to head off the war brewing between Kenya and South Africa, ages ago.

He sipped at the water while Aditi sat on the edge of the bed, watching him caringly.

"You've given Adri a lot to think about," she said.

Jordan smiled wanly. "I hope he can do what I'm going to ask him to do."

At last Adri's three-dimensional image spoke. "Friend Jordan, your news troubles me. I confess that I expected better from your people. Please tell me how I can help you."

Jordan did precisely that.

nEW YORK CiTY

++

++

vera Griffin stood by the one narrow window of the
otero Network's control center and watched the sun
coming up over the skyscrapers that lined manhattan's
East Side.

Smiling at the sight, she thought idly, The town so big they
named it twice: New York, New York.

It was Friday morning, the end of the workweek and the last
time she'd have to work the graveyard shift. On Monday she was
going to start in her new position. After four years of dedicated
drudgery in the control center, she would be a producer at last, with
an office of her own. Producer of a dinky little human-interest segment of the network's evening news, it was true, and her office
would be nothing more than a cubicle, but it was her first step
up the ladder that led to the executive suite and real, substantive
success.

I'll have to move to Boston, she knew, to corporate headquarters. All right, I'll make the move. Beantown or Podunk, I'll move
to where my career takes me. But still she gazed fondly at the wall
of towers that rose to the sky.

She was a diminutive woman, slim and doll-like, with lank brown
hair she had once thought of as mousy but now was attractively
coifed and highlighted with touches of gold. Even for the grave-
yard shift she dressed stylishly: no dungarees and sweatshirts for
her, you never knew when one of the corporate suits might pop into

the control center. It was rare but it happened; once Carlos Otero himself had appeared unexpectedly in the studio. When he did Vera looked like an up-and-coming young future executive. Determined. Knowledgeable. Charming.

"Hey Vera, you better look at this."

She turned at the sound of the man's voice. One of the grave-yard crew, assigned to monitoring the four dozen screens that showed the network's news feeds from around the world.

Vera's eyes went wide. Every screen was showing the same thing! Some middle-aged guy with silver hair and a trim mustache, speaking earnestly as he stared into the camera. She recognized the man as Jordan Kell, the star traveler who had led the mission to New Earth and returned with an alien wife.

She hurried to her workstation while the man was saying, "You may remember that I returned three weeks ago from our expedition to New Earth, the planet orbiting the star Sirius."

"What's going on?" she demanded as she slid into her chair.

"He's on every friggin' feed," her assistant said. "Even the other networks. The private chatter channels, too!"

"He's going out on the air?"

Her assistant pointed to the monitor that showed what the network was broadcasting. Jordan Kell was there, too.

"Jesus!" she gulped. "Pull him off! Take him down!"

Other crew people were shouting frantically into the voice-activating pin mikes that controlled their consoles. None of their screens changed in the slightest. Some crew people were even tapping at their antiquated keyboards. Pounding on them. Nothing changed—Jordan Kell kept speaking intently, his face utterly serious.

"I've taken this extraordinary step of intervening on your tele-casts because we face an extraordinary challenge. The World Council wants to ignore this challenge, but I feel that you—the people of Earth—should know about it, understand it, and decide what you want to do about it."

Phones started jangling. Vera knew who was calling. The suits, the executives who've had their morning coffees interrupted by this . . . this . . . invader.

"The solar system is going to be flooded by a lethal wave of gamma radiation," Jordan Kell was saying. "It will kill all life on Earth and every other part of the solar system, unless we act to protect ourselves."

Her assistant shoved a phone receiver in front of her nose. "It's the chief of programming!" he yelped, his face flushed.

Vera took the phone.

"What the hell's going on down there?" her boss fairly screamed. "Our regular netcasts are off the air, for chrissake!"

"It's some nut case," Vera answered. "He's somehow taken control of all our channels."

"Get him off the air! Now!"

"We're trying."

"Get it done!"

"Yessir."

But half an hour later, Vera had to face the fact that no matter what she tried, Jordan Kell remained on the air. Every channel. It was scant consolation that he was on the competition's channels, as well.

It was almost lunchtime in Barcelona when one of her aides tiptoed into her conference room and stood nervously at Anita Halleck's elbow.

Halleck was in the midst of a sensitive meeting with representatives of the Latin American Alliance, a power bloc that controlled enough seats on the World Council to force a vote of confidence upon her.

Halleck ignored the aide's fidgeting as long as she could, then finally asked her visitors to forgive the interruption.

Before she could ask the man why he dared break into her

meeting, he leaned over and whispered into her ear, "It's Jordan Kell. He's on every video broadcast all around the world!"

"What?"

"He's speaking about the death wave."

Halleck shot to her feet. "Excuse me," she said to the startled men and women seated around the conference table. "Something has come up."

Leaving the Latin Americans gaping at her, Halleck followed her aide back to her private office. There, in the three-dimensional viewer on the wall opposite her desk, sat Jordan Kell, his face grave, his voice solemn.

". . . unless we decide to help them, these intelligent creatures will be wiped out by the death wave, driven into extinction because we failed to act."

"Get Rudy Castiglione in here," she snapped. Her aide bolted for the door.

Kell appeared to be in a bare-walled sitting room, probably in that air base at Tarragona, Halleck thought. Yet somehow he was speaking on the World Council's private communications channel. From the way he was speaking, Halleck realized that he must be on all the public channels, as well.

She called to her phone for her chief of communications. It took a few seconds, but the woman's harried face finally appeared on the phone screen.

Pushing a disheveled lock of hair from her eyes, the comm chief didn't wait for Halleck's obvious question.

"He's on every channel!" she said, her voice close to panic.

"How can that be?" Halleck demanded.

"I don't know! I've got my entire staff trying to track it down. The phones are jammed; calls from video broadcasters, private chat networks, all across the world!"

Through it all, Kell still appeared on her viewer, speaking calmly, evenly. "This is a crisis of interstellar proportions. Earth and all the human settlements throughout the solar system are in danger. So are other worlds, other planetary systems scattered among the stars where intelligent species exist. If we don't act, those creatures will die. If we don't act, the human race will die."

Halleck could hear her pulse thundering in her ears. The anger that seethed through her, though, slowly faded as she marveled at what this man Kell was accomplishing. With the help of his alien wife. Every broadcast channel on the planet! she marveled. I've got to get control of this technology. Which means I've got to get Kell under my control. Him, and his alien woman.

Nashville

++
++

Hamilton cree flew to Nashville on his three-day weekend holiday to see his brothers for the first time since christmas.

The family reunion took place at Jeff's home, a rambling single-story ranch-type house sitting close to the massive levee that kept the Cumberland River within its banks. Farther south and west the lower Mississippi had been engulfed in what people now called the Sea of Mexico. Nashville had barely saved itself from being drowned, like New Orleans and Baton Rouge and so many other cities had been.

Hamilton was the only unmarried man of the four brothers, and the house rang with the shrieks and laughter of his six nieces and nephews.

Happily stuffed with the dinner his sisters-in-law had made, and the beer that brother Hank had brought with him from his distributorship, Hamilton sat in relaxed comfort in Jeff's man cave: territory forbidden to wives and children.

"You see that broadcast the starman made?" asked Washington. He was the closest to Hamilton's age, only two years older. He didn't look much like his namesake: Wash was short, with curly dark hair and a noticeable beer belly.

"Had to see it," Ham replied, from his seat on the sofa between Wash and Hank. "He was on every channel."

"Yeah," said Hank. "Even on my chat line."

"How'd he do that?" Jeff wondered, from the recliner he had cranked halfway back.

"You'll hafta ask him, I guess," Wash said.

"I looked him up on different search engines," said Hank. "Jordan Kell. Used to be some kind of diplomat. They sent him to places where a war or some sort of violence was breakin' out and he'd try to calm ever'body down."

"His wife got killed in one of those scrapes," Wash said.

"I didn't know that," Ham admitted.

"So now he's married to a pretty little thing from New Earth."

"Guess they are just like humans, after all."

With a shrug, Wash said, "They must screw like humans, at least."

"I don't know," Jeff said, in his superior oldest-son tone. "Maybe they do it different."

That led to several minutes of speculation and lewd jokes.

Hamilton almost admitted to his brothers that he'd like to meet this star traveler, face-to-face, see this guy who can close down public bridges just so he and his alien wife can take a look around. Ask him where he gets so high and mighty.

Hank changed the subject. "Hambone, you still lookin' for a job?"

Hamilton hunched his shoulders. "Sort of. Only got a few days until I'm finished with my mandatory service."

"This outfit I'm workin' for up in Chicago, they use a private security firm."

"Rent-a-cop?"

"Yeah, but they're damned good. Topflight outfit. And they're lookin' for people."

"Private security," Hamilton mused.

"Pay's good, and with your police background you'd be a shoo-in. You oughtta go see them."

"Maybe I should," Hamilton agreed.

tarragona air force base

Jordan took a long swallow of cool, tart grapefruit juice.

"Thank you," he said to Aditi, handing her the empty glass. "I've done quite a lot of talking this morning, haven't I?"

She nodded, smiling. "About an hour's worth. That's not so much. I understand human politicians have spoken for days on end, sometimes."

He got up from the cushioned bench and stretched his arms over his head while Aditi carried the glass back to the kitchen. Tendons cracked satisfactorily and Jordan felt his back muscles relax.

"I hope what I've said does some good."

"We'll soon find out."

"Yes." Stepping to the room's only window, Jordan admitted, "I'm rather surprised that no one's burst in here and tried to shut me up."

As if in answer, he saw an unmarked gray sedan screech to a stop down on the street outside. Castiglione bolted out of its rear door.

A small truck pulled up behind the sedan and a dozen men in air force uniforms piled out of it. An officer bustled out of its cab and started waving his arms, directing the men to surround the building.

"The air police are here," Jordan said as he heard Castiglione thumping up the steps to their quarters.

He knocked once, then opened the door and entered the sitting room. For once, he was not smiling.

"You're a very tricky fellow," Castiglione said, without preamble.

Jordan shrugged. "I think the people have a right to know the truth."

Castiglione noticed Aditi in the kitchen. With a slight bow, he said, "I suppose you had something to do with this as well."

"Something," she replied, almost saucily.

Turning back to Jordan, Castiglione eased into a grudging smile. "Every broadcast channel all around the world," he said, nearly admiringly. "How did you do it?"

Jordan quoted, " 'Any sufficiently advanced technology is indistinguishable from magic.' "

"Very erudite," said Castiglione. "I've heard that one before, somewhere."

"Arthur C. Clarke," Jordan explained. "Twentieth-century writer and futurist. English, you know."

Castiglione's face grew serious again. "I'm afraid you've made Anita Halleck very angry."

"I'm sorry to hear that."

"I should be angry with you, as well. I've had to run back here from Barcelona on a supersonic military jet. You've upset my plans for the day."

"My regrets," Jordan said.

Castiglione looked toward Aditi again. "She wants to see you. Both of you. Immediately."

"I'll be happy to see her again. You may recall that I asked you about speaking with her yesterday."

"Yes, I remember," Castiglione replied thinly. Then he smiled again. "Please allow me to offer a quotation for this occasion."

"By all means," said Jordan.

"Be careful of what you wish for. You might get it."

WORLD COUNCIL HEADQUARTERS

Anita Halleck appeared cool, unruffled as she sat at her massive curved desk of ebony and brushed chrome. Its surface was clear, Jordan saw. The hallmark of a capable executive, he remembered. Shift the work to your underlings.

Halleck's office was more than commodious: the desk was in one corner, flanked by sweeping windows that looked out on the busy avenues of Barcelona. Four comfortable burgundy leather armchairs were arranged in a shallow semicircle in front of it. An oval conference table took up the far corner of the room; a pair of sumptuous couches were arranged across from it, a curved glass coffee table between them. Jordan thought the recliner in the remaining corner looked like a therapy chair.

Castiglione ushered Jordan and Aditi into the office. No one else. No police or security guards. Yet Jordan felt as if he and his wife were under arrest, facing angry, suspicious, powerful authority.

He sensed a tautness beneath Halleck's outwardly calm appearance, a tightness of the mouth, a hard expression in her eyes.

Instead of inviting them to sit down, Halleck asked, "How did you do that? Commandeering all the video channels all around the world; even the private chat channels."

Before Jordan could reply, Aditi said, "Our communications engineers will be happy to explain it to you."

"They will?" Surprised.

With a nod, Aditi replied, "Our policy has always been to answer all your questions completely and honestly. But only the questions you have learned to ask."

Halleck frowned at that.

"May we sit down?" Jordan asked.

"Of course," said Halleck, gesturing brusquely to the armchairs.

They sat, Aditi between the two men. Castiglione made a show of looking at his wristwatch. "Should we have tea?" he asked.

"Not for me," said Jordan. "I'm here to discuss what the World Council plans to do about the death wave."

Halleck frowned at him. "You're here," she said firmly, "to hear what we've decided to do about *you*. This business of broadcasting your story all over the world—"

"Plus Selene and the other lunar communities," Aditi informed her. "And the settlements in the Asteroid Belt and elsewhere."

"Through the entire solar system," Castiglione muttered.

"Of course."

Pointing a finger at Aditi, Halleck asked, "You did this?"

"With help from my people on New Earth."

Before Halleck could respond to that, Jordan said, "You might as well face the fact that you can't keep us muzzled. I intend to tell the truth to the people of Earth—to all the human beings in the solar system. The problem is too big to be hushed up."

Halleck glared at him.

"The people have a right to know," Jordan continued. "They have a right to make their opinions known to the World Council."

"So you're going to play on their emotions, to try to force the Council to do what you want," said Halleck.

"I'm going to explain the situation to them, fully and honestly. Then we'll see what they decide."

The ghost of a smile crept across Halleck's face. "And you think that they'll go into a panic over a problem that won't affect us for two thousand years?"

"I'm hoping," Jordan said, "that they'll have the decency to try to save intelligent species who will be destroyed by the death wave in another century or two—unless we act to save them."

"Who are these intelligent species?" Castiglione demanded. "Where are they?"

"Our astronomers can explain that to you," said Aditi.

Jordan said, "There are at least six intelligent species within five hundred light-years of Earth. All of them appear to be pretechnological in their development. They are intelligent, but they haven't yet developed high technology. No electricity. No space travel. No interstellar communications."

"Then how do you know of them?"

"Our Predecessors have sent scouts throughout this sector of the galaxy," Aditi said. "Once they detected the death wave, they began searching for intelligent species that would be endangered."

Jordan added, "Life in the universe is commonplace, apparently. But intelligence is very rare. It's our duty to help intelligent creatures to survive the death wave."

"Our duty," Halleck echoed.

"Our moral obligation," Jordan insisted. But he did not tell her the rest of it. He did not tell Halleck and Castiglione that most intelligent civilizations destroy themselves, one way or the other. He did not tell them that intelligence often leads to a dead end.

carlos otero was accustomed to getting what he wanted. He believed himself to be a self-made man, starting soon after graduating Harvard with nothing more than the local communications company that his father and uncles had bequeathed him. From that small beginning he had built the Otero Network, a news and entertainment empire that reached halfway across the solar system.

And yet, Otero said to himself, this man Kell had taken over all his broadcast centers, even the one all the way out in the habitats orbiting the planet Saturn, commandeered them all to tell his tale of impending doom.

Otero admired the man's daring, but feared his abilities. Standing at the floor-to-ceiling window of his office, on the top floor of Boston's tallest tower, Otero scowled unhappily at the city spread at his feet.

He was a solidly built man in the prime of life, his luxuriant hair and full mustache handsomely dark, his body well muscled. He generally won at any game he played, from golf to arm wrestling—even when he played against people who did not owe their living to him. He had a bright, flashing smile and used it often, especially with willing, eager women.

But this morning he stood alone in his office, unsmiling, hands clasped behind his back, brooding over the report his head of engineering had sent him.

Otero had asked his top engineer a simple question: How did this man Kell manage to take over all the broadcast facilities in the solar system?

The answer unsettled Otero badly. We don't know, his top engineer had reported. We simply cannot determine how Kell took command of the entire Otero Network, and all the other broadcast facilities from Mercury to Saturn, as well.

That kind of power is dangerous, Otero knew. If he can step in and take over all our communications, where does that leave us? Where does that leave me? Impotent. Helpless.

On the other hand, he thought, if we can somehow get Kell to work with us, for us, what a coup that would be! The star traveler, exclusively on Otero Network! I could give him carte blanche, let him tell his story about the wave of radiation or whatever it is that's approaching us. I could make him an interplanetary media star.

And his wife, an alien from another star. What a sensation I could make of her!

Abruptly, Otero turned away from the window and strode to his desk. "Get me Anita Halleck," he commanded his voice-activated phone.

He loathed the chairwoman of the World Council. They had butted heads more than once, usually over matters of communications policy and freedom of speech. Halleck wanted to control the solar system's communications—for the good of the people, she maintained. For her own power, Otero knew.

But now, this Jordan Kell, this man who has returned from the stars, he is a threat to us both. Until I can figure out how to use him against Halleck, I'll have to work with the bitch to see to it that neither Kell nor anyone else can usurp my network again.

In Barcelona, Anita Halleck smiled thinly at Jordan Kell and the human-looking alien sitting beside him.

"You understand, of course, that it's no trivial matter to build starships and send teams out to these civilizations that you claim are endangered."

Jordan nodded politely. "Not trivial, but well within the capabilities of the World Council, I should think."

"You realize, I presume," Halleck said evenly, "that our resources are already stretched close to the limit on damming the meltwater flow from Greenland. If the Gulf Stream is diverted, Western Europe's climate will become Siberian."

"Including the British Isles," Castiglione added, almost vindictively.

Jordan nodded. "Still, we must build the starships and save those alien worlds. It would be inhuman to stand by and let them die."

"What you don't seem to understand," said Halleck, "is that we have our own problems to deal with. You can't expect us to go out on an interstellar crusade."

Sitting on Aditi's other side, Castiglione asked, "Why the urgency? You say that the death wave won't reach their worlds for centuries."

"And won't reach our vicinity for two thousand years," Halleck added.

Jordan stifled the reply that immediately leapt to his mind. He refrained from telling them what he thought of their kick-the-can-down-the-road attitude.

Instead, he said, "I know that the World Council has worked very hard to alleviate the effects of the global climate warming."

"It's our number one priority," said Halleck.

"Yet if the world's governments had acted when the climate warming first became noticeable, nearly three hundred years ago, those effects could have been prevented."

"There was no World Council then," Castiglione pointed out. "No international government at all."

"But the nations of the world were warned about the climate change. Scientists organized international meetings, put out detailed reports."

"Which were not acted upon," Halleck admitted. "Until it was too late. The main reason the World Council was established was to deal with the climate change and its effects."

"And in the meantime coastal cities were flooded. Farmlands parched. The very geography of planet Earth was drastically changed. Millions died. Tens of millions were displaced."

Her face grim, Halleck said, "That wasn't our fault. We have worked very hard to alleviate the effects of the global warming. It hasn't been easy—"

"If the world's political leaders had acted when the scientists first warned of the consequences," Jordan insisted, "most of those effects could have been prevented."

Castiglione got the point. "You're saying that we should act now about the problem of the death wave. We shouldn't wait, even though there's plenty of time."

"Indeed," said Jordan. "There's much to be done."

Focusing on Aditi, Halleck asked, "You can communicate with your people on New Earth? Eight light-years away?"

"Eight point six," Jordan muttered.

"Yes," Aditi answered. "There is a time lag of about an hour, but I can arrange for your technical experts to speak with our communications technicians, our astronomers, whoever you wish."

"And they'll answer our questions."

Aditi nodded. "We will hold nothing back. We want to be fully cooperative."

"I see," Halleck murmured.

"How soon could we start communicating?" Castiglione asked.

"Right away. Today. Now."

Halleck eased back in her plushly cushioned desk chair. "Very well," she said, "we'll begin right now. Rudy, why you don't take Mrs. Kell to meet our communications engineers?"

Castiglione looked surprised. "Now?"

"Now," Halleck answered. "My administrative assistant, in the outer office, will set up the meeting for you."

With a questioning expression on his handsome face, Castiglione got to his feet, then offered his arm to Aditi. "Come, lovely lady. We will astound some of the world's top communications experts."

Jordan pushed himself up from his chair, but Halleck said, "Please stay, Mr. Kell. We have to discuss this matter of building the starships you want."

Jordan stood uncertainly for a moment, then reached out for Aditi's hand. "I'll see you later, dear."

Aditi smiled at him. "Later," she half-whispered.

Halleck said, "She'll be perfectly all right, Mr. Kell. Rudy will take good care of her."

As Jordan sank back into his chair he thought, That's what I'm worried about.

barcelona

+++
+++

Once Aditi and Castiglione left her office, Halleck called for two council members to join her and Jordan: Janos Rudaki, the former astrophysicist, and Deborah Adler, an Austrian-born economist.

The four of them sat around the oval conference table, ostensibly to discuss building starships.

Rudaki reminded Jordan of a badger: compact, strong, dark. His suit looked as though it hadn't been pressed in years; his thick mop of black hair seemed uncombed.

"I have a personal interest in this," he said in his slightly rasping voice. "My daughter is still on New Earth. Perhaps, if she will not return here, I might go to see her."

Halleck said firmly, "You have responsibilities here, on the Council, Professor."

Rudaki waved a hand. "It's about time for me to retire, don't you think?"

"No. Decidedly not. I want you reelected next year, not some interloping newcomer." And she looked directly at Jordan.

"It's nice to be wanted," Rudaki muttered.

Jordan kept his silence.

Deborah Adler was considerably younger. Tall and full-figured, she was wearing a drab gray calf-length dress, without any jewelry nor makeup that Jordan could detect. Yet she still looked appealing, somehow. Is it the sadness in her eyes? Jordan wondered. She seemed almost like a little lost waif, on the verge of tears. But so would I be, I suppose, Jordan told himself, if I were descended from people who'd been driven from their homeland by the Nuclear Holocaust.

She was an economist, according to Halleck. A sad woman whose field of study was the so-called dismal science, Jordan thought, watching her.

"I can call up the cost figures for the vehicle we sent to Sirius," she said, her voice low but steady. "I don't recall the exact amount, but it was close to four billion international dollars."

"I should think we could do better," Jordan said. "After all, we have access now to the energy screens that Aditi's people have developed."

"But they are not propulsion systems," Rudaki pointed out.

"The basic technology can be adapted for propulsion," said Jordan. "We should consult Mitchell Thornberry about that. I believe he and his people are already looking into the propulsion question."

"Thornberry?" Halleck asked. "He's the one who patented the energy screen technology. He's made himself quite wealthy from this alien technology."

"The people of New Earth also gave Mitch a complete education about the basic physics behind the energy screens. We need Mitch to join this project."

With a wintry smile, Halleck said, "We don't have a project yet, Mr. Kell. This is merely a preliminary discussion."

"Yes, but once we get started, Mitch will be of inestimable value."

Halleck nodded.

Adler said, "I'll call up the cost figures for the Sirius mission. We can use them as a baseline."

"Times six," Halleck pointed out.

"I'll call Thornberry," Jordan volunteered. "Mitch will be happy to sink his teeth into the challenge of propelling starships."

"All in good time, Mr. Kell. Remember, what we're doing today is quite preliminary."

And Jordan remembered that, except for their one dinner in Chicago, he hadn't seen Mitch Thornberry at all since their return to Earth. Nor even conversed with him by phone or computer link.

Is Halleck deliberately keeping us apart? he wondered.

The meeting ended, and Halleck gave them all her thanks as she returned to her desk. Jordan thought about asking Rudaki and Adler to join him and Aditi for dinner, but then he realized that he didn't know where Aditi was, nor where he and she were going to spend the night.

Back to the air base? No, he decided. I won't go. I'll demand that Halleck give us back the hotel suite they whisked us away from.

As Adler and Rudaki headed for the door, Jordan turned to Halleck, seated now at her desk, and asked, "Where is Aditi? And where will we be spending the night?"

With an impatient flutter of her hand, Halleck replied, "See my assistant, in the outer office. She'll take care of you."

Jordan had to admit that Halleck's assistant did indeed take care of him. She was a youngish Kenyan, elegantly slim, her tightly kinked hair arranged in cornrows, her voice betraying just a hint of an Oxford accent.

With a few quick phone calls the young woman reserved a suite in the same hotel across the square from the Gothic cathedral, got a Spanish Air Force jet to fly his and Aditi's belongings to the hotel, and arranged for a pair of security people to drive Jordan to the hotel.

Before he left the World Council offices, though, Jordan asked the woman, "And my wife? Where is she?"

Her deeply brown eyes widened slightly. "Why, she's with Signore Castiglione, sir."

"And where might that be? I need to tell her that we'll be staying at the hotel again."

"I'll see to that, Mr. Kell. I'll tell her to call you there."

Feeling more than a little nettled, Jordan said, "I'd prefer to do that myself. Please tell me where she is."

"With Signore Castiglione."

"Here in this building, I presume."

"No sir. They're at the communications center, downtown. It's not far from your hotel, actually."

Before Jordan could react to that, she went on, "It's a highly secure facility, sir. You have to have a special clearance to gain access to it, even on the telephone."

"Then how—"

"I'll see to it, Mr. Kell. You go with your escort to the hotel, and I'll have Mrs. Kell meet you there."

I'm being stonewalled, Jordan realized. By this young slip of a Kenyan.

Two security men entered the office. Both young, trim, with short blond hair and wearing identical navy blue blazers over pearl gray slacks. They stood like patient robots by the door.

Trying to keep from frowning, Jordan said to Halleck's assistant, "Well, thank you, then. I'll expect my wife to meet me at the hotel."

Yet when Jordan got to the luxurious suite, Aditi was not there. Nor had there been a phone message from her.

communications center

++++ ++++ ++++ ++++ ++++ ++++ ++++ ++++ ++++ ++++

++++ ++++ ++++ ++++ ++++ ++++ ++++ ++++ ++++ ++++

"This is an incredible complex," Castiglione was explaining as he led Aditi along an elevated catwalk.

Below them, Aditi could see row upon row of workstations, each console monitored by a man or woman staring intently at the screens flashing images or data. The walls beyond the consoles were larger screens, many of them reaching from the floor to the ceiling, two stories above. The entire vast area seemed to thrum with electric energy.

She walked carefully, to avoid trapping the heels of her shoes in the open metal gridwork of the catwalk.

"From up on the street this structure looks like a nondescript office building," Castiglione was saying, "but down here, in this hardened underground complex, this is the nerve center of the World Council."

Aditi nodded. "They are in touch with all the Council operations around the world?"

Gesturing to a group of consoles set next to the giant wall screens, Castiglione said, "Not merely around the world: they're talking to Selene and the other lunar communities," his pointing finger moved, "the Mars exploration base, the rock rats' center on Ceres, the solar energy base at Mercury, and there," his extended arm shifted again, "the habitats in orbit around Saturn."

"Not Jupiter?" Aditi asked.

Castiglione frowned. "Yes, there must be at least one console talking with the scoopship operators in Jupiter orbit. Ah! There it is. See, on that screen by the corner."

Aditi saw a blur of colors, bands of muted pink and yellow.

As they neared the end of the walkway, Castiglione said, "It takes more than two hours to communicate back and forth with Saturn."

"Your systems are limited to the speed of light," said Aditi.

"Yes. But that will soon change, eh?"

"If that's what you want."

His smile was dazzling. "That's what we want, dear lady. Instant communications."

"It isn't instant," Aditi replied. Before Castiglione could react she went on, "But at the distance between here and Saturn it will seem almost instantaneous."

They had reached the metal door at the end of the walkway. As Castiglione tapped out the security code on the wall-mounted keypad he explained, "This complex was started back when nuclear war was an all-too-real threat. Israel and half the Middle East were destroyed. But down here we're safe from almost anything."

"I suppose that's good," said Aditi, wondering what his *almost* included.

"Indeed it is." The door popped slightly ajar and Aditi felt a breath of cooler air coming from it. Pushing the metal door all the way open, Castiglione ushered Aditi through with a grandiose sweep of his arm.

As the door closed once again behind them, the buzzing hum of the communications center cut off. Aditi saw they were in a quiet, hushed corridor, thickly carpeted, with closed doors on either side. No pictures or decorations of any kind on its blank, off-white walls.

"This is also part of your communications complex?" she asked.

"An extension of it," said Castiglione. "This is where the scientists do their research. We are constantly working to improve our communications capabilities."

"What kind of improvements are they working on?"

As they walked along the corridor, Castiglione answered, "Oh . . . security measures, mostly. Countering attempts to access classified channels. Working to extend our monitoring network."

"Monitoring?"

With a vague wave of his hand Castiglione replied, "We have to keep watch on the people, of course. For their own safety. And to catch criminals and such before they can do harm."

"I see," said Aditi. Yet she thought, Before they can do harm. They're monitoring their own people. And she remembered the cameras and microphones hidden in the quarters she and Jordan had been given at the air base.

"Here we are," said Castiglione. Leaning forward slightly, he spoke his name into the minuscule speaker grille on one of the doors along the corridor. The door was marked PHYSIOLOGY LABORATORY.

"What is this place?" Aditi asked as the door slid open noiselessly.

"Dr. Frankenheimer will explain everything to you," Castiglione replied as he gestured Aditi through the door.

They stepped into a small anteroom, empty except for cushioned benches set against two of its walls. The walls themselves were bare, eggshell white. How drab, Aditi thought. She remembered the swirling colors that decorated the walls of public buildings back on New Earth.

The inner door opened, and a short, slim, sandy-haired man smiled shyly at them.

"Hello. I am Dr. Oswald Frankenheimer."

Aditi accepted his extended hand. Frankenheimer seemed young, almost fuzzy-cheeked.

"My friends call me Ozzie," said Frankenheimer, "although I'm afraid a good number of them also call me Dr. Frankenstein—behind my back."

Puzzled, Aditi asked, "Dr. Frankenstein?"

Castiglione explained, "A famous old novel about a scientist who created a living man out of parts from dead cadavers."

"A monster," Frankenheimer added.

"Oh."

His smile dimming noticeably, Frankenheimer said, "I'm not involved in anything like that, Mrs. Kell, please believe me."

"Then what are you involved in?" she asked.

"Brain physiology," he said. "Please, come into my office and I'll try to explain it all to you."

With Castiglione trailing behind them, Aditi followed the scientist along a short corridor and, at its end, a large windowless office with a desk, several comfortable chairs, and blank walls that glowed a pearly gray. Frankenheimer gestured to one of the chairs. As Aditi sat on it, he pulled up another chair next to hers. Castiglione remained standing by the door, his arms crossed over his chest.

Leaning slightly toward Aditi, Frankenheimer began earnestly, "You have extraordinary capabilities, and we would like to understand them."

"We?" asked Aditi.

Frankenheimer glanced at Castiglione before answering, "My staff here at the laboratory, Mrs. Kell . . . and myself, of course."

Aditi said, "I see."

"Me too," Castiglione added. "Faster-than-light communications!"

"And I presume," Frankenheimer continued, "that it was you who enabled your husband to effectively take over all the communications channels on Earth this morning."

"And off-Earth, as well," said Castiglione.

Aditi looked from Frankenheimer to Castiglione and back again. "You want to learn how this is done."

"Yes!" In unison.

Touching her left temple, Aditi said, "I have a communications device implanted in my brain. It's been there since . . . since I was born."

Eagerly, Frankenheimer said, "We'd like to examine it." Before Aditi could reply, he clarified, "It would be a completely noninvasive examination, I assure you. Neutrino tomography, just to map your brain and the device."

Feeling a bit uncertain, Aditi asked, "Completely noninvasive?"

"Yes. Certainly."

She drew in a little breath, then said, "I'd like to have my husband present when you do this."

"That won't be possible," Castiglione said.

"Not possible? Why not?"

Looking slightly uncomfortable, Castiglione said, "Mr. Kell does not have a security clearance. Without a clearance he cannot enter this complex."

"But I don't have a security clearance," Aditi said.

"Ah, but you are a special case," said Castiglione.

Frankenheimer interjected, "You are the subject of our investigation."

Suppressing a frown, Aditi said, "Suppose I refuse to allow you to probe my brain."

"I'm afraid we would have to insist, dear lady," Castiglione said.

Frankenheimer was starting to look truly distressed. "It's very important," he said. "Ms. Halleck has insisted that we learn how your FTL communications work."

Forcing a smile, Aditi said, "But I don't know how it works."

"You don't?"

"No, I don't. Do you know how your computer works? Or an airplane? You use such devices, but you can't explain how they work, can you?"

"I can explain the general principles," Frankenheimer said.

Aditi said, "I can put you in contact with our technical people. I'm sure they could explain how the communicators work."

Before Frankenheimer could reply, Castiglione said, "You mean you could set up a two-way communications link between here and New Earth?"

"There would be a time lag," said Aditi. "About an hour."

"That would be acceptable," Frankenheimer said, looking eager.

++
++++ +++++++++++++++++++++++++++++++++++++++

Anita Halleck, meanwhile, was smiling across her desk at Carlos Otero. The network owner sat glowering at her like a dark thundercloud.

Otero was in his office in Boston, but the holographic phone link made it appear as if he were sitting in the same room with Halleck.

"You can't keep him under wraps like this," he said, nearly growling. "He's news, for god's sake! The star traveler!"

"Do you want him disrupting your network again?" Halleck challenged. "Do you want him shooting off like a loose cannon again?"

"I want him on Otero Network."

Halleck bit back the refusal that immediately sprang to her mind. Instead, she drew in a calming breath and realized that it would be better to have Otero as an ally than an enemy. Far better.

Slowly, carefully, she replied, "I think that might be arranged, Carlos."

Otero's mustachioed face broke into a happily surprised grin. "It could?"

"Under the proper circumstances."

"What do you mean?"

"You can have Kell appearing on your network exclusively. But not live. Let him say anything he wants to, but our security people will edit his speech. We will allow only the edited version to go out on the air."

Otero's expression darkened. "Only the sanitized version."

"Yes. He can talk about this death wave all he wants to. And about the other worlds that he wants to save from it. But nothing about the new technologies that the aliens have developed. Nothing about his wife or her people."

"Why not? That's news! People would be extremely interested—"

"Too interested," said Halleck. "I don't want the general public expecting miracles from New Earth. We've got to be very careful about how we allow alien technology to be introduced here."

"Like the ban on nanotechnology."

Halleck nodded. "Very much like the ban on nanotech. New technology can be dangerous."

Rubbing his swarthy chin, Otero muttered, "You want to control how much new technology is introduced to Earth."

"Control it very carefully," Halleck said. "Control it so that it helps us to regulate the situation instead of letting everything run wild."

"Protect the people from themselves."

"Exactly."

Otero leaned back in his chair and smiled at the head of the World Council. Remembering that Anita Halleck's body teemed with nanomachines that were forbidden to everyone else on Earth, he said, "But Kell can appear on Otero Network."

"Should be quite a feather in your cap, Carlos."

"Yes. It will be."

Her expression hardening, Halleck said, "But Kell and that alien wife of his are to be kept separated. We can't have him taking over your network—and all the others. That must not happen again."

"Of course not," Otero agreed.

GRAND HOTEL

Jordan paced the spacious sitting room of his hotel suite. Aditi was not there, and four phone calls to Halleck's office had gotten him nothing more than polite requests to be patient.

"I'm sure Mrs. Kell will be with you by the dinner hour," said Halleck's dark-eyed assistant.

Jordan frowned at her image in the phone screen. Dinner hour in Barcelona was around ten P.M., he recalled.

"Where is she?" he demanded.

"With Signore Castiglione" was the only answer he got.

They've separated us, Jordan realized. Halleck is smart enough to realize that without Aditi I'm impotent. I can't reach Adri on New Earth without her. I can't even reach Mitch Thornberry, wherever he is.

Feeling more desperate with each pace across the luxuriously furnished room, Jordan finally decided, Maybe I can reach Professor Rudaki. Perhaps he could be of some help.

Somewhat to his surprise, his phone call to Rudaki was allowed to go through. The professor's dour expression brightened when he saw Kell's image.

"Mr. Kell. I am honored."

Jordan unconsciously reverted to his old diplomatic demeanor. "Thank you, sir. I am flattered."

Rudaki was seated in what appeared to be a smallish office,

crammed with tiny plastic boxes that Jordan assumed held information chips. Books, he imagined; reports, images from telescopes and spaceborn sensors. His desk was heaped high with them.

Looking curious, the professor asked, "To what do I owe this pleasant surprise?"

Jordan realized that he was still standing. Heading for one of the brightly covered couches, he said, "I'm feeling a little desperate, sir."

"Desperate?"

As he sank into the couch's yielding cushions, Jordan explained, "Apparently Anita Halleck has decided to keep my wife and me apart."

Rudaki's rumpled face pulled into a frown. "What did you expect? You frightened her out of her wits when you usurped all the communications channels."

"She's not out of her wits," Jordan said. "She's very much in command of her wits, I'm afraid."

Nodding gruffly, Rudaki agreed, "She's no fool. She guessed that your remarkable performance was as much your wife's doing as yours. So she has decided to keep the two of you separated."

"I don't like that," said Jordan.

"But what can you do about it?"

"I was hoping that you, as a Council member, might help us."

Rudaki broke into a rueful grin. "Halleck runs the Council with an iron hand. If we were to vote twenty to zero against her, she would declare that she won the vote."

"You mean that she's become a dictator?"

"Not quite. But you know the old adage, Power corrupts . . ."

". . . and absolute power corrupts absolutely," Jordan finished.

"I'm afraid she is heading in that direction."

"And this man Castiglione? Where does he fit in?"

"He's her lackey. A charming rogue. He does her dirty work."

A pang of alarm hit Jordan. "He's with my wife."

Rudaki hesitated before replying, "I didn't mean that he would harm her. But if Halleck wants to keep you separated from your wife, Castiglione is perfectly capable of seeing to it."

"What can I do about it?"

"Nothing, I'm afraid."

"Can you help us?"

Again the professor hesitated. After several heartbeats he said, "I can speak to her about it. But I doubt that it would do much good. As I said, that performance of yours really frightened her."

Jordan nodded. But he thought, Did I frighten Halleck, or did I make the mistake of showing her what Aditi's people can do? Would she allow us to be together if I promise to show her how to use Aditi's communications technology?

Dr. Frankenheimer stared in awe at Adri's image on his wall viewer. He was still seated beside Aditi, in front of the desk in his office. Castiglione had quietly taken the chair on Aditi's other side. All three of them had turned their chairs to face the three-dimensional viewer built into the wall.

It was like looking into another room. Adri sat smiling and apparently relaxed in a comfortably padded chair in what Aditi recognized as his office, on the top floor of the civic center in New Earth's only city. It was a spacious room, devoid of the trappings of power: simply an airy room with wide windows that looked out on the city's quiet streets and stately buildings. No desk, no hierarchical arrangement of furniture, only comfortable chairs and small couches scattered across the tiled floor.

The expression on Frankenheimer's youthful face was a mixture of wonderment and curiosity: his mouth hung slightly open; his light brown eyes were wide and totally focused on the alien.

Instead of his usual robe Adri wore a loose-fitting shirt of pale blue that hung over darker slacks. He held a small, furry, round-eyed pet in his lap, stroking it absently. Aditi recognized that as a sign that Adri was far from relaxed: he was actually nervous, concerned.

Half apologetically, Adri was saying in his soft voice, "I'm sorry that the time lag between our world and yours makes a true conversation so difficult. But as I understand it, you would like to learn how our communications technology works."

"Yes!" Frankenheimer cried. Then he looked embarrassed when he realized that his word could not reach New Earth for an hour.

Adri went on, unperturbed, "I will gladly put you in touch with our communications technicians, of course. But you should also contact Mitchell Thornberry, who is on your own planet. Professor Thornberry received a full education in physics while he was here on New Earth, and I'm sure he can teach your people the basics of our communications technology."

Frankenheimer turned to Aditi, who nodded her agreement.

"If there is anything else I can help you with, please do not hesitate to ask me. We intend to be as helpful as we can."

Aditi said, "Thank you, Adri. You've been helpful already."

Adri's image dissolved. The wall went back to a blank glowing gray.

Castiglione smiled grandly at Frankenheimer. "Are you satisfied?"

Looking almost like a man waking from a dream, Frankenheimer said faintly, "It seems like a good beginning."

Aditi confirmed, "As Adri said, we intend to be as helpful as we can." She got to her feet and said to Castiglione, "Look at the time! Can you take me back to my husband, please? He'll be worried about me."

"I'm afraid that will be impossible, dear one."

"Impossible? Why? I want—"

"Lovely one," Castiglione said, "you are our only link with New Earth. We can't risk allowing you to leave this complex. It can be dangerous out there."

"Dangerous?"

"You are an object of curiosity—and fear. There are too many excitable people out there, too many fanatics."

"Then I'm a prisoner here?"

With a smile meant to be charming, Castiglione said, "Let us say you are our guest, beautiful one. Not a prisoner. A highly valued guest."

It amounts to the same thing, Aditi realized.

north dakota

"so this is where you've squirreled yourself away," Thornberry said, looking past Paul Longyear's lean, high-cheeked face to the treeless grassland stretching out to the distant rolling hills.

"My people's homeland," said Longyear, with some bitterness in his voice.

Longyear was a biologist who had been stunned to find that the aliens of New Earth were just as human as he was. For centuries, the intelligent machines that Aditi called the Predecessors had sent scouting missions to Earth to collect DNA samples, from which they created the humanoids that greeted Longyear and the other members of Jordan Kell's expedition to Sirius.

"Not such a bad spot," Thornberry said. "From all I'd read about the United States' treatment of Native Americans I'd expected your reservation to be nothing but rocks and sand."

Longyear stretched out one arm and swept it across the horizon. "Before the whites invaded our territory," he said, "the Sioux Nation ranged all across this land. They followed the buffalo herds for a thousand miles. Now we're penned into this reservation."

Thornberry, thickset and jowly, was wearing a tan leather jacket over his white shirt and jeans. Longyear wore a checkered flannel shirt and almost identical jeans tucked into worn, scuffed boots. His jet black hair was braided into a long queue that ran down his back halfway to his belt.

As they walked slowly along a streamlet that bubbled over a pebbled bed, Thornberry said, "I thought you'd be at your university, not out here."

Longyear shook his head. "I got the feeling that I was being watched. Everywhere I went, they were watching me."

His beefy face breaking into a quizzical smile, Thornberry said, "You're not accustomed to being famous."

"Famous? Me?"

"You're one of the star travelers, m'boy. You've been to New Earth. Of course people stare at you." Lowering his voice to a conspiratorial half-whisper, Thornberry added, " 'Tis a great way to find willing women, it is. That, and finding yourself to be a multimillionaire."

Longyear did not smile. "I'm no multimillionaire. Besides, it wasn't that kind of a thing. I got the feeling the government was watching me, listening to everything I said. I had no privacy, not really."

"You're pretty young to be a paranoid."

"It's not paranoia. They *were* watching me. Following every step I took. Like they wanted to know exactly where I was, every minute of the day or night, what I was saying, what I was thinking."

Thornberry rubbed his jaw. "Y'know, I got that feeling, too. I even spoke to Jordan about it, when we had dinner in Chicago."

"I should have gone with you," Longyear admitted. "It would've been good to see Jordan again."

"He and Aditi send their regards."

Longyear walked along the edge of the stream for a few silent moments. Finally, he asked Thornberry, "So, Mitch, what brings you here? And don't tell me you missed my company."

"I did, you know. And that's a fact."

"But there's more, isn't there?"

Thornberry's normal little smile faded. "There is. I think you're right. We are being watched. And listened to."

Longyear actually smiled. "So who's the paranoid now?"

"I tried to phone Jordan yesterday," Thornberry said, utterly serious. "I got a digitized message saying he's not available."

"You mean they won't let you through to him."

Thornberry nodded.

"That's why I came here," Longyear said. "I can be free here, among my own people."

"Nobody from the government's come looking for you?"

"Oh, a half-dozen security people have come sniffing around. But my people don't tell them anything. I've even seen a couple of drones flying by; I go to ground then."

"Go to ground?"

"Indoors," Longyear said.

Casting an eye toward the nearly cloudless sky, Thornberry said, "Y'know, they probably have satellites surveilling this area."

"Nothing I can do about that."

"Well, there's something I can do, b'god. I'm going back to Chicago and start raising a rumpus. I'm a wealthy man now, and they can't bottle me up."

"You think not?" Longyear asked.

Thornberry hesitated before answering, "I hope not."

Castiglione led Aditi along a thickly carpeted corridor, explaining, "When this complex was originally built, back when nuclear war was a reality, it was constructed to hold more than a thousand people in safety and comfort for a year or more with no contact with the world outside."

Aditi asked, "Your people actually used nuclear weapons on each other?"

"Sadly, yes. Only a few, but that was enough to kill millions. That's when the politicians finally formed the World Council—to control international affairs and get rid of all the remaining nuclear weapons."

"The World Council accomplished that?"

"Oh, yes. It took some time, and there were a few very tense confrontations, but today we have a nuclear-free world."

"That's good," said Aditi.

Flashing a bright smile, Castiglione continued, "But we had already built this marvelous underground complex. Built it and staffed it. Little did we know that one day it would serve to house a visitor from another star."

Aditi did not smile back. Very seriously she said, "I would much rather be with my husband."

"In time, dear one, all in good time," Castiglione said easily. "For the present, you will live here in some comfort."

He stopped at an unmarked door, tapped on the keypad on the wall, and the door slid open. With a flourish, Castiglione ushered Aditi into the apartment.

"Your home away from home," he said grandly.

Aditi stepped into the living room. It was small, but comfortably furnished. She recognized a viewer for three-dimensional broadcasts on one wall. Through an open door she saw a neatly prepared bedroom.

"We've taken the liberty of bringing your clothes from the air base. You'll find them in the bedroom closet and drawers. If you need anything else, just tell me."

"I see."

Still smiling, Castiglione went on, "We have a fairly good restaurant facility here, as well. Would you kindly join me for dinner?"

"It's been a long day," Aditi said, "and I'm quite tired."

"I understand." Pointing to the telephone console on the end table by the sofa, Castiglione said, "You can order dinner brought here."

"Thank you."

"I'll see you in the morning."

"Very well."

Aditi stood in the middle of the room as Castiglione smiled his way out. As soon as the door slid closed she tried to contact Adri, on New Earth.

grand hotel

+++
+++

Jordan tried to open the door of his hotel suite. Locked. He frowned, and felt simmering anger rising within him. Don't lose your cool, old man, he said to himself. Then he banged the door with his fist.

A voice from the speaker set into the ceiling asked, "Mr. Kell, how can I help you?"

"I'd like to go down to the restaurant. I'm hungry."

"Sir, I'm afraid that's not possible. You can order dinner brought to your suite."

"I'm not allowed to leave the suite?"

"Not at this time, sir."

Jordan stood there, thinking, They've got me under lock and key. And they're watching me. It's a prison. A very luxurious prison, true enough, but a prison nonetheless.

Wishing that Aditi were with him, wondering where she was and how she was faring, he went to the phone and grudgingly ordered dinner. Within minutes it was brought to his room by an impassive robot. Once the machine had deposited the dinner tray on the sitting room's coffee table and left, Jordan sat down to eat.

And think.

They're watching me in here, and they've probably got cameras out in the corridor. I'm on the tenth floor, and the window doesn't open. I'd have to shatter it to get out, and then it's a ten-story drop to the street.

So how do I get out of here?

He chewed on that question as he slowly, methodically chewed his way through dinner. Halleck's people must have the entire hotel under continuous surveillance, he figured. No doubt there's a team of security people on hand to take care of any emergencies.

Well, he told himself, I suppose I'll have to create an emergency and see how far I can get. I'm certainly not going to sit here like a good little prisoner.

He finished his coffee, then reached for the tiny snifter of cognac. Its top was sealed, but the plastic cover popped off easily enough. Jordan tossed down the cognac and got to his feet.

Time to act, he told himself.

He went to the bedroom and pulled a lightweight checkered jacket from the closet, then returned to the sitting room and mentally counted off the seconds until the door slid open and a serving robot wheeled into the room.

"Are you finished with your dinner, sir?"

You can see that I'm finished, Jordan replied silently. Aloud, he asked, "Have you been waiting outside my door all this time?"

"No, sir. That would be inefficient. I was directed to your room when the controllers calculated that you would be finished by the time I reached your suite."

"I see." To himself, he added, So they are watching me in here, just as I thought.

Extending two of its four arms toward the dinner tray on the coffee table, the robot asked again, "Are you finished with your dinner, sir?"

"Yes," said Jordan. "Quite finished."

He watched as the robot deftly picked up the tray, then pivoted and began trundling toward the door, which slid open as it approached.

Jordan walked a step behind the blocky machine and went out into the corridor with it. The robot ignored him and headed down the corridor, in the direction opposite to the elevator bank.

Service elevator, Jordan thought. It must use a service elevator.

Sure enough, the robot went through an unmarked door at the far end of the corridor and into a small room with bare concrete walls that held an ice machine, several bins that Jordan didn't recognize, an obvious laundry chute, two black elevator doors, and another door marked EMERGENCY EXIT.

Still holding the dinner tray in two hands covered in synthetic skin, the robot used its third hand to touch the elevator call button.

A voice from the speaker set into the ceiling suddenly blared, "Mr. Kell, you are in a restricted area. Please return to your suite."

Jordan looked up and saw a tiny red light glowering at him: another surveillance camera.

"Sorry," he said easily. "I'm just curious."

"Please return to your suite, Mr. Kell."

"Of course."

But instead Jordan pushed through the emergency exit. As he expected, it opened onto a stairway of bare gray concrete steps.

He started down the steps. As soon as he reached the next landing, the same overhead voice said, "Mr. Kell, you are not authorized to leave your suite. Please return."

Hurrying down the next flight, Jordan said, "I always take a constitutional after dinner." Inwardly he smiled at the small pun: I'm exerting my constitutional right to freedom by taking a constitutional walk.

He got down four flights of the stairs before a pair of security agents came clattering up the stairs toward him. A young man and a slightly older woman, both in dark blue suits and white turtleneck shirts.

"Where do you think you're going?" the woman demanded, from the landing below.

Jordan saw that their hands were empty, but that didn't mean they weren't carrying weapons beneath their jackets.

Remembering his youthful lessons in self-defense, Jordan recalled that surprise and speed were the best way to attack. Surprise and speed, he repeated silently, hoping that his two-century-old reflexes were still good enough to serve.

He said nothing as the two of them came up the steps toward him. That's right, he said to himself, come and get the old man. He felt an odd tingle of anticipation.

As the pair of them climbed to within two steps of him, Jordan lashed out with a kick squarely to the man's chest that knocked him backward, tumbling down the steps. He smacked the back of his head against the concrete wall with a sickening thud and went slack, his eyes rolling up. The woman looked shocked for an instant, then reached into her jacket. Jordan pinned her arms and wrestled her to the stair's railing.

She tried to knee him in the groin, but Jordan bent her back over the stair rail. She looked down the stairwell, her eyes widening with sudden fright.

"It's a long way down," he growled at her.

She let her body relax and Jordan pulled her back onto the stairs. Immediately she slipped one hand free of Jordan's grip and aimed an elbow at his head. Jordan ducked and stamped as hard as he could on her foot. She yowled and Jordan grabbed at her jacket. He pulled out the pistol that had been holstered under her arm.

She froze for an instant and Jordan realized he didn't know how to use the pistol. It looked strange to him, small, deadly, oddly shaped. A tranquilizer gun, he guessed.

She swung at him again and without thinking about it he whacked her across the temple with the gun. Her legs folded and she sank to the steps, unconscious.

Puffing from exertion, feeling strangely exhilarated, Jordan congratulated himself, Not bad for a two-hundred-year-old.

He stuffed the pistol into the waistband of his slacks and started down the stairs again. The male security agent was moaning and writhing.

It's just a matter of minutes before they send reinforcements,

Jordan knew. He raced down the steps, toward the hotel's lobby level.

But then he skidded to a stop. They'll be waiting for me in the lobby, he thought. I'll be walking into their arms.

Slower, more carefully, he went as far as the mezzanine level and tried the door. It opened onto another service area, virtually identical to the one on his floor. A maintenance robot was emptying one of the bins into a rolling cart, totally oblivious to Jordan's presence.

He pushed through the door and found himself on the well-carpeted mezzanine. Nearly a dozen people were walking along, chatting, laughing. A grand curving staircase leading down to the lobby was only a dozen paces away from where he stood.

As casually as he could manage, Jordan slipped in among the people who were heading toward the stairs. The men were wearing suits or sports jackets; the women stylish dresses. Jordan was glad he'd thought to put on his jacket—he blended in with the others better, and it hid the gun stuck in his trousers' waistband.

He saw a trio of security people down on the lobby floor, all in the same dark jackets and white turtlenecks, threading through the crowd, hurrying toward the service area. One of them had his hand to his ear.

They're telling him that I got off the stairwell at the mezzanine level, Jordan guessed as he started down the gracefully curved stairs. Stay with the crowd, he told himself. Don't run, don't do anything to call attention to yourself.

As he reached the lobby floor, he glanced sidelong at the security team. They rushed past him, nearly within arm's reach, and started up the stairs toward the mezzanine. Another pair of guards stationed themselves at the elevator bank.

Get to the main entrance before they put guards on it, Jordan told himself. They might have the entire hotel under surveillance, but it takes time to get orders from the monitoring center to the security teams stationed around the hotel. You've got to move faster than they do.

Staying with the crowd that was heading toward the hotel's main entrance, Jordan could feel his heart thumping beneath his ribs. He turned to the elderly gentleman beside him and said, in Spanish, "It seems like a beautiful evening."

"Yes," the older man replied graciously. "There should be no rain until after midnight."

The hotel's entrance was wide. Steady streams of people were entering the lobby and leaving it. Jordan counted four robots standing impassively just outside the entrance, and a single human doorman in splendid uniform smiling at the people climbing out of taxicabs and limousines.

Jordan stepped through the entrance, turned to his right, and started walking down the crowded street.

To where? he asked himself. I've got no money and I don't dare use the credit chip that the government gave me; it could be traced in a matter of minutes.

Alone on the busy streets of Barcelona, Jordan realized that he was free for the time being. But what should I do next?

cΩmmuΩicΩtiΩΩⁿ cΩmplΩx

Aditi picked at the dinner she had ordered, her attention focused on the viewer built into the wall of
the living room where she sat.

Perhaps this underground complex is shielded too heavily for
my call to get through, she worried. She knew that the communicator in her brain operated on dark energy, completely different
from the electromagnetic frequencies used on Earth, but still she
feared—

"Hello, Aditi." Adri's face, lined with age, smiled gently at her.

She gushed out a relieved sigh. In the three-dimensional viewer,
Adri appeared to be walking along the stone path that ran along the
perimeter of their city on New Earth, out in the open on a bright
cloudless day. He wore a floor-length robe of forest green, with
fine golden traceries bedecking it.

Before she could say anything, Adri suggested, "Perhaps you had
better talk to me and tell me what has happened to you since we
last spoke. From your latest message, I presume that you are alone.
They have separated you from Jordan?"

As swiftly and concisely as she could, Aditi explained what was
happening to her and Jordan. She tried to keep her voice calm, tried
to recite only the facts. But she found herself trembling with emo-
tion: fear, resentment, even anger. By the time she was finished she
felt weary, drained.

The viewer went blank. She knew it would take about an hour

for her words to reach Adri, and his reply to return to her. She went to the lavatory, showered and prepared for sleep, thinking that Castiglione could walk into her apartment whenever he chose to. Aditi wondered what she would do if he chose to barge in on her at this time of night.

By the time she returned to the sitting room, Adri's three-dimensional image was once again in the viewer. The old man had sat himself down on one of the stone benches that lined the curved perimeter walkway, his hands clasped on his lap. Once Aditi explained the situation to him, he shook his head slightly.

"The humans must be very afraid of you," he said, "to keep you isolated. I presume that they understand you can contact me whenever you wish."

Aditi nodded, even though she knew that Adri would not see her gesture for an hour.

Continuing unperturbed, Adri said, "We must not lose sight of the major objectives: to save as many of the intelligent civilizations as we can, and to save Earth itself and the other human settlements in Earth's system."

But how can we do that if Earth's leaders refuse to act? Aditi wondered silently.

"It would seem," Adri went on, "that your task is to convince Earth's leaders to act, without delay. But it is very difficult to make them see the need for prompt action. They are still steeped in their ancient ways, still distrustful of strangers, still eager to seek advantages that will promote their own interests."

Adri slowly rose to his feet. "We must find a way to make them see the need to protect themselves and the other intelligent species that are in danger. Quite frankly, Aditi, I don't know how to do that. You are there, on the scene, among them. You must find the way. You and Jordan, together."

"But we're not together!" Aditi blurted. "They've separated us!"

"I wish I could help you," Adri continued. "If I think of anything that might be helpful, I will contact you. In the meantime, you must act as wisely as you can."

The viewer went dark. Aditi sat in the underground apartment, alone.

Jordan walked along Las Ramblas, enjoying his newfound freedom even though he half-expected a team of security agents to surround him at any moment.

What to do? he asked himself repeatedly. Where can I go?

Las Ramblas was crowded with people, even though it was nearing midnight. Restaurants and bars were open, brightly lit. Crowds clustered outside theaters that offered everything from flamenco dancers to historical dramas.

Aditi, Jordan said to himself. Where is Aditi? What have they done with her?

I need help, he knew. The only person he could think of who might be willing to help him was Mitchell Thornberry. But Mitch is in Chicago, Jordan knew. I need help here, right now.

Then he remembered Professor Rudaki. Maybe he'd be willing to help me. He wasn't much help when I phoned him earlier, but who else can I turn to?

Jordan found a curbside bench that was occupied only by a pair of youngsters who seemed oblivious to everyone and everything except each other. He sat at the other end of the bench and wondered how he could locate Rudaki's address.

I can't risk calling him, or even using my phone to find his address, Jordan reasoned. Halleck's people probably monitor all communications and they'll pinpoint my location immediately.

With some trepidation, he said in Spanish to the young couple on the other end of the bench, "Excuse me, please. Could you kindly help me?"

The two youngsters looked surprised, shocked almost, to be pulled out of their private universe.

Trying to appear befuddled, Jordan said, "I can't get my communicator to function properly. Could you please find an address for me?"

The young man smiled. Jordan thought, In his eyes I must seem like a dotty old coot.

"Certainly, sir," the lad said.

Within less than a minute the youngster found Rudaki's address and even showed Jordan a street map of how to get there. Too far to walk, Jordan realized.

"A million thanks," he said as he got up from the bench.

"It's nothing," said the young man, turning back to his young woman.

Jordan walked away and looked down the crowded avenue for a taxi. No cash and I can't use a credit chip. With a shake of his head and an almost rueful little grin, Jordan told himself, Imitate the action of the tiger. Be bold. Display no doubts. A confident attitude had helped him in other scrapes all those years ago, when he had been a diplomat sent to trouble spots around the world.

He waved to an approaching taxi. It glided to curbside and Jordan ducked into it. It was a tiny vehicle, with only two seats. No human driver, the cab was automated. Jordan smiled to himself. At least I won't cheat a workingman out of his fare.

He directed the cab to within five blocks of Rudaki's address. It was a quiet suburban area, hardly any traffic. The sidewalks were lined with trees, and empty of pedestrians. A nice, peaceful, upscale residential neighborhood, Jordan thought. Good.

When he tried to get out, though, he found that the taxi's door would not unlock.

"The fare is twelve international dollars," said the synthesized voice from the cab's dashboard speaker, in Spanish.

"I'm afraid I don't have any money with me," Jordan replied in English.

Switching to English, the nonhuman voice repeated, "The fare is twelve international dollars."

"I don't have any money with me," Jordan repeated.

"This vehicle is equipped to accept credit charges."

"No credit chip, either."

For several moments the cab remained silent. Jordan tried both doors; still locked. Then a distinctly nettled woman's voice issued from the speaker grille. "You don't have a credit chip?"

"I'm afraid not."

"Remain in the cab, then. I am dispatching a security car to take care of you. They'll be with you in a few minutes."

Jordan glanced around the cab's interior. There was a transparent plastic panel in the roof, marked EMERGENCIA.

Well, he said to himself, this is an emergency if there ever was one.

Wondering if the cab was equipped with a security camera, he reached up and flicked the latch of the emergency panel. A shrill warning whistle erupted. Quickly, Jordan pushed the panel open, then stood up and climbed out of the cab. As he dropped down onto the street, he heard the woman's voice over the wail of the alarm, "The security car will be with you in less than a minute. Please remain seated."

Not bloody likely, Jordan said to himself as he hurried away from the taxi. He saw a pair of headlights approaching from two blocks up the otherwise empty street, so he turned at the corner. As he slipped behind one of the curbside trees the gray unmarked sedan went past him and pulled to a stop behind the taxi. Jordan walked as fast as he could toward Rudaki's house.

JANOS RUDAKI

It was the smallest house on the block, but it still looked luxurious to Jordan as he stood before its gate of intricately decorated metal spikes. Two stories high, with a gabled roof. Set well back from the street. Gracious trees and thick flowering bushes adorning the front lawn.

Rudaki's doing well for himself, Jordan thought as he leaned on the call button set beside the gate. Being a World Council member must pay considerably better than being a university professor.

There were lights on in two of the second-floor windows, he saw. A figure passed by one of them.

"Yes?" Rudaki's querulous voice. "Who is it?"

Jordan hesitated. Should I give him my name? What if he calls the police?

"Well?" Impatiently.

"It's Jordan Kell, Professor. I need your help."

"Kell? At this time of night?"

"I'm in trouble and I need your help, sir."

Jordan heard grumbling, and a woman's sleepy voice. At last the gate's lock clicked and Rudaki said, "Come in. I'll meet you at the front door."

As Jordan hurried up the walk to the front door of the house he felt a few drops of rain pattering down on him. Glancing at his wrist, he saw it was precisely midnight. Do they control the weather? he wondered.

Lightning flashed across the dark sky and a roll of thunder growled as Jordan reached the door. In the light of the overhead lamp he saw that the door was made of wood, with a schematic of the solar system carved into it.

Grateful for the overhang protecting him from the increasingly heavy downpour, Jordan saw lights come on inside the house. The door opened at last and there stood Janos Rudaki in a disheveled maroon bathrobe, his heavy brows knitted, his expression dour, wary.

"Come in, Mr. Kell," the astrophysicist said. "Get out of the rain."

Half an hour later, fortified by a healthy slug of Spanish brandy, Jordan sat in Rudaki's study, unfolding his story.

"So I was hoping that you could help me to reach Mitchell Thornberry, in Chicago," he said.

The room was small, intimate. Astronomical photographs covered the walls. Data chips were strewn everywhere: in the bookshelves, on the couches and ottomans; stacks of them were lined haphazardly against the wall next to the professor's desk.

Jordan sat in a comfortably upholstered armchair in the only uncluttered corner of the room, Rudaki in a similar chair, facing him. Like Jordan, he held an almost-empty brandy snifter in one hand. The bottle rested on a small table beside his chair.

His expression still cheerless, Rudaki said, "You've set yourself against the most powerful woman in the solar system. Halleck wants control of your wife's FTL communications technology."

"She can have it," Jordan replied. "Aditi's people have no intention of hiding it from her. We're here to help the human race."

"Just like that?" Rudaki countered. "No strings? You want nothing in return?"

"I want the World Council to begin taking steps to protect the solar system from the death wave—"

"Which won't be a problem for two thousand years."

"And to protect the other worlds that are endangered by the approaching radiation."

"Worlds that we know nothing about. Our searches for intelligent life among the stars have revealed nothing—except for your aliens of New Earth."

"The intelligent species on those planets are preindustrial. They haven't achieved the level of technology that can create the kind of signatures you've been looking for. No radio or telephone. Not even telegraph signals."

Rudaki shook his head in disbelief.

"I can get the astronomers of New Earth to show you their evidence," Jordan said, feeling a bit desperate. "Those worlds are out there, believe me. Those intelligent creatures are in danger of extinction!"

Rudaki sank back in his chair and almost smiled. "You are very passionate about this, I'll give you that much."

"This isn't a game," Jordan snapped. "It's not some intellectual exercise. Lives are at stake. Whole civilizations!"

"And just how do you intend to make Halleck do what you want?"

Jordan hesitated. Then, "I don't know. The only course I can imagine is to go public with the story. Tell the truth to the people and let them decide."

"You tried that once and it frightened Halleck very badly."

"And she's separated me from my wife." Jordan didn't give voice to the fear that he felt. *What are they doing to Aditi? What do they want of her?*

With a dejected shake of his head, Rudaki said, "You can't fight Halleck. She's too powerful."

"I've got to try," said Jordan. "Perhaps . . . perhaps you might help me?"

"Me?" Rudaki looked shocked. "I'm an old academic who was dragooned onto the Council by the global lottery Halleck initiated. She won't even let me resign!"

"You want to resign?"

"I've put in enough time on the Council. Look around this room! My work in astrophysics is moribund. I can't even go to New Earth and join my daughter."

And I can't even be with my wife, Jordan thought.

In her apartment deep inside the communications complex, Aditi was again speaking to Adri on New Earth.

"They are eager to learn how our communications technology works. Could you set up a meeting with our best technicians? I think that would help to ease their fears about us . . . and it would encourage them to allow Jordan and me to be together again."

She glanced at the digital clock set into the wall beneath the holographic viewer and saw that it was well past one A.M. No wonder I feel sleepy.

To Adri's inert image, she said, "I know that you can't reply for more than an hour. I'm going to sleep now. I hope your response will be waiting for me when I wake up."

But as she arose tiredly from the couch on which she'd been sitting, she heard a rap on the apartment's door.

Puzzled, alarmed, she flicked her eyes to the screen that showed who was at her door. It was a robot, bearing a tray of bottles and glasses.

"Go away," she called. "I'm retiring for the night."

Castiglione stepped into the screen's view, smiling softly.

"Aditi, I brought you a nightcap."

"I don't drink alcoholic beverages," she said, stretching the truth slightly. "And I'm preparing to go to sleep."

The door slid open and Castiglione stepped into the room, his smile turning brighter.

"Our security people are worried about you," he said. "You've turned off all their surveillance devices. They can't see what you're up to."

"I want my privacy," Aditi said.

Castiglione nodded. "That's fine. But we must make certain that you're all right."

"You can see that I am. Now please go."

Instead, Castiglione turned and beckoned to the robot, which trundled in from the hall.

"I thought we might share a nightcap before retiring."

Aditi drew herself up to her full height, barely as tall as Castiglione's shoulder. "I don't want a nightcap. I want to go to sleep."

His smile turning almost into a leer, Castiglione asked, "Alone?"

Aditi slapped his face as hard as she could. "Get out!"

Castiglione looked shocked. Aditi could see the white imprint of her fingers on his reddened cheek.

"Out," Aditi repeated.

Without another word, Castiglione turned and left the room, the robot rolling along behind him. Aditi slid the door shut and leaned against it. But he can come in here any time he wants to, she thought. Any time he wants to.

barcelona, el prat airport

The flight to London was scheduled to take off at seven a.m. As he stepped out of the chauffeured car at the terminal's curb, Jordan half expected a squad of police or security agents to descend on him any moment.

He had slept at Rudaki's house, and the professor had provided him with a handsome traveler's check to cover his expenses.

"Old-fashioned, using paper," Rudaki had said as he handed Jordan the check. "But it's not traceable by their usual means."

"This is terribly good of you," Jordan said.

"I'm afraid that's all I can do for you." With a crooked little smile, the professor had said, "The money comes from a fund that's available to members of the World Council. In a sense, your trip will be financed by Anita Halleck." His smile fading, he had added, "I hope she won't be able to trace it."

Jordan appreciated the irony of that as he left the chauffeured car Rudaki had provided him and headed straight to the airport's money exchange booth.

Now he forced himself to sit and wait for the plane to London to take off. He was booked on a London-to-Chicago flight later in the day.

What's happened to Aditi? he asked himself, over and over again. Is she all right?

* * *

Aditi was also sitting tensely, on the living room sofa in the apartment where she'd spent the night, watching Adri's lean, aged face in the holographic viewer.

"I have set up a lecture-demonstration by the leader of our communications department," the old man was saying. "If you can get your communications technicians to provide me with a time that would be convenient for them, we can begin their education."

Adri's image froze and Aditi realized he was waiting for her response.

She nodded, knowing he wouldn't see her reaction for an hour. "One further thing, Adri," she said, lowering her voice even though she knew all the surveillance devices in the apartment had been disabled. "Can you help to get me out of this complex? I want to be free. I want to find Jordan and be with him."

Anita Halleck was livid. The chief of her security department stood before her desk like a guilty little schoolboy, his head hanging low, while she fulminated.

"Gone! Escaped from the hotel! How is that possible? How could one man get through your security system and waltz out of that hotel? Didn't you have him under surveillance? Didn't you have a team of agents covering the hotel?"

His voice so low Halleck could barely hear it, the security chief said merely, "He got past our people. We have camera views of him every step of the way, but he beat up two of our people and slipped out of the hotel before my team could stop him."

"Fire them!" Halleck snapped. "Fire each and every one of them!"

"I'm afraid that's not possible, ma'am. Their employment contracts—"

"I don't care what their contracts say! Get rid of them! Transfer them to Timbuktu or Mars if you can't fire them!"

"Yes, Madame Chairwoman."

"And find Jordan Kell! Wherever he is, I want him found and brought here to me."

Licking his lips, the security chief said, "We checked all the taxicab trips throughout the city at that time of night."

"And?"

"There was one trip where the customer didn't pay his fare; he got out of the cab through the overhead emergency exit and left, just a couple of minutes before midnight."

"That could be him."

"Yes'm. I personally analyzed the street map of the area where he left the cab. It's an upscale residential neighborhood."

"Kell doesn't know anyone in Barcelona," Halleck said.

"He's met the Council members, hasn't he?"

"Yes."

"Councilman Rudaki lives a few blocks from where Kell left the cab. Assuming it was Kell. We have voice recordings from his talking to the cab's computer. They're pretty weak but my people are trying to see if they match Kell's speech patterns."

"Rudaki," Halleck murmured. "He went to Rudaki's home?"

"It's a possibility."

"You get a team to his house immediately. Search the premises, cellar to attic." Turning to her desktop phone console, Halleck commanded, "Get Professor Rudaki and tell him I want to see him here, in my office, immediately."

treasure island

+++

+++

"Just call me Walt," said the black man.

"Walt," Nick Motrenko repeated.

The two of them were sitting side by side on a concrete bench on the edge of a pathetically small public park in the middle of a dilapidated public housing project. Nick's home, provided rent-free by the state of California, was one of two thousand identical one-bedroom houses that covered the island, manufactured in a fully automated factory and transported to this island in the bay with hardly a single human being involved.

At the end of the shabby street Nick could see the Bay Bridge and the incessant stream of traffic flowing along, cars and buses and trucks, most of them shiny new, each of them with somewhere to go, some job or duty or rendezvous to fulfill.

Walt was wearing a gray shirt and dark slacks. They looked almost like prison-issue clothes to Nick. Shabby, but not as bad as that crummy bathrobe he'd been wearing the first time they'd met. Somehow his beard looked neater, less scruffy. He must have shaved a day or two ago, Nick thought. Yet he smelled rancid, unwashed.

Nick looked into the black man's red-rimmed eyes and saw a deep discontent there. And something more, something darker. Resentment. That was it, Nick realized. Walt feels the same kind of resentment that I do.

"Walter James Edgerton is the name my parents gave me," said

Walt. "Sounds very genteel, doesn't it? Walter James Edgerton." Smiling, he seemed to roll the name on his tongue, tasting it like a choice morsel. Then his expression hardened. "That's the name the government knows me by. The name I haven't used since I left prison. You're the first person I've told my full name to in more than ten years, Nick."

Nick had offered his house to Walt, but the black man had gently refused. "Public housing is filled with sensors. Within minutes of my entering under your roof, the government would identify me and send a team of social workers to gently but firmly bring me back into their system."

"You've been living on the streets for more than ten years?" Nick asked.

"It's not that difficult," Walt answered. "People are kind. Most people."

"Is there anything you need?" Nick asked. He'd already brought Walt an improvised lunch out of his own refrigerator: the two men had shared thin sandwiches and beer on the park bench.

"Where is Rachel this morning?" Walt asked.

Nick shrugged. "She works for the public library in downtown Oakland. That's how we met, in the library where she works."

"A lovely young woman," Walt murmured.

"Yeah." Silently he added, *Hands off*, but he had the feeling it was already too late for that.

Very earnestly, the black man said, "I want you to understand, Nick, that I have never come on to Rachel. I've never tried to get her into my bed." Then he smiled and added, "Of course, I don't have a bed to call my own."

Nick nodded, then remembered that he hadn't needed a bed to have sex with Rachel.

"She tells me you're concerned about the star traveler."

Surprised by the sudden change of subject, Nick said, "Jordan Kell, yeah. Him and his alien wife."

"What bothers you about him?"

"The government's protecting him. Keeping him away from people who want to interview him."

"Like you."

"Yeah. I've applied to interview him for my blog and all I get is excuses."

Walt nodded slowly. "I suppose everybody wants to interview him."

"Yeah, but nobody's getting to see him. They've got him hidden away someplace. Ever since that first news break when they returned from New Earth, nobody's even seen him."

"I understand he was in New Mexico, briefly."

"Yeah, I heard that, too. But why New Mexico? What was he doing there? What's he up to? Why's the government hiding him?"

For a long moment Walt held his silence. At last he said, "Maybe he wants to stay hidden. Maybe the government is doing what *he* tells *them* to do."

Nick had never considered that possibility. "You think?"

"Who knows?"

Bitterness simmering inside him, Nick growled, "They're up to something. They're keeping him away from us, him and his alien wife."

"Or he's keeping himself and his alien wife away from us," Walt said, his voice a low purr.

"Either way, it's a fucking conspiracy, that's what it is. The government's in contact with aliens, and they won't let us ordinary citizens know what's going on!"

"There's more here than meets the eye," Walt agreed.

"Yeah."

"What do you think you should do about it?"

Nick started to answer, but found that he had nothing to say. "I don't know," he admitted, feeling weak, helpless, and hating himself for it.

But Walt smiled, sphinxlike. "I think perhaps I can help you, Nick, my friend."

"Yeah?"

"Remember what I said when we first met. Rise and strike."

so much of his life was based on fiction and deception that walt sometimes had difficulty separating the
true from the not-so-true.

He had indeed been arrested and jailed when he was fourteen.
Not for hacking into the school system's examinations, but for at-
tempting to blackmail his middle school principal, threatening to
reveal that they had had sex together (which was false) unless she
altered his grades (which were less than admirable).

His trial was so brief that he didn't realize it was over until
the judge declared him guilty and sentenced him to five years in a
corrective school.

It was there that his talents blossomed. Walt obtained con-
traband narcotics for his fellow teenaged jailbirds, he sold forbidden phones and notebooks to them, he learned how to smuggle
prostitutes—male as well as female—into their cells.

He himself remained a virgin. He was never raped. He never
hunted down his nonexistent violator. He never killed anyone.

But one fine day (actually it was raining hard all morning) he
was taken from his cell and brought to a conference room. Waiting for him there was a tall, broad-shouldered blond woman with a
generous figure and a face that would have been beautiful if she
would only smile.

But she was deadly serious. She offered Walt freedom and even
a decent income if he would cooperate with the World Council

security agency, of which she was a high-ranking member. A recruiter, she called herself, working to find and stop criminals before they could harm society.

So Walt became an *agent provocateur*. At first he had been thrilled about it. His job was to mix with the young and disaffected, the unemployed, unemployable youthful men and women who lived on government subsidies. Find the ones who were willing to commit crimes and see to it that the police apprehended these potential criminals before they could do much harm to society.

It meant living like a smelly unshaven bum much of the time. But Walt didn't mind that too much. It was part of the deception, part of the role he was playing. He found that there were plenty of young women who were willing to trade sex for adventure, for advancement, for staving off the loneliness of their threadbare existences.

Over the years, Walt became a guru, wandering across the country, meeting youngsters who were desperately seeking guidance and friendship, searching for some goal in their cheerless lives. He began to believe he was honestly doing good among the kids growing up in the public housing projects and dark streets of their overcrowded cities.

He kept a neat little apartment for himself in Oakland, California, and repaired to it in between assignments. He worked off and on at writing his autobiography, partly accurate, mostly fiction.

Then he got an urgent call from Barcelona, from the woman who had originally recruited him.

"People are frightened of this star traveler," she had told him. "They're afraid we're going to be taken over by aliens."

Walt had never considered that possibility. Neither had anyone he'd met or worked with.

"There must be terrorist groups scheming to assassinate him,"

Gilda Nordquist went on. "We've got to identify them and find out what they're up to."

Walt understood what she was saying. She expected him to produce a terrorist cell that would try to assassinate the star traveler. And if they succeeded, so much the better.

Chicago

+++++ +++++ +++++ +++++ +++++ +++++ +++++ +++++ +++++ +++++ +++++ +++++

+++++ +++++ +++++ +++++ +++++ +++++ +++++ +++++ +++++ +++++ +++++

The flight from London to Chicago was by rocketplane, of course. Forty-five minutes from liftoff to touchdown. Yet as he sat in the softly yielding recliner chair and watched the atmosphere's thin layer of blue hugging the curved horizon, Jordan wondered why no one had invented a better system for long-distance transportation.

They're still using rockets, he mused. Probably not chemical rockets, they must have come up with something more efficient than that, but basically this vehicle isn't that much different from the clipperships we used before I left for New Earth.

Well, maybe Mitch can adapt the energy screen technology for propulsion. Use dark energy instead of brute force rockets. He said he was looking into that.

The display screen on the bulkhead of his private compartment lit up with the image of a smiling young woman in the airline's sky-blue uniform who said, "We are beginning our descent into Chicago's Banks Aerospaceport . . ."

She looked faintly Asian, although her eyes were sky blue. A mixture of different stock, he concluded; the whole human race was slowly blending. That's good. Then he remembered that almost everyone on Earth carried a percentage of Neanderthal genes. We've been blending for a long time, he realized.

Jordan tuned her out of his attention. All she was really saying was that he should buckle his safety harness. As he did so, he recalled that he didn't know Thornberry's address: neither his home nor his place of business. I'll have to look him up in a local directory.

To Jordan's surprise, however, Mitchell Thornberry was standing at the gate when he entered the terminal building. The Irish roboticist was wearing a neatly buttoned vest over a long-sleeved silver shirt and darker slacks. The vest's colors shifted as Thornberry moved through the arriving crowd toward him; the colors melded and swirled like an art display.

A knowing grin split Thornberry's jowly face as he stuck out his hand. "Welcome back to Chicago, Jordan."

"Mitch," said Jordan, clasping his friend's hand gratefully. "How did you know—"

"Professor Rudaki called me. Said you were heading here, out of London. There's only two flights a day from London, and the next one's not due until evening, so I figured you'd be on this one."

"You should be a detective," Jordan bantered.

As they started to head for the exit, Thornberry said, "Rudaki told me you've run into trouble with the head of the World Council."

"I'm afraid I'm something of a fugitive, Mitch. And they've separated me from Aditi."

Thornberry's face darkened. "They can't do that."

"They've done it. I don't know where she is or how she is."

"Well, we'll see about *that*," Thornberry said as he shooed Jordan with one hand toward the crowded corridor that led out of the terminal.

Janos Rudaki sat in his study, his eyes focused on the astronomical journal displayed on his wall screen, his ears listening to the heavy footfalls of the louts who were searching his home. His wife had fled to her room, unwilling to watch these strangers poking everywhere. The serving robots had been herded into the kitchen, where a trio of stern-looking security agents were going through their memory chips.

Rudaki sat and waited for the security agents to finish. He knew how to deal with such intrusions. There was nothing for them to find, so let them look until they got tired.

At last the head of the security team—a muscular-looking man with short-cropped sandy hair and a trim, slightly darker beard—appeared at his doorway.

"May I come in?" he asked in a deep, flat voice.

Rudaki looked up from his reading. "You're asking permission?"

"I am being polite, Councilman."

"Come in, then. Sit. Make yourself comfortable."

The security agent stepped into the room but remained standing.

"You found nothing," said Rudaki.

"Nothing."

With a shrug, Rudaki said, "I told you so. He was here last night. He slept in the guest suite. He left this morning, quite early."

"And went where?"

"I don't know," Rudaki lied.

"He hasn't used his credit account."

"So you have no idea of where he is."

"He can't get far without money."

Rudaki hunched his shoulders again. Then he asked, "Tell me, just why are you searching for him? Is he under arrest or something?"

"Something," said the agent.

"What?"

"You should discuss that with Chairwoman Halleck, sir."

"I already have, while your people were thumping through my home. She says Kell is supposed to be under protective custody."

"That's my understanding."

"And his wife?"

"She's safe."

"Under protective custody?"

"Yes."

Rudaki took in a deep breath and pushed himself to his feet. He fretted about his phone call to Mitchell Thornberry, in Chicago. Sooner or later the security forces would listen to it. With a mental shrug he told himself, So be it. They can't arrest a Council member for phoning someone. I hope.

"Well," he said to the security man, "if you're finished here then I suppose you should leave. I have a meeting with Halleck scheduled for later this afternoon. I'll be sure to tell her how thorough your team has been."

If the security man caught the irony in the professor's voice, he gave no evidence of it.

communications complex

with some misgivings, Aditi walked with Castiglione and Dr. Frankenheimer down a long corridor. She saw that the doors on either side were unmarked, and the corridor ended in a double door, also unmarked.

Castiglione was wearing a fitted military-style tunic, complete with epaulettes. Frankenheimer was in ordinary street clothes: a collarless tan checkered jacket that somehow complemented his thinning light brown hair and round, youthful face. Aditi had found a sunny yellow blouse and midnight blue skirt among the clothes that had been delivered to her apartment in the communications complex.

Castiglione was chatting cheerfully as though he had forgotten about the slap in the face Aditi had given him the night before, or at least put it out of his mind for the time being.

"Don't be worried, lovely one. The procedure is totally painless. Isn't that correct, Doctor?"

Frankenheimer nodded. But while Castiglione was smiling toothily, the neurophysiologist's boyish face looked quite serious, concerned.

"It's a completely noninvasive procedure, Mrs. Kell," he assured her. "You won't feel a thing. And it won't affect your brain at all. It's just . . . well, taking a picture of what's inside your skull."

"With neutrinos?" Aditi asked. "I thought they didn't interact with matter."

His brows knitting slightly, Frankenheimer said, "They don't, hardly at all. But if you produce enough of them you can get useful information from the relatively few interactions they do have."

Before Aditi could respond, he added, "You should talk to a physicist about it, I suppose. I merely use what they've built."

Mitchell Thornberry, Aditi thought. Mitch would understand it.

Castiglione laughed. "You should go through the procedure with me first." To Aditi he said, "That will show you there's nothing to fear."

"I'm not afraid," Aditi said. It was almost true.

"Good." Castiglione cocked his head slightly, then added, "I suppose a picture of what's inside my head would show that it's empty."

No, Aditi retorted silently. An image of your brain would show filth.

The inside of the imaging laboratory reminded Aditi a little of her own educational center back on New Earth. It was a small room, slightly colder than the corridor outside. A set of consoles lined one wall, a desk and several plastic chairs stood along the wall opposite. In the center was a recliner and behind the chair rose a metal arch studded with lights and display screens. She saw tracks set into the floor on either side of the recliner.

Castiglione fell silent; he stood by the door and crossed his arms over his chest. Frankenheimer led Aditi to the recliner chair.

"This arch contains the neutrino scanner," he explained. "It will slide along these tracks and take a three-dimensional image of your brain."

"I understand," said Aditi.

"If you'll just sit in the chair and relax, this should be over within a few minutes."

Aditi sat, wondering what Frankenheimer's reaction would be if she shut down the scanner's electrical circuitry. No, she decided. Let them go ahead with this procedure. I want to get this over with. I don't want to frustrate them. Or frighten them.

She cranked the chair down to its reclined position and closed her eyes. Just as she did so, she heard a phone chime. Opening her eyes, she saw Castiglione putting his phone to his ear, his smile suddenly gone.

Janos Rudaki sat before Anita Halleck's imposing desk.

"It was good of you to come on such short notice," she said, with a forced smile.

Rudaki grimaced slightly. "I thought it would be better to answer your summons than to have you send another squad of hooligans to my home."

Halleck's brows rose. "The search team disturbed you?"

"My wife. She's very sensitive. But to tell the truth, your search team was very polite, very careful. Outside of one little ornamental dish given to me by the late king of Sweden, they didn't break a thing."

"I'm sorry for that."

"I appreciate your concern." His fleshy face contracting into a frown, Rudaki asked, "But tell me, what is so important about this man Kell? Why do you want to put him in protective custody?"

Halleck's eyes shifted from Rudaki to the dark holographic viewer set in the wall across her office, then back to the professor again.

"A man who can insert himself into every electronic broadcast across the solar system? He could be dangerous."

"Perhaps," Rudaki conceded. "But it seems to me that all he wants is for us to build a few starships."

"He wants to control the World Council," Halleck snapped. Before Rudaki could react she went on, "And his alien wife holds the secret of faster-than-light communications—as you yourself pointed out at the last Council meeting."

"According to Kell, the aliens are quite willing to give us such technology."

"He told you that?"

"We had a long conversation last night. He does not appreciate your attempts to keep him under your thumb. Nor your separating him from his wife."

"That can't be helped."

"Can't it? My sainted old grandmother used to tell me you catch more flies with honey than with vinegar."

Halleck went silent for a moment, studying Rudaki's face. "What are you suggesting?"

"Nothing," the professor answered. "Only that it would be better to have Kell's willing cooperation than to make an enemy of him, don't you think?"

"His willing cooperation."

"Unite him with his wife. From what he tells me, the aliens on New Earth will willingly explain their FTL communications technology to us."

Halleck slowly nodded, but she was thinking, This man doesn't understand anything. I can't let Kell be reunited with his wife. If they can take control of every broadcast channel in the solar system, what else might he be capable of doing with her helping him? No, they've got to be kept separate.

Rudaki was watching her with an expectant smile on his usually dour face. Makes him look like an old clown, Halleck thought. He's sheltered Kell. He probably knows where Kell's gone, although he denies it.

She let out a long, sighing breath. "Perhaps you're right, Professor," Halleck said. "Perhaps I have been overly cautious. If Kell is willing to cooperate . . ." She let the thought dangle.

"I'm sure he will, if you allow him to be with his wife," Rudaki assured her.

"But we don't know where Kell is," Halleck pointed out. "How can we bring about this reunion if we don't know where he is?"

Rudaki started to answer, but hesitated before speaking a word.

He's thinking it over, Halleck judged. He knows where Kell has gone, but he's not going to tell me. Not willingly.

The professor finally said, "Perhaps you should try contacting the other men who returned from New Earth with him. If anyone knows where Kell is, one of them is the most likely."

Halleck nodded. "Yes. Of course."

But she was thinking, You know where he's gone, little man. And you're going to tell me.

The brain scan was completed in less than a minute. Aditi sat up straight as Castiglione came to her, looking unhappy.

"Your husband has disappeared," he said, his voice flat, almost accusing.

"Disappeared?" Aditi asked.

"Apparently he just walked out of the hotel we had put him in, right past an entire team of security guards."

Aditi kept her face from smiling, but inwardly she exulted, Jordan's gotten away from them!

A sly smile sneaking across his face, Castiglione asked, "Would you happen to know where he might have gone?"

She shook her head and answered as innocently as she could, "I haven't the faintest idea."

It was difficult to keep from laughing.

Frankenheimer, meanwhile, was staring at the three-dimensional image of Aditi's brain.

"Where's your communicator?" he asked. "There's no device showing."

Glad of the opportunity to change the subject, Aditi got up from the recliner and stepped to the neurophysiologist's side. "You're looking for an artificial mechanism," she said. "The system is composed of neural fibers, the same as my brain cells."

His boyish face twisting into a frown, Frankenheimer grumbled, "Then how am I supposed to see what the device is?"

Castiglione bent over Frankenheimer's other shoulder. "It's not an artificial device?"

"It's not a *natural* device," Aditi corrected. "But it's composed of the same type of cells as the rest of my brain: neurons, glial cells, the rest."

For the first time since she'd met him, Frankenheimer looked annoyed. "Then how am I supposed to see what the device is like?"

Aditi pursed her lips for a moment, then replied, "Perhaps, if you allow me to work your imager . . ."

"You could highlight the communicator's cells?"

"I can try," she said.

Frankenheimer got up from the little wheeled chair. "Go right ahead," he said.

Aditi took the chair. Frankenheimer unclipped the pin mike from his shirt and handed it to her.

As he started to explain the voice-activated control system, Aditi said, "I watched you working it. I think I understand how to do it."

Frankenheimer glanced at Castiglione, then answered, "Very well. Go right ahead."

Standing behind Aditi, Castiglione frowned unhappily. Kell just waltzes away from the team that was supposed to be holding him, and she can operate the imager after merely watching Frankenheimer use it for a few minutes.

That's eerie. These people are . . . frightening.

ChiCago

"All this is yours?" Jordan asked.

"That it is," said Thornberry, with a happy smile. "That it is."

They had just stepped out of the elevator that had carried them to the fiftieth floor of a downtown Chicago office building. Jordan saw that Thornberry Enterprises, Ltd., took up the entire floor, from one sweeping windowall to the other, opposite. The area was open, no partitions between the desks and workstations, and plenty of space between them. Men and women were sitting at individual stations or clustered in little groups around circular conference tables. A few were standing beside a row of food- and drink-dispensing machines, chatting pleasantly.

"It's quiet," Jordan remarked.

"Ah, that's the acoustic oscillators' doing. Damps down the sounds of conversations, y'know. And we use low-power energy screens instead of walls and partitions. That's better, don't you think?"

He started to lead Jordan across the wide room, nodding and greeting his employees more like a friendly paterfamilias than a corporate boss. No one paid any special attention to Jordan. They all seemed relaxed, cheerful.

Jordan felt pleased with the informality, the lack of hierarchy. Then he noticed a row of bigger, more imposing desks along the far wall, next to a broad window that looked out on Lake Michigan.

Leading him toward one of the unoccupied desks, Thornberry said, "Officer country." Pointing, "That's my desk, there."

Jordan felt a brief tingle as they came up to his desk, and all the buzzing hum of conversations cut off. Energy screens instead of walls, he realized. Quite effective. I suppose Mitch could make the screens go opaque if he wanted to.

"This is where I do me deep thinking," said Thornberry. Instead of sitting behind the desk, he plopped himself in one of the softly yielding upholstered chairs arranged in front of it. Jordan sat next to him.

"Very impressive, Mitch," he said.

"'Tis rather grand, isn't it?" Thornberry said, grinning happily. Waving toward his employees on the other side of the energy screen, he said, "They do the work and I rake in the profits. Capitalism at its best."

Jordan laughed with him. Then he asked, "Which group is working on your propulsion ideas? I'd like to talk with them."

"Ah, that'd be the physicists. They're not here. I've got them in their own location, where they can argue and quarrel with each other without bothering anyone."

"And do experiments without endangering anyone but themselves."

"That too," said Thornberry. His smile fading, he said, "I wish Aditi could give them an education in physics the way she did me. An hour or so in her teaching machine and I learned centuries' worth of physics, just like that." He snapped his fingers.

"Maybe we can build such teaching machines here," Jordan said.

"Not before I get a patent for them!"

"The rich get richer."

"Money buys power, Jordan me lad. And power is what you need to fight against Halleck and her World Council."

"I don't want to fight against her," Jordan insisted. "I just want to be with Aditi—and to start them to prepare for the death wave."

Thornberry's usual little smile vanished. Very seriously, he asked, "You'll be willing to give Halleck the FTL communications technology?"

"Certainly."

Thornberry drummed his fingertips against his thigh for a moment. Then, "I wonder if she'll be satisfied with that."

Jordan understood. "Give her an inch and she'll want a mile."

"I shouldn't be surprised."

"So we should offer the communications technology to the full Council, not to her alone."

"That might help."

"And only after Aditi is back with me."

Thornberry nodded. "She'll probably want your promise not to go to the news media again."

"But, Mitch, I've got to let the people—"

The phone console on Thornberry's desk interrupted, "Incoming call from Chairwoman Halleck, sir."

Jordan felt a pang of alarm. *Does she know I'm here? Does she have Mitch's offices bugged?* Then a new fear struck him. *Has Mitch betrayed me?*

"Audio only," Thornberry said, his tone dark, hard.

Anita Halleck's three-dimensional image took form between Thornberry's desk and the window, solid and completely realistic. She appeared to be sitting in her own office in Barcelona.

"Mr. Thornberry," she said, almost pleasantly. "Is there something wrong with your video?"

"We're working on it," Thornberry replied, in a flat, almost dismissive tone.

"I see," Halleck said.

Jordan hoped that she didn't.

In a somewhat lighter manner, Thornberry asked, "To what do I owe the honor of your call, Madame Chairwoman?"

Her dark eyes narrowing slightly, Halleck said, "We're trying to locate Jordan Kell. He left the hotel we had him quartered in and—*poof!*—he's disappeared."

"Really?"

"We don't know where he is and, naturally, we are concerned for his safety."

"Naturally."

"Has he contacted you?"

Thornberry glanced at Jordan, then replied, "He hasn't called me. Not at all."

Halleck frowned slightly. "I see. Well, if he does, please tell him that we're terribly concerned about him. We wouldn't want anything to happen to him."

"Of course not," Thornberry said. Then, with a crooked little grin, he asked, "And Mrs. Kell? I presume she's with him?"

"No. She's here, in Barcelona. She's quite safe."

That means they've got her in their hands, Jordan thought.

"Well now," said Thornberry, "if Jordan calls me I'll be sure to tell him that you're worried about him."

"You do that," said Halleck. And her image disappeared.

Thornberry scowled at the empty air. Turning to Jordan, he growled, "She'll have her security goons crawling over this place before another hour passes. We've got to get you to somewhere safe."

Nodding, Jordan said, "Yes. But where?"

Anita Halleck asked her deputy director of security, "was he telling the truth?"

The woman sitting before Halleck's desk was Gilda Nordquist: young, large-boned, statuesque, flaxen hair braided tightly, wearing a short-skirted dress of glittering metallic fabric. She reminded Halleck of a Valkyrie, strong and dedicated. On her lap rested a small electronics box, not much bigger than a personal phone. She was squinting at the varicolored curves wriggling across its screen.

Nordquist raised her head to look directly at Halleck. "The scanner is analyzing his voice tremors," she said, in a voice as clear and vibrant as a Nordic stream. "It's too bad we got no video; his eye movements would have been useful in determining if he were lying to you."

"Maybe that's why he killed the video," Halleck said.

"Probably. The scanner should be finished with its analysis in a few seconds."

As Halleck waited impatiently, she thought that perhaps she should relieve the oaf who had allowed Jordan Kell to escape and hand his position of security director to Nordquist.

The box beeped once. Nordquist looked down at its screen again. "He wasn't obviously lying," she reported.

"What does that mean?" Halleck demanded.

"Mr. Thornberry's vocal patterns don't show the kind of stress that's associated with outright lying. There's some stress there, yes, but that might be simply from the fact that he was speaking to the chairwoman of the World Council."

"Was he telling the truth or wasn't he?"

"I'd say he was, within the limits of the context of his words."

Halleck frowned. Why can't she give me a definite answer? Was Thornberry lying when he said he hadn't heard from Kell?

Seeing the annoyance in the set of the chairwoman's jaw, Nordquist explained, "What Mr. Thornberry said to you was truthful, but it might not be the entire truth. He said that Mr. Kell did not call him, and that's probably the truth. But it doesn't mean that he doesn't know where Mr. Kell is."

"I've already dispatched a security team to search his premises," Halleck said.

Nodding, Nordquist murmured, "Always a good maneuver. Even if they don't find anything, they might frighten him into admitting his guilt."

"Where else could Kell have gone?" Halleck asked the empty air. "He doesn't know anybody; he's been off-Earth for nearly two hundred years."

"Douglas Stavenger?" Nordquist suggested.

"How would he get to Selene?"

"How did he get out of Barcelona?"

Halleck thought about that for several silent moments. At last she leveled an index finger at Nordquist and said, "You go to Selene. See Stavenger, face-to-face. Even if he hasn't taken Kell under his wing, there's always the possibility that he'd be tempted to do so. Him and his independent nation of Selene! You make him understand that Kell is a fugitive, and I want him in custody."

Nordquist picked the scanner off her lap and got to her feet. "I'm on my way," she said, her expression stern.

As the Valkyrie swept out of her office, Halleck mused, If she can locate Kell, I'll make her director of security.

* * *

The World Council's communications complex was a mere five-minute ride from the Council's headquarters through the deep tunnel system that connected the two buildings.

In his office at the underground complex, Oswald Frankenheimer stared at the wall-screen image of Aditi's brain.

Castiglione, sitting to one side of Frankenheimer's desk, asked, "Well?"

Without taking his eyes from the intricate tracings of neurons, Frankenheimer said, almost in a whisper, "I could get a Nobel out of this."

"Nobel Prize?" Castiglione's expression was more amused than interested.

"If I can disentangle the communicator in her brain from the other cells, isolate and identify which cells she uses to communicate with her people on New Earth . . ." His voice sank too low for Castiglione to hear.

"You'd open her skull?"

Frankenheimer pulled his attention from the wall screen. "Open her skull? Are you insane? She's not some experimental animal, for god's sake! She's much too valuable for that."

"Then how . . . ?"

With the patience he would show when explaining fundamentals to a teenaged student, Frankenheimer said, "We get her to communicate with New Earth while she's in the neutrino scanner. Then we can see which neurons are activated, which cells are part of the communications device and which are not."

"Ah," said Castiglione. "I see."

"And we go on from there, mapping the cells that are activated."

"This will tell you how the device works?"

"Not entirely. But it'll be a start."

Castiglione pondered that for all of five seconds. "I understand that our own communications techies will be receiving tutorials from New Earth."

"Yes, the first one is scheduled for later today."

"If they learn how to build such devices, you won't have to probe Aditi's brain."

Frankenheimer shook his head so violently his hair flew askew. "No! You don't understand!"

"Understand what? If they willingly tell us how—"

"I want to understand this technology from first principles," Frankenheimer insisted. "It's one thing to make copies on a monkey-see, monkey-do basis. But we need to *understand* how this technology works, understand it so that we can build such devices for ourselves, without help from New Earth."

"But the end result is the same, isn't it?"

"No it's not! If we learn how to create such technology for ourselves, we don't need New Earth's experts handing us the technology like superior beings handing a gift to benighted children. We'll know just as much as they know. We'll be independent of them, not dependent."

"Oh. So that's it."

But Castiglione was thinking, And you, Dr. Frankenstein, go on to win the Nobel Prize—using Aditi as your experimental animal.

Gilda Nordquist

She had been raised in Stockholm—"the Venice of the North." Her father was the chief engineer in the state-owned firm responsible for building the intricate system of dams and breakwaters that saved the city from the rising sea levels of the greenhouse warming.

Her mother had died of cancer when Gilda was barely five, but her father had his wife's body frozen in the hope that her disease could one day be cured and she would be returned to him.

She had always excelled in her studies, and received her degree in international law when she was merely twenty. She accepted the World Council's invitation to join their security agency. That's when she started learning how to break the law.

Tall, blond, good-looking in an outdoorsy, athletic way, Gilda Nordquist became an expert at spying on Earth's citizens, and using undercover agents to provoke susceptible people into becoming criminals.

Neither she nor the men and women she worked with considered what they were doing to be illegal. Extra-legal, at worst, they told themselves.

"The world is filled with potential criminals," said her mentor, a narrow-eyed Korean who successfully bedded Nordquist during her first year in Barcelona. "Our task is to identify them, control them, and *use* them to help keep order and harmony in society."

Thus Nordquist became a recruiter of criminals. "Better to have them working for us than against us," the Korean told her, time and again, until she believed it fully.

She would scan police reports and court hearings, seeking petty thieves and swindlers whom she—and the psychotechnicians and police detectives who worked with her—could turn into informers and recruiters.

Dozens, hundreds, thousands of serious criminals were apprehended by the simple expedient of luring them into committing crimes and then swooping them into prison. The general public saw their police departments triumphing over the forces of anarchy and danger. The bewildered criminals, pawns in a global scheme they seldom comprehended, disappeared into prisons and cryonic freezers.

Nordquist was convinced that she was helping to maintain law and order. Crimes were committed, of course, but the criminals were put away before they could strike twice. The world order was protected, even strengthened.

It wasn't long, however, before a woman of Nordquist's intelligence and ambition began to seek better things for herself. She started to climb through the World Council's security bureaucracy. By the time she was named deputy director, and she had set her sights on the directorship, her opportunity came to her—from the stars.

ChiCago

Looking decidedly unhappy, Thornberry said to Jordan, "Halleck will be sending a team to search this place, she will. And my house up on the lake shore, too, I'll wager."

"I should get out of here before they arrive," Jordan said.

With a heavy sigh, Thornberry agreed, "That you should. I'm sorry. I'll do my best to get this straightened out."

"I appreciate it, Mitch. But for the moment, I've got to find a hideaway."

"Paul's in North Dakota, on his people's reservation."

Jordan nodded. "That might be a good place."

"Kind of obvious, though."

With a shrug, Jordan said, "I don't know anyone else. All my friends from before our mission to New Earth haven't seen me for nearly two hundred years. I can't just suddenly pop in on them."

Jabbing a finger at the phone console on his desk, Thornberry commanded, "I'll call Paul Longyear. His personal phone."

Jordan felt nervous. How long will it take for Halleck to get a security team here? This is the United States, of course. They'll have to get a court order before they can start searching the place. But that won't stop them from putting a security cordon around the building that would pick me up as I tried to leave.

"Paul's not answering his phone," Thornberry grumbled.

Jordan got to his feet. "I'd better be leaving."

"Do you have a phone?"

"Yes, but I'm sure Halleck's people could trace it easily."

Thornberry pushed his chair back and got up, too. "Come on up to the roof, then. I'll arrange a private jumpjet to fly you to Paul's reservation and I'll give you a new phone, so you can talk with the man—whenever he deigns to answer his damned phone."

It wasn't until the jumpjet was nearly at Bismarck that Paul Long-year finally returned Jordan's call.

The biologist's lean, dark-eyed face broke into a rare smile once he saw Jordan on his phone's screen.

"Jordan! Good to see you."

Jordan couldn't help smiling back at him. But he said, "Paul, I'm in a bit of a jam. I need your help."

"What's wrong?"

As Jordan swiftly outlined his situation, Longyear's expression grew more and more somber.

"Separated you from Aditi?" he said at last. "They can't do that!"

"They've done it. Halleck is using the fear of alien contact to pursue her own interests."

Longyear said tightly, "I'll pick you up at the Bismarck airport."

"Good. Thanks."

The jumpjet arrived at the airport before Longyear did. Jordan spent an anxious hour sitting in the terminal building's lobby, watching the main entrance, expecting a team of security agents to burst in at any moment.

As he tensely waited he kept asking himself, How can I reach Aditi? How is she? Where are they holding her? How can I get to her?

The lobby was quiet, uncrowded; only a few travelers were coming through it. Jordan paid no attention to the elderly, oversized Native American who entered the terminal, then stood just inside the main entrance, scanning the area with his hooded eyes. The man wore a nondescript plaid shirt, baggy work pants, scuffed boots, and a broad-brimmed black hat tilted back on his head. His face was copper-red, his expression stony.

After sweeping the lobby visually, the man walked straight toward Jordan, who rose to his feet uncertainly as the burly Native American approached.

He's certainly not dressed like a security man, Jordan thought. But still . . .

"Jordan Kell?" the elderly man asked, in a low rumble.

"Yes."

"I'm Paul Longyear's uncle. He's waiting for you outside, in the pickup."

Jordan puffed out a relieved breath and started walking alongside the man. He was massive: not fat, just large, solid, straining the clothes he wore. Jordan got the image of a retired athlete.

"I didn't catch your name," Jordan said.

The man almost smiled. "I didn't give it. It's George Twelvetoes."

"Twelvetoes."

"All the men in my family are born with six toes on each foot."

"That's unusual," said Jordan.

"Not in my family."

Twelvetoes led Jordan out into the airport's parking lot. It was a warm and sunny day, dry with a soft breeze blowing. Off in a far corner of the lot a battered old pickup truck was baking in the sunshine. As they approached it, Jordan recognized Paul Longyear sitting in its cab.

Longyear stepped down onto the blacktop and extended his hand to Jordan. "Good to see you, Jordan," he said with a warm smile.

"It's good of you to come all this way to pick me up," said Jordan.

The three men climbed into the truck: Twelvetoes behind the wheel, Longyear in the middle. The electric motor made hardly any noise at all as they drove off the parking lot and followed the signs to the highway.

Jordan went through his litany again as Longyear nodded solemnly, listening. Twelvetoes said nothing and kept his eyes on the road.

"So what do you intend to do, Jordan?" Longyear asked as they accelerated onto the interstate.

"I need to get to the news media," said Jordan. "I need to tell the people about the death wave and the other civilizations that we've got to save."

For several moments Longyear said nothing. He glanced at his uncle, who still stared straight ahead, then turned back to Jordan.

"That's about what we expected," Longyear said. Before Jordan could reply, he went on, "Uncle George and I talked about the problem on our way to the airport to pick you up. We think you ought to stay with us on the reservation for the time being."

Jordan shook his head. "I appreciate the offer, but I need to get in contact with the major news media."

With a wry smile, Longyear said, "We don't live in teepees anymore, Jordan. We have our own holographic broadcasting station. They can make contact with the media networks for you."

"They can?"

Twelvetoes, without taking his eyes from the road, deadpanned, "Red man make heap big medicine. BIG smoke signals!"

All three men broke into laughter.

In Barcelona, Gilda Nordquist dropped in to the satellite surveillance center of the communications complex.

The surveillance center always reminded her of what it must be like inside the head of a giant insect. Dozens of display screens lined the walls, making the place look like colossal multifaceted eyes.

"I only have a minute," she told the pouchy-faced operator on duty there. "I'm on my way to Selene."

"Flying to the Moon," the operator said. *"Quelle romantique."*

"You don't know the half of it," Nordquist said, smiling coldly.

"So what can I do for you, boss lady?"

"There's a big Indian reservation in North Dakota."

"Native American," the operator said. "The Yanks haven't called them Indians for centuries. And there are several reservations in the state of North Dakota."

Ignoring the correction, Nordquist said, "Find the one that Dr. Paul Longyear has squirreled himself in. Scan the area between it and the nearest major airport. Plus the reservation itself, of course."

"What am I supposed to be looking for?"

"Jordan Kell. His vitals are on file."

"He's the star traveler, isn't he?"

"That's right."

"And he's on an Indian reservation?"

Nordquist resisted the urge to throw the correction back at the operator. Instead she said, "Search also for Paul Longyear. He was also on the star mission and his vitals are on file, as well."

"Aren't everybody's?"

"Almost," Nordquist conceded. "We're working on adding the few we don't have yet."

"Kell and Longyear," the operator said.

"Twenty-four/seven. I want to find them. Call me immediately when you do."

"On the Moon?"

"Yes. Immediately."

"You're sure Kell's out there?"

"I have a pretty strong hunch that he is. Or will be, sooner or later."

"What the hell's the star traveler doing out in the middle of no-where?"

"That's what I want to find out," said Nordquist.

+++

+++

тhe pickup truck turned off the interstate and started up a secondary road.

"тhis is the way to the reservation?" ̩ordan asked.

Longyear nodded. "Back road. Not the main entrance."

Jordan thought: Paul rode to the airport in his uncle's truck and stayed in it while he sent his uncle to find me.

"You think they're scanning the area with satellites?" he asked Longyear.

The biologist replied, "Could be. No sense aiding and abetting them."

"That's a term the police use about criminals."

His expression bleak, Longyear said, "That's how you're being treated, isn't it? Like a criminal."

"I suppose so," Jordan admitted.

The road was reasonably straight as it cut through a heavily wooded area.

"I didn't realize there were forests in this region. I thought it was all treeless prairie," said Jordan.

"The Great American Desert," said Longyear. "That's what Pike and the other early white explorers called it. Not a tree for hundreds of miles."

"Plenty of trees now."

Waving a hand, Longyear said, "This has all been planted in the past century or so. Climate change has actually helped this area: more rain, warmer winters."

Jordan's personal phone buzzed. Automatically, he pulled it from his trousers pocket, then hesitated.

"Might be the government," he muttered. "The World Council or the police, trying to track me."

Longyear smiled grimly. "You're starting to think like a criminal."

"A fugitive," Jordan corrected. Then he looked at the phone's screen to see who was calling.

Aditi!

Without an instant's hesitation he clicked the phone on. "Aditi? Is it you?"

"Jordan." Her lovely face beamed at him.

"You're all right?"

"I'm fine. Forgive me for calling you like this. I didn't call earlier because I was afraid Halleck's security people would trace the call and find out where you are."

Feeling torn between seeing his wife for the first time in days and fearing that the security forces would locate him, Jordan merely repeated, "You're all right?"

Aditi smiled, almost mischievously. "I heard that you had gotten away from the security guards. Apparently Halleck is very angry that you broke free."

"Darling, I'm afraid we should cut this call short."

"No need," she said, her smile warming. "I contacted Adri and he's connected us. Neither the World Council nor anyone else on Earth can intercept this call."

Jordan's jaw sagged open. Recovering, he asked, "You mean this call is being relayed through New Earth? Eight light-years away?"

"No, but we're using a frequency that no one on Earth even knows about. Completely private, only you and me. Isn't that wonderful?"

"It's wonderful to see your face, Aditi. To hear your voice."

"And to see you, Jordan."

"Where are you?"

"Still in Barcelona. They're keeping me in an underground complex, not far from the World Council's headquarters."

As the truck rolled through the young forest, Jordan and Aditi told each other what they had been going through for the past few days.

"They've scanned your brain?" Jordan asked.

"Yes. Adri has arranged for our communications people to educate the technicians here on Earth, but Dr. Frankenheimer still wants to study the communicator in my brain."

"And you're cooperating?"

"I don't have much choice. But it's been painless, and the poor man is really excited to be learning so much."

"I imagine he is," Jordan said, thinking that everyone he and Aditi had met since returning to Earth was trying to gain new knowledge from them. No, not knowledge, he realized. Power.

He asked Aditi, "How can I contact you, dear?"

Her expression sobered. "I'm afraid you can't, not unless you want to have the security police locate you. I'm using the frequency that my implanted communicator operates on."

"And Castiglione and the others don't know it?"

"No. They can't detect it."

"All right, then," Jordan said. "But could you please call me at least once every day?"

"Of course," Aditi answered. "Every hour, if I could."

"I miss you, darling."

"And I miss you, Jordan. I hope we can be together soon."

Unconsciously, he nodded. "I'll be working on that. And waiting for your next call."

"I love you, Jordan."

Suddenly realizing that Longyear and his uncle could hear everything the two of them said, Jordan lowered his voice slightly. "I love you, too, Aditi. And I'll be with you as soon as I possibly can."

"That will be good."

"It'll be wonderful."

"Yes."

"Good-bye."

"*Au revoir.*"

The phone screen went dark. Jordan stared at it for several silent moments, smiling as he wondered how much French she had picked up.

Longyear pointed to a roadside sign that flashed by. "Five more miles and we'll be at the reservation."

"Good," said Jordan as he slipped the phone back into his pocket. But he was wondering about his wife being held a captive back in Barcelona. With Castiglione.

Mitchell Thornberry was trying to smile at the three-dimensional image of Anita Halleck hovering across the desk from him. It looked as if the World Council chairwoman was sitting in his office.

Smile, he told himself. Be a jolly old elf.

Halleck was smiling, too: a thin, patently forced curve of her lips. "I see you've got your video feed working again," she was saying.

"That I have," said Thornberry.

"Was Kell in your office the last time we spoke?"

Thornberry hesitated. He had heard of the voice analyzers and scanners that security people used to determine if someone was lying or not.

"Why do you ask?" he replied.

"Kell is a fugitive. We're trying to find him."

"Is he a criminal, then?"

"We want to keep him in protective custody. For his own safety. There's already been one attempt on his life."

Thornberry forced his smile wider. "Well then, if you can't find him, with all the fine resources you have at your beck and call, then I imagine the crackbrain killers can't find him, either."

"You think so? That's rather naive, isn't it?"

More seriously, Thornberry said, "I'm going to appeal to the International Court of Justice to enjoin you from holding Jordan in custody. It's not right. It's an infringement on his freedom."

"You'd rather see him assassinated by some fanatic?"

"I'd rather see him free."

Halleck said, "Aiding a fugitive is a criminal offense, you know."

"Tell that to me lawyers," Thornberry snapped.

"If you know where he is, it would be best if you tell me."

"And how should I know where he is?"

Halleck let her distaste show on her face. "Mr. Thornberry, you have become quite wealthy from alien technology. But you're not so powerful that the World Council can't freeze your assets and examine your dealings, down to the smallest detail."

"You can tell that to me lawyers, as well," Thornberry said, snapping his fingers to cut off the phone connection.

Halleck's image disappeared and Thornberry said to himself, I'd better speak to me lawyers, m'self, by God.

KTBF

++
++

"You're the starman," said Lester Youngeagle, outright awe clear in his voice, his face, his eyes.

station KTBR was housed in a modest plastic-walled building, shaped like a bright white mound hugging the earth. Tornadoes were a frequent threat, Longyear had explained to Jordan as they drove up to it, and the building's aerodynamic design allowed the wind to slip by it without much resistance.

"No windows," he had pointed out as his uncle parked the truck. "Nothing for the wind to grab hold of."

"Who thought up the design?" Jordan had asked.

With a hint of pride in his voice, Longyear had replied, "Our people have designed hogans this way for millennia. We know how to live with tornadoes, better than the whites with their bricks and frame houses."

Once they entered the building, the young female receptionist had summoned Youngeagle. He can't be much more than twenty, Jordan thought as he shook hands with the young man. Youngeagle was not quite Jordan's height, but stocky, thickset, with skin the color of burnt tobacco leaf, wide-set deeply brown eyes and jet black hair hanging down to his collar. He was wearing a white shirt, its sleeves rolled up past his elbows, and well-faded jeans.

"I saw that broadcast you did a coupla days ago," Youngeagle said, once they had shaken hands. "Every damned station on Earth! Wow! How'd you do that?"

"Alien technology," Jordan said. "It's one of the gifts we can offer to the people of Earth."

As he led Jordan, Longyear, and Uncle Twelvetoes down the building's central corridor, Youngeagle asked, "So what brings you here? What can I do for you?"

Jordan said, "Anything you do for me might get you in trouble with the World Council. As far as they're concerned, I'm a fugitive."

"So you're hiding out here, on the reservation."

"That's right."

They passed a big, open studio, dark and empty. Four 3-D cameras stood idle in the middle of the floor. Each corner of the area was decorated differently: a library, a news desk, an angle of smart screens showing weather maps that reached up to the lights hanging from the ceiling, and what looked to Jordan like a fake classroom. A scattering of lights came on automatically as they entered the area.

"We do most of our broadcasts from one of these sets or another," Youngeagle explained as he led them to the library set.

"You're not broadcasting now?" Jordan asked.

"Network feed. We'll go on the air again with the local news at six."

Gesturing to the sofa and armchairs in the library corner, Youngeagle said, "This is the most comfortable spot in the building."

Jordan and Longyear took the sofa, Youngeagle one of the upholstered chairs. Twelvetoes remained standing, off to one side.

Leaning forward intently, Youngeagle asked, "So what can I do for you?"

"Can you put me in touch with the people who run the major news networks?"

Youngeagle flinched backward slightly. "I wish I could. I wish I knew some of those birds. But I'm only the general manager of a small station out in the wilderness."

"Oh," said Jordan. "I see."

With a forlorn little shake of his head, Youngeagle said, "Just about the only person I know in the New York end of the business is a gal I met at a conference last year. Her name's Vera something . . . Vera Griffin, that's it."

"She's with the news media?"

"The Otero Network. She's only a junior manager in Otero's control center, but she's bright and ambitious."

"Well," he said to Youngeagle, "she'll have to do."

Turning to Longyear, sitting beside him, Jordan said, "It's a start."

nordquist and stavenger

Gilda Nordquist rode a commercial rocket to the moon, sitting amidst the tourists and schoolchildren who were on their way to selene or the more adult attractions of the Hell Crater entertainment complex.

The man seated beside her was an astronomer, heading for the Farside Observatory. He tried to engage Nordquist in conversation, but she quieted him soon enough with her flat, monosyllabic responses. Men, she thought. Always on the prowl.

Commercial flights did not coast to the Moon; that would mean taking several days to reach their destination. Instead, they accelerated at less than half a g—half the gravitational force experienced on the Earth's surface—halfway to the Moon, then reversed and slowed their approach so that they landed on the lunar surface in a matter of hours, not days. The passengers experienced zero gravity only for the few minutes of the turnaround.

Still, Nordquist was dismayed that two of the children and several adults moaned and gagged while briefly weightless. At least no one upchucked, she thought gratefully, recalling the sickening smell of vomit from earlier flights to orbital zero-g facilities. The astronomer beside her took zero-g in stride. He must be a veteran traveler, she thought.

To her surprise, Douglas Stavenger himself was waiting for her at the end of the flexible passageway that connected the spacecraft's hatch to the air lock of Selene's Armstrong Spaceport, smiling warmly, wearing a plain gray set of coveralls, much like most of the other permanent Luniks.

She walked carefully in the light lunar gravity, not wanting to stumble and make a fool of herself. Once she reached him, Stavenger extended his arm and she took it gratefully.

"You've never been to the Moon before, have you?" he asked—solicitously, it seemed to her.

"This is my first time," she admitted.

"You're doing fine." And he led her slowly into the terminal's main area.

Stavenger was beginning to look his age, she thought. Even with his body teeming with nanomachines, there were crinkles in the corners of his eyes and his once-dark hair was peppered with gray. She saw that she was several centimeters taller than he, but he still was handsome and broad-shouldered.

"It's so good of you to meet me personally," Nordquist said, actually feeling impressed.

As they walked past the lines of other passengers filing through the immigration inspections, Stavenger smiled boyishly.

"I don't have much of a staff," he explained. "I haven't been an official member of Selene's government for ages."

Nordquist picked up his slight emphasis on the word "official." Stavenger had been Selene's leader back in the early days, when the community was still known as Moonbase. He had led the short, sharp battle for independence against the old United Nations a century before Nordquist had been born. For all that time he had been the power behind the throne of Selene; he had no official position, he merely was the man who made the effective decisions.

"But you're a member of the World Council," she said to him. "That's quite an honor."

He smiled at her. "Anita Halleck's rubber stamp," he said. The smile told her that he didn't mean for her to take the remark seriously. But still, she thought, he'd said it.

They rode the tram through the tunnel that linked the space-port to the mostly underground community of Selene. Stavenger assumed—correctly—that Nordquist wasn't interested in the usual tourist attractions in the Grand Plaza. He knew she hadn't come to the Moon for low-*g* acrobatics or flying like a bird on rented wings with nothing but her own muscle power.

He took her directly to his home: a snug set of rooms nestled deep in Selene's warren of tunnels.

Stavenger ushered her into a smallish room furnished with comfortable chairs; its walls were covered with smartscreens that glowed softly. No desk, Nordquist noted. No signs of authority; he doesn't need to impress visitors, he's impressive on his own.

Once they had settled into padded chairs facing each other, Stavenger got straight to the subject. "I assume your visit here has to do with Jordan Kell."

"You assume correctly," Nordquist responded. "He's slipped away from the security team that was guarding him."

Surprised, Stavenger blurted, "He did?"

"Yes. Apparently he spent last night with Professor Rudaki, but now he's gone."

"You don't know where he is?"

"No, we don't."

"Rudaki doesn't know where he's gone?"

"If he does, he's not admitting it."

Stavenger fought down the urge to smile. Anita's security people can't run roughshod over a Council member the way they would over an ordinary citizen, he knew.

"And Kell's wife?" he asked.

Nordquist replied, "She's safely in the Council's communications complex. One of our research scientists is studying the communications device that's implanted in her brain."

"Oh?"

Her face taut, Nordquist explained, "That's the device that allowed Kell to take over every broadcast station in the solar system."

"Yes," Stavenger said, nearly smiling. "Even our own system here in Selene carried Kell's little speech."

"We'd like to know how they did that."

"They? You mean Kell and his wife?"

"Yes. And, of course, that device in her skull can send and receive messages faster than light."

Stavenger leaned back in his chair. "Anita must be very interested in that."

"Indeed she is."

"You know," he said, "I was the one who got Anita active in public service, ages ago. She's come a long way since then."

Nordquist started to reply, thought better of it, and merely nodded.

"She's very ambitious," Stavenger said.

"She has enormous responsibilities."

"And no intention of stepping down as head of the World Council."

"She's facing reelection next year."

"She'll win easily." Suddenly Stavenger's eyes narrowed. "Unless Kell runs against her."

Nordquist's jaw sagged open. "Run against her? He can't! He's a fugitive!"

"Has he been charged with a crime?"

"No . . . but he's escaped from protective custody."

"And Anita's trying to get him back, keep him bottled up, prevent him from talking to the public."

"It's *protective* custody," Nordquist insisted. "There are plenty of fanatics out there who'd try to kill him."

"Or use him for their own purposes."

Nordquist sat up straight, stiff-backed. "Mr. Stavenger, I'm here to remind you that aiding a hunted fugitive is a breach of the law—even on the Moon."

Strangely, Stavenger broke into a low chuckle. "We're not harboring Kell here in Selene. You can assure Anita of that." Then he sobered and added, "Although, if he showed up here, I imagine our governing council would be tempted to grant him asylum."

"You can't do that!"

"Selene is an independent nation, Ms. Nordquist. We make our own decisions."

"You'd better not decide to harbor Kell. Or his wife. Make certain that your governing council understands that."

"What would Anita do if we did harbor him?"

Nordquist hesitated only a heartbeat before answering, "The first thing she'd do is cut off all commerce between Earth and Selene. That's the *first* step. There would be more to follow, I assure you."

Stavenger muttered, "Yes, I assume there would be."

"Kell's not worth going to war."

"Freedom is," said Stavenger.

GRIFFIN AND OTERO

"Lester Youngeagle?" Vera Griffin was sitting in the cubicle that had been assigned to her as the new producer of the "Neighbors and Friends" segment of the evening news show.

As she had expected, her promotion meant she had to move to the network headquarters, in Boston. With a mixture of anticipation and reluctance she had made the move, and now she sat in her new cubicle, its partitions bare and impersonal, surprised that this young Native American she had met more than a year ago was calling her.

Griffin was wearing a stylish shifting-hued blouse and trim dark slacks: hardly a producer's outfit, she thought. She had simply grabbed the first clothes she could yank out of her travel bag this first morning in Boston and hurried from her new apartment to her new office.

Youngeagle's three-dimensional image hovered in front of her desk. In his shirtsleeves, he appeared to be sitting at a desk as well. Smaller than her own, she noted. It looked old, hard-used.

"Yes, I remember you," Griffin said, checking her directory of names as she spoke. "The . . . uh, the conference last year in Spokane."

"That's right," said Youngeagle, obviously pleased that she remembered him. "How are you?"

"I'm fine. What's with you? Are you in Boston?"

Youngeagle shook his head. "No, I'm still in North Dakota."

"So what are you calling about?"

Lowering his voice a notch, Youngeagle replied, "I've got a bombshell of a story for you."

One thing that Griffin had learned in the few days since the network had announced that she would be a producer was that everyone had a story they wanted to get on the air.

"A bombshell?" she asked wearily.

"Jordan Kell," whispered Youngeagle.

"The starman!"

"The guy who took over every broadcast outlet on Earth."

And the rest of the solar system, Griffin added silently. Excitedly.

"You know where he is?" she asked.

Grinning like a successful conspirator, Youngeagle said, "He's right here on the reservation, with me."

"That's in Nebraska?"

"North Dakota."

"What's he doing there?"

"He wants to talk to a network executive. I figured you'd know more about that than I do."

The image of Carlos Otero flashed through Griffin's mind. "Yes," she said. "I do."

It took most of the day for Griffin to battle her way through the layers of Otero's protective staff. The Big Boss seldom made time for a newly promoted minor producer. But Griffin insisted that she had the inside track on a story that was so big she would only talk to Otero himself about it.

Where the staff flunkies she had argued with were hard-faced and sharp-voiced—even Otero's personal assistant had practically sneered at her—the Big Boss himself smiled genially as the assistant ushered Griffin into his airport-sized office.

"It's *Vera* Griffin, isn't it?" Otero asked as he got to his feet and came around his massive carved ironwood desk, extending a hand to her.

Griffin nodded and smiled back as she plowed across the thick carpet. You know damned well what my first name is, she was thinking. You've got my whole dossier on your desk screen.

Otero radiated power. He was much bigger than Griffin: taller and wider, looking splendid in a light gray suit that fitted him perfectly. His gleaming smile looked genuine, though, and his outstretched hand was big enough to swallow Griffin's diminutive one easily.

Gesturing to the pair of luxurious armchairs in the conversation corner of his office, Otero said, "Have a seat, Vera. And tell me what's so important that you can only speak about it to me."

As they sat down, Griffin said, "The starman."

Otero's eyes widened. "Jordan Kell? What about him?"

"I know where he is. And he wants to talk to you."

The Big Boss eased back in his chair, his smile broader, more genuine. "Does he?"

"Yes. He's hiding out from the World Council's security agents. They're hunting for him."

In a few swift moments, Griffin outlined what Lester Youngeagle had told her. Before she finished Otero had sprung out of his chair and started pacing excitedly.

"And Anita Halleck is holding his wife, too? Incommunicado?" Otero asked from halfway across the spacious office.

"Yes. In Barcelona. And she's got her people searching for Kell."

"If we could get him on our network," he enthused, "it'd be a coup for Otero Network. And a nice black eye for Halleck."

"An exclusive for the network."

Rubbing his swarthy jaw, Otero said, "This is dynamite. It's a hydrogen bomb, by god!"

"It will make an enemy of Anita Halleck," Griffin warned.

Returning to his chair and perching on its front four inches,

Otero said, "She's already our enemy. She's an enemy of freedom of the news media. Has been for a long time."

"I suppose so. But . . . she's got a lot of power, doesn't she?"

"So do we," Otero countered. "We can bring in all the major networks if she tries to muscle us. We could knock her off the World Council next year."

"That means we won't have an exclusive about Kell."

Otero shrugged his heavy shoulders. "His first appearance will be our exclusive. Then we'll graciously offer the other networks to share his future appearances. Halleck can't fight the whole news industry."

"I suppose not," Griffin said uncertainly.

"We'll insist that Halleck release Kell's wife. This alien from New Earth. We'll put her on the air with him! It'll be terrific!"

Griffin swallowed hard, then said, "And I could produce the show."

Nodding happily, Otero consented. "I'll put you in tandem with one of our more experienced producers." He gazed up at the smooth panels of the ceiling. "We'll hire a troop of armed guards to protect Kell. That'll erase Halleck's claim that he's got to be kept safe from possible fanatics and assassins."

"It'll be good publicity for the network," Griffin agreed.

"We'll twist Halleck's tail, but good!"

It took another quarter of an hour for Griffin to get the Big Boss to dictate a memo outlining their plans to meet Kell and set up an interview between him and their top news personality.

"No," Otero said, his voice quivering with excitement. "*I'll* interview him. Me. Myself."

Griffin clapped her hands together like a little girl. "That would be terrific! And I'll produce the show."

After another few minutes of eager planning, Griffin got to her feet and hurried toward the door.

"I've got a lot to do, a lot to prepare," she said, by way of taking her leave.

Otero watched the diminutive young woman leave his office, glowing with satisfaction. Like a little daughter, he thought. I'm like a father to her.

Once he was alone in his enormous office, he went back to his desk and called up his favorite quotation. It was from an ancient dramatic show from back in the days of radio, before three-dimensional broadcasting and even before flat television. Otero had run across it in a history class when he'd been a student in college. It was corny, but it had stuck in his mind all these years. Now he played the ancient recording, the closest thing he had to a credo:

In a scratchy old audio recording a crack-of-doom voice proclaimed, *"The freedom of the press is like a flaming sword. Hold it high. Use it wisely. Guard it well."*

Guard it well, Otero thought. If I go through with this Kell business, Anita Halleck's going to declare war on me.

Guard it well.

albuquerque

Hamilton cree felt strangely sentimental as he neatly folded his uniform and placed it into the box resting on the locker room bench.

The last time I'll wear it, he said to himself. For five years I've been a New Mexico Highway Patrol officer, and now it's all over.

A pair of his fellow officers were watching him from several lockers away, both wearing nothing but fuzzy white towels around their midsections.

"So where're you going, Ham?" asked one of them.

"Chicago," Hamilton answered, hardly looking up at them. And he realized that in five years he had barely made any friends among the men and women he worked with. Five years, and he was still practically a stranger among them.

"What's in Chicago?" asked the other.

"Women," said the first. "City women with big boobs and easy ways."

"Hey, we got women here," the other officer argued.

"Prairie dogs."

"Not so loud," the man said, grinning. "The women's lockers are just on the other side of the wall."

"The wall you drilled a peephole through."

"Not me!"

"Somebody did."

"Not that much to see."

"Yeah, but Chicago's different. Ham's going to be surrounded by adoring women, ain'tcha Ham?"

Hamilton said wistfully, "Could be."

As he pulled on the trousers of his brand-new suit, he noticed that half a dozen other guys had come up behind the half-naked pair. All of them were wearing nothing but towels, too.

"So, aside from easygoing women, what's in Chicago, Ham?"

"A job. A real job."

"What, bouncer in a whorehouse?"

Hamilton shook his head and felt his cheeks redden. "Naw. Private security firm."

"You're gonna be a rent-a-cop?"

"Unicorn Recovery Agency."

"Unicorn?"

"They screw virgins, don't they?"

Hamilton reached into his locker for the bolo tie his father had given him the day he'd left home for New Mexico. Five years ago. The old man had died a few months later and Ham had to fight the Highway Patrol's brass to get a few days off to go back east for the funeral.

"Well, you look great in your new suit, Ham."

"Thanks." He pulled on the jacket and studied himself in the mirror inside his locker door. Not bad, he thought.

But the first of the towel-clad officers knitted his brows and said, "I think your suit's a little dirty, though. Don't you guys agree?"

"Dirty? Whattaya mean, I just took it out of the box."

Suddenly they made a rush at him. Half a dozen half-naked Highway Patrol officers grabbed him, kicking and thrashing, and carried him into the shower.

Hamilton realized what they were doing and stopped struggling against them. They held him under the shower, soaking him and his new suit.

Hamilton just stood there, grinning at them. They like me, he realized. This is their way of saying good-bye.

He almost wished he wasn't leaving them. Almost.

barcelona

AS SOON AS SHE RETURNED FROM THE MOON, GILDA NORD-
QUIST WENT STRAIGHT TO THE SATELLITE MONITORING CENTER
IN THE UNDERGROUND COMMUNICATIONS COMPLEX. I might
as well still be at Selene, she said to herself as she strode through
the windowless corridors, stopping only to peer into the scanners
that checked her retinal pattern at every security door.

None of the men or women walking along the corridors recognized her. Good, she thought. But once I'm head of the security
division they'll get acquainted with my face. Then she thought, Or
maybe I should remain anonymous, unknown. Keep everyone
guessing.

The same overweight, jowly man was sitting at the center of
the insect-eye set of display screens. His shirt looked wrinkled,
sweaty, as if he'd slept in it. Does he ever leave this room? Nordquist wondered.

"What have you found about Jordan Kell?" she asked, without
any polite preliminaries.

"He's on the reservation, all right," the unkempt man said.
"They're keeping him indoors as much as possible, but I've got a
good track on him and his accomplice, Paul Longyear. Whenever
they step out into the open, one of our satellites pings me."

"He's still there, then."

"They both are."

"Good. If he moves off the reservation, inform me immediately."

"You and the Seventh Cavalry."

"What?"

The man chuckled softly. "Nothing. A little joke, that's all."

"This isn't funny. It's very important. Top priority."

"A memo to that effect would help me explain the costs I'm running up for you."

"You'll get it before the day's over."

Nordquist left the pudgy little man sitting amidst his display screens and headed for Anita Halleck's office.

Jordan Kell was impressed with the hospitality that Paul Longyear and his people had shown him. They had put him up in a comfortable bedroom in the ranch-style home of Paul's parents, both of them teachers at the local high school.

The bedroom had been Paul's when he was growing up. Now he had a small home of his own, less than a kilometer away, but Jordan recognized the university banner still tacked to the wall over the narrow bed, and the digital reader that lay on the bureau where Paul had left it.

He glanced at his watch. Too early for Aditi to call, he knew. She usually calls well after dinnertime. Still he wondered how she was, what she was doing, what Halleck's minions—especially that oily Castiglione—were doing with her.

"Dinner's ready," Mrs. Longyear called from the kitchen.

Jordan walked down the short corridor that led to the dining room. Paul's father was already seated at the head of the table. Mrs. Longyear was depositing a steaming platter of roast chicken in front of him.

Quanah Longyear was a good-natured man approaching his fifth retirement opportunity. He had spent his adult life teaching Native American children the history of their ancestors, alongside the history of the nation that surrounded them. His hair was silver, his smile cheery; he had none of the suspicious, uneasy attitude that his son carried around with him.

Mrs. Longyear—Karolyn—was a mixture of Irish and Native American: fair skin, graying hair, warmly gracious.

As he took the chair opposite Mrs. Longyear, Jordan said to them, "It's awfully good of you to take me in like this."

"It's no imposition," said Mrs. Longyear. "We're glad to do it. We don't get many visitors from outside the reservation, you know."

Her husband nodded agreement as he passed the platter of chicken to Jordan. "Paul says you're in some trouble with the World Council."

"I'm afraid they want to keep me in custody," Jordan said, putting the platter down and picking a thigh. The food smelled delicious, with a hint of tangy spice.

"Why's that?" Longyear asked.

"They don't want me to talk to the news media."

"Why's that?"

As he handed the platter to Mrs. Longyear, Jordan answered, "I want the Council to start working now on the problem of the death wave—"

"Death wave?" Mrs. Longyear blurted.

So Jordan spent most of the dinner explaining what he had learned on New Earth, and how the World Council was putting off the decisions it had to make.

"So that's why we've had drones flying over the reservation," said Longyear.

"I'm afraid it's because of me, yes."

"And Paul's involved in this?" his wife asked, looking alarmed for the first time.

"Peripherally. It's really me they're after."

"Tribal council's complained to the federal government about those drones. They've entered our airspace without permission." Longyear's easy smile had morphed into a troubled frown.

Mrs. Longyear looked anxious, too. "You mean that there are whole civilizations on other worlds that might be wiped out? Extinguished?"

"If we don't help them, yes."

"And this death wave is heading our way?" Longyear asked.

"It will be here in two thousand years."

"That's a long time."

"I know," Jordan conceded. "But we should start preparing for it now, don't you think?"

Longyear pursed his lips. "No sense waiting until the last minute, I suppose. But two thousand years . . ."

Mrs. Longyear asked, "Those other people, on their own planets—the death wave will hit them a lot sooner, you say?"

"Yes. We barely have enough time to reach them, even if we start right now."

"We ought to help them," she said.

"I agree," said Jordan.

"So do I," Longyear said. "But there's not much we can do if the World Council doesn't want to act."

"There's something I can do," Jordan said. Then he added, "Perhaps."

Mrs. Longyear said, "Helping those people would be the right thing to do."

Longyear nodded agreement, but said, "Well, right now the best thing we can do is dig into our dinner before it gets cold."

DOUGLAS STAVENGER

++
++

After Gilda Nordquist's brief, unsettling visit, Stavenger decided that he had to talk with Jordan Kell, but he didn't know how to reach the man.

If he's slipped through Anita's security people, he won't be easy to find, Stavenger realized. Then he remembered that Nordquist claimed Kell had spent a night at Councilman Rudaki's home. So he called Rudaki.

Looking uncomfortable, Rudaki grudgingly admitted that Kell had headed for Chicago. "But he's not there now, I'm sure," the councilman insisted.

Chicago meant Mitchell Thornberry, the multimillionaire scientist/businessman who had been to New Earth with Kell.

Thornberry seemed uneasy, too. "I shouldn't talk about that. I've got too many World Council security boyos snooping through me offices as it is. And they're listening to me phone calls, you can be sure of that."

"I understand," Stavenger said, admiring the man's stubborn loyalty to his friend. "Thanks, anyway."

"I wish there was some way I could help," Thornberry said, looking almost embarrassed.

"I understand," Stavenger repeated.

Less than half an hour later, Stavenger's phone buzzed. "Answer," he called out. The phone's screen remained blank but a man's voice—Thornberry's, it sounded like—called out a twelve-figure number. Then the call abruptly cut off.

Stavenger ordered his phone to trace the origin of the call: Digby O'Dell's Pub, in Chicago. With a smile, he understood that Thornberry had made the call from a phone that the World Council security agents were unlikely to be monitoring. I hope he had a pint of Guinness while he was there, Stavenger said to himself.

In the Longyear home, Jordan had just slipped into Paul's old bed when his pocketphone rang. Startled, he remembered that it was the phone Mitch had given him. Could Aditi be calling on that number?

He leaned over and picked the phone from the bedside table. The holographic viewer across the room showed a man sitting in an easy chair. Jordan immediately recognized him: Douglas Stavenger.

"Hello, Mr. Kell," Stavenger said, his face serious, almost stern.

"Mr. Stavenger," said Jordan. "How did you ever find this number?"

Stavenger explained Thornberry's secretive assistance, ending with, "So the chances of our being overheard by security agents are pretty low."

"But not zero."

"No," Stavenger admitted. "Not zero."

The three-second lag between their words told Jordan that Stavenger was indeed on the Moon.

"I can make it zero," said Jordan.

Later that night, when Aditi called him, Jordan asked her to set up a link between him and Stavenger, at Selene.

"Why does he want to speak with you?" she asked, her beautiful face taut with concern.

"I'm not sure, dearest," Jordan replied, "but I'm certain that

Mitch helped him locate me, and he's just as wary of Halleck's eavesdropping as we are."

"You don't think he's working for Halleck?"

"No, I honestly don't. Everything I've ever heard about Stavenger tells me he's fought to keep Selene free of domination by the World Council."

Aditi looked doubtful, but she said, "I'll ask Adri to help me set up the link. Give me a few hours."

It was nearing two A.M. when the holographic viewer in the Longyear bedroom chimed, waking Jordan, and lit up to show Douglas Stavenger sitting in a cushioned chair in a windowless room, looking halfway between pleased and puzzled.

"Mr. Kell," he began.

"Jordan."

Stavenger smiled tentatively and said, "Fine. I'm Doug."

"My wife explained the FTL link to you?" Jordan asked.

"Sort of. I'm not sure how it works, but apparently it's eliminated the time lag between here and Earth."

"And it can't be tapped."

His smile widening, Stavenger said, "That's a great advantage. We can talk without being overheard."

"So, now that you've found me, what do you want to talk to me about?"

"I want you to know that the independent nation of Selene would undoubtedly offer you sanctuary, if you could get here. And your wife, too, of course."

"That's very kind of you, but I don't see how I could avail myself of your offer, at the moment."

"Not everyone on the World Council approves of the way Anita Halleck is treating you."

Smiling ruefully, Jordan said, "I just don't understand what she's afraid of. Surely she doesn't believe this alien invasion twaddle."

"She's afraid of *you*, Mr. Kell. She's afraid you're after her chair."

"Nonsense."

"That's not the way she sees it."

"I'm no threat to her. I'm not interested in politics."

Stavenger's smile turned skeptical. "I believe it was Pericles who said that the Athenians regarded a man who takes no interest in politics not as a harmless man, but as a useless man."

Jordan puffed out a breath. "You mean that I'm involved in politics whether I like it or not."

"You should be."

"The World Council is very powerful, isn't it?"

Nodding, Stavenger said, "And Anita is making it more powerful every year. She's been gathering all the threads of power into her own hands ever since she became the Council's chairwoman."

His face tightening into a frown, Jordan asked, "But why? Why is she doing this? How can the Council and the rest of the world's people allow her to?"

history lesson

Stavenger leaned back in his cushioned chair.

"You've got to understand that the world council has faced some tremendous problems over the past two centuries. First the global climate reached a tipping point and greenhouse floods swamped coastlines everywhere. Millions were killed. Hundreds of millions were suddenly homeless."

"I know," said Jordan. "I was one of the people who worked to find new homes for the refugees, to build new cities."

"Wars broke out. The Middle East was devastated by nuclear strikes and counterstrikes. Biological warfare nearly depopulated the Indian subcontinent."

And killed Miriam, Jordan thought, feeling the stab of pain all over again. I let her come to Kashmir with me, and the bioweapons killed her.

"People wanted safety. They wanted order. They needed new homes, new lives, new ways of earning a living."

And I ran away, off to New Earth, Jordan remembered. I couldn't face living on the world that had killed my wife.

If Stavenger saw the pain on Jordan's face he made no sign of it. He continued, "The World Council was created to deal with those problems. National governments on Earth were more than willing to pass the responsibility on to the World Council. Selene and the other human settlements throughout the solar system were more than willing to help."

"Yes, I understand that," said Jordan. "But how was Halleck able to build a virtual dictatorship out of that?"

Looking grim, Stavenger answered, "When people are hungry, homeless, frightened, they will give up their liberties for food, for shelter, for hope."

"I suppose that's right."

"Oh, there wasn't any grand plan to it, no design to create an authoritarian government. Not at first. The World Council was merely coordinating international efforts to help the refugees."

"But?"

"But taxes had to be raised. Safety regulations had to be put in place. And enforced. There was no takeover of political power by the World Council. But an army of safety engineers, of child care workers and psychotechnicians, of bureaucrats, set up a web of rules and enforcements that gradually assumed control over almost every aspect of the people's lives."

"And froze it all in place," Jordan muttered.

"Technology played a part in it. With the world's work force decimated by the floods and other climate changes, it was necessary to turn to automation. Robots took over jobs and became so good at them that soon enough robots became preferred over human workers. An enormous social welfare system arose: the retirement age was relentlessly lowered. People became dependent on their governments for their pensions, their livelihoods."

"All around the world."

"All around the world," Stavenger echoed. "We in Selene and some of the other off-world settlements tried to point out that the World Council's system wouldn't work, not in the long run, but nobody on Earth would listen to us. Things were getting better. Thanks to space resources and industries, the global economy actually started growing again."

"Population certainly grew," Jordan said.

"Yes. And the bigger the population, the more need for control: safety regulations, security controls, economic management."

"And now they're locked into the system," Jordan said.

"The World Council's first priority became to protect the people. And to protect them, it was necessary to watch over them constantly. To eliminate crime, it was necessary to monitor people, to catch the malcontents and mentally unsound *before* they could harm society."

Jordan simply shook his head. "There's a dead end up ahead, isn't there?"

"Not necessarily. Not as long as new crises can be found. The Greenland meltdown is a godsend for Halleck. A new crisis that threatens the climate of Western Europe."

"Then why doesn't she see the death wave as a crisis?"

"Because it's two thousand years in the future. An eternity."

"Not for those other worlds."

"They're not real, not to Halleck or most of the Council. Not to the vast majority of Earth's people."

Jordan fell silent for several moments, thinking hard. At last he looked back at Stavenger and said, "Then I'll have to make it real."

His smile breaking out again, Stavenger said, "Yes, I think you will. And to accomplish that, you'll have to get yourself elected to the World Council."

"Me? The World Council . . ."

"The Council needs your voice, Jordan. You could be the nucleus of a new movement, a counter to Halleck's drive to be empress."

escape

++

++

Jordan couldn't sleep after his talk with Stavenger. Get myself elected to the world council, he thought. Challenge Halleck directly. Become a politician.

He shook his head. How strange the world is. Halleck's actions are forcing me to take the one course that she wants me to avoid most of all.

For every action, he thought, remembering Newton's law, there is an equal and opposite reaction.

Glancing at the window, he saw that dawn was starting to brighten the sky. Briefly he thought about taking a walk outside. Through the room's curtained window he could see a nearly full Moon grinning lopsidedly as it settled toward the hilly horizon.

No, he decided. The less I'm outside the less chance for a surveillance satellite to spot me. Even in the dark of night, he had the eerie feeling that they were watching for him.

I'm getting just as paranoid as Paul, he told himself. But then he repeated the old dictum: Even paranoids have enemies.

According to Longyear, the tribal council had complained to the U.S. Bureau of Indian Affairs about drones flitting across the reservation. The government officials claimed they had not authorized any drone flights, but the FAA confirmed that several drones had indeed penetrated the reservation's airspace.

Halleck's World Council at work, Jordan knew. The matter was being discussed by U.S. Department of State officials and World

Council bureaucrats. In the meantime, Jordan stayed indoors as much as possible.

Suddenly Aditi's lovely face took form in the holographic viewer, smiling at him.

"Hello, Jordan dearest."

"Aditi! You're up early. Or have you been up all night?"

"It's almost lunchtime here in Barcelona," she said. With a dimpled grin she added, "Dr. Frankenheimer expects me in his laboratory in an hour or so."

"How are you, darling?" Jordan asked. And for the next half hour he was lost in the joy of talking with her.

After a while, Aditi told him, "I think Dr. Frankenheimer is using me as a check on the information our technicians are giving to his technicians. He wants to be able to build a copy of my communicator by himself, without waiting for the technicians to learn how to do it."

"He's looking for a Nobel Prize," Jordan muttered, wondering in the back of his mind if this link Adri had set up for them was really safe from tracing.

Aditi didn't seem to have any such worries. "And you, Jordan, how did your talk with Mr. Stavenger go?"

"He wants me to run for election to the World Council."

Her eyes lit up. "Of course! That way you could fight Halleck openly."

"I'm not sure that I'm cut out to be a politician."

"Of course you are," Aditi insisted. "You'll make a wonderful councilman."

He sighed. "I wish we were together."

"So do I, dearest," said Aditi. "So do I."

Glancing around the small, snug bedroom, Jordan said, "I'm waiting for Youngeagle to set up a meeting with the head of the Otero Network. Still staying indoors as much as possible."

"But the World Council can't take you away against your will," she said.

With a rueful smile, Jordan said, "And they can't keep you in custody, either. But they're doing it."

"I don't mind that. Working with Dr. Frankenheimer is interesting." Then Aditi added, "But I miss you."

Jordan nodded. "It's lonely without you, darling."

"Lonely."

Trying to smile, he said, "Well, if everything works out right, we'll be together again—sooner or later."

Aditi said, "Sooner." But Jordan saw the doubt in her eyes.

"I'll get you," he promised. "No matter where you are, I'll come to you."

"Yes," she answered, with a smile that warmed his heart.

The Sun was just climbing over the rim of the distant hills as Paul Longyear and his uncle Twelvetoes huddled with Jordan in the living room of Longyear's parents' house.

Lester Youngeagle was there, too, practically quivering with the news that he had contacted the Otero Network and Carlos Otero himself was flying to St. Louis to meet Jordan.

But first they had to smuggle Jordan out of the reservation and to the airport at Bismarck.

"There'll be six pickups altogether," Longyear was saying, rehearsing the plan for spiriting Jordan off the reservation. "They should be arriving in ten, fifteen minutes."

"Five plus mine," said Twelvetoes.

"Each of the five other trucks will have at least two men in them. They'll all come in here—"

"It'll be crowded," Twelvetoes said.

Casting a glowering eye at his uncle, Longyear continued, "Then we all go out. I've got an extra hat I'll loan you, so the satellites won't be able to see your face."

"We'll all be wearing hats," Twelvetoes said. "To the satellites we'll look like an old-fashioned posse."

Longyear resumed, "Jordan, you come with Uncle and me. The others all drive to five different reservation gates. That'll give the satellite monitors plenty to look at."

"And where do we go?" Jordan asked.

"The reservation offices. They've got a covered parking garage. You get out there, wait about an hour, and then an official reservation school bus will pick you up."

"Won't that be rather conspicuous?" Jordan asked.

"Hide in plain sight," said Twelvetoes.

"The bus goes every morning from the reservation offices to four different schools," Longyear explained. "While you're riding around, I'll drive my own car to the last school on your route. You'll transfer to my car and I'll drive you off the reservation, to the airport and your meeting with this news media head man."

"Carlos Otero," Youngeagle reminded him.

Jordan nodded. The plan sounded like it could work. Keep me out of the satellite cameras' view, he told himself, while giving the satellite monitors plenty to look at.

Still, the thought of spending more than an hour in a bus full of spirited schoolchildren sounded less than appealing to him.

The school bus turned out to be noisy, but fun. Jordan felt a little self-conscious in the black wide-brimmed hat Longyear had given him, as if the hat were wearing him, rather than vice versa. He sat up front, just behind the driver—a stolid, corpulent Native American woman wearing a windbreaker despite the bright warm weather. He used the driver's microphone to talk to the kids about the stars.

Their ages ran from kindergarten to sixth grade, and this was the one day of the week when they had to show up in their class-rooms and interact with their live teachers. The other days they worked at home and communicated digitally.

Jordan found them to be lively, bright, and intensely interested in what he had to tell them. Practically every one of them put away their digital readers and game players to shower questions on the star traveler. As he talked about his experiences on New Earth, he wondered how such curious children could metamorphose into sullen, uncommunicative teenagers. Is it hormones? he asked himself. Or does the educational system somehow beat the curiosity out of them?

"So who knows how far the star Sirius is from Earth?" Jordan asked.

"A gazillion kilometers," said a grinning first-grader.

More seriously, an older girl answered, "Eight point six light-years."

"Very good," Jordan said. "And how many kilometers are there in a light-year?"

By the time they reached the last school on the bus's route, Jordan was happy but nearly exhausted. How do teachers put up with all this energy and curiosity? he asked himself.

Longyear was waiting in a sleek, bright blue sports car, and whisked Jordan off the reservation to the airport at Bismarck. Jordan gave the hat back to Longyear and thanked him for his help.

"I don't know what I would have done without you, Paul."

Breaking into a rare grin, Longyear answered, "When you get the missions to those other worlds started, make sure I get a slot on one of them."

"I will."

Once they reached the airport they embraced like brothers, and then Jordan hurried into the terminal to catch the flight to St. Louis, trying not to look over his shoulder for World Council agents sent to bring him back to Barcelona.

At St. Louis's Lindbergh Airport, a pair of corporate executives in three-piece gray suits greeted him and drove him to the terminal for private planes. They led him to a twin engine, swept-wing plane bearing on its tail the logo of Otero Network.

Standing just inside the plane's hatch, almost filling the space, stood Carlos Otero, a beaming smile on his dark, mustachioed face.

"Jordan Kell," Otero said, extending both hands as Jordan hustled up the stairs to him. "You don't know how happy I am to meet you."

"I'm very pleased to meet you, sir," said Jordan, accepting a vigorous pumping of his arm.

Leading Jordan down the aisle of the plushly outfitted jet, Otero gestured to a tiny, almost doll-like young woman standing before the built-in bar.

"Vera Griffin," he said, a little pompously, "this is Jordan Kell, the starman."

"How do you do?" said Jordan, accepting her outstretched hand. She smiled and stared at him, idol worship radiating from her tawny eyes.

"Vera's going to be the associate producer of your interview," Otero said.

Jordan heard the plane's engines begin to whine softly. Electric engines, he thought. Then one of the crew closed the main hatch and the faint sound cut off entirely.

As the plane began taxiing toward a runway, Jordan asked, "Where are we heading?"

"Corporate headquarters," said Otero, gesturing to the plush seats. "Boston, Massachusetts. Land of the bean and the cod. The Hub of the Universe."

the hub

"The way to do this," Otero was saying, "is to produce a news special about you. But we don't announce that you'll be making an appearance. We emphasize that you've disappeared, that not even the World Council knows where you are. Then, once the show begins—*wham!*—there you are, live."

The electrojet plane was winging to Boston, flying high above a smooth gray blanket of clouds. Otero was relaxed in a plush chair, a glass of tequila in one meaty hand. Vera Griffin had been sipping slowly at a tall glass of iced tea, her eyes never leaving Jordan, who had accepted a glass of grapefruit juice from the uniformed flight attendant who served as bartender.

Otero had then dismissed the flight attendant and they began to make plans for the special show and Jordan's unannounced appearance.

Leaning earnestly toward Otero, across the aisle from his own seat, Jordan said, "I want Halleck to release my wife. She's being held—"

"I know, I know," Otero said impatiently. "From what my snoops tell me, your wife is cooperating with the scientists in Barcelona."

"She can still cooperate without being imprisoned," Jordan grumbled.

Jabbing a finger at him, Griffin said excitedly, "That's what we want on the show! That kind of indignation. Get the viewers sore at the Powers That Be."

Otero nodded happily.

"All right," Jordan agreed. "But let's remember that the prime reason for this appearance is to tell the public about the death wave and the other worlds that are in imminent danger from it. Worlds we've got to help."

Otero's swarthy face grew somber. "One thing you've got to realize, Jordan, is that *telling* people something is nowhere near as impressive as *showing* it to them."

"Yes," Griffin agreed. "We don't want this show to be a bunch of talking heads. We need visuals."

"Visuals—from worlds that are light-years away?"

Otero waved a meaty hand. "Oh, I suppose we could 'gin up some very realistic-looking animation. Computer graphics. That sort of thing."

"We've got to give the audience something to look at," Griffin emphasized.

"Something they've never seen before," Otero added.

With a slightly bitter smile, Jordan said, "My handsome countenance won't be enough, eh?"

"For maybe five minutes," Griffin said, straight-faced.

"Three, tops," said Otero, grinning. "Remember, this is show business."

"I thought this was to be a news broadcast," Jordan said.

"Oh, it's news all right," Otero replied. "But even the news is show business, too. Show business, first and foremost."

"We've lost track of him," Gilda Nordquist admitted.

Sitting behind her sleekly imposing desk, Anita Halleck looked grim. Like an empress who's about to order heads to roll, Nordquist thought.

"How did that happen?" she asked, her voice tight, holding her anger in check—barely.

Nordquist was standing in front of the desk. Halleck had not invited her to sit in one of the comfortable chairs arrayed on either side of her.

"He must have had half the reservation helping him," Nordquist reported. "We were tracking half a dozen pickup trucks, but it turns out he wasn't in any of them."

"No trace of him?"

With a shake of her head, Nordquist said, "I can only assume that he's left the reservation."

"And gone where?"

For the first time, Nordquist saw a ray of hope for herself. "You know we regularly keep a watch on key people. So I queried the heuristic program about who Kell might have gone to. It came up with an interesting correlation."

"What is it?"

"Carlos Otero flew out to St. Louis yesterday. He stayed only a few minutes, never left the airport, then flew directly back to his corporate headquarters in Boston."

Halleck's expression grew thoughtful. "Did he?"

"He might have gone there to pick up Kell and bring him back to his own surroundings."

Halleck gestured to the armchairs in front of her desk. "How can we determine if he did that?"

As she gratefully sank into one of the chairs, Nordquist answered, "I have people checking with the airport authorities in St. Louis and New York. Nothing official, of course; the Americans aren't accustomed to being interrogated by World Council security agents."

"Not yet," Halleck murmured.

Otero had insisted that Jordan stay in his own home, a rambling old residence in Concord that had been built to Otero's own ideas of what a wealthy Mexican landowner's hacienda would look like.

Burnished dark wood beams supported the ceiling of the over-sized living room. The floors were tiled, with boldly patterned area rugs scattered here and there. More colorful tiles adorned the walls. The furniture was large and overstuffed, upholstered with gaudy patterns. Flowers were everywhere: in vases on the side tables, in pots dangling from the ceiling. The dining room table could hold twenty. Jordan felt as if he had stepped into a spare-no-expense Hollywood set.

Otero personally showed him through room after room, even the enclosed silver-inlaid swimming pool with its retractable roof.

"It's rather overwhelming," he admitted when Otero asked him what he thought of the place. Then he tactfully added, "Splendid, though. Magnificent."

Smiling hugely, Otero said, "I think it was Churchill or one of those British clowns who said, 'Nothing succeeds like excess.'"

Remembering his old training as a diplomat, Jordan smiled back and murmured, "You've certainly succeeded, then."

At last Otero led Jordan to the wing of the house that held the guest quarters. It was a full suite: sitting room, dining area, bed-room, lavatory finished in green marble, and even a small garden with a graceful willow tree. Through the foliage surrounding the garden Jordan could see the quiet street that led down to the town's center and the famous bridge where the Minutemen had battled the Redcoats.

To Jordan's surprise, the guest suite was decorated in starkly modernistic style: ergonomic chairs and a fire-engine-red sectional sofa.

"My interior decorator begged me to let him do the suite in a different style from the rest of the house," Otero said. "What do you think of it?"

"It's . . . interesting," said Jordan.

With a shake of his head, Otero complained, "It's not warm, like the rest of the house."

"It will be fine," Jordan assured him.

Otero headed for the suite's front door, apologizing that he couldn't have dinner with Jordan.

"I've got to be at a banquet that my own PR people arranged, in the city," he explained. "I can't very well back out of it. Some of the most important business leaders on Earth will be there."

"I understand," said Jordan.

"Officially," Otero confided, "it's a gathering of multinational corporate heads. We're supposed to be discussing international business trends. But what we're really going to talk about is next year's election for head of the World Council."

Jordan nodded. "Anita Halleck's running for reelection, isn't she?"

"Against nothing but token opposition," said Otero. Allowing a slight smile to lighten his face, he added, "But we're trying to change that."

"You're not happy with her leadership?"

Otero abruptly turned from the door and settled his bulk onto the sectional sofa. Jordan sat in the skeletal chair next to it.

"Listen," Otero began. "Halleck has been running the Council for too long. Just because people have extended their life spans to centuries doesn't mean that she should stay in office forever."

"You don't have term limits?" Jordan asked.

"We do, but she put through an amendment that excludes her from it. She's determined to stay in office for as long as she chooses, so long as she gets reelected every ten years."

"I see."

"She gets more dictatorial every year," Otero said, his expression darkening. "Look at what she's doing to you and your wife."

"And once she gets her hands on faster-than-light communications she'll be able to tighten her grip throughout the solar system."

Nodding unhappily, Otero said, "So you see why this dinner

meeting is important." Before Jordan could reply, he went on, "And why this show we're doing with you is even more important. Vital! We can't allow Halleck to keep you bottled up. We've got to get your story across to the public!"

Jordan said, "I agree completely." But he was thinking, I hope I can stay out of Halleck's clutches long enough to do the show.

Then a new thought hit him: And what happens to Aditi when I do the show?

aditi

Jordan had dinner brought to him in the guest suite. As he ate, barely tasting the food and wine, he wondered if Aditi could reach him in this new location. She had explained to Jordan that the New Earth FTL system tracked his wrist communicator, so that it didn't matter where he was, she would be able to find him.

Yes, he said to himself. But is the system really that good? Can it avoid detection by Halleck's people?

And overriding every other consideration: What will they do to Aditi if I go through with Otero's broadcast? This whole mess started when I made that broadcast last week. What will Halleck's reaction be when I show up on the air again?

"Hello, dear Jordan."

He snapped his attention to the holographic viewer built into the sitting room wall. Aditi appeared to be sitting there, across the room from him, near enough to touch, to hold.

"Hello, darling," he said as he got up from the dining table and went to the sectional sofa. "How are you?"

"I'm fine," she said, smiling a little. "They're treating me quite well. But how are you? And where are you?"

Wondering if he could answer his wife's question without Halleck's people listening in, Jordan plunged ahead anyway. "I'm in the Boston area, a guest at the home of the owner of the Otero Broadcasting Network."

"It looks rather magnificent," Aditi said.

"Stylish," Jordan agreed. "But it's just another prison, really. I can't go outside for fear of being spotted by World Council agents."

"How did you get to Boston? Why are you there?"

Jordan explained about the special show that Otero was planning.

"I'm going to rattle Anita Halleck's cage," he said, surprised at the heat seething within him.

Aditi giggled. "We're the ones in cages."

"I intend to put an end to that."

"You're going to run for the World Council seat?"

He nodded. "If I can get out from under Halleck's insistence on putting me in protective custody."

"Wonderful!" Aditi clapped her hands happily. But then she added, "I miss you, Jordan."

He wanted to get up from the sofa and cross the room to embrace her. She looked so real, so lovely, so desirable.

But all he could do was reply, "I miss you, too, dearest."

Sensing his discontent, Aditi said, "Tell me about the show you're going to do."

Jordan explained what he wanted to do, then repeated to her Otero's dictum that he had to show the viewers the alien worlds, not merely talk about them.

"I'll ask Adri about that," she said.

Jordan asked, "Do you think he has imagery of other worlds?"

"Our astronomers do, I'm sure. The Predecessors sent scouts to many worlds, landers as well as orbiters."

"That would be wonderful!"

Looking pleased that she could be of help, Aditi said, "I'll ask Adri about it as soon as we finish our talking."

It took hours before they finished.

* * *

Anita Halleck was not accustomed to waiting. When she summoned someone, that person came to her immediately. Not Rudy Castiglione, though. The handsome, roguish Italian was always late for his appointments. Not terribly late: just a few minutes, never more than a quarter of an hour. Just enough to establish some slight measure of independence. And Halleck allowed him to get away with it. Rudy was too charming to chastise. And too useful.

Halleck was pacing impatiently across the carpeted floor of the study in her home on Barcelona's outskirts. It was nearly midnight; the weather forecast called for rain between midnight and three A.M. Despite her irritation, Halleck smiled to herself. If Rudy doesn't get here soon he's going to get wet.

"Signore Castiglione has arrived, Madam Chairwoman," announced the digitized voice of the house's communications system. The human servants were all in their quarters. Halleck wanted no witnesses to Castiglione visiting this late at night. The chairwoman of the World Council has to be above reproach, she believed. Above even the slightest hint of misbehavior.

On the display screen built into the cozy little room's bookshelf-lined wall, she watched Castiglione striding gracefully up the wide staircase and heading straight toward the study—which adjoined Halleck's bedroom.

He opened the door and peeked in, a slightly sheepish expression on his handsome face.

"I know I'm late," he said, one hand behind his back as he stepped into the room. "I saw these on Las Ramblas and stopped to get them for you."

With a flourish, he whipped a bouquet of exotic-looking colorful flowers from behind his back. "They're from the jungles of Brazil. I thought you might like them."

"They're beautiful, Rudy," she said, her inflection as flat as the communications system's. "Put them down somewhere. We have a problem to discuss."

"Problem?"

"Jordan Kell has apparently gone to Boston. My security people believe he's with Carlos Otero."

Castiglione laid the flowers on an end table and walked toward her, his lips pursed.

"Otero? That could be trouble."

"We've got to stop Kell from going public again. He's got to be contained."

"And you want me to, uh . . . contain him."

"That's right."

"No questions asked? I can use whatever means necessary?"

"Within limits. I don't want anyone murdered, or an urban riot, for god's sake. You've got to be discreet."

Castiglione nodded. "All right. I'll go to Boston."

"Good. Have you been there before?"

"Ages ago. As a student I played a football match there—although the Americans called it soccer. An odd sort of people."

"Very well," said Halleck. "Get to Boston and bring Kell back here."

With a sigh, Castiglione said, "We could have had this discussion over a secure phone call. There wasn't any need for me to come all the way out here. And now it's started to rain."

Halleck looked into his softly dark eyes and saw an expectation there.

The shadow of a smile curling her lips, she said, "Well, as long as you're here, I suppose you ought to stay the night."

Castiglione's answering smile was incandescent.

preparations

morning in concord, massachusetts.

Jordan stood beneath the graceful willow tree in the garden outside his bedroom, watching the buildup of going-to-work traffic on the street beyond the hedge. Cars and the occasional bus flowed along quietly, their electric engines purring softly. Not much of a morning rush, he thought. It's actually rather peaceful.

Otero had arranged a date with a tailor for Jordan. He had brought only the clothes on his back, and the network owner wanted him to look stylish, attractive. Although he laundered the shirt, slacks, and underwear he'd been wearing before going to bed, Jordan had to admit they were beginning to look shabby.

Glancing at his wrist, Jordan saw that the tailor was due in another half hour. Stepping back into the bedroom, he decided to finish his morning coffee and then stand to be measured.

"Friend Jordan."

Adri's tall, lean figure stood in the bedroom's holographic viewer. Wearing a full-length softly creased robe of grayish blue, the old man appeared to be walking in a park thick with brightly colored flowers.

"I know your responses to me will take an hour to reach here," Adri said in his soft, slightly sibilant voice, "so if you don't mind I will talk while you listen."

Jordan hurried to the sitting room and dropped onto the sectional sofa. Adri was on the viewer there, as well, of course. Jordan saw a small, furry, big-eyed head peeking out of the folds of Adri's robe. One of his pets.

"Aditi has told me that you require imagery of some of the worlds our exploratory spacecraft have observed. I can send you such images, although many of them—images of worlds that have been destroyed by the death wave—will undoubtedly be quite disturbing to you."

The more disturbing the better, Jordan replied silently.

"I presume you have equipment that can record the images. Otherwise we will have to arrange to send them to you at the time you are actually making your presentation. That might be a little tricky, you know."

His eyes riveted on Adri's seamed face, Jordan tapped the phone console on the sofa's end table and canceled his tailor's appointment.

Carlos Otero's personal assistant was Elizabeth Beauregard, a short, stocky, highly intelligent woman who was known to Otero's top staff people as Betty the Bodyguard—or even Betty the Bitch. She had worked for Otero for nearly ten years and had seen more than her share of importunate people who simply *had to* see the Big Boss: connivers and con men, ardent champions of Noble Causes who wanted to bend Otero's ear about how much good he could do—for them. Intensely serious people who had the inside information on scandals, on government cover-ups, on imminent disasters and hidden treasures. Beautiful, impatient, smoldering women eager to have Otero smile upon them.

Betty the Bodyguard sized them up and put them down. Only rarely did she allow someone—anyone—to break through and see the Big Boss. Her instincts seldom failed her. When she did allow someone to get past her, as she had with Vera Griffin little more than a week ago, it almost always worked out well.

Now she was facing a smiling, smooth-talking, devilishly

attractive Italian from the World Council. Rudolfo Castiglione claimed to be a personal assistant to Anita Halleck herself, and he flashed impressive credentials along with his killer smile.

But Elizabeth Beauregard knew that her boss loathed Anita Halleck, and thought the World Council was a gaggle of collectivists who were determined to establish a global tyranny. No, an interplanetary tyranny.

Sitting at her immaculately clean desk, Betty looked up at Castiglione and said in her unemotional, no-nonsense voice, "I'm very sorry, sir, but Mr. Otero has a totally full calendar. He gave me strict orders not to add a single item to his schedule."

Castiglione's smile did not diminish by a single watt. "Not even an urgent request from the chairwoman of the World Council?"

Blinking her brown eyes at him, Betty replied, "I could lose my job, sir."

"But this is *important*," Castiglione insisted.

Betty knew that sometimes appearing to bend a little could disarm an insistent visitor. She said, "Perhaps if you could tell me what this is all about . . ."

Castiglione drew himself up to his full height. "It concerns the starman, Jordan Kell."

"Oh," she said. "Then you'd probably want to talk with Vera Griffin."

"Who is she?"

"The producer of a show we're going to do about New Earth and this death wave that's supposed to be coming our way."

Castiglione's brows knit slightly as he thought it over. After a few heartbeats, he said, "Very well, then. I'll talk with her."

Betty the Bodyguard kept herself from smiling. But she was thinking, The old deflection routine. Palm them off on one of the péons and keep the boss happy.

Then she added, And it'll serve Ms. Griffin right; her and her goddamned persistence.

EVIDENCE

Jordan Kell slumped back on the sofa in the guest suite's sitting room, aghast at the images in the holographic viewer, unable to tear his eyes away from the utter devastation he was seeing.

From slightly more than eight light-years away, the astronomers of New Earth were sending him the images they had amassed of planets overtaken by the deadly wave of gamma radiation flowing through the galaxy.

He recognized Elyse Rudaki's voice describing the scenes he'd been watching since morning. Ordinarily warm and vibrant, the astrophysicist's voice was trembling on the brink of tears. Jordan felt close to tears himself as he gaped, slack-jawed, at what had once been a living, thriving civilization.

Now it was a charnel house.

"It must have been done in a few hours," Rudaki was saying. "A whole world, slaughtered."

Puppies, Jordan thought. They look like . . . puppies.

Not really, his rational mind countered. Puppies don't have six legs. Puppies don't sprawl in heaps and mounds of death.

Yet the inhabitants of that world reminded Jordan uncannily of prairie dogs or meerkats: puppies, really. Small and furry, with six limbs; four for walking, two for grasping. Jordan saw pincerlike hands at the ends of those upper limbs.

They had built cities, of a sort: aboveground structures made of sun-dried mud bricks, most of them no more than two stories high, although here and there a slender tower rose somewhat higher. They must have had a much more complex system underground, a warren of tunnels and dens. But they were intelligent enough to start building cities aboveground.

The cities were intact, undamaged, frozen in time. And all around them lay the intelligent creatures who had built them— dead, every one of them. Tongues lolling from their mouths, eyes staring blankly. They piled together as if trying to comfort one another, huddling instinctively in the last moments of their lives.

A whole world, utterly dead.

"The gamma radiation reached far enough belowground to kill those who remained in the tunnels," Elyse Rudaki's voice was saying, choking back sobs. "Even the bacteria that normally decompose dead tissue were killed by the gamma radiation, so there's no rotting of the bodies. They're p-perfectly preserved."

The planet orbited a greenish star, and its sky was a sickly pale gray. The satellite view moved across the landscape. Everything was dead. Jordan recognized what must have once been the equivalent of trees: bare, burned black, limbs twisted and pleading.

"Perhaps some of them survived the gamma wave," Rudaki went on, "for a while. Maybe they were too deep underground for the radiation to reach them. But with all the vegetation dead, all the other animals killed, they couldn't have lasted very long."

Jordan wanted to ask where this planet was, how far it was from Earth, when the death wave did its deadly work. But then he realized, What difference does it make? Nothing can change what happened there.

Rudaki was saying dolefully, "The astronomers here on New Earth have estimated that at least a million young civilizations have already been destroyed by the death wave." Her voice nearly broke as she added, "Nothing can stop it."

*   *   *

In Boston, Vera Griffin was sitting at the desk in her cubicle, staring up at the devilishly handsome Rudolfo Castiglione.

"Mr. Otero's personal assistant, Ms. Beauregard, told me to speak to you," Castiglione was saying as he stood before her desk. As he spoke he quickly took in the cubicle's décor—or lack of it: bare partitions, a delicate little curved desk, a set of bookcases that were empty, two cushioned chairs that looked as if they'd been purchased from a discount furniture store.

Vera Griffin herself appeared to be young: quite slim, stylishly dressed and coiffed, her soft brown eyes studying him intently. Good, thought Castiglione. She can be charmed out of her shoes, no doubt. And out of her clothes, most likely.

Gesturing to one of the chairs, Griffin said, "Please make yourself comfortable. You said this is about the star traveler?"

Castiglione sat and leaned back casually. "Yes. Jordan Kell."

"We're doing a show about him."

"So I've heard." Castiglione allowed his smile to contract slightly. "You know, he's a fugitive from custody."

Her eyes went wide. "Really?"

"Yes. I'm trying to find him."

"What's he done?"

Nonchalantly, Castiglione replied, "Oh, there are no criminal charges against him. The World Council decided to put him in protective custody after some terrorists made an attempt on his life."

"They tried to kill him?"

"Yes. We want to protect him. It's for his own safety, you know."

Griffin thought, What a show it would make if we could get an assassination attempt! Maybe we could re-create what actually happened. But a real attack would be terrific!

"So you see that it's important that we locate the man," Castiglione was saying.

I'll have to tell Mr. Otero about this, Griffin realized. Maybe we should hire some security people.

Watching the emotions playing across her face, Castiglione said, "You do know where he is, don't you?"

Griffin actually flinched, as if he'd slapped her. "No, I don't," she answered. Too quickly, in Castiglione's view.

"Really?"

"Really," she said. Then, more slowly, "But perhaps Mr. Otero does. Let me ask him about it."

His smile returning, Castiglione said, "Please do."

Griffin went through the motions of phoning Otero's office, keeping the phone's handset to her ear, so Castiglione couldn't hear the other end of the conversation.

After a few seconds, Griffin nodded and said into the phone, "Okay. I'll come up at five o'clock."

Castiglione nodded and smiled as he replaced the handset. "And perhaps after you've met with Otero you and I could have a drink together. I'm all alone here in Boston and I don't know anyone in town."

Griffin smiled back and nodded. "That would be fine."

I've got her, Castiglione said to himself. And she'll lead me to Kell, one way or the other.

barcelona

Aditi felt tired as she entered the sitting room of her apartment in the underground communications complex. She had spent the day with Frankenheimer, using the communicator implanted in her brain to contact Adri and others on New Earth.

The physiologist seemed rapt with delight as he studied the neutrino tomographs of Aditi's brain while she talked to people more than eight light-years distant. He traced circuits in her brain that interlaced with the natural network of neurons.

While Aditi grew more weary of the tests, Frankenheimer became more excited.

"Your communicator is made of neuronal tissue," he exclaimed at the end of one hour-long call to New Earth.

Nodding, she agreed, "Yes, it is natural tissue, grown from stem cells just like the rest of my brain."

"And it grows and develops just like the rest of your brain."

"Yes, of course."

"Of course," Frankenheimer echoed. "It's just as natural as your heart's beating—to you."

"It's been part of me all my life," she said.

Looking at Aditi like a little boy asking for candy, Frankenheimer said, "Could . . . would your people on New Earth show me how to make a communicator for someone here?"

"Someone? Who?"

"A test subject." He licked his lips, then added, "Myself, I suppose."

Aditi said, "I could find out for you."

"Could you? That would be great!"

"I'll ask my people this evening."

"Great," Frankenheimer repeated. "Wonderful."

Now Aditi lounged back on the bed, too tired and emotionally spent to order dinner for herself. She recognized the eager glow of ambition in Frankenheimer's eyes. Can I trust him with a communicator? she wondered. I'll have to ask Adri about that.

But first I need to talk to Jordan.

Jordan was also feeling close to exhaustion. He had spent the entire day staring at the images New Earth's astronomers had sent to him. Dead worlds. Whole planets wiped clean of life, down to the bacteria. A world of creatures who reminded him of butterflies: utterly devastated, their beautiful winged bodies strewn across the rocks and sands of their dead world. A planet covered with mats of biological matter that formed a worldwide mind: totally destroyed by the lethal gamma wave. Planet after planet, intelligent species after intelligent species, civilization after civilization, erased as if they had never existed.

Otero wants visuals to show the public, Jordan told himself; now we've got plenty. But can we show it? Will it be too upsetting, too demoralizing, too soul-wrenching?

As he rubbed his aching brow, an ancient quotation came to him: "Ye shall know the truth, and the truth shall set you free."

From the Bible, somewhere, Jordan remembered. Knowledge is always preferable to ignorance. No matter how painful, no matter what the consequences, the truth shall set you free.

He hoped that was right.

Glancing at the clock set into the wall below the holographic viewer, Jordan saw that it was nearly dinnertime. *Otero will expect me downstairs, and I'll have a lot to show him.*

Then Aditi appeared in the viewer, sitting up on her bed fully clothed. She looked drawn, worn, pale.

"What's the matter, darling?" Jordan blurted.

She smiled wanly. "I was going to ask you that same question, Jordan. You look . . . troubled."

"So do you."

They spent the next several minutes explaining the events of the day, the reasons for their weary melancholy.

"Yes," Aditi said mournfully, "watching the dead worlds can be very depressing."

"You've seen them?"

"A few."

With a determined shake of his head, Jordan said, "We've got to prevent that from happening to more planets, more intelligent creatures."

"Of course."

"Of course," he echoed.

"But getting the World Council to act won't be easy, Jordan. You'll have to move the whole world, all its people."

"*We'll* have to move the world," Jordan corrected.

"That's still only two of us."

"But with you beside me, dearest, I can move mountains."

She smiled wanly. "We can try, at least."

"Lord, I miss you, Aditi."

"And I miss you, too, Jordan. I hope we can be together soon."

"It can't be soon enough."

With a troubled shake of her head, Aditi half-whispered, "I never thought I could feel so . . . so empty."

Jordan could see on her face the pain he himself felt.

Forcing a bitter smile, he changed the subject. "So your scientist friend wants a communicator for himself."

"Yes," Aditi replied. "It would require major surgery to implant one in his brain."

"Couldn't it be outside the body, a device like a phone?"

"I suppose it could."

Jordan pursed his lips, then suggested, "Perhaps your people on New Earth could work with Mitch, here in Chicago. It could become a new product line for him."

Aditi actually giggled. "And make him even richer."

"And open up new jobs for people," Jordan countered.

"I'll talk to Adri about it," she said.

"Fine." Glancing at the clock again, Jordan said, "I'm afraid I'm expected for dinner."

"Go ahead, darling. I'm going to put in a call to Adri and then go to sleep."

"Pleasant dreams, my dear."

"And to you," she said. "Dream of me."

"I always do."

San Francisco

++

++

union square was filled with tourists, working citizens enjoying their lunches in the smiling sunshine, and jobless nobodies like Nick Motrenko, who had nothing better to do.

But Walt had other ideas.

Rachel was sitting beside Nick on one of the benches. A couple of teenagers zoomed past on souped-up rollerboards, laughing as they weaved through the pedestrian traffic, startling the older walkers. Nick saw one elderly gentleman yank a phone from his jacket, his face twisted with anger.

"Calling the cops," he said to Rachel.

"But the square's a police-free zone," she protested.

"Not if somebody files a complaint."

Sure enough, within less than a minute a blue-anodized drone swooped over the square and the rollerboarding teens stopped, picked up their boards, and headed out of the square.

Just the threat of cops makes them leave, Nick realized.

"Where is Walt?" Rachel wondered. "He said he'd be here at noon."

"It's only five after . . . Hey, there he is."

If he weren't so tall, they might not have recognized him. Walt was wearing a regular suit; he looked almost like a businessman or even a politician, despite his height and scrawniness. His hair looked as if it'd been freshly cut, he was clean-shaven and smiling brightly.

On his arm was a brassy-looking redheaded woman, very young, dressed in a tight sweater and clinging miniskirt, with a capacious tote bag slung over her shoulder.

Nick got to his feet as the pair of them approached. Slowly, uncertainly, Rachel got up, too.

"Hello there," Walt called out, in his deep, strong voice. He stopped in front of Nick and Rachel and introduced, "This is Delores, otherwise known as Dee Dee. Dee, meet Rachel and Nick."

Dee Dee smiled perfunctorily as Nick tried to avoid staring at her generous breasts. Her hair was brick red. Can't be natural, Nick thought.

Walt stepped past a worn old KEEP OFF THE GRASS sign and headed for the shade of a tree. "Lovely morning, isn't it," he said as he hunkered down and sat on the grass. Dee Dee sat beside him. Rachel and Nick sat also, making a little circle at the base of the tree.

"You look wonderful," Rachel said to Walt. "All dressed up and all."

Walt beamed happily. "I'm in disguise," he said.

Nick thought he was probably shacked up with Dee Dee. Getting regular sex makes a guy happy, he knew.

"Dee Dee works for the police department," Walt said.

Before Nick could respond, Dee Dee said, "I'm a clerk in the property section." Her voice was nasal, irritating.

Walt went on, "And she has brought us a gift."

"It's from the department's inventory," said Dee Dee, as she opened the clasp on her tote bag and spread its top wide.

Nick peered into the bag. "It's a gun!"

Rachel looked startled.

Still smiling, Walt explained, "As far as the police department's records are concerned, this gun never existed. My clever little Dee Dee has erased it from their inventory."

Nick knew better than to take it from the bag. Someone might see it.

Walt was going on, "The pistol is almost entirely plastic. Very difficult to spot it with ordinary security sensors."

"Why do we need a gun?" Rachel asked.

His smile going even wider, "Why, someday we might decide to rise and strike." He focused his red-rimmed eyes on Nick. "Perhaps we will save our world from the aliens with a well-placed assassination."

boston

"once this was the tallest building in the entire state," said vera criffin. "They named this restaurant the Top of the Hub. you could see clear into New Hampshire from here."

Sitting across the candlelit table from her, Castiglione could see little outside the restaurant's sweeping windows except a forest of other office towers.

He had no desire to make small talk with this woman. Not yet.

"What was Mr. Otero's reaction when you told him that I need to speak to him personally?"

Griffin dimpled into an almost-guilty smile. "He doesn't like the World Council very much. He thinks you should leave Jordan Kell alone."

Arching a brow at her, Castiglione said, "Leave him alone to be attacked by fanatics? Murdered by terrorists? That doesn't make much sense."

She shrugged her slim shoulders. "That's what Mr. Otero believes. I'm in no position to argue with him about it."

Castiglione accepted defeat graciously. "Well, let's forget him and Jordan Kell and everything else. You tell me the story of your life and I'll tell you the story of mine."

Griffin nodded happily. "You first."

Castiglione was only partway through a heavily edited autobiography by the time they finished dinner, went down to the street, and walked leisurely up to Beacon Hill and Griffin's shabby studio apartment.

It was while they were in bed together that she finally admitted that Jordan Kell himself would make a surprise appearance on the show she was producing and sit for an interview with Carlos Otero.

Castiglione lay beside her in the darkness, and as Griffin snored lightly in a happy slumber, he wondered how he could stop this show from going on the air.

But first I've got to get out of this bed and back to my hotel, he said to himself.

After dinner, Jordan showed Carlos Otero some of the imagery that Elyse Rudaki had sent him. The two men sat together in Otero's man cave, where one entire wall was a holographic viewer.

For nearly two hours they watched planet after devastated planet, worlds scrubbed clean of all life by the passage of the death wave. They sat side by side, in yieldingly comfortable wing chairs, lit only by the glow from the viewer, and watched death spreading across the galaxy.

Elyse Rudaki's voice nearly broke into sobs more than once. "There's so many of them," she said in a tear-choked whisper. "So many."

Otero said nothing, his eyes fixed on the scenes of desolation, the glass of mezcal in his hand untouched. Jordan had drained his scotch long ago, but sat riveted in his chair, unable to get up and pour himself more.

At last the three-dimensional display went dark, and the room's scattered lamps came on again softly.

Otero put his untouched drink down on the table next to his chair, then turned to Jordan.

"Those are actual images, not computer generated?"

"Actual images," said Jordan.

"They're not fakes? Not touched up? Enhanced?"

Jordan said evenly, "Those are the images recorded by space-craft that the Predecessors sent to worlds engulfed by the gamma wave."

Unmoved, Otero said, "You know that if there's any trickery here, any falsification of any kind, no matter how trivial, some wise-ass techie will figure it out and beat us over the head with the evidence. That could destroy us."

Fighting down a surge of irritation, Jordan replied, "The astronomers of New Earth are not charlatans. What reason could they have to enhance those images? Aren't they horrific enough for you?"

Otero nodded grimly. "I'll get my technical people to go over them. We have to be a thousand percent certain about these images before we show them on the air."

Jordan replied tightly, "Very well."

At last Otero reached for his drink. "This is powerful stuff."

"It's real."

"And this death wave could do the same thing to us, here on Earth?"

"When it gets here."

"In two thousand years."

Jordan said, "Two thousand or two million: once it gets here it will kill every living creature in the solar system, unless you're adequately protected."

"And your aliens can protect us?"

"They can show you how to protect yourselves."

Otero gulped at his mezcal.

Once he woke up in his hotel room, Rudolfo Castiglione called Anita Halleck. But not before ordering his breakfast—and a dozen roses to be delivered to Vera Griffin's desk at the Otero Network headquarters. No name, no card. She'll know who they're from, he told himself.

Halleck looked impatient. "I only have a few minutes before another damnable budget meeting."

"I think I've found Jordan Kell," Castiglione said, almost offhandedly, as he reached for a croissant.

"Where?"

"Carlos Otero is sheltering him," Castiglione said, munching on the croissant. "I don't know exactly where, but Otero has him, I'm sure."

"Get to him! Warn him that he's harboring a wanted fugitive."

"It's not that easy, my dear. So far, he's refused to see me."

"I'll call him myself," Halleck said. "He can't refuse to talk to *me*."

"I suppose not. In the meantime, I'm going to try a back-channel approach."

"Back channel?"

"Strictly unofficial. Off the record. But perhaps I can get to see Kell that way."

"And what good will that do?"

With a knowing smile, Castiglione said, "Once I meet with him and know for certain where he is, we can call in a security team to take him."

Halleck smiled back. "Rudy, you're little short of despicable."

He put on a pained expression. "Little short? Where have I failed?"

As he had expected, the roses castiglione had sent to vera griffin had bowled her over.

"It was so sweet of you!" she gushed when he called her later in the morning. "Everybody in the office wants to know who my boyfriend is."

Wincing slightly at the word "boyfriend," Castiglione said, "Then you'll come to dinner with me this evening?"

Her face radiating happiness in the tiny screen of his wrist communicator, Griffin replied, "Sure! Where?"

"You pick the place. I'll find it."

Now, while the setting sun cast long shadows along Beacon Hill's narrow streets, Castiglione located the restaurant that she had picked for dinner. It was on a corner only a few blocks from the Massachusetts State House. He knew he was early for their date, so he walked up the sloping street to take a look at the golden-domed redbrick building.

Even with the marble columns adorning its front it looked small, pedestrian, to his eyes. It's no Castel Gandolfo, he thought with an amused shrug.

He noticed a statue on the front lawn: a seated woman, wearing what appeared to be a very plain dress. Then he saw that she was a Quaker. The inscription on the statue's base read: *Mary Dyer, Witness for Religious Freedom. Hanged June 1, 1660.*

Castiglione blinked at the inscription. Americans, he thought. Strange people. Strange sense of humor.

He got back to the restaurant just in time to see Griffin hurrying up the street to meet him. He smiled his full wattage at her and offered his arm to lead her into the pathetically unsophisticated eatery.

Castiglione suffered through what passed for seafood and listened to Griffin chatter about her arduous day. She did not mention Jordan Kell and he did not ask about him. He smiled and nodded in the right places, biding his time.

After dinner they took a taxicab to Castiglione's waterfront hotel. At the quiet little piano bar back of the lobby they had a drink, then went to the elevator bank and up to Castiglione's room.

"What a beautiful view!" she exclaimed, crossing the carpeted floor to look out at the harbor and, across the water, the aerospaceport.

He came up behind her and slid his arms around her. "A beautiful view, indeed," he said as he turned her around and kissed her deeply.

Later, in bed, the only light coming from the window, Castiglione said very softly, "Vera, I need you to set up a meeting for me with Jordan Kell."

She tried to evade the idea, tried to convince him that she didn't know where Kell was, but he persevered—gently, but firmly—and in the end she said, "I'll try, Rudy. For you."

"That's wonderful," he breathed.

"But I'll be taking a big risk. I could lose my job."

He understood where she was going. "Perhaps I could help you to get a job with the World Council's broadcasting department."

"Really?"

"In Barcelona," he said. "It's a much livelier city than Boston."

"Barcelona! Wow!"

Castiglione smiled in the darkness. Once I meet with Kell I can get rid of this woman. But in the meantime . . .

He pulled her naked body next to his.

Just as she had done every morning since arriving at the communications complex, Aditi walked alongside her security escort toward Frankenheimer's laboratory. They never sent the same person twice to walk her through the underground corridors. She knew the layout well enough to go alone, but every morning a young man or woman was waiting for her when she opened her apartment door, always dressed in a gray or darker jacket, a white turtleneck shirt, and navy blue slacks.

As she walked, Aditi thought, Frankenheimer wants a communicator for himself, wants it badly. It's time for me to make a demand for something in return.

She knew precisely what she would ask for.

Frankenheimer was waiting for her in his lab, all boyish enthusiasm.

"What did your people on New Earth say about producing a communicator for me?" he asked eagerly.

Aditi looked into his soft brown eyes and responded truthfully, "They don't like the idea of implanting a device in your brain."

"Oh?"

"It would require major surgery. That could be risky."

Frankenheimer nodded. "Yours was implanted in your brain in infancy."

"In utero," Aditi corrected. "It's a bit late for that, in your case."

The physiologist looked crestfallen. But he quickly asked, "Does the device have to be in my brain? Maybe it could be implanted somewhere else in my body."

"Or it could be completely external, like a wristwatch or a pocket computer."

"You can do that?"

"They can, I believe."

"Okay! Great!"

"But first there's something I'd like you to do for me," Aditi said.

"Sure! What is it?"

"I want to be reunited with my husband. We've been kept apart long enough."

Spreading his arms in a gesture of helplessness, Frankenheimer bleated, "That's out of my area. I don't have anything to do with that."

"Then kindly find someone who does," Aditi said, her voice low but iron hard. "I'm not going on with the work you want done until Jordan and I are reunited."

Otero Studio Six

"And this is where your interview with mr. otero will take place," vera Griffin was saying.

Jordan stood in the doorway of the studio. Even empty and barely lit, it looked enormous. They could produce *War and Peace* in here, he thought.

The cavernous room looked more like an empty airplane hangar than anything else. Vast and echoing. Several three-dimensional cameras stood clustered in a far corner. Strips of lights ran along the ceiling, high above. Most of them were off. The huge studio was deep in shadows, with only pools of light here and there. Jordan spotted a bare metal stairway along one wall and, looking up, saw that it led to what must be a control booth. It was dark now, unoccupied.

Griffin walked him across the nearly empty floor, toward a corner that was lit from overhead. A pair of comfortable armchairs faced each other, with a small round table between them.

"Mr. Otero will sit there," Griffin pointed, "and you here. You'll chat together without interruption. We'll edit your conversation before it goes out on the air, of course."

"No," said Jordan.

"No?"

"I'd rather do the interview live, with no editing, no cuts."

"Mr. Otero wants—"

"I'm sure that Mr. Otero will see the benefits of a live broadcast," Jordan insisted.

Looking very uncertain, Griffin said, "I . . . I can ask him about it."

"I'll speak to him about it this evening, over dinner."

Griffin said nothing for a couple of heartbeats, then at last asked, "You and Mr. Otero are getting along well together, aren't you?"

"Reasonably well, thank you," said Jordan. "He's a very intelligent man—and a gracious host."

Biting her lip, Griffin nodded. Then she said, all in a rush, "I've taken the liberty of inviting a man from the World Council to talk with you this morning."

"The World Council?"

"He'll be here in a minute or so." Seeing the apprehension on Jordan's face, she added, "It's all very unofficial, very private."

Jordan's mind was racing. *A man from the World Council. A security agent? Are they going to try to put me back under their custody? Of course they are! Has Otero sold me out? I've got to get out of here!*

The same door from which they had entered the studio opened once again, and a trim figure of a man strode across the wide emptiness toward them. Jordan heard the click of his boots on the bare concrete of the floor, approaching him, coming nearer.

As the man finally stepped into the fully lighted area where Jordan stood, he recognized Rudolfo Castiglione, smiling and handsome as ever, but his sea-green eyes were cold, mirthless.

"Ah, Mr. Kell," said Castiglione, "we meet again, at last."

Ignoring his proffered hand, Jordan said, "To what do I owe this unexpected honor?"

Castiglione glanced at the two comfortable-looking chairs, then turned to Griffin. "Vera, my lovely, could you please give us a few minutes of privacy? I must speak to Mr. Kell alone."

Griffin's eyes went wide with surprise, but she quickly recovered and said, "Certainly, Rudy."

As she hurried back toward the stairway that led up to the control booth, Castiglione said to Jordan, "An interesting woman."

"I suppose you find all women interesting," said Jordan.

Chuckling, Castiglione agreed. "Women are like wine. No matter how much you know, there is still so much to be learned."

Jordan said nothing. He heard Griffin clattering up the metal steps, in the shadowy distance. If that's really the control booth up there, he thought, she'll probably be able to eavesdrop on every word we say.

Castiglione gestured to the armchairs. "Let's be comfortable, shall we?"

"By all means," said Jordan. He saw one window of the control booth light up. She'll be listening to us, all right.

They sat, facing each other.

Crossing his legs, looking completely relaxed, Castiglione said, "The World Council wants you back in protective custody, Mr. Kell."

"I don't need your protective custody and I don't want it. I'm quite satisfied with where I am."

"There's already been an attempt on your life."

"Which was staged. I wouldn't be surprised if you arranged it yourself."

Castiglione laughed, a trifle nervously, Jordan thought.

Then he said, "Your wife is quite happy in our custody."

Jordan suppressed an urge to bash his face in. "I want to be with her. You have no right to keep her imprisoned."

"Imprisoned?" Castiglione looked shocked. "She's not in a prison. She's very comfortable and she's working quite willingly with our scientists."

Jordan realized that Castiglione didn't know that Aditi talked with him every night. He decided not to reveal that information to him.

"She can work voluntarily with your scientists while we live together. In a reasonable hotel, not some guarded government facility, no matter how comfortable it might be."

"And the danger to your life? And hers?"

Leaning forward slightly to tap Castiglione on the knee, Jordan replied, "The only danger you're worried about is my talking to the general public about the death wave."

Castiglione admitted, "Anita Halleck is quite concerned about that, it's true."

"Well, you can tell her that I will be speaking to the largest audience the Otero Network can reach. Within the next few days. And there's nothing she can do about it."

"Nothing? You underestimate her."

"I'm not a criminal. There is no legitimate reason for the World Council to put me in custody. I have my rights as a citizen of Great Britain and of Earth."

"What if I told you that you could make your broadcast while in protective custody? You could speak to the public, we have no objection to that."

"Speak freely? Live? Without editing?"

Castiglione waved a hand in the air. "I believe that could be arranged."

Smiling thinly, Jordan said, "Well, I have that arrangement here, with Carlos Otero himself. I don't have to accept your . . . eh, *hospitality* for it."

"Our hospitality," Castiglione said, his expression hardening, "seems quite acceptable to your wife."

"I want her back with me. There's no reason for Halleck to hold her."

"Ah, there we have the crux of the situation. The only way you can be reunited with her is to accept our protective custody. It's for your own good, after all."

"No, it's for *your* good. For Anita Halleck's good. Not mine. Not Aditi's. If you don't release her, I'll tell the world that you're holding her prisoner."

"That would be a mistake, Mr. Kell. Don't force Anita Halleck's hand. She can be quite ruthless, you know."

"You're threatening me?"

"No. Not at all. But I'm warning you that your actions could put your wife in danger. Grave danger."

Jordan felt the icy cold that always gripped him when he became truly angry. Through gritted teeth he told Castiglione, "If anything happens to Aditi I'll hold you and Halleck responsible. Both of you."

"Very noble, I'm sure," Castiglione said, with a pitying little smile. "But quite useless. There's nothing you can do—"

Jordan sprang out of his chair and gripped Castiglione's throat with one hand.

"Never drive an enemy to desperation," he hissed, squeezing hard, slowly lifting Castiglione off his chair. Gasping for breath, Castiglione fluttered his arms at Jordan's iron-hard grip, in vain.

"If anything happens to my wife, I'll kill you," Jordan promised. "Both of you."

He released Castiglione, who dropped, coughing and sputtering, to his knees.

"You go back to Barcelona and tell Halleck that," Jordan fairly snarled. "And tell her to watch me on Otero Network."

With that, Jordan turned and marched out of the studio, heading for Carlos Otero's office.

barcelona

"Are those finger marks on your throat?" Anita Halleck asked as she stared at Castiglione's image in her desktop phone screen.

"Yes," Castiglione replied, his voice harsh, rasping. "The bastard nearly strangled me."

Halleck slumped back in her desk chair. "What happened?"

"He got upset . . . about his wife."

"Upset?"

"Homicidal, almost," Castiglione croaked. "He caught me by surprise."

Halleck listened to Castiglione's telling of his meeting with Jordan Kell.

"So he's sensitive about his wife, is he?"

"Very," said Castiglione, rubbing his throat.

"We can use that."

"Yes, for certain. But be careful! He's like an unexploded bomb about her. One instant he's perfectly fine, then—*boom!*—he goes off."

Halleck smiled coldly. "Well, I won't have any private meetings with him, that's for sure. In the meantime, perhaps we could arrest him for assault."

Castiglione shook his head. "It's a trivial charge, and—"

"Attempted murder?"

"The local authorities would have to arrest him, and he'd be out on bail in a few hours. We couldn't hold him."

"Too bad," said Halleck. "At any rate, I suppose I should have a serious talk with Carlos Otero."

Leaning back comfortably in his desk chair, Otero was actually smiling as Jordan told him about his meeting with Castiglione.

"You throttled him?"

"I lost my temper," Jordan admitted, almost sheepishly.

Before Otero could reply, he saw his desktop phone screen flashing yellow, with the name ANITA HALLECK printed out across its face.

"Oh, oh," he murmured. "Here she is now."

"Halleck?"

Nodding, Otero instructed the phone to project Halleck's image onto the three-dimensional viewer built into the wall across his office.

The chairwoman of the World Council sat behind her desk, wearing a sky blue blouse and a somber, grim expression. Her eyes widened momentarily as she saw Jordan seated before Otero's desk, but she quickly recovered from her surprise.

"I'm pleased to see you both," she said in a voice that could etch steel.

"And it's always a delight to see you, Anita," Otero replied, grinning.

"You're harboring a fugitive, Carlos. That isn't wise."

"Mr. Kell is a fugitive? What crime has he been charged with?"

"He was in protective custody, as you well know."

Jordan spoke up. "That's an honor I respectfully decline. And I'd like my wife to be released, too."

"Impossible," Halleck snapped. "She's working willingly with our scientists."

Leaning both his beefy forearms on his desktop, Otero said, "It wouldn't look good for you if Mr. Kell complained on worldwide video that you're holding his wife captive."

"It wouldn't be good for you, Carlos, if you go through with your plan to put Mr. Kell on your network."

Otero waved a dismissive hand in the air. "My lawyers tell me that we're perfectly within our rights. Mr. Kell is not a criminal. Neither is his wife."

"Your lawyers will get their chance to represent you in court, after we've arrested you for breaching the security laws."

"See you in court, then," Otero said. "After my interview with Mr. Kell."

"Carlos, you can't—"

"Just a minute," Jordan interrupted. "We're getting away from the important point. There's a wave of death heading toward Earth—"

"Which won't be here for another two thousand years," Halleck scoffed.

"But it will engulf other worlds, it will wipe out other intelligent creatures."

"So you say."

Otero, his face dead serious, said, "So we will *show* on our program. We have some very frightening evidence to put on the air."

Leveling a finger at him, Halleck said, "If you try to put this scaremongering material on the air, I'll have the electrical power supply from the power satellites cut off for all of Massachusetts, all of New England, if need be!"

Otero laughed. "That would be a grand feather in your cap, wouldn't it? That would win you a lot of votes for your reelection next year."

"No, it will be *you* who causes the blackout, by trying to broadcast alien propaganda."

"Propaganda?" Jordan yelped.

"I am not going to allow alien propaganda to be foisted on the general public," Halleck said. "For all I know, Mr. Kell, you are a willing agent for the aliens in their scheme to take over the Earth."

"That's ridiculous!"

Otero was still smiling, more broadly than ever. "This is great! We'll get more viewers than ever if they're scared of an alien invasion."

Halleck started to snap out a reply, but checked herself. She drew in a breath and then, very deliberately, she said to Jordan, "If you want to see your wife again, Mr. Kell, don't go through with this broadcast."

And her image winked out.

Once the connection was cut, Anita Halleck allowed her iron-hard self-control to loosen. She slumped in her desk chair and laid her head on the desktop.

He's a madman, she told herself. Jordan Kell is absolutely insane with this idea of saving alien worlds from the death wave. Maybe he actually is working for the aliens. Maybe this is all some convoluted plot . . .

She stopped and sat up straight. The worst sin in politics, she reminded herself, is to believe your own propaganda.

Kell's going to go through with his broadcast and Otero's going to make it possible. All right, let them. Don't try to stop them, use them. Turn them to your own advantage.

And she remembered another dictum about politics: Don't get mad, get even.

I'll destroy Otero if it takes me the rest of my life! she vowed.

Then she saw that Gilda Nordquist had called. Her message line said, *Urgent, re Mrs. Kell.* Nothing more. But that was enough to get Halleck to return her call.

"we'd better put your show on the air as soon as we can," otero told jordan, "before нalleck figures out a way to stop us."

Still seated before Otero's desk, Jordan asked, "Can she actually cut off the electrical power from the satellites?"

With a grim smile, Otero said, "She'd have to declare a state of emergency first. That would take some time, perhaps a few days."

"And the whole region would go into a blackout."

"She's not going to do that. The repercussions would ruin her."

"I wonder," Jordan mused.

"The way to prevent it," Otero said, "is to get you on the air before she can act."

"I'm ready whenever you are."

Drumming his fingers on his desktop, Otero muttered, "I'd wanted a big publicity buildup for your show, but we don't have the time for that now. I'll tell my programming chief to put your show on as a special, cancel our regular prime-time programming for tomorrow evening."

Jordan watched as Otero considered the pros and cons of the idea. At last he nodded once, firmly, his mind made up.

To his phone, Otero commanded, "Get me McKinley."

His mustachioed face breaking into an almost boyish grin, Otero said, "Damn the torpedoes! Full steam ahead!"

* * *

It was already night in Barcelona. Anita Halleck stood by the floor-to-ceiling windows of her office and watched the lights of the city twinkling in the darkness.

Why does Kell have to be so stubborn? she asked herself for the hundredth time. Why is he doing this to me?

And the answer came to her as it had the other ninety-nine times: Kell wants my job. He wants to be chairman of the World Council. He's spent his life as a diplomat and then he went off to New Earth. Everybody in the world recognized his name, his face. The popular vote would be a landslide for him and the Council would have no choice but to appoint him chairman.

And where does that leave me? Out in the cold, after so many years of hard work and faithful service. I *deserve* to head the World Council! I've earned the job. I've led them through the second greenhouse floods, rebuilt whole cities, established a global economic order, moved millions of refugees to safety; I've seen to it that they were fed, that they found decent homes and incomes for themselves, schools for their children.

And now this ex-diplomat, this star traveler, is going to snatch my position away from me? Never!

It's a plot, a damned plot by the aliens. They get Kell to take over the World Council and then they start taking over our world. All this talk about a death wave and saving other planets is a ruse, a sham to hide their real motivation. They want to take over Earth and Jordan Kell is their Judas goat.

"Gilda Nordquist," the phone announced.

Halleck snapped her attention back to the present, to this moment, here in her office where she held the power to move people.

"Send her in."

Nordquist strode into the office, tall and broad-shouldered. She's built like an Olympic swimmer, Halleck thought. Although Olympic athletes don't wear skintight mid-thigh dresses of glittering metallic fabric.

Gesturing to the chairs in front of her desk, Halleck said, "There's a problem with Mrs. Kell?"

Nordquist's open, clear-eyed face looked serious. Not troubled, as far as Halleck could see, but she was concerned about something.

"She refuses to work with Frankenheimer anymore unless we let her get back together with her husband."

"Frankenheimer?" Halleck asked.

"The scientist who's been working with her on the aliens' communications system. She's been cooperating with him, even put him in contact with the alien engineers on New Earth. But all of a sudden she says she won't do any more until she's reunited with Kell."

"The little bitch!"

"Frankenheimer wants to continue with the work," Nordquist continued, calm and unemotional. "He's drooling over the prospect of constructing an FTL communicator for himself."

"For the World Council," Halleck corrected.

"Yes, of course. But he can't do anything unless Mrs. Kell cooperates with him."

"And she won't cooperate unless we let her reunite with Kell." Nordquist nodded.

"Meanwhile, Kell's planning to do a broadcast on the Otero Network. He'll bring out every maniac and fanatic in the world."

Nordquist said nothing.

Halleck murmured, "I've been talking with the Americans on the Council. They all have this silly allegiance to what they call 'freedom of the press.'"

"An outmoded term."

"But it's like a sacred commandment to them."

For a long moment neither woman spoke a word. Halleck was searching in her mind for a way to stop Kell's broadcast and get his alien wife working again with the scientists. Nordquist merely sat, watching the stream of emotions flowing across the chairwoman's face.

At last Nordquist said, "I may have a way to solve the problem."

"You do?"

"Move Mrs. Kell to an orbital facility, where she'll be totally dependent on us. Bring Kell to the facility so they can be reunited. Don't let either one of them leave the facility."

Halleck shook her head. "He'd see through that. He'd refuse to go."

"Not if you tell him that the two of them can leave the facility and return to Earth whenever they wish."

"Do you think he'd be foolish enough to believe that?"

"Apparently he loves his wife and wants to be with her. We can at least dangle that carrot before his eyes."

"And if he goes for it . . ."

"The two of them stay in the orbital facility, incommunicado, for as long as we choose."

Halleck thought it over for another few moments. Then, "It's worth a try."

"Good."

"Let's do it. Get Frankenheimer to move his laboratory to orbit."

"And there's one more thing you have to do, if you please."

Looking surprised, Halleck asked, "What?"

"Promote me to head of the security section and get rid of the incompetent oaf who's in charge now."

With a laugh, Halleck said, "Done." Before Nordquist could react, though, she added, "Once you get Kell and his alien wife into orbit."

Otero Studio Six

The control booth felt hot, stuffy, with so many corporate executives jammed into it. Vera Griffin was nervous as she wormed the communicator into her right ear. Mr. Otero himself was standing right behind her chair, with Jordan Kell at his side.

The network had blanketed the airwaves with announcements of the special show about the death wave and promises of showing actual imagery of alien planets. The programming chief expected a record audience for the show. If anything went wrong, if the executives' high expectations weren't met, Griffin knew her career as a producer would be finished before it began.

Rudy's offered to take me to Barcelona, she reminded herself. But then she wondered how reliable Castiglione would be. *He's the type to leave me when I need him most,* she realized.

As she watched the lights going on down on the studio floor, she heard a woman's voice behind her say, almost timidly, "Mr. Otero, it's time for you to go to Makeup, sir."

Otero's voice had a smile in it as he replied, "Do you think I really *need* makeup?"

"Well . . . I . . . uh, I think we should let the makeup director decide that, sir."

With a dramatic sigh, Otero responded, "Oh, I suppose I should, shouldn't I?"

"And you, too, Mr. Kell," the woman said, her tone suddenly unyielding. "Makeup."

For the next hour Griffin operated on autopilot, making certain that the set below this crowded, oppressive booth was correctly lit, the imagery that they intended to show was ready, every technician and camera and microphone and speck of dust was in place and operating properly.

Out of the corner of her eye she saw the screen that was showing what the network was sending out over the air. Puffery about alien worlds, and the death wave, and the fact that Carlos Otero himself—founder and head of Otero Network—was personally going to host this very special show. With a surprise guest.

Otero walked onto the set, looking younger than he would have without makeup. He smiled at the crew as he took one of the comfortably upholstered chairs beneath the lights. Jordan Kell stood off to one side, in the shadows.

Griffin checked the clock, bit her lip almost painfully, then counted down, "Five seconds . . . four . . . three . . ."

Otero put on his best fatherly smile as the floor director pointed his fingers like a pistol at him.

"Good evening," he began, "and welcome to this special presentation of Otero Network."

The cue screen's lettering was large enough for Otero to read without squinting.

"More than a month ago, three of the people we sent to New Earth almost two centuries ago returned home, together with a young woman from that distant world. They brought with them some very disturbing information . . ."

Aditi was watching the three-dimensional broadcast when someone rapped on her apartment door. Glancing at the ID screen, she saw that it was Rudolfo Castiglione.

She felt a pang of alarm. What's he doing here at this time of the night?

Before she could get up from the couch on which she'd been sitting, Castiglione opened the door and stepped in. Two bulky humanoid robots trundled in behind him.

"Please pardon this intrusion, dear lady."

Aditi got to her feet. "I'm watching the show—"

"About the death wave, yes, I know. Half the world is watching it, apparently. Your husband is going to appear on it, you know."

Aditi started to reply, but checked herself. If she admitted that she knew Jordan was slated to be on the show, it would reveal to Castiglione and the others that she'd been in communication with him.

"Is he?" she asked.

With a theatrical sigh, Castiglione said, "You know, he isn't making many friends among the Council members."

Aditi swallowed the retort she wanted to make.

"The chairwoman, especially," Castiglione added.

Pointing to the robots standing silently just inside the doorway, Aditi asked, "And what are they here for?"

"To pack your belongings."

"I'm leaving? Now, in the middle of the night?"

Nodding, Castiglione replied smoothly. "To a new laboratory, in orbit. Dr. Frankenheimer wants to calibrate the speed with which your communications travel. He says the messages travel too fast to get a good measurement here on Earth."

"But orbit is only a few hundred kilometers—"

"Not a near-Earth orbit. This facility is in one of the habitats at the L-5 position, in the same orbit as the Moon. That's almost four hundred thousand kilometers, I believe."

They want to separate me farther from Jordan! Aditi realized.

"I won't go," she said.

Castiglione smiled at her. "First you say you want to leave this facility and now you say you won't go? Come now, dear lady."

"You can't force me to go."

"Ah, I'm afraid that we can. And we will, if it becomes necessary." Raising a finger to silence Aditi before she could say a word, Castiglione went on, "But you may be happy to know that we have invited your husband to join you there. You can be reunited at last."

"Jordan will see through your little trap."

"Trap?" Castiglione put on an air of wounded innocence. "All we're trying to do is to bring you two together. Where you can both be safe."

He motioned to the robots, which rolled past him and headed into the bedroom.

A little more conciliatory, Aditi asked, "Has Jordan agreed to come?"

"He hasn't been asked yet. But I'm sure he'll agree. I'm certain that he wants to be with you, wherever you are."

dead worlds

Good god, Otero said to himself, after all these years I finally discover that I'm a ham.

He was enjoying himself, enjoying sitting there in the studio with the cameras on him and speaking earnestly to the vast unseen audience around the world.

"While this deadly wave of radiation is still two thousand years away from Earth and the rest of our solar system," he was reading from the prompter, "it has already engulfed thousands of other worlds, other planetary systems, and wiped them clean of all life."

The monitor screen, positioned to one side of the floor director, showed a view of a star field, thousands upon thousands of bright gleaming stars strewn against the black of infinity.

"To tell you more of the challenge we face," Otero said as the cameras focused on him once more, "we have the man who has been to the stars, the leader of our expedition to New Earth, Mr. Jordan Kell!"

Jordan felt the director's tap on his shoulder and stepped into the lighted area, while Otero rose to his feet and extended his hand. Jordan smiled tightly. Look pleased but concerned, the director had whispered to him.

There was no applause, no audience to give a reaction. Otero gripped Jordan's hand strongly with an expression on his mustachioed face that said, *We're in this together, friend.*

Once they sat facing one another, Otero said, "Before we get into the problems that the death wave presents, could you tell us a bit about New Earth, its people, the civilization you found on that planet?"

Jordan nodded. He and Otero and the network's writers had gone over this scenario.

"It's an extraordinary story," Jordan began. "Quite beyond anything we expected to find."

For the next half hour, Jordan spoke about New Earth and its human inhabitants, while the monitor screen showed the images that he had brought back with him of the aliens and their city.

"They're completely human?" Otero asked.

"Completely," said Jordan. "Just as human as you and I. In fact, I've married one of them."

The monitor showed Aditi and Jordan together, in the city on New Earth.

Following the script, Otero asked, "And where is your beautiful wife now?"

His expression tightening, Jordan replied, "She's being held in some secure facility by the World Council."

"Being held? You mean she's in prison?"

"They call it protective custody. Anita Halleck and her fellow Council members apparently feel that Aditi and I are in danger here on Earth. They claim that fanatics, terrorists will try to assassinate us."

"You don't believe that?" Otero asked.

"Hardly. I think that Halleck wants to keep us separated because she doesn't want us to tell the people about the death wave that's approaching us—and other worlds that harbor intelligent life, as well."

Otero rubbed his swarthy chin. "Well, this is your opportunity to speak the truth to the people. We have well over a hundred million viewers watching you right now."

Jordan turned to face the cameras directly. "While it's true that the death wave won't reach Earth for two thousand years, there are other worlds that bear intelligent civilizations lying much closer to the wave front. We've got to help them! If we don't, they'll be wiped out, just as so many intelligent species have already been killed by the death wave."

Hamilton Cree sat in his new apartment in Chicago and stared at the holographic viewer. Dead worlds. He watched scenes of death on other worlds. Cities where the streets were piled with bodies. They looked more like oversized lizards than humans, but they were dead, all of them, sprawled in grotesque agony everywhere. Other worlds where neatly squared-off fields lay blackened and lifeless beneath a warm sunny sky. Creatures that were giant worms stretched across the ashes of what had once been a village; now it was a silent collection of mounds on a cemetery world.

Through it all, Jordan Kell's measured, somber voice intoned, "This is what will happen to the worlds that are in the path of the death wave, unless we help them. We've got to build the starships and go out to save these civilizations. The creatures living on those worlds don't know that they are threatened with extinction. They won't know it until the death wave reaches their worlds, and by then it will be too late."

The view cut to Kell's face: totally serious, almost pleading. "Thanks to the people of New Earth, we have the technology to protect ourselves from the death wave. But there are more than half a dozen other worlds that we can reach—we *must* reach—before the death wave engulfs them. As I said, we have the technology. Do we have the heart, the will, to save other intelligent creatures from the death wave?"

Cree slowly shook his head. That's a lot to swallow, he thought. How do we know he's telling the truth? How do we know these images he's showing are real?

Real or not, they were certainly disturbing. Whole worlds killed off. Why would Kell or anybody else want to show us that if it wasn't true?

Back in the studio, Otero was asking, "If these creatures on these other worlds are intelligent, why can't they protect themselves against the death wave?"

Jordan was sitting tensely in the armchair. He saw Otero looking at him, sensed the people up in the control booth, the viewers across the world and through the solar system. The whole human race was involved in this, whether they knew it or not. Whether they liked it or not.

"These other civilizations aren't as advanced as we are. They don't have electricity yet, no radio, no airplanes, no spaceflight. They have no way of knowing they're facing death."

Before Otero could respond, Jordan went on, "We ourselves wouldn't know about the death wave if we hadn't made contact with the people of New Earth. They are part of a civilization that's much, much older than ours. They've graciously given us the technology we need to shield ourselves from the death wave."

"Then why don't they go out and save these other worlds?" Otero asked. "Why do we have to do it?"

responsibility

+++++ +++++ +++++ +++++ +++++ +++++ +++++ +++++ +++++ +++++
+++++ +++++ +++++ +++++ +++++ +++++ +++++ +++++ +++++ +++++

Jordan stared at Otero as he tried to frame his answer.

"The people of New Earth are few, and their race is very ancient. Their Predecessors—"

"Intelligent machines," Otero interrupted.

"Yes," said Jordan. "Intelligent machines that represent a civilization that is millions of years older than our own. Those machines built New Earth—built the planet and populated it with humanlike people to attract our attention. They wanted to warn us about the death wave and they asked our help in saving other worlds."

"The New Earthers can't do the job by themselves, then," Otero said.

"That's right. They need us. They need our strength, our vigor, our courage."

"But these machines—these Predecessors, as they're called—can't they do the job?"

"For the past several thousand years the Predecessors have spread themselves through the Milky Way to save endangered civilizations. But the machines are millions of years old; they're not immortal. The one that built New Earth has died. Its intention was to get us to carry on the work of saving the intelligent species in our region of the galaxy.

"It lived long enough to pass the torch to us. Now it's up to us to save those other worlds. And ourselves, of course."

Hunching forward in his seat, Otero asked, "Why us? Why can't someone else do the job?"

"Because there isn't anybody else," Jordan replied. "Like it or not, we're the most advanced civilization in this sector of the Milky Way galaxy."

"Except for the New Earthers."

"They're not strong enough. They were created specifically to recruit us to save the others. As I said, we have the strength and the tools. The question is, do we have the heart, the *will* to save the others?"

"I wonder," said Otero.

"We have to do it. Intelligence is very rare in the universe. There are only six other intelligent species in our area—six, out of millions of stars and planetary systems. We can't just let them die! That would be inhuman."

Despite himself, Otero felt awed. "That . . . that's a big responsibility."

"Yes. But I believe we're up to it. I believe that the human race can face this challenge and overcome it. With the help of the technology that New Earth has given us, we can save those creatures—and ourselves."

"It all depends on the World Council, doesn't it?"

"No," Jordan contradicted. "It depends on the people of Earth and the rest of the solar system. The World Council represents the people—or at least it should. The people must tell the World Council that we've got to do our best to save the intelligent creatures who face extinction."

Sitting alone in her darkened office, Anita Halleck watched Jordan's earnest face with seething fury rising inside her.

He wants my job, she said to herself. All this noble talk about saving other worlds is a sham, a smokescreen he's using to keep people from understanding his real motivation. He wants to be the next chairman of the World Council.

Well, he's not going to get away with it!

She snapped an order to her phone console and within a heartbeat Rudolfo Castiglione was smiling handsomely at her from the holographic viewer built into the wall.

"Is she packed and ready?" Halleck asked.

"Almost," said Castiglione.

Halleck could see the alien woman sitting on a couch, looking like a lost and frightened little waif. Good, she thought. Keep her under control.

But suddenly Aditi got to her feet and stepped to Castiglione's side. "Ms. Halleck, I don't want to go to your orbital habitat. I want to be released, to be free to join my husband."

Halleck made a sweet smile. "And so you will be, Mrs. Kell. We're about to invite your husband to join you in the habitat. It's a very delightful location. I'm sure you'll both be quite happy there."

"He won't come," Aditi said, her expression defiant. "He'll see through your little ruse."

Her brows rising in feigned surprise, Halleck said, "If he refuses to join you, that won't be our fault, will it?"

Aditi glared at her.

"In the meantime, you're going to the habitat, along with Dr. Frankenheimer and several of his staff. And Signore Castiglione, of course."

In his home in the lunar city of Selene, deep below the airless surface of the Moon, Douglas Stavenger watched every second of Jordan's presentation. He sat in stunned silence as he saw the images of the dead worlds, piles of living creatures sprawled on the ground, whole worlds absolutely still, silent, scrubbed of all life.

"He's right," Stavenger murmured to his wife, sitting beside him.

Edith Elgin was a veteran of the news media business. "That's powerful stuff," she agreed.

Stavenger ordered the holographic viewer to shut down. The living room lights came up, but softly, muted to their evening level.

"The next meeting of the World Council is going to be a free-for-all," Stavenger said, almost grinning. "It'll be tough for Halleck to hold them all in control."

"Especially you," said Edith.

"Me? I'm just representing Selene, strictly an ex-officio member of the Council. I don't even have a vote."

"So what are you going to do?"

He made a little shrug. "I think tomorrow I'll ask the chairman of Selene's executive committee if we can't offer the World Council a starship."

"For free?"

"As a gesture toward helping solve the death wave crisis. Building a copy of the ship that went out to Sirius shouldn't be that expensive, not when we use nanomachines to build it."

"A gesture? Or a kick in Halleck's backside to get her moving in the right direction?"

Stavenger chuckled. "The secret of a successful politician, Edie, is to never do anything for just one reason."

"And how many reasons do you have in mind?"

"A few," he replied, almost innocently. "The biggest one, of course, is to use the crisis as a stimulus to move the human race beyond the confines of the solar system, out to the stars."

habitat gandhi

with castiglione sitting beside her, aditi fretted that she couldn't call jordan and tell him where she was going.

The passenger cabin of the spacecraft had no windows, but the forward bulkhead was almost entirely taken up by a three-dimensional viewer. It showed the habitat that they would soon be docking with. To Aditi it looked like nothing more than a large section of pipe, slowly rotating along its long axis.

Castiglione was playing at being a tour guide. "*Gandhi* is one of the oldest habitats in the Earth-Moon system. It was built by the Indian government, back when space endeavors were mostly run by governments, instead of private corporations."

Aditi saw that indeed the cylinder looked old, its metal surface dull and pitted, the Hindi script painted along its flank faded and somehow tired-looking.

"It's more than ten kilometers long," Castiglione explained, "and four klicks wide, if I remember correctly."

"It rotates to produce a feeling of gravity inside," Aditi said, to show Castiglione that she wasn't totally ignorant.

"Yes, correct. Along the inner surface you'll feel an entirely normal gravity, just a few percent less than Earth's."

"A few percent less?"

With an easy smile, Castiglione replied, "Yes. It makes you feel just a trifle lighter, stronger. The psychotechnicians claim it's good for your mental outlook. There are quite a few elderly people who've come up to these orbital habitats to retire. Some of them are more than two hundred years old."

Aditi nodded absently. Jordan's more than two hundred years old, she thought to herself, although most of that time he's spent in cryonic suspension, during the flights to New Earth and back.

Castiglione had not been more than a dozen meters away from her side since he'd come into her apartment in the underground Barcelona complex and directed the robots to pack her things. Aditi had drowsed for most of the flight to *Gandhi*, with the Italian in the seat beside her.

Frankenheimer and four of his assistants were also aboard the spacecraft, sitting behind her. The scientist did not look at all happy about being uprooted from his laboratory.

"But it will take days for all the necessary equipment to be hauled up from Barcelona," he had complained. "My wife's birthday is next week, for god's sake!"

"That can't be helped," Castiglione had replied, a trifle loftily. "Orders from the top. A-one security procedure."

Frankenheimer had grumbled but gone along. The chance to measure precisely how fast Aditi's FTL communicator worked was too tempting to ignore.

Now, as they approached *Gandhi*, Aditi saw that its slowly rotating length was studded with antennas, docking ports, pods of one sort or another. And several long rows of windows ran its length, glinting as they caught the sun.

"The habitat is completely self-sufficient," Castiglione described, as if reciting from a guidebook. "Much of the interior is farmland, to support the population."

"How many people live inside?" Aditi asked.

Castiglione frowned slightly, trying to remember. "It was designed to house one hundred thousand, I believe. But you know the Indians: they've allowed many more than the designed capacity to pack themselves into the habitat."

"How could they—"

"Corruption, pure and simple, dear lady. Officials are paid to look the other way and whole families are smuggled into the habitat."

"Our arrival will add six more people to their population," Aditi mused. Then she added, "But we won't be there permanently, of course."

With a shrug, Castiglione said, "Probably not."

It was close to midnight in Boston. Jordan and Otero were having a drink together in Otero's office. Well deserved, Jordan thought, after two hours of being on camera.

They sat in a pair of comfortable recliners in a corner of the outsized office, tired and feeling slightly deflated. Through the long windows across the way Jordan could see the lights of Boston: office towers, mostly, but there was a slice of the old Boston Common showing. Jordan remembered riding the swan boats there as a child visitor to America.

A continually fluctuating set of numbers was scrolling on one of the wall screens. Otero's eyes never strayed far from the display. He had pulled his bolo tie loose and kicked off his loafers.

"Damned near fifty percent of the global audience was watching us!" he exclaimed between gulps of his tequila. "And that's not counting the off-world watchers."

"I presume that's good," said Jordan.

"Good? It's fantastic! You're a vid star, Jordan."

Reaching out to clink his glass of scotch against Otero's glass, Jordan said, "And so are you, Carlos."

Otero laughed. But then he said, "Now we see what the critics have to say. The pundits and opinion-shapers." His voice dripped with contempt.

The phone on Otero's desk announced, "Vera Griffin to see you, sir."

With a pleased smile, Otero said, "Let her in."

The door opened and Griffin stepped through. In Jordan's eyes, she looked almost like a waif, slim and small and vulnerable. But she strode across the thickly carpeted office with sure, determined steps. He saw that Otero remained seated as she approached, so—with some misgivings—he did, too.

"Mr. McKinley says that more than a hundred news organizations want to interview Mr. Kell," she announced happily.

Otero grinned up at her. "And why hasn't McKinley come in person to deliver the good news?"

"He's still fielding requests," Griffin replied. "Besides, I'm the producer of the show. He talks to me first."

Turning to Jordan, Otero asked, "How do you want to handle this?"

"I'd be happy to be interviewed."

"One at a time, or all at once, like a news conference?"

"Which do you recommend?"

Griffin broke in with, "Like a news conference. I can arrange it."

"That's McKinley's area," Otero said with a mock scowl.

"I meant that I could produce the show. We could put it on the air."

"Certainly," said Otero. "My phone tells me that four other major network chiefs have called."

"Requests to rerun your interview?"

With a slight shake of his head, Otero said, "If I know these pigeons, what they're after is some way to get Jordan on their own networks."

"Feeding frenzy," Griffin said.

"Yes," said Otero. Turning to Jordan, "You're now a very famous person. I'm going to have to get you some protection."

"Protection?" Jordan echoed.

"Halleck isn't entirely wrong about security," Otero said. "News reporters, bloggers, self-important media analysts and commentators—they're all going to be hounding you now."

"The price of fame," Jordan muttered.

"Yes, but in with them there could be a few crazies, fanatics who want to kill you. You're going to need protection wherever you go."

mitchell thornberry

No matter how palatial his home on the lakefront above chicago, mitchell thornberry found himself reminiscing about his old digs at trinity college. The friendly old ramshackle residences, the people on the campus and outside in the streets of Dublin, the pubs, the chat.

Enough of that, he told himself. You're a wealthy man now, you've got to take the sour with the sweet.

Looking around at his spacious bedroom, with the tall windows that gave a view of Lake Michigan sparkling in the moonlight, Thornberry chuckled softly to himself. The sour is pretty damned sweet, he thought. That it is.

Alone in his twelve-room house except for the serving robots, he'd watched Jordan's program from beginning to end. The early minutes, when they showed images from New Earth, almost made Thornberry nostalgic for the alien world.

But then Jordan had revealed that the World Council was keeping Aditi separated from him. Protective custody indeed! Keeping a man's wife apart from him.

Thornberry fumed over that even while he stared, aghast, at the scenes of devastation that Jordan had shown. Once the program ended Thornberry put through two phone calls: one to the chief of the American delegation to the World Council, and one to his friend and fellow star traveler, Jordan Kell.

He didn't expect to have either call returned at this time of the night. Get yourself a good night's sleep, Mitchell me boy, he told himself. Tomorrow you start working to help Jordan.

He called for his butler robot to bring him a glass of Paddy Irish whiskey. One of Ireland's many contributions to civilization, he thought, and a grand consolation in times of trouble. Wrestling with the World Council isn't going to be easy, he knew.

Thornberry pulled off his clothes, then went to the bathroom, brushed his teeth and urinated, and finally settled himself in bed. As he reached for the glass that the butler had left on the bed table the phone announced, "Jordan Kell, returning your call."

Surprised, Thornberry commanded the phone to accept the call. Jordan appeared in the holographic viewer at the foot of the bed.

"Mitch," he said, his brows rising slightly, "I should have waited until the morning."

"No, no, no," Thornberry replied. "I'm glad you called."

Jordan was also in a bedroom somewhere; looked like a private home, expensive, elegant. He was sitting in an angular chair by a heavily draped window.

"How are you, Mitch?"

"I'm grand. I saw your show. Impressive."

"Thank you."

"The World Council is keeping you separated from Aditi?"

"I'm afraid so."

"That's criminal! What can I do to help?"

Jordan hesitated, then answered in a rush, "You can get me nominated for a seat on the World Council."

Aditi's breath gusted out of her when she stepped out into the open interior of habitat *Gandhi*.

With Castiglione leading her and Frankenheimer's little team of scientists, she had gone from the spacecraft that had carried them to the habitat into a sizable air lock chamber and then through a series of offices and corridors. Officials checked the digital information about the new arrivals and politely ushered them through a set of scanners that quickly and efficiently probed their physical health.

Satisfied that the newcomers did not pose any health hazards for the habitat, a dark-skinned young guide in a crisp tan uniform led them to still another doorway and with a smile and a slight bow, said, "Welcome to habitat *Gandhi*."

Aditi followed the young guide through the doorway and onto a path bedecked with three-meter-high flowering shrubbery on either side. She could smell gardenias and jasmine in the air; it was like walking through a corridor of flowers.

Castiglione explained with a smile: "We are now inside the habitat—inside that big pipe we saw on our approach." The young guide immediately took over. "The inner surface of the cylinder has been carefully landscaped. Most of it is devoted to farmlands, with towns and villages spaced among them. The people live in comfortable homes or apartments. Most of them work in the community in which they live, unless they are retired. Even the retirees find many ways to occupy their time, however."

They stepped past the shrubbery and into an open area. That's when the air gushed out of Aditi's lungs.

A panorama of green countryside stretched before her startled eyes, kilometer after kilometer of neatly squared farmland, with white-walled villages dotted here and there. In the distance she could see a larger community, a town with red-roofed buildings and slim towers rising above the ground.

There was no horizon: the land *curved* up and up until Aditi was staring overhead at more green fields and villages hanging effortlessly above her.

The young guide said, "Nearly a quarter of a million souls reside in this habitat. They live and work in this man-made world."

"And they make babies," Castiglione added, almost sneering.

Their guide's facial expression hardened. "It is very important to maintain our population at a sustainable level. Births are strictly controlled, to balance deaths. We have no population boom here. We are not ignorant savages."

"Of course," said Castiglione, in a more conciliatory tone.

The guide led them to a trio of brightly colored minibuses, parked next to the flowering hedges. Gesturing the six of them aboard the closest bus, he explained, "We will now go to the town in which you will live. It is not very far."

Nick Motrenko stared at his laptop screen. He read the message again:

> The Otero Network invites you to a news conference to be held in Boston, Massachusetts, to interview Mr. Jordan Kell, the star traveler.
>
> If you are interested in participating in the interview, please contact Douglas McKinley at . . .

Nick put through the call immediately. The next thing he did was to call Walt. Despite his disdain for worldly goods, Walt carried a phone wherever he went, like ordinary people did.

"In Boston, eh?" Walt asked. "I would have thought they'd do it in New York, or maybe Barcelona."

"It'll be in Boston!" Nick replied, excited. "Live! I'll be in the same room with him!"

Walt did not mention that it was his connection to the World Council bureaucracy that won Nick the invitation. Instead, he asked, "Can you bring anyone with you?"

Nick was surprised at that. Walt wants to see the starman for himself, he guessed.

"Two, besides me."

Walt nodded happily. "Good. You'll bring Rachel, of course. And Dee Dee."

"Dee Dee?"

"And the little item she purloined from the police department's warehouse."

concord, massachusetts

It's been a long day, Jordan said to himself as he walked tiredly to the lavatory of his suite in Otero's home. I hope it's been a productive one.

It worried him that he hadn't heard from Aditi the night before. What's happened to her? Why didn't she call?

As he reached for his toothbrush, though, he started thinking about how Mitch Thornberry could help him to get Aditi free of Halleck's so-called protective custody.

Thanks to Carlos, I've shown that I can appear on global video whenever I want to. There's no point in Halleck keeping Aditi and me separated. But will that be enough to actually get her to release Aditi? Is there more than logic involved here?

Of course there is, he realized. There's Halleck's ego. And her sense of power.

A politician's power depends on what he—or she—can make other people do. Halleck thinks that by controlling Aditi she can control me. I've just shown her that she's wrong. How will she react?

And how will she react to Mitch getting me nominated for a seat on the Council? That will bring things to a boil, no question. But if I win a Council seat, she won't be able to keep Aditi and me separated.

As he returned to the bedroom, the holographic viewer on the far wall glowed to life, and there was Aditi, sitting in a room that looked unfamiliar to him. His wife smiled at him.

"Hello, Jordan."

"Aditi! Dearest. How are you? *Where* are you?"

Swiftly, Aditi explained her trip to habitat *Gandhi*.

Jordan sank onto the padded bench at the foot of his bed. "Four hundred thousand kilometers away," he muttered.

"Once we were more than eight light-years apart," Aditi reminded him.

"That was before we met. I have no intention of staying separated from you any longer than I have to."

"Castiglione claims you're going to be invited to join me, here."

"Then Halleck will have us both under her control."

"You won't come?"

Jordan clenched both his fists. With cold, deliberate anger rising inside him, he said, "I'll come. But not to stay there. I'll come to take you away with me."

First thing the next morning, in Chicago, Hamilton Cree reported to his new boss.

The innocuously named Unicorn Recovery Agency was housed on the twenty-seventh floor of one of Chicago's many combined business-residential towers. Cree's apartment was on the fortieth floor of the same building: only a one-room studio, but it was new and almost luxurious, compared to the dump he had been renting in Albuquerque.

Gonna be easy for me to get to work, he told himself, with a grin. Short commute. Just drop down the elevator chute.

His boss was a retired veteran of the Defense Intelligence Agency, a short, surly-looking Hispanic with mahogany skin, his black, tightly curled hair hanging down to his collar. Despite his lack of height, his shoulders were heavy and wide, like a professional football player. It made him look like a small, truculent rhinoceros,

Cree thought, although the man's nose was little more than a per-
forated wart.

The office was modest and spare. The only decoration was a
nameplate on the desk: COLONEL TÓMAS PALOMA, with a tiny out-
line of a dove after the name. Cree understood enough Spanish to
know that *paloma* was a slang term for prostitute, but he didn't
let a smile crack his sober expression as he stood stiffly before the
desk.

"You don't have a jacket?" Paloma asked, his tone just a bit above
a snarl. Paloma was in a three-piece business suit, dark gray with
silver pinstripes.

Standing before the desk in his shirtsleeves, Cree answered,
"Yessir. It's at my desk."

Paloma nodded. "Good. See that you're properly dressed at all
times. We run a tight ship here."

Cree suppressed a groan. "Yessir."

Gesturing to the hard wooden chair in front of his desk, Paloma
said, "Sit down." With a glance at his desktop computer screen, he
continued, "You have a very good record with the NMHP."

Cree said nothing.

"You actually met this star traveler, Jordan Kell?"

"I didn't really meet him. I was on a security detail when he visited the Rio Grande Gorge, above Taos."

"But you'd recognize him if you saw him again?"

With a nod, "Yes, I would. And his wife, too."

Paloma studied Cree's face for several heartbeats, then made up
his mind. "Good. We're putting together a security team to protect Kell. You'll be on it."

"Thanks."

The trace of a smile flickered across Paloma's dark face. "Twenty-
four/seven. Where he goest, thou goest. *Comprende?*"

"*Yo comprende,*" said Cree.

Paloma's frown could have soured milk. "I hope you're better at
security than you are at Spanish."

* * *

Vera Griffin felt as if she were in some vid production of a spy thriller. She left the network offices after a morning of wrestling with McKinley and his public relations staff and headed off by herself to her lunch date with Castiglione.

McKinley, of course, wanted to handle all the interviews with Jordan Kell with his own staff. He did not want Griffin involved at all.

"This is the PR department's territory," he exclaimed, just about every ten minutes during their stormy meeting, while his six staffers—three women and three men, all in bright colors—nodded their heads in metronome unison.

And each time Griffin answered in her little girl voice, "Mr. Otero himself has told me to stay with Mr. Kell and oversee all the arrangements you make."

Her little girl voice had helped her through many stormy confrontations in the past. But McKinley wasn't buying it.

"*I* run the PR department, not you."

"Of course you do, Mr. McKinley. But, you see, I'm in the midst of negotiating an agreement with the other three multinational networks for Mr. Kell's future appearances to be shared by us all."

In the end, McKinley had reluctantly agreed to give Griffin a veto power over all the interviews his people set up for Jordan Kell. And he also okayed the two dozen bloggers and chat hosts that Vera had added to the list of network news anchors.

"Amateurs," he had groused.

"Self-employed interviewers," Griffin had countered.

McKinley and his staff had finally left Griffin's tiny office, muttering among themselves.

Now, as she walked into the restaurant for her lunch with Castiglione, her wrist phone tingled her arm.

It was Castiglione, his handsome face looking sad, almost desolate. "I can't make it to lunch with you, sweet one. My duties have taken me into space. I'm aboard a habitat in the L5 location."

Griffin almost felt relieved. Rudy's fun, but he's going to dump me sooner or later, she told herself as she watched his face in the minuscule phone screen, nattering away about how important his work was.

Then he said, "But I need you to do a favor for me, if you can. I need to speak to Jordan Kell as quickly as you can arrange it."

"Of course, Rudy," she said. He gave her his contact number and clicked off.

He's in an orbital habitat with Kell's wife, Griffin thought as she absently allowed the maître d' to lead her to a table for two, far in the rear of the restaurant. I wonder how Kell will react to that.

"Luncheon for one," the maître d' murmured as he held out a chair for her.

And Griffin wondered what it would be like to have lunch with Jordan Kell.

invitations

It was as if they were sitting in the same room, thanks to the three-dimensional communications link. Mitchell Thornberry was in his office in Chicago, however, while Anita Halleck was reclining in a therapy chair in her home outside Barcelona.

It was just past six P.M. in Chicago. Through his office window, Thornberry could see sailboats cutting through the waves of a choppy Lake Michigan. It had rained earlier in the afternoon, and off on the horizon thunderclouds were rearing their ominous dark heads against a graying sky.

Thornberry had peeled off his jacket and pulled his tie loose. He had been thinking about tugging his shirt out from his trousers when the phone announced that the chairwoman of the World Council was calling.

"It's good of you to answer my call so quickly, Ms. Halleck," Thornberry said, with a gruff good cheer that he did not really feel. Be nice to the lady, he told himself. Don't twist her knickers. "Why, it must be after midnight where you are."

Halleck smiled minimally. "The trouble with the World Council is that its business encompasses the whole world—and all its time zones."

"Well, I appreciate your calling," Thornberry reiterated.

"My assistant told me that you were inquiring about Mrs. Kell."

"Aditi," Thornberry said. "Yes. According to Jordan, you're keeping her in protective custody, against her will."

There was a slight lag in their communications link, while the messages went up to a relay satellite in geosynchronous orbit and then back to the ground again. Halleck felt her chair's welcome heat and massage on her back as she smiled perfunctorily at the camera on the wall across her room.

"'Against her will' is putting it rather strongly," she said. "She's working quite willingly with a team of our scientists."

"And where would that be?" Thornberry asked.

"At a facility where she's safe from attack by fanatics and loonies."

"But she'd rather be with her husband, you know."

"Of course. That's only natural."

Thornberry realized what Halleck was doing: Agree with everything, but give nothing, not a millimeter.

"Must she be kept separated from him?" he asked.

"No, not at all. As a matter of fact, we are extending an invitation to Mr. Kell to join his wife at our secure facility."

"Are you now?"

"Yes indeed. We have no desire to keep them separated," Halleck said, with near-perfect sincerity.

"Well, I didn't know that," said Thornberry.

Halleck went on, "So you see, Mr. Thornberry, it's up to Mr. Kell himself to end this separation. All he has to do is to accept our invitation."

"Would you be willing to allow Aditi to join Jordan where he is now? He's perfectly safe, and I understand that a private security team is being put together for him."

"I'm afraid that would be rather impractical. After all, Mrs. Kell is working with a team of dedicated scientists. It would be far better if he came to where she is."

"At your facility."

"At our facility."

"And just where might that be?"

Halleck hesitated a heartbeat longer than the communications lag required. Then, "I'm sorry, Mr. Thornberry, but I can't tell you the location. Even the Council's chairwoman has to obey the security regulations."

Thornberry puffed out a sigh. "But you've invited Jordan to come to your facility and be with Aditi again."

"I believe he's being invited right now, as we speak."

"Is he now."

A hint of a smile curling her lips, Halleck said slowly, "You know, Mr. Thornberry, the work that Mrs. Kell and our scientists are doing should be of some interest to you."

"Really?"

"They're working on a technology that the aliens use: faster-than-light communications. That could make a profitable product line for you, eventually."

Thornberry immediately realized, She's trying to bribe me!

He said, "I suppose it could."

"I'm sure the Council could grant you licensing rights, once we've got the technology in hand."

"Exclusive rights?" Thornberry heard himself ask.

"Probably."

"Well, I suppose that's all to the good, then."

"I'm glad that you see it that way."

With a reluctant smile, Thornberry said, "Well, thanks again for answering my call."

"It was a pleasure to speak with you," said Halleck.

"Oh! I nearly forgot."

"What?"

"It would've been a grand foolishness for me to talk so pleasantly with you and then forget to give you the news."

"What news?"

"I want you to know that I've placed Jordan's name in nomination for next year's election to the World Council. Both the American and the European delegations have accepted his nomination very happily."

The shocked expression on Halleck's face warmed Thornberry's Irish heart. But his brain scolded him, There go your chances for an exclusive license on the FTL communications technology.

"Rudolfo Castiglione calling for you, sir," said the phone in Jordan's bedroom.

Jordan had just finished dinner with Otero, Vera Griffin, and McKinley, the network's public relations director. He sensed that there was bad blood between McKinley and Griffin, but Otero took it all cheerfully as they outlined the plans they were making for his news conference.

"We'll have every major network there," said McKinley proudly.

"And some of the world's most important bloggers and chatters," Griffin added.

"Good," said Otero, like a happy grandfather, sitting at the head of the table.

Jordan took it all in, thinking, It's only good if I can get Aditi out of Halleck's hands. Mitch has told her that I'm standing for election to the World Council and she must be furious about that.

The dinner ended at last and Jordan repaired to his suite, hoping that Aditi would call him. Instead, he got Castiglione.

The Italian appeared to be sitting in a comfortable living room, leaning back in a recliner with his legs crossed.

"Good evening, Mr. Kell," he said.

"To what do I owe the pleasure of your call?" Jordan asked, with a diplomat's sham goodwill.

Turning his smile to full wattage, Castiglione replied, "I have good news for you. I have finally convinced the Powers That Be to invite you to join your wife at the facility where she now resides."

The Powers That Be are Anita Halleck, Jordan knew. And the

facility was in a space habitat out at the L5 location, but he wasn't going to let Castiglione know that he knew where she was.

As innocently as he could manage, Jordan asked, "And where might that be? I take it you've moved her from Barcelona."

It took several seconds for Castiglione to reply. The communications lag, Jordan realized. Even at the speed of light, communications take a few seconds to cover the distance between Earth and L5.

Castiglione answered at last, "No, she is no longer in Barcelona. In fact, she is no longer on Earth."

Jordan's expression darkened. "You've moved her to an orbital facility. Against her will, I'm sure."

"She would prefer to be with you, of course. So I have convinced Halleck that it would be best to reunite the two of you." Grinning, he added, "It's the romantic in me."

"Very romantic," said Jordan. "If I go there, when will we be allowed to leave?"

With a shrug, Castiglione said, "When your wife's work with our team of scientists is finished, I suppose."

"Is that a promise that I can rely on?"

"Let us say that it is a possibility that depends on several factors."

"Such as?"

"Such as your giving up this attempt to get yourself elected to the World Council."

There it is, Jordan thought. Out in the open at last.

"If I do that," he asked, "then Aditi and I will be allowed to leave your facility and end this ridiculous farce of protective security?"

"It is not a farce, I assure you. Our security people have tracked several groups that want to assassinate you."

"I have my own security team now."

"No private organization has the power and the capability of the World Council's security organization."

"Perhaps," Jordan conceded.

"You will come? It seems a shame to keep you two separated."

"The separation wasn't our idea."

"True enough. But now you have the opportunity to end it."

"At the cost of my freedom."

Castiglione didn't reply for many moments. At last, his smile gone, he leaned forward slightly and warned, "This may be the only chance you get to be with your wife once again. Don't be stubborn."

Jordan let his head droop slightly, then he looked up and said softly, "I suppose you're right."

Castiglione's grin reappeared. "As the Americans say, you can't fight city hall."

"I suppose not," said Jordan. "All right, I have a news conference scheduled for tomorrow. I'll be ready to go to Aditi the day after."

"Good!" said Castiglione. "Excellent!"

"You'll make arrangements for my transportation?"

"Of course."

"Very well. I'll join Aditi in two days' time, then," Jordan said. To himself he added, Or sooner.

news conference

sitting in a small anteroom next to the studio where the news conference would take place, Jordan saw on the wall screen that there were nearly a hundred news correspondents, bloggers, and chatroom hosts seated out there.

Impressive, he thought. But he was more concerned with the arrangements that Otero and his security team had made to spirit him up to habitat *Gandhi* immediately after the conference.

I've got to get there without Halleck's people knowing it. I've got to spring Aditi free of their clutches.

A pair of private security guards sat in the small room with him: two hard-eyed men, wearing identical dark jackets and whipcord jeans. And more of their cohorts were outside in the studio, Jordan knew.

"Can I ask you a question, sir?" asked one of them. He was tall and lean, with brooding brown eyes and sandy hair cut militarily short.

"Certainly," said Jordan. "And my name is Jordan."

The man broke into a guarded smile. "Mine's Hamilton. Hamilton Cree."

"What do you want to know, Hamilton?"

Looking almost troubled, Cree said, "I was with the Highway Patrol detail when you and your wife visited the Rio Grande Gorge, a couple weeks ago."

Oh-oh, Jordan thought. *He wants to find out how human Aditi is.*

Instead, Cree asked, "Why'd you go to the gorge?"

Jordan felt his brows rise. "Why? Because it's one of my favorite places on Earth. I first saw it long before you were born, when I was in the States helping to resettle refugees from the first greenhouse floods."

"You just wanted to see it? Like a tourist?"

"That's right. I wanted my wife to see it. I've got to admit, though, that I was somewhat embarrassed with the officials closing the bridge to everyone else. I thought that was a bit much, actually."

Cree nodded slowly. "Yeah. So did I."

"So you're working with the Unicorn Recovery Agency now?"

Glancing at the tiny unicorn emblem on his jacket's breast pocket, Cree said, "Right. Beats being a Highway Patrol cop."

Just then Vera Griffin sailed through the door. "It's showtime!" she announced, looking excited, eager.

Jordan got to his feet, as did the two security men. *Time to face the music,* he said to himself as they headed for the studio.

Carlos Otero watched the news conference from his office, pleased that the rows of seats that had been set across the studio floor were almost entirely filled with interviewers. Eyeing the men and women standing on either side of the seated interviewers, he noted with satisfaction that the Unicorn team was being properly unobtrusive.

The first handful of questions were softballs, asking what New Earth was really like and how Jordan felt when he realized the planet was inhabited by humanlike people.

Then one of the women asked how he felt about being kept separated from his wife.

Unsmiling, Jordan said, "Not good. Not good at all."

The correspondent countered, "But the World Council people

say that it's necessary, for her protection. And you should be in protective custody, as well."

Jordan replied, "Whenever a politician wants to control a person, she claims it's necessary for the person's security. Well, I don't want the World Council's protection, not for me and not for my wife. I want to be free, and above all, I want to be with her."

Tensing in his desk chair, Otero shook his head. Don't let your temper show, Jordan, he warned silently. Remember, you've agreed with Castiglione to go up to the habitat to be with your wife. That's our cover story. Don't screw it up.

Standing to one side of the rows of seated newspeople, Hamilton Cree saw that a trio of younger people—two women and a man, seated in one of the rearmost rows—had their heads together. They seemed to be ignoring the questions and answers and were busy doing something, their heads bent over, their hands moving on their laps.

Typing? Cree wondered. Instead of recording what was being said? Just like kids, he thought, more than a little disgusted. Tweeting in the middle of the conference.

Nick Motrenko's hands were shaking as he and Rachel put together the plastic pistol that Dee Dee had brought with her. Just as Walt had predicted, they had gotten the gun through the security scanners by breaking it down to three separate pieces, carried by the three of them.

Now they had to put it together, while the starman was standing up at the head of the room, answering questions.

Not for much longer, Nick told himself. As soon as we get this pistol together, I'm going to shoot the traitor, this big shot who's sold us out to the aliens.

"Rise and strike," he heard Walt's voice in his head. "Rise and strike."

I'm going to be famous, Nick thought happily.

Jordan was standing at the head of the studio, behind a lectern that had been set up on a makeshift platform, answering their questions.

A large, seriously overweight man rose slowly to his feet as if the struggle against gravity took all his strength.

"Tad Chatsworth, of Chatsworth's Chat Corner," he identified himself.

Jordan nodded and smiled.

"Why should we believe you?" Chatsworth challenged, his jowly face dead serious. "Why should we believe that these aliens are friendly and want to help us? What if there's no death wave, and it's only a scheme by those aliens to take us over?"

Dead silence for several heartbeats. Then someone in the crowd of correspondents giggled.

"The death wave is very real," Jordan said, his tone somber, grave. "I wish it weren't, but it is. Some of our world's best astronomers have reviewed the evidence that the astronomers of New Earth have amassed, and they unanimously agree that the wave of lethal gamma radiation is spreading across the Milky Way galaxy at the speed of light."

"Evidence can be faked," Chatsworth said.

"You should talk with the astronomers. They're convinced. I am, too."

"I just don't believe it. I don't believe *you*."

As politely as he could manage, Jordan asked, "And just what is it that you do believe?"

"I believe the aliens are trying to take us over, and you're helping them. Your name has just been placed in nomination for next year's World Council elections. You want to be head of the

Council, and from there you'll let the aliens take over our solar system."

Before Jordan could reply, a younger man in the rear of the room jumped to his feet and aimed a pistol at him.

assassination

+++
+++

Everything seemed to happen at once.

Standing on the stage at the front of the studio, Jordan saw the young man aim the pistol at him. An equally young woman got to her feet beside him, screaming, "Kill the alien-loving bastard!" From the side of the studio one of the security people whipped a gun from beneath his jacket.

Jordan stood frozen at the lectern, his mind inanely telling him to duck behind the lectern but his body unable to respond. The gun was pointed right at him, its muzzle looking like a tunnel to eternity.

This is no ruse! Jordan realized. They really want to kill me!

He saw the pistol's muzzle erupt in smoke and heard something whip past his ear like an angry bee. People were diving to the floor, yelling. The lectern shattered into a thousand pieces. One of the news correspondents grabbed at the gunman while the security man off to the side pushed through the crowd, pistol in hand, knocking people over as he rushed for the would-be assassin.

The studio was filled with shouts, screams, curses. The gunman seemed to collapse while the woman beside him clawed at the correspondent who had wrapped his arms around the man. The security guard reached them as a second security man came in from the opposite direction and pulled the screeching woman off the correspondent's back.

And then it was all over. People got up off the floor, dazedly. Overturned chairs were set right again. Several more security people had two young women in their grip. The gunman lay sprawled across several chairs; unconscious or dead, Jordan couldn't tell which.

Then someone said, "You're bleeding, Mr. Kell."

Jordan looked down and saw that his shirt was soaked with blood. The lectern was smashed to splinters. People were on their feet, gaping.

From his office, Otero watched the whole incredible episode, thinking, This is all going out on the air, live! A real assassination attempt! And we've got it all on camera!

The security team hurried Jordan, his hand pressed to his bleeding side, to the small infirmary on a lower floor of the Otero Network building.

Walking beside Jordan, Hamilton Cree said, "It doesn't look too bad."

Jordan thought of Mercutio's line from *Romeo and Juliet* and quoted, " 'No, 'tis not so deep as a well, nor so wide as a church door . . .' "

"If I had reacted faster . . ."

"You did fine," Jordan said. "Is he . . . did you kill him?"

Cree shook his head. "Nerve jangler. Paralyzed him. We're not allowed to carry lethal weapons."

"But they do."

One of the other security men, older, grimmer, said, "The three of those nitwits carried their gun in separate pieces, mostly plastic. Didn't set off the scanner alarm. Then they put it together once they were seated in the studio."

"Who are they? Why did they want to kill me?"

"We'll find out, don't worry."

A registered nurse and a diagnostic robot were waiting for them at the one-room infirmary.

"I don't think it's very bad," Jordan said to the nurse.

"Let's see," she said.

They laid him on the examining table and cut away his blood-soaked shirt. The robot ran its metal arm, filled with beeping, chirping sensors, up and down Jordan's body.

"No internal injuries," its synthesized voice pronounced.

The nurse bent over Jordan's abdomen, a tweezers in one hand. "This may twinge a bit," she muttered.

It did twinge, but only for a moment. The nurse held up the tweezers, a bloody sliver of wood in its grip.

Hamilton Cree said, "He had a semiautomatic pistol. Got off three shots. Two of 'em hit the lectern and shattered it. You got hit by a splinter."

"And that's it?" Jordan asked.

"That's it," said the nurse, beaming happily.

Carlos Otero burst into the tiny room. "Jordan, you're a hero! That idiot was firing at you and you stood there, strong as a rock. A hero!"

Jordan confessed, "I was too petrified to move."

Otero laughed heartily. "It all went out live, every damned network in the solar system is rerunning it."

"What about the shooter?"

"The police have him and his two girlfriends," said the elder Unicorn man. "They'll fill 'em with babble juice and get to the bottom of this."

"Every newsman in the solar system wants to interview you, Jordan," Otero said. "McKinley's people are going crazy fielding all the calls."

"No," said Jordan. Before Otero could react, he went on, "I've been too badly wounded to be interviewed. You're taking me to a private hospital. No visitors."

Otero's mouth popped open, but it was Cree who caught on first. "Perfect cover. We sneak you onto a shuttle, incognito, and take you to the *Gandhi* habitat."

"And we start now," Jordan said.

Preparations

"You speak Hindi?" asked the elder security man.

Jordan nodded, bringing a frown to the makeup woman's round face.

"A little," he answered. "Enough to get along." And he remembered the war in Kashmir. *The war I was supposed to stop. The war that killed Miriam.* The memory of his wife's death brought a stab of pain, but it was muted, softened, almost as if it had happened to someone else, in another life. Still, the pain lurked there.

The makeup woman complained, "You've got to keep still. Otherwise you'll smear the color."

"Sorry," Jordan said, properly sheepish.

He was sitting in the barber's chair in the Otero building's makeup room. The other two chairs were empty and the only people in the room besides Jordan and the makeup woman were a trio of Unicorn agents. More security people were out in the corridor, guarding the door.

As far as the general public was concerned, Jordan Kell had been seriously injured by the assassination attempt and was being whisked to a private medical facility, under heavy guard. Actually, he had never left the Otero building.

The heavyset woman stepped back to survey her handiwork. Jordan looked into the mirror and saw that his face was now as dark as a native Gujarati's and his silver hair had been transformed into deep black. His cheekbones had been sharpened, made more angular.

The elder Unicorn agent pulled a small black box from his jacket pocket, saying, "These contact lenses will show the proper retinal patterns to the scanners when you go through customs on *Gandhi*. The machines will think you're Lakshmi Ramajandran, a Unicorn employee who's vacationing at the habitat."

"He's a security man?"

The agent made a sour face. "He's an accountant, a bean counter."

Looking at the image of the real Ramajandran on the viewscreen set up on the shelf beneath the wall mirror, Jordan muttered, "I hope you don't have to break my nose."

"Nope," said the makeup woman. "Just a little prosthesis and you'll look just as ugly as he is."

Gilda Nordquist was not accustomed to being stonewalled.

"Surely you could at least tell me where Mr. Kell has been taken," she said to the image on her phone screen.

The flinty-eyed Unicorn executive replied evenly, "I'm sorry, ma'am, but we feel it's necessary to keep Mr. Kell under wraps, for the time being."

"But I represent the World Council," Nordquist reminded him, trying to keep the frustration from showing in her face or her tone. "We can demand that you reveal his whereabouts."

The man hiked his thin brows a little. "I suppose you could ask Mr. Otero himself, or maybe go to the International Court of Justice and—"

"That would take days, perhaps even weeks."

"For what it's worth," the man said, "Mr. Kell has agreed to our arrangements." A trace of a smile curled the corners of his mouth. "Apparently, he doesn't want you people to put him in protective custody."

"But he agreed to come to our facility on the space habitat, to be with his wife."

The man shook his head. "He's not going anywhere. Not for a while, at least."

Nordquist abruptly cut the connection, thinking, Now I'll have to get a team to ferret out Kell's location. And what then? Can the Americans keep him out of our hands? I'll have to ask the legal department about that.

And, she knew, she'd have to tell Anita Halleck about this latest kink in the road. Too bad the assassin didn't kill the troublesome sonofabitch.

In the headquarters of the Boston Police Department, local and federal police detectives crowded the three interrogation rooms where the would-be assassin and his two female companions had been taken. A trio of World Council security agents were also there, one in each room.

Nick Motrenko still looked woozy from the paralysis charge that Cree had fired into his neck. A matronly Boston Police Department nurse brandished a hypospray syringe, while one of the detectives rolled up Motrenko's sleeve.

"Whass that?" Motrenko mumbled.

"Just something to wake you up," said the detective.

"It won't hurt a bit," the nurse reassured him.

Motrenko flinched when the cold metal touched his skin, but once the stimulant hissed into his bloodstream he perked up; his eyes focused on the men and women around him.

"Did I get him?"

"Clean miss," said one of the detectives.

"You're a lousy shot, kid."

"I never fired a gun before," Motrenko admitted.

"You blasted the lectern pretty good."

"But I didn't kill him."

"Why'd you want to kill him?"

Motrenko looked up at them with disbelief. "Why? He's a traitor! He's selling us out to the aliens!"

The World Council agent leaned in between a pair of Boston detectives and asked stonily, "What makes you think that?"

Within half an hour they got Nick's story of Jordan Kell's selling out the human race and the impending alien takeover. Motrenko earnestly pleaded with them to "do something" about the coming alien invasion. It wasn't until he realized that they all thought he was slightly daft that he thought to claim his rights and demand a lawyer.

By nightfall Jordan and three Unicorn agents—including Hamilton Cree—were at Logan Aerospaceport, lining up to board the rocket shuttle that would take them to habitat *Gandhi*. They were all traveling as tourists. Jordan saw that Cree was several places ahead of him in line, the other two agents were behind him.

The Unicorn men were all in casual clothes: colorful short-sleeved shirts and trim dark slacks. Jordan was dressed as a Gujurati workingman, in a hip-length white tunic and slightly baggy tan slacks.

He placed his travel visa on the electronic scanner's plate, then stood before the optical scanner that registered his retinal pattern. Despite himself, he held his breath. The machine beeped and flashed a green light. Suppressing a grin, Jordan headed down the access tube that led to the shuttle's main hatch.

This was an overnight flight that accelerated at slightly less than one *g* halfway to its destination, then decelerated to a zero-*g* rendezvous with the gigantic habitat. Before liftoff the passengers had to watch a safety video that emphasized they would experience weightlessness—near-zero gravity—only for the few minutes of turnaround and during the final approach to the habitat's air lock.

The shuttle lifted off with a shuddering roar that pressed

Jordan deep into his cushioned seat. The video screen built into the seatback in front of him showed the Earth falling away. The sky turned from blue to black, and in a few minutes the vibrations smoothed out and he felt comfortable again.

"We're on course and on time," came the captain's reassuring voice. "Next stop: habitat *Gandhi.*"

Most of the passengers cranked their seats back and tried to sleep. The woman next to him slipped a blindfold over her eyes, Jordan saw.

He tilted his seat back and slid a set of smart glasses over his eyes. Their frames included tiny speakers that he could hear through bone conduction. To the travelers around him, Jordan seemed to be drowsing off.

But actually he was waiting for Aditi to call him.

inTELLigEnCE

"You've had a long day," said Frankenheimer.

"So have you," Aditi replied.

They were sitting together at a table in the small dining room on the ground floor of the building where Frankenheimer and his team had set up their equipment. Between them, the crumbs and crusts of their dinners lay on a clutter of plates; their glasses were nearly empty. The room was deserted except for the two of them. Robots had placed the chairs on the tops of all the other tables and wet-vacuumed the rest of the floor. Now a single robot stood by the door to the kitchen, silently waiting for them to leave.

Frankenheimer smiled tiredly. It made his roundish face look like a teenaged boy's, Aditi thought.

"A long day," he said, "but a very successful one."

"You've confirmed the measurement?"

"More than seventy-five thousand times the speed of light," he said, awe in his voice. "Seventy-five *thousand* times faster than light! That's how fast your communications travel."

Nodding, Aditi said, "Back on New Earth, one of the physicists told me that once you break through the light-speed barrier, there's no physical limit to how fast information can be transmitted."

"Seventy-five thousand," Frankenheimer repeated, as he reached for his wineglass. He drained it, put it down on the tabletop with a thump, then pushed his chair back and got to his feet, a trifle unsteadily.

"I don't know about you, ma'am, but I'm going to sleep. Tomorrow we repeat the test and see if we get the same results."

Aditi rose also, smiling as she said, "Good night, then."

"G'night." And he toddled off, leaving Aditi alone.

She watched him go, then turned and said to the robot standing patiently by the wall, "You can clean up now."

The robot stirred to life and trundled toward the table. Aditi headed for the door and her own bedroom, on the top floor of the building.

Time to call Jordan, she said to herself.

Jordan had nearly drowsed off when he heard Aditi whispering his name.

"Are you there?" he whispered back. He looked sharply at the passenger next to him; she was deeply asleep. Good, he thought.

"I'm here, dearest." And Aditi's image took form in the smart glasses he was wearing.

"Where are you?"

"In the habitat. Frankenheimer and his staff have commandeered a whole building to conduct their experiments. But where are you?"

"In a shuttle rocket, heading toward you."

"Really?" The delight in her voice thrilled Jordan.

"Really," he said.

"How soon? When will you get here?"

"We're scheduled to dock at ten in the morning, your time."

"Wonderful!"

"But it's a very large habitat. I need to know exactly where you are."

Aditi's smile thinned. "By ten A.M. we'll be doing more tests of the communicator that Frankenheimer has built. I'll try to include you into the receiving loop."

"You can do that?"

"I think so. I'll try."

"Then I can track you," Jordan said.

"Yes. Right."

"If not I'll tear down the whole habitat until I find you."

She laughed. "You're bringing an army with you?"

"Three men."

"I don't think that will be enough."

Glancing at the woman sleeping beside him once again, Jordan asked, "How many security people are guarding you?"

"Only a few," said Aditi. "Not more than six, I think. They believe that keeping me on this habitat, so far from Earth, is good-enough protection."

"Not for long," Jordan promised.

Rudolfo Castiglione was not accustomed to being rebuffed. To begin with, he chose his women carefully. Like a shark searching for prey, he sensed the inner vibrations of a woman who was vulnerable to his charm. Old or young, rich or poor, as long as they were physically desirable he knew he could put up with their emotional quirks and demands. After all, these encounters were not intended to last long. Ships that pass in the night, he thought. Or fish that feed the prowling shark.

Yet this alien woman had rebuffed him, in no uncertain terms. His cheek still stung from the memory of the slap she had given him. His pride stung still more.

Well, it's been long enough, he thought. I've escorted her here to the dismal space habitat. I've been the perfect gentleman. While she's been spending her days with Dr. Frankenheimer and his geeks, I've allowed her to spend her nights alone.

An interesting woman. No matter how we bug her quarters, within a minute of her entering the rooms all the sensors go dead. A pity. It would have been interesting to watch her shower and prepare for bed. Perhaps even informative.

Tomorrow night I shall try again. I will be pleasant and witty. She must be lonely. I will console her. I will tell her that I am lonely, too. I will ask her out to dinner, take her to the finest restaurant in this dreary space settlement. There must be a place that doesn't specialize in that overspiced Indian cuisine. A nice Italian restaurant, or even a French one. We will drink wine. We will be friends, two lonely souls cast away, far from home.

I will make her mine. One way or the other. I will remove the memory of that slap.

He smiled inwardly. The shark is circling its prey, he thought. And coming closer with each circle.

COUNTERINTELLIGENCE

"It's good of you to meet with me," said Gilda Nordquist.

"I'm always happy to cooperate with the authorities," Vera Griffin replied in her meekest little girl voice.

Nordquist was in Barcelona and Griffin in her office in the Otero Network building in downtown Boston. Yet the holographic viewers in their respective offices made it appear that they were in the same room, seated facing each other from behind their respective desks.

They made a dissimilar pair: Nordquist the blond, broad-shouldered female Viking warrior; Griffin the elfin, stylishly dressed child-woman, looking concerned, troubled, almost frightened.

"You were the producer of Jordan Kell's news interview," Nordquist stated. It wasn't a question.

"That's right."

"You witnessed the assassination attempt."

"Yes, I did. From the control booth, up above the studio floor."

"But you saw the whole thing."

"Yes, of course."

"You could identify the shooter?"

Griffin allowed a small smile to break her mask of vulnerability. "We have it all recorded. The local police already have a copy of the whole incident."

"Please forward a copy to me, personally," said Nordquist.

"Certainly."

"Where is Mr. Kell now?" Nordquist tried to ask that key question in the same tone as all the others, but Griffin noted a slight rise in the intensity of her voice.

"I don't know," Griffin answered honestly. "Mr. Otero himself has taken charge of his whereabouts."

"He's in a hospital?"

"Mr. Otero told me that he's in a private medical facility."

"In the Boston area?"

"I presume so."

"With private security guards."

"Yes."

Nordquist hesitated, her eyes flicking to the screens off to one side of the 3-D viewer. Eye movement, vocal intonation, body tremors: apparently Griffin was telling the truth.

"How badly hurt was he?"

Griffin hesitated. This is the World Council asking the questions, she knew. Mr. Otero viewed the World Council as a pack of collectivists working to destroy American freedoms and establish a dictatorship across the whole solar system. Yet Griffin herself looked on the World Council as the force of international law, of stability and order, of safety despite the enormous upheavals of the climate shift.

And, perhaps, the World Council represented an opportunity for her to advance her career.

She answered, "From what I could see, he didn't seem so badly wounded. I mean, he walked with the security people to the elevator and then along the hallway to the infirmary. They didn't have to carry him or call for a stretcher or anything like that."

"But he was wounded?"

"His shirt looked bloody, from what I could see. But he stayed on his feet the whole time."

"How close did you get to him?"

"I rushed down to the infirmary, but the security people wouldn't let me in."

Nordquist's pale blue eyes narrowed. "Was Mr. Otero there?"

"Not then. A little later, I think. He went down to the infirmary, and then the security guards took Mr. Kell away."

"To the hospital."

Nodding, Griffin replied, "That's what they told me."

Pouncing on the slight uncertainty in her reply, Nordquist snapped, "You don't believe that?"

Griffin hesitated. The last thing she wanted to do was to make Otero angry with her. But the next-to-last thing was to give this World Council woman some excuse to arrest her.

"I . . . I'm not sure," she said, reverting to her little girl voice.

"What do you mean?"

"I don't really know, but . . ."

"But what?"

"There were a bunch of security people in the hallway just outside the makeup room," Griffin said. "About a half hour after the shooting. Maybe more like forty-five minutes after."

"In front of the makeup room?"

"I don't know why, but they wouldn't let anybody in there."

"And where was Kell at that time?"

"Still in the infirmary, I guess."

"You guess?"

"I don't know. There were security people all over the place. They wouldn't let anybody near Mr. Kell."

Nordquist kept on asking questions and Griffin kept on being cooperative, but it was clear that she didn't know anything more.

After closing down the link to Boston, Nordquist rocked back in her commodious swivel chair, thinking: Kell didn't seem that badly injured. Somebody was in the makeup room. What if they whisked Kell from the infirmary to the makeup room? Why? To disguise him.

What if they didn't take him to a hospital? Instead, Otero helped ferret him out of the building. To go where?

The answer leaped up in Nordquist's mind. He's gone to habitat *Gandhi*! He's gone to get his wife away from us!

habitat Gandhi

"This is *big*," said Hamilton Cree.

He and his two cohorts were standing with Jordan just inside the entryway to the interior of the cylindrical habitat. Before them stretched kilometer after kilometer of tidy green fields, with streams meandering through them and little villages standing like toy towns here and there. Off in the hazy distance the fields ended at what looked like a huge metal cap, but the fields rose up and curved overhead in a complete circle.

Their guide, an almost painfully thin, gray-haired, dark-skinned Bengali, smiled brightly. "It is an inside-out world," he said, in lilting English. Pointing to the long, bright window that ran the length of the cylinder, he added, "Welcome the new day and your arrival in habitat *Gandhi*."

Jordan replied in Hindi, "Thank you."

The guide's smile got even brighter. "It is nothing."

It was unusual to see a person who looked so old. Jordan wondered if the man's religious beliefs forbade rejuvenation therapies. Whatever his age, he seemed sprightly enough as he led them to a gaudily colored minibus. There was no driver; the bus was fully automated. Jordan took the front seat, hoping their guide wouldn't test his Hindi vocabulary too far. The guide sat on the opposite side of the aisle while Cree and the other two security agents took seats behind them.

"We are going to a very fine hotel," said the guide, after telling the voice-recognition system their destination. "Very fine indeed."

The practically noiseless electric engine started up and they were on their way through the gracefully curving roads that threaded from village to village, heading for the biggest town in the habitat and the very fine hotel they'd been booked into.

By noon Jordan had unpacked his meager travel bag and was pacing his hotel room impatiently. He had removed the prostheses that the makeup woman had applied, and thoroughly washed up. Lakshmi Ramajandran was gone; Jordan Kell had reappeared.

There was a holographic viewer on one wall of his hotel room, but Aditi had not contacted him. Nor did he pick up any signal from the communications test that she was involved in.

She's probably surrounded by the technical team she's been working with, he told himself. Be patient.

Still, he paced nervously.

The room's phone buzzed. Startled, Jordan called out, "Answer!"

Cree's somber face appeared on the phone's screen. "We're ready to move whenever you give the word," he said.

Sitting on the edge of the bed, Jordan replied, "I have no idea when the word might come through. You might as well go out and see the local sights. I'll call you if anything turns up."

Cree shrugged. "Not much of a town. Shouldn't take more than ten minutes to take in the local sights."

With a sardonic smile, Jordan said, "I'm sure you'll find something interesting. I'll stay here and wait for a call."

"He's gone to the habitat?" asked Anita Halleck.

Nordquist said, "I'm sure of it."

Halleck was on her way to a committee meeting. Nordquist paced alongside her down the long, crowded corridor, followed by a phalanx of Halleck's aides and sycophants. The two women made a striking sight: Halleck youthfully vigorous, sleek, long-legged, wearing a trousered suit of royal blue, her chestnut hair coiled atop her head; Nordquist several centimeters taller, athletically built, blond braids hanging down her back, pale-eyed, in a glittering metallic sheath.

"Why would he go to the habitat?" Halleck demanded. "He agreed to let us take him there."

"He went on his own so he could find his wife and get her away from us," Nordquist answered.

"You're sure of this? You have evidence?"

Without breaking stride, Nordquist shook her head. "Just a hunch, but it all adds up. We're checking the passenger manifests and the visual imagery of everyone who boarded a shuttle for *Gandhi* since yesterday."

"The time of the shooting."

"That's right."

Halleck fell silent for several hurried strides. Then, "If you find any shred that he's already gone to the habitat, any speck of evidence at all, I want you to take a team up there and *find him*!"

"I should put a team together and go to the habitat right now. No sense wasting time. I can still review the passenger lists while I'm on the way."

"How long would it take you to get there?"

"High-priority flight? Six hours, maybe less."

"That fast?"

"It'd be a high-*g* boost," Nordquist said. With just a hint of a smile she added, "The guys won't like it. They're always worried about straining their testicles."

Halleck smiled back at her. "Do it."

Castiglione was bored by the scientists' work. It's like watching a Wagner opera, he thought: hours of tedium interrupted by moments of brilliance.

The tedium was getting on his nerves.

Frankenheimer and his aides were tinkering with an assemblage of equipment that was far beyond Castiglione's understanding or interest. That pile of junk is supposed to do the same things that Aditi can do in her head? he wondered.

Aditi was sitting quietly in one corner of the cluttered room, while Frankenheimer and his people puttered around the incomprehensible heap of electronic hardware scattered across a tabletop. Something had gone wrong with their first attempt to communicate with their colleagues back in Barcelona, and now the nerds were frantically replacing microscopic components and thumbnail-sized circuit chips.

Aditi watched patiently, her lips moving now and then. She's talking to her people on New Earth, Castiglione realized. Eight light-years away, and she's having a conversation with them.

So what? he asked himself. Tonight she's going to have a conversation with me. And I'll be much closer to her than her friends on New Earth.

Still pacing impatiently in his hotel bedroom, Jordan was startled to see Adri's seamed, bald face appear in the holographic viewer. The old man seemed to be sitting in a park somewhere in the aliens' city on New Earth.

"Friend Jordan."

"Adri! This is a surprise."

"I'm afraid it still takes an hour or so for your words to reach me, so if you don't mind, I will tell you what Aditi wants you to know," Adri said, in his slightly sibilant, paper-thin voice.

Jordan nodded.

"By the way, your brother Brandon sends his regards, as do the others of your group."

Good, Jordan replied silently. But what of Aditi?

As if he could read Jordan's mind, Adri went on, "Aditi is well, but the communication device that your scientists have built has broken down. They are trying to fix it. That's why she hasn't contacted you directly."

Relief washing through him, Jordan asked, "Can you show me where in the habitat she is located?" Then he mentally kicked himself, realizing that Adri wouldn't hear the question for an hour.

But he was saying, "She wants you to know where she is being held."

Adri's image was replaced by a graphic showing habitat *Gandhi*'s interior layout. One of the buildings was highlighted by a blinking yellow cursor.

That's where she is, Jordan said to himself. Unconsciously clenching his fists, Jordan said, "Tell her I'll come to her. Tonight."

PLANS OF ATTACK

From her private compartment aboard a world council executive rocket, heading for the habitat at a strenuous two gs, Nordquist sifted through the ID imagery of every passenger who had booked a flight to *Gandhi* in the past thirty-six hours.

The security team flying with her was seated in the general passenger section, the men glued to their seats, looking tense about the strain imposed by the ship's heavy acceleration.

Nordquist was using comparative graphics to try to spot Jordan Kell among the *Gandhi*-bound travelers. Her handheld computer was linked to the display screen on the bulkhead of her compartment. Even so, she felt thankful that the computer was voice activated, and she didn't have to move her hands. Weighing twice as much as usual, even breathing was laborious, almost painful.

As each image came up on the screen, she superimposed an image of Kell's face. Only one ID picture came close to matching. It showed the same basic bone structure as Kell's, although the man's skin and hair were much darker and his nose was larger and bent crookedly. It looked like it had been broken and never properly repaired. Same jawline, though. Almost the same cheekbones.

Calling for the retinal scans, she saw that the traveler's did not match Kell's at all. Contact lenses, she thought. They can fool the stupid scanners with contact lenses.

She stared at the facial image. Lakshmi Ramajandran, the data bar across the bottom of the screen said. From the state of Gujurat, in India, now working as an accountant for the U.S. security firm Unicorn Recovery Agency.

Jordan Kell. She was certain of it.

Nordquist put in a call to the head of security aboard habitat *Gandhi*.

"Looks sort of like a castle," muttered Hamilton Cree.

He and Jordan and the other two Unicorn operatives had pedaled on electrobikes from the town where their hotel was located to this village, some five kilometers away. It had been an easy bike ride: the winding road was quite flat, no inclines steeper than a few degrees. The bicycles were freely available in storage racks at almost every street corner.

Now they stood on the edge of a park—grassy grounds with well-tended shrubs and small trees—and studied the gray stone building across the wide lawn through digitally boosted binoculars. Its front door was elaborately carved wood, its walls covered with intricate high reliefs of animals, sword-armed men, voluptuous women.

Jordan peered at the narrow windows set into its walls amid all the sculptures. "According to the tour guide information, it was originally built to be a replica of a temple in India, for a tourist attraction, but the World Council took it over to be used as a residence for their people."

"That means a lot of World Council people inside," said Cree.

Jordan shook his head. "I wonder. Aditi told me there's no more than a half-dozen security people there."

"Plus the scientists," said one of the Unicorn agents.

"Geek guys," Cree said, with a slight grin. "No trouble from them."

It was nearing nightfall inside the giant habitat. The solar win-

dows that ran the length of the cylinder were slowly, almost reluctantly closing, like the eyes of a sleepy child.

Aditi had contacted Jordan, at last, toward the end of the day.

"Castiglione has asked me to dinner," she had told Jordan. "And
I've agreed."

"You agreed?"

With an almost impish smile, she had answered, "I thought it
would be impolite to refuse." Her face turning more serious, she
added, "Besides, I don't want to arouse his suspicions. We'll have
dinner and I'll thank him very politely and retire to my room."

"Alone," Jordan had snapped.

Her smile had returned. "Of course alone. Until you get here."

So Jordan had fidgeted and bristled all through the early evening. Cree and his two cohorts had gone to dinner, then rejoined
Jordan for the bike ride to the building where Aditi was returning—
with Castiglione.

"It'll be full night soon," Cree said, gesturing toward the slowly
closing windows.

Jordan nodded. They had decided to wait until dark. Even with
high-tech sensors, darkness provided a cloak for intruders—at least
emotionally.

How our emotions control us, Jordan thought as he waited impatiently. We still prefer to do our skulking in the dark.

One of the other Unicorn men held a palm-sized scanner in his
hand. "No cameras or motion detectors," he muttered to Cree. "At
least none that this handheld can spot."

"That building wasn't designed to repel attackers," Jordan said.

"We're only four guys," said Cree. "They won't need fancy electronics to stop us."

They had already decided that they would approach the building once it was fully dark, creeping across the park toward its far
side, away from the main entrance. Jordan would scale the ornate
carvings to the top floor and go in through one of the windows up
there. He knew that Aditi's bedroom was on the top floor. The

three Unicorn men would then go to the front door and pound on it until someone opened it: a diversion that Jordan hoped would keep their security guards on the ground floor while he and Aditi scrambled down from the window. Then they would return to the hotel that Otero's people had booked for them. With Aditi.

It should work, Jordan told himself as he crouched in the shadow of a large rhododendron bush with his three cohorts. Looking at the ornately carved walls, he thought, I can climb to the top floor, even in the dark. But then he wondered, Can Aditi make it down?

Grimly he determined, I'll bring her down even if I have to carry her on my back.

As they started to get to their feet, though, Cree gripped Jordan's shoulder and pulled him back down behind the foliage.

"Somebody's coming," he hissed.

Jordan saw one of the habitat's glaringly colored minibuses pulling up to the building's front door. It stopped and two people got out: Aditi and Castiglione.

All through dinner at the posh Mediterranean-style restaurant that Castiglione had picked, Aditi tried to disguise her anxiety about Jordan's expected attempt to rescue her. She spoke little through the many courses of the meal and sipped meagerly at the wines that were placed at their elbows.

If Castiglione noticed that she was tense, he gave no sign of it. More likely, Aditi thought, he's attributing it to my being nervous because of him.

Castiglione chattered away cheerily, smiling, telling jokes, speaking of his many accomplishments in the service of the World Council.

"Anita Halleck herself depends on me," he boasted. "Whenever she has a difficult or important task to be done, she calls on me."

Aditi said, "Is it so difficult to look after me?"

"Not at all, my beautiful one. But it is very, very important."

She realized that almost anything she said, short of an outright insult, would make him think she was enjoying his company. She felt appalled at the depths of the man's ego.

Castiglione was thinking, I'm being the perfect gentleman: witty, interesting, intelligent. If only she would drink a little more of the wine.

The dinner ended at last and the restaurant's maître d' summoned one of the habitat's minibuses to take them back to their quarters.

As the automated minibus pulled up to their building's front door, Aditi realized that this was the most dangerous part of the evening.

She stopped at the door, Castiglione beside her, while the bus drove away.

"Look up," he said softly.

Aditi saw that the landscape curving overhead was dotted with lights: roads, buildings, homes scattered across the darkened fields.

"It looks like stars," she said.

"Some people have seen patterns in the lights," Castiglione told her. "They've created artificial constellations in their minds." With a laugh, he added, "They even cast horoscopes on them!"

"How interesting."

"And beautiful."

Aditi avoided looking directly at him. "Well, it was a lovely dinner, Rudy. Thank you so much."

As he opened the heavy wooden door, Castiglione purred, "The evening is far from over, lovely one. In fact, it's just beginning."

Jordan watched the two of them enter the building. Turning to Cree, he said, "Let's go. Now."

Cree nodded agreement and the four men hurried across the darkened greenery of the park to the base of the building's side wall.

"We'll wait here and make sure you get up to the top okay," said Cree.

With a crooked grin, Jordan added, "And catch me if I fall."

Cree chuckled softly.

Jordan peeled off the jacket he'd been wearing and handed it to Cree. Like the others, he was wearing a dark blue turtleneck shirt.

"All right then," he said. "It's time to go."

"You're sure you don't want a gun?" Cree asked. "They're not lethal."

Jordan shook his head. "No, I'm not a trained marksman, like you. I don't want my wife in the middle of a firefight."

In the shadows, Jordan couldn't make out the expression on Cree's face. But he heard his disappointment. "Well . . . good luck, then."

"Thanks."

Jordan gripped an elephant's tusk in one hand and the outstretched arm of a warrior in the other and started to climb.

One step at a time, he told himself. Don't hurry, be careful. But his overriding thought was to get to Aditi before Castiglione tried to force himself upon her.

"I want a full security team surrounding that building, at once," Nordquist almost shouted at the man in the screen of her shuttle compartment.

He was brown-skinned, wearing a tunic with a stiff high collar, smiling blandly at her. "I will put your request through to the head of our security department."

"I thought you were the head of the security department!"

"Oh, no. Not so. I am only the acting head. The actual security director is at home, having dinner with his family."

Nordquist said, "As acting head of the department you can surely order a security detail to surround that building."

"I can, yes, certainly I can. But what if my chief disapproves of what I have done? What if he believes that I have overstepped my authority? What then?"

"But this is an emergency!"

"What is the nature of the emergency, please?"

Between the rocket's enervatingly high gravity that made every motion a struggle and this bureaucrat's obtuseness, Nordquist was ready to scream.

"The chairwoman of the World Council wants Jordan Kell placed in protective custody. It's a direct order from the chair of the World Council!"

"I understand," said the bureaucrat, still smiling insipidly. "But this is not a dangerous situation, is it? There is no threat of violence or physical danger."

Thinking of the physical danger she would like to expose this moron to, Nordquist said through gritted teeth, "Put me through to your department head, then."

The man looked startled. "At his home? At his dinner?"

"Yes! Now!"

Blinking rapidly, the man said, very reluctantly, "If you insist."

Nordquist wanted to pound the armrests of her seat, but the doubled gravity forestalled that. Glancing at the digital clock read-out in the corner of the display screen, she saw that her shuttle would be docking at the habitat in another hour. *We'll rush to that building and grab Kell before he can get away. With my own assault team. To hell with these bureaucrats!*

There's something about being watched by men who are younger and more athletic than you are that brings out the best in a man, Jordan thought as he sweatily climbed the ornate wall carvings.

Reaching from one figure to the next, his shoes barely maintaining traction as he scaled the wall, Jordan knew that Cree and his buddies were watching him and probably thinking that they could make this climb much better than he could. He felt the spool of hair-thin buckyball cable in his pants pocket. *At least the way down will be easier than this bloody ascent, even if I have to carry Aditi on my back.*

Looking up, though, he saw that the window he was aiming for still seemed to be a hundred miles away.

"There's no need for you to come all the way up to my room," Aditi was saying.

Castiglione was at her side as she walked up the curving staircase that led to her top-floor bedroom.

"It's nothing," he said, waving an insouciant hand in the air. "I feel as though I'm escorting a beautiful princess to the castle tower where her chamber lies."

Aditi knew that Castiglione was quartered in the floor below her own. She wondered if a slap in the face would stop him tonight. *Where is Jordan?* she asked herself.

Castiglione was chattering away as if he had no idea of what was going through her mind. "Besides, fair one, there is a surprise waiting for you once we get to your chamber."

"A surprise?"

"You'll see." The man's smile was almost leering.

Aditi thought that the surprise she most wanted was to have Jordan waiting for her. Adri must have shown him where I'm quartered, she said to herself. Jordan must be on his way to me.

But then she wondered if her husband would be stepping into a trap. Once Halleck has us both in her hands, what then?

They reached the door to her room. Castiglione was smiling toothily beside her.

"Allow me," he said as he opened the unlocked door and pushed it wide.

Aditi's quarters consisted of a single room. It was very spacious, with two narrow screened windows and a scattering of furniture that looked to her as if the pieces had been picked hurriedly and slapped in place by someone with little sense of style. Still, it was comfortable enough. The king-sized bed off in the far corner, away from the windows, was neatly made up. A human-form robot stood next to the lavatory door, inert until commanded into labor.

There was a comfortable couch just big enough for two across from the bed. Aditi saw that a champagne bucket and two fluted glasses had been placed on the coffee table in front of it.

"Oh," she gasped.

"Surprised?" Castiglione asked, stepping into the room. "It's only the local wine, but I'm told it's quite good."

"Rudy, I've already had too much wine," Aditi said, still hanging back in the doorway. "I'm tired, and—"

He grasped her wrist and tugged her into the room. "And you want to go to bed," he said. "So do I."

action

+++
+++

chandra Natarajan was the director of security for habitat *Gandhi*. He was a very large man, in every physical sense: almost two full meters tall, dark of skin, round of face and belly, he outweighed any two of his soft-spoken, submissive assistants. He was given to laughter, and enjoyed his life in the habitat, where his duties were almost entirely pro forma and he could spend plenty of time with his much shorter but equally round wife and their seven children.

So it was something of a rude shock when his assistant phoned him in the middle of dinner and told him that the acting security chief of the World Council was making demands upon him.

Seated at the head of his dinner table, Natarajan bellowed at the holographic image in the wall viewer, "Can't you see I'm having dinner with my family?" His voice could be even larger than his girth, when he chose.

The assistant writhed with a combination of dread and shame. "But she was most insistent, sir. She demands that we—"

"Demands? Of me?"

"Not you personally, of course . . ."

Natarajan saw that his wife and all seven of his children were staring at him, absolutely silent, awestruck at his justifiable anger.

"She wants us to have the old temple surrounded?"

"Yes, sir. I know it's unusual, but—"

"Surround it, then."

"Sir?"

His tone moderating a bit, Natarajan said, "We are always happy to cooperate with the World Council. Surround the temple. Nobody in or out."

"Yessir!"

More ominously, he growled, "And let me get back to my dinner." Silently, he added, You toad.

The window was within arm's reach, Jordan saw. Steady now, old man, he told himself. Wouldn't do to get this far and then fall like a stupid ass.

As he stretched his arm to the windowsill, he saw his wristwatch. Only six minutes had elapsed since he'd started climbing. Seems like six hours, he thought.

The window was screened, he saw. Why screened, he wondered, in this artificial habitat? Then he remembered the farm fields and pasturelands he had seen. They must have insects, just as we do on Earth. And old-fashioned screens instead of energy barriers. Are they being faithful to the original temple's design or merely behind the times? Is Mitch's company restricting its sales to Earth?

Very well, then. Clambering to the window, Jordan carefully planted both feet on the sill and rose to his full height, gripping the window's edges. He didn't dare look down. Cree and his team are watching, he told himself. They'll give me five minutes to find Aditi and then they'll go around front and start making a rumpus.

Holding on to the sides of the stone frame as firmly as he could, he kicked at the screen. It buckled. Jordan drew in a breath and then kicked again, harder. The screen clattered to the floor of the room inside.

He froze for an instant, then realized that even if the noise attracted someone, it would be better to meet him inside the room rather than balancing perilously on this windowsill.

He stepped down onto the floor of the darkened room and realized he was soaked with sweat. No more climbing for you, old boy, he said to himself.

Aside from the faint nighttime glow coming from the window, the only light in the room was from the crack beneath the door that led out, he presumed, into a corridor. Peering into the shadows, Jordan saw that the room looked like an oversized closet, or perhaps a storeroom. Boxes stacked up along one wall, and a little desk jammed against the other.

He tiptoed to the door and listened. Nothing outside. Wait! He heard voices, muffled by the door's thickness, but discernible as a man's and a woman's. Aditi!

Opening the door a crack, he saw one of the rooms down the hall had its door open. Aditi's voice was coming from there. The other voice was Castiglione's, he felt certain.

Glancing up and down the hallway, he saw that all the other doors were closed. Lord knows how many men are behind those doors, he thought. Well . . . imitate the action of the tiger.

Jordan tiptoed noiselessly down the hallway.

Aditi was saying, "I don't want any wine. I want you to leave. Now."

And Castiglione replied, "No more coyness, beautiful one. You are alone here. I have given the security guards strict orders to stay on the ground floor. Now be reasonable. You are attracted to me, aren't you?"

Stepping through the open doorway, too angry to speak a word, Jordan pushed the door shut. Aditi's eyes went wide at the sight of him. Castiglione whirled around when he heard the door click shut.

"That's my wife you're speaking to," Jordan choked out.

Castiglione quickly recovered from his surprise. "Jordan Kell! So you've come to be with your wife."

"I've come to take her away from you."

A sly smile snaking across his face, Castiglione asked, "And how do you propose to do that? There are half a dozen security guards downstairs."

"They'll be busy," Jordan said, advancing toward Castiglione. Aditi stood immobile, like a statue, her eyes riveted on Jordan.

"Even so," Castiglione said, "I can take care of you myself." And he whipped a slim pistol from beneath his jacket.

Jordan saw that it wasn't a tranquilizer gun: it fired bullets. It could kill. He felt suddenly defenseless. And stupid.

"It wouldn't do for you to kill me," he heard himself argue. "Halleck wouldn't like being responsible for the death of the star traveler. What kind of protective custody would that be?"

His smile turning disdainful, Castiglione said, "Oh, I won't have to kill you. Just cripple you with a shot in the leg. Kneecapping, I believe it's called."

Aditi's face radiated smoldering fury. She turned and yanked the wine bottle from its ice bucket. The noise made Castiglione turn his head toward her. Jordan leaped at him as Aditi swung the bottle with both hands at his face.

Castiglione reflexively raised his arm to block Aditi's swing as Jordan hit him with a rugby block and grabbed for the pistol. The gun went off with a *pop, pop, pop* sound as all three of them tumbled to the floor.

Castiglione shoved Aditi off him but Jordan grabbed for the gun and tried to wrestle it out of his hand. Again the pistol fired, up into the air. Castiglione swung his free fist into Jordan's ribs and the air exploded out of Jordan's lungs. But he still kept both his hands on Castiglione's wrist, twisting it as hard as he could.

Aditi got to her knees and swung the bottle again, at Castiglione's face. He screamed as the bottle crunched his nose. Jordan at last yanked the gun free and jammed it into the man's bleeding face.

"My nose," Castiglione bleated. He lapsed into Italian. Jordan recognized a blistering string of choice profanity.

Staggering to his feet, Jordan held the pistol on Castiglione's supine figure, puffing, "I've never killed a man, but I wouldn't mind starting with you."

Then he saw that Aditi was bleeding.

escape

cree pounded on the wooden front door of the temple until an angry-faced man yanked it open. He was obviously one of the world council security guards, Cree immediately recognized: burly, tightly curled auburn hair cut flat as a drill field, jacket flapping across his taut midsection.

"Who the hell are you?" he demanded in international English. "What the hell do you want?"

"We want to see the temple," Cree said, smiling as though he were drunk. Over the man's shoulder he could see the temple's entryway, with a fancy spiral staircase winding upstairs.

"This isn't a tourist attraction anymore. Go home."

"Home's a zillion kilometers from here."

A slight *pop, pop, pop* sound, from somewhere above. The guard looked up over his shoulder. "What was that?" he yelled into the depths of the entryway.

"Sounded like a gun going off," said another guard, walking into the light, his head craning up the curving staircase.

"Better get up," said the man at the door.

Pulling his pistol from beneath his jacket, Cree said, "Take it easy, pal." He reached into the guard's jacket and yanked his gun from its holster. "You too, buddy."

Cree's two companions disarmed the other World Council agent.

"How many others inside?" he asked.

"You can't get away with this," the big redhead snarled. "We're with the World Council, you dumb shit!"

With a lazy smile, Cree said, "Yeah, and it's gonna look great on your dossier that you let a private security agent take you."

"Aditi!" Jordan blurted.

"It's only a scratch," she said. But her left hand was clamped on her upper right arm. Blood was seeping through her fingers down the arm, dripping onto the carpet.

Turning to Castiglione, still flat on his back, Jordan snarled, "I ought to kill you!"

Aditi stepped toward Jordan. "It was an accident, Jordan. He didn't mean to hurt me."

No, Jordan thought. He meant to hurt me. To cripple me. With a smile on his face.

"We've got to get out of here," he said to Aditi. "Can you walk?"

"Yes, of course."

"Come on, then." He slid an arm around her shoulder and started for the door.

"What about Rudy?" Aditi asked.

Turning back to Castiglione, who still had both hands pressed to his broken nose and tears streaming down his cheeks, Jordan demanded, "Give me your phone."

Castiglione fumbled in his trousers pocket and pulled out the slim, oblong device. Jordan bent down and took it from his hand, then straightened and looked around the room. Spotting the phone console on the bedside table, he fired at it. It shattered on his first shot.

"Let's go," he said to Aditi.

"Where?"

Yes, where, Jordan asked himself. I can't expect her to climb down the outside wall with her arm hurt. She won't even be able to hold on to me if I try to rappel down on the buckyball cable.

Pointing with the pistol, Jordan asked again, "Can you walk?"

"Yes!"

"Down to the ground floor, then," he said, hoping that Cree and his two partners had neutralized the World Council security team.

The winding stone stairs looked endless, but in less than two minutes they reached their base and the entryway, where Cree and his men were holding six others, including two women, at bay.

"Let's get out of here," Jordan said to him as he stepped onto the entryway's stone floor, still holding one arm around Aditi's slim waist.

"She's hurt," Cree said.

"Yes. Come on, we've got to get away."

"I've already called for a minibus."

"Good."

The leader of the World Council team said, "Where do you think you're going? You can't get off this habitat and you can't hide in it for long."

Jordan almost smiled. "You underestimate the power of the news media."

An automated minibus was pulling up the driveway as they left the building. Cree's men had taken the security team's guns and phones, but Jordan knew it was only a matter of minutes—perhaps less—before other security guards would come swarming over the area.

They bundled into the minibus, Aditi's arm still bleeding. Cree gave the guidance system the name of the hotel where they were staying and the brightly colored vehicle started smoothly toward the main road.

As they reached the gently curved road they passed another bus heading in the opposite direction, toward the temple. It was gray and marked SECURITY.

Cree grinned sternly. "Local cops. Somebody must have called them."

"Call the hotel," Jordan told him. "Tell them we need a doctor."

* * *

When Nordquist finally arrived at the temple she found a down-cast team of security agents and a badly rattled Castiglione. Pressing an ice-filled towel to his broken nose, Castiglione moaned, "They've ruined my face. Ruined it."

Nordquist huffed, "Stem cell therapy will repair the damage. Where are Kell and his wife?"

The redheaded leader of the security squad said, "I heard him say something about a hotel."

"Which hotel?"

The man shrugged. Nordquist glared at him, but thought, There can't be more than a half-dozen hotels in this habitat. As long as I can keep anyone from leaving this artificial world, I've got him trapped.

Stalemate

The Hindu doctor smiled cautiously as he told Jordan, "It was merely a graze. Small caliber. I have administered therapeutic nanomachines and—"

"Nanomachines?" Jordan snapped. "Aren't they illegal?"

"On Earth, yes, of course. But not here."

Aditi was lying on the bed of Jordan's hotel room, her upper right arm swathed in a spray-on bandage. The doctor stood beside Jordan at the bed's side. He was small, hardly up to Jordan's shoulder, and very slim. His nearly black skin looked shiny, as though oiled. It stood in stark contrast to his white shirt and trousers.

"The nanomachines will deactivate themselves in twelve hours," he was telling Jordan. "Then you will be free to return to Earth."

"And she'll be all right?"

With a bright smile, the doctor answered, "Perfectly recovered. Completely recovered. Not even a scar."

Then we can return to Earth, Jordan thought. If we can get out of this habitat. If they allow us to leave.

To the doctor he said, "I see. Thank you very much."

"Thank you," said the doctor, with a little bow.

As Jordan showed him to the door, the doctor said, "You realize, of course, that I shall have to report this to the security people. A gunshot wound, after all. Very unusual. Very rare."

"I understand," said Jordan.

Once he had shooed the doctor out, Jordan rushed back to Aditi's side.

"How do you feel?" he asked, leaning over her.

She smiled and patted the bed with her left hand. "You can sit beside me, darling. I'm fine."

He sat gingerly on the edge of the bed and took Aditi's good hand in both of his. "I'm so sorry—"

"There's no reason for you to be contrite. You rescued me, and I love you."

"I love you, too, dearest. But I'm afraid I haven't really rescued you from anything. Not yet."

A heavy rap on the door. Jordan thought, That doesn't sound like Cree. Frowning, he got up and went to the door.

A huge dark man filled the doorway, peering past Jordan, at Aditi. Behind him, Jordan saw, was a strong-looking blond woman wearing a skintight sheath of glittering silver. A black giant and a Nordic princess, Jordan thought.

"I am Chandra Natarajan," the dark Goliath said, his voice stern, "director of security for this habitat."

Before Jordan could reply, Natarajan half-turned and introduced, "And this is Gilda Nordquist, acting director of the World Council's security department."

Without bothering to ask permission, Natarajan pushed past Jordan and stepped into the room, with Nordquist right behind him.

Feeling nettled, Jordan said, "I presume you know who we are."

Natarajan suddenly broke into a jovial grin. "You are not Lakshmi Ramajandran, that is for certain."

Jordan dipped his chin. "Yes, that's true."

Nordquist said, "You came into this habitat under a false identity and forcibly took her," she pointed to Aditi, "from our protective custody."

"I didn't want your protective custody," Aditi said, propping herself on her good elbow.

"That's neither here nor there," Nordquist said.

"No, that's the central issue," Jordan countered. "We don't want the World Council's protective custody. We want to be free."

"Free to spread your propaganda."

"Free to tell the truth."

Natarajan spread his arms, as if to separate the two of them. "Enough bickering!" he snapped. "Whatever differences you have back on Earth are of no consequence here on habitat *Gandhi*."

"You can't be serious," Nordquist said.

"I am quite serious. Totally serious." Pointing at Jordan, he said, "This man claims neither he nor the woman there accept your protective custody. The laws of this habitat allow them their freedom—as long as they follow our laws."

"But—"

"No buts!" Natarajan said, making a slicing motion with both his hands, palms down. "Habitat *Gandhi* is a member in good standing of the World Council, but we are not a colony nor a possession. We govern ourselves. If you can show that these two are criminals, we will of course allow you to take them back into your custody and return them to Earth. Otherwise they are free to remain here as visitors."

Jordan asked Nordquist, "Are there any criminal charges against us?"

"No. The World Council wants to protect you against would-be assassins." Leveling a finger at Jordan, she added, "There have already been two attempts on your lives, for god's sake!"

Glancing at Aditi, Jordan retorted, "We would rather take our chances with private security protection than be hidden away in some World Council prison."

"Prison?" Nordquist fairly shouted. "Neither one of you was ever in a prison."

"We were deprived of our freedom of movement," Jordan argued. "Kept from speaking to the public."

"Your wife was working with our scientists. Voluntarily."

Aditi said, "But I was kept from leaving your underground center. And then taken up here, whether I wanted to go or not."

Before Nordquist could respond, Jordan said, "Tell Halleck that we neither want nor need her protective custody. We want to be free."

Almost smiling, Nordquist said, "Very well. You can be free. As long as you remain in this habitat."

"But we want to return to Earth."

"Impossible."

Aditi asked, "Will we be allowed to make broadcasts to Earth?"

"Of course," said Nordquist. "Under our supervision."

"That's hardly freedom of speech," said Jordan.

Nordquist replied, "Freedom to spread propaganda, to dupe the public, is against both sound policy and the public interest."

"Your interest," Jordan countered. "Halleck's interest."

"Enough discussion," said Nordquist. "You can stay here in *Gandhi* . . . under World Council protection. Whether you like it or not."

STONE WALLS DO NOT
A PRISON MAKE . . .

+++
+++

CARLOS OTERO LOOKED GLOOMY, JORDAN THOUGHT.

SITTING NEXT TO THE HOTEL ROOM'S BED, WHERE ADITI LAY, HE WATCHED OTERO IN THE HOLOGRAPHIC VIEWER. THE network owner was apparently in his office: Jordan could see the towers of Boston through the window behind Otero, and a slice of the harbor glittering in the morning sun.

"Halleck is being her bitchy best," Otero was saying gloomily. "She's referred our complaint to the World Council's legal department. It'll take weeks before they even convene a hearing. Months, maybe."

"And in the meantime, we're bottled up here in this habitat," Jordan said.

With a mournful shake of his head, Otero said, "They're not going to allow you off the habitat, Jordan. She's blocking all traffic to and from *Gandhi*."

"She can do that? Legally?"

With a nod, Otero said, "My legal department tells me she can. She's apparently declared an emergency and invoked some regulation about inspecting all flights into and out of the habitat. She's not stopping any flights, just inspecting the passengers to make sure you two aren't aboard any of them."

"And this is within the Council's legal powers?"

"Yes, dammit. The International Transportation Safety Commission. One of Halleck's bureaucracies."

Jordan glanced at Aditi, who was sitting up in the bed. Turning back to Otero, he said, "Well, I suppose we'll have to stay here, for the time being."

"One other thing," Otero said, his expression morphing from unhappy to angry. "She's put an injunction on us doing any broadcasts from *Gandhi*."

"That muzzles us!"

"It certainly does. I've got my legal people protesting it, but again, it'll take weeks to get to a court hearing."

"She really wants to keep us from speaking to the public."

"That she does," Otero said. "The first act of a tyrant: muzzle the news media."

Once Jordan ended his doleful conversation with Otero, he turned back to Aditi, and was surprised to find her smiling cheerfully.

"You're not upset?"

With a little shrug, she said, "Not very much. Should I be?"

"We're penned in here."

"We can turn this into a second honeymoon. Or our first, really. We never had an actual honeymoon, if you recall."

Smiling back at her, Jordan said, "That would be wonderful, except that we can't allow Halleck to keep us muzzled like this. We've got to be able to tell the people the truth."

Aditi's face grew more serious. "Jordan, have you considered the possibility that your people don't want to be bothered with the truth?"

"Not bothered?"

"They live prosperous lives. They have the illusion of freedom. They take for granted that the World Council watches over them, protects them, takes care of them."

"And we're trying to shake them loose from that idea."

"We're trying to make them accept a responsibility that they don't really want to accept."

"So Halleck is right and we're wrong?"

"No," Aditi said. "But she's in tune with what your people feel. We're trying to make them change. Change is always painful, Jordan."

Reluctantly he admitted, "I suppose you're right."

"So what do you want to do about it?"

He thought it over for all of a heartbeat. "Well . . . at least we're together. That's the most important thing."

"No," said Aditi, quite seriously. "The most important thing is to get the people of Earth to save those worlds that will soon be engulfed by the death wave."

He stared at her. "Yes, that's so. But how do we do it?"

Aditi broke into a sunny smile. "I believe your people have an old adage, 'You shall know the truth, and the truth shall set you free.'"

Mitchell Thornberry was flattered that the chairwoman of the World Council had invited him to Barcelona. Just a quick trip for a face-to-face meeting. But being asked to meet personally with Anita Halleck was an unexpected honor.

Honor or command appearance? he asked himself as the rocketplane arced high above the curving horizon. Looking through the narrow window next to his seat, Thornberry saw the onionskin layer of blue atmosphere. How thin it looks, he said to himself. The lives of twenty-some billion people depend on that thin slice of air.

The plane landed smoothly at Barcelona's aerospaceport and a quartet of World Council flunkies met him inside the terminal to whisk him to his meeting with Halleck.

To Thornberry's surprise, they did not go downtown to the Council headquarters, but out into the hills at the edge of the city, to an impressive mansion.

The flunkies left him at the door, where a stiffly dignified butler in solemn black livery led him through a long corridor to the back of the sizable house.

Anita Halleck was sitting in a chaise longue on a patio by an Olympic-sized swimming pool, wearing shorts and a shapeless green pullover. Thornberry suddenly felt overdressed in his wine red jacket and off-white slacks. No one else was present, only a serving robot standing beside a wheeled cart bristling with bottles.

Halleck got to her feet as Thornberry approached and the butler headed back inside the house.

Extending her hand, she smiled and said, "How good of you to come and see me on such short notice."

For a ridiculous moment Thornberry felt that she expected him to kiss her hand. He took it in his own and replied, "I'm somewhat mystified as to why you want to see me in person."

Instead of replying, Halleck gestured to the rolling bar. "I believe your preference is Paddy's whiskey?"

The robot stirred to life and lifted a bottle of Paddy's from the collection.

She knows I like Paddy's, Thornberry thought. There's not much about me she doesn't know, I'm sure.

Thornberry took the proffered drink and settled himself on a cushioned chair next to Halleck's lounge. He saw there was a tall glass of something pink and cool-looking on the small table between them. The trees on the other side of the pool were casting long late-afternoon shadows across the patio.

"As I said, I'm mystified as to why you've invited me here," Thornberry repeated. Quickly he added, "Pleased, of course. But mystified."

Halleck smiled coolly. "I wanted to speak to you in private about Jordan Kell and his wife."

"Aditi."

"Yes, the alien woman. She's been working with a group of our scientists, you know. They're developing the technology for faster-than-light communications."

Thornberry nodded. "And how is their work coming along, may I ask?"

"Of course you may. They've built a prototype system."

"Have they now? And it works?"

Nodding, Halleck said, "Many thousands of times faster than light. We'll be able to have practically instantaneous communications throughout the entire solar system."

"That's grand!"

"It should open quite a sizable market."

"Indeed it should."

Pursing her lips momentarily, Halleck asked, "I want to continue our conversation about developing the commercial market for FTL communications systems."

Without an eyeblink's hesitation Thornberry said, "Certainly!"

"I believe that I can convince the Council to grant you an exclusive license to develop the technology for commercial use."

"For how long a period?"

Halleck hesitated just long enough to make Thornberry realize she was toying with him. At last she answered, "Shall we say . . . five years?"

"Ten would be better. Eight, at least. After all, we'd have to sink a lot of capital into new manufacturing facilities and infrastructure, and—"

"Six years?"

"Eight," Thornberry said.

"Eight years for exclusive rights," she mused. "I suppose I could get that through the Council."

"That'd be grand!"

"If I'm still the Council's chair after next year's elections."

Thornberry instantly recognized what she wanted. "I'm afraid it's too late for me to withdraw Jordan's nomination, you know."

"I understand," said Halleck. "But you don't have to give him your support, do you? He'll be nominated, but without your support he'll have a difficult time winning the election."

His brows furrowing, Thornberry said, "Jordan's a friend. We've been through a lot together."

"But you'll be too busy setting up your FTL business to spend much time—or money—on the election campaign, won't you?"

For several heartbeats Thornberry did not reply. At last he said, in a low voice, "I suppose so."

The two of them chatted on as the shadows of dusk enveloped the patio. Thornberry understood why she wanted this meeting face-to-face, with no witnesses. *She's handing me a fortune! With no competition! But the price is to hang Jordan out to dry.*

Ah well, he told himself, *maybe Jordan can get himself elected without my help.*

Halleck watched the expression on his face as the evening darkened. *How transparent he is,* she thought. *I've got him now. He won't dream of helping Kell and his alien wife, even if they find a way to return to Earth. Mitchell Thornberry is on my side now.*

+++

+++++ +++

Gazing at Aditi, sitting up in the hotel room bed, Jordan echoed her words, "'You shall know the truth, and the truth shall set you free.'"

"It's from your Bible," she said.

"Yes, I know. But I don't see how it applies to us."

Still smiling at him, Aditi said, "Halleck can't prevent you from broadcasting your message."

Realizing her meaning, Jordan said, "Ah, you mean you can use Adri's help to get me on the air."

"Yes. It doesn't matter where we are. I can contact Adri and—"

He interrupted, "The last time we did that it frightened Halleck so badly that she separated us and put us under protective custody."

"She can't do that now. Can she?"

"I wouldn't want to push her too hard. There's no telling what she can or can't do."

Aditi's expression grew more serious. Then, "What if, instead of taking over all the communications systems in the solar system, we simply contacted Mr. Otero and you spoke over his network. That's what the two of you planned to do anyway, isn't it?"

Jordan broke into a grin. "That's right. I could broadcast from here, over the Otero Network."

"But we'd still have our honeymoon, wouldn't we?"

"We will indeed!"

* * *

Nick Motrenko asked, "So what's going to happen to us?"

The court-appointed public defender looked as if he were handling soiled diapers. He was a youngish New Englander, spare and hollow-cheeked, with a Phi Beta Kappa key decorating the lapel of his dark gray suit.

Nick was sitting across the table from him, in a bare little conference room in the Boston lockup, with Rachel and Dee Dee on either side of him. Rachel looked worried, Dee Dee sullen.

"The three of you spilled your guts under interrogation," the attorney said, almost accusingly.

"They put something in the water," Nick replied angrily. "Made us talk. Like I was drugged."

"That's not legal, is it?" Dee Dee asked.

"They can't use anything you said in court, but the information is valuable in their investigation. Who's this man Walt?"

Rachel said, "He's a guru, like a holy man."

With a gloomy shake of his head, the public defender said, "Inciting you to attempt murder: some holy man." Turning to Nick he asked, "Where's he live? How can I get in contact with him?"

Nick stared blankly at the lawyer. "I don't know. He doesn't have a real address."

"He's a wanderer," said Rachel.

The attorney gave her a disapproving frown. "If you could help the police track him down, it'll go easier on you at your trial."

"Well, we can't," said Nick.

"I suppose if the police psychotechnicians couldn't get it out of you under interrogation you really don't know how to find him."

"He contacted us," Rachel said.

The attorney shook his head again.

"So what happens now?" Nick asked.

"You'll go to trial, be found guilty of attempted murder, and be sent to the freezers."

"Freezers?" Rachel asked.

Looking annoyed at having to explain something so common-place, the attorney said, "The state's official policy is that a crime such as yours—attempted murder—is caused by a mental or emotional defect that science doesn't know how to cure. So they freeze your body until science eventually comes up with a cure. That way the state doesn't have to feed you or house you. For just a few cents' worth of electricity per year they can keep you frozen indefinitely."

"Indefinitely?" Rachel asked, her voice quavering.

"Like someone who has an incurable disease," the attorney said. "You stay frozen until they find a cure."

Dee Dee said, in a disgusted tone, "And they haven't found a cure. Bodies have been in the freezers for a century. More."

"You mean we might never get out?" Nick asked.

"Nobody has," Dee Dee said.

"You've got to get us out of that!" Rachel demanded, shuddering. "You can't let them freeze us!"

The attorney folded his hands on the tabletop and gave her a hard look. "Look," he said. "I'm a public defender. That means my job is first and foremost to defend the public against breaches of the law."

"But we're not criminals," Nick protested.

"You tried to kill a man, for Christ's sake! With millions of eye-witnesses watching! I'll try to get the best deal for you that I can, but you're going into the freezers, like it or not."

Rachel broke into sobs.

"Unless . . ." said the attorney.

Nick grasped at the word. "Unless?"

"Unless you cooperate with the authorities. Tell them where you got the gun. Who helped you. That sort of thing."

With a glance at Dee Dee, Nick told the attorney, "It was all my idea. I know this starman is working for the aliens. They oughtta give me a medal for trying to save the human race."

"You're not going to get a medal," said the attorney. "You're going to get a drawer in the freezer facility."

"But what about the news media? I want to talk to them, tell them my story. We're going to be invaded by the aliens!"

The public defender shook his head. "No news coverage. That would just stir up other nitwits to try the same thing. We've got to protect the public."

"So we get frozen," said Dee Dee.

Nick stared blankly at him, seemingly in shock. "No news coverage?" he asked, his voice pleading. "I don't get to tell my story?"

"You've had your fifteen minutes of being famous," said the public defender. "Your time's up."

Carlos Otero was having dinner alone in his home in Concord when the hologram viewer in his dining room lit up to show Jordan Kell.

He was somewhat surprised, but once Kell explained that they could do more interviews despite the World Council's interdiction on broadcasts from habitat *Gandhi*, he asked, "You can do this?"

"Yes, thanks to her." Jordan gestured to Aditi, sitting beside him.

Otero broke into a wide, beaming smile. "This is going to drive Halleck up the wall!"

Aditi asked, "It won't get you in trouble, will it?"

With a shake of his head, Otero replied, "It shouldn't. We're not breaking any laws, just evading the blackout she's clamped on the habitat." He broke into hearty laughter. "My god! You'll be able to campaign for election to the World Council from where you are. She'll go crazy!"

Jordan forced a small return smile. He wondered what Halleck's reaction would be when he started making broadcasts. She won't go crazy, he thought. But she'll get very, very angry.

broadcast

"so it's up to you," Jordan said earnestly, looking squarely into Aditi's handheld phone, propped up on the coffee table in front of him, "to decide what we human beings should do to help the people who will be wiped out unless we act to save them."

In the three-dimensional viewer across their hotel room he saw himself sitting in front of a backdrop of the swirling star clouds of the Milky Way galaxy.

"The people of these other worlds do not look human, of course, but they are intelligent, and they have as much a right to life as you and I. We can't just sit here idly and let them die. That would be inhuman."

The holographic scene changed from Jordan's intent face to a view of a planet in space, with two large moons hanging nearby.

"This is one of the worlds in danger," Jordan said. "It orbits a faint red star nearly two hundred light-years from Earth. That means that it will take four hundred years for a spacecraft traveling at fifty percent of light speed to reach it."

The view shifted again. Now it showed greenly forested mountains with sparkling streams tumbling down their flanks. And in the distance, graceful towers that resembled minarets.

"These views were taken from robotic spacecraft that surveyed this planet many centuries ago. The people who live here have not yet discovered electricity or even steam power. But they have built a civilization that exists in harmony with their environment."

The scene shifted to show the city more closely. Its streets were busy with traffic. Creatures that looked curiously like oversized salamanders walked on their hind legs, dressed in colorful draperies. Four-legged reptilian animals pulled wagons. The city looked to Jordan's eyes like a medieval community, prosperous and busy.

"They have no idea that the death wave is hurtling toward them at the speed of light. If we sent a rescue mission to this world, it would barely get there before the death wave kills every living thing on it."

Jordan saw his own face once more in the viewer. "If we don't act, and act soon, those people will be totally destroyed by the death wave. And so will the intelligent creatures of five other worlds.

"Can we let them die? Or should we use our strength and our courage to save them? It's up to you to decide."

Anita Halleck slapped her hands together with a vicious crack and her holographic viewer went dark.

Turning to Gilda Nordquist, sitting off to one side of her desk, Halleck said, "We're going to have to get rid of that alien bitch."

"Kill her?" Nordquist asked, slightly alarmed.

"Freeze her, kill her, send her to the other end of the galaxy— as long as she's with Kell he can thumb his nose at us."

Nordquist hesitated for a moment, then said, "But they're protected by a private security team. And then there's *Gandhi*'s own security forces."

"Which are a joke."

"Yes, but you can't get at her while they're in the habitat. You can't just invade a sovereign territory."

Halleck's frown slowly morphed into a vicious smile. "Then we'll simply have to end our isolation of *Gandhi* and allow Kell and his wife to return to Earth."

Nordquist nodded. "Plenty of would-be assassins here."

"Talk to Rudy Castiglione. He's got a score to settle with the two of them."

Nick Motrenko watched Kell's appearance over the 3-D viewer in the jail's common room, with Rachel and Dee Dee sitting on either side of him.

The three of them were treated almost like royalty by the other inmates. In a makeshift community of felons, where social rank was decided by the seriousness of one's crime, attempted murderers were practically like royalty. The jailhouse population of sneak thieves, con artists, burglars, strong-arm bullies, and rapists treated Nick and his two women with some deference. It helped that almost all the inmates were young, hardly anyone much older than Nick himself. Modern society had weeded out the habitual criminals, the professionals and psychotics, and tucked them away in freezers. Now the police concentrated on catching petty crooks before they graduated to more serious crimes.

Once Kell's show was finished, Rachel asked Nick, "Do you believe him? I mean, about that world being in danger?"

Dee Dee said, "Looked pretty real."

"It could've all been faked," Nick said. "They can make anything look real."

A tall, thatch-haired young man with a strong jaw and pale green eyes leaned into their conversation. "Looked real to me."

Nick was about to tell him to butt out when the youngster said, "I used to work in graphics and special effects. It'd take a helluva lot of effort to make a scene look so real. I mean, even the trees in the background were all different, no two alike."

"How'd you get in here?" Nick demanded.

The kid actually blushed. "I was faking alibis for guys arrested for burglaries. Showed them miles away from the scene of the crime."

"And?" Dee Dee asked.

He shrugged. "I got careless. Let a couple details slip and the police experts spotted 'em. So here I am."

"Are they going to freeze you?" asked Rachel, real concern in her voice.

"Nah. I'm going to a reeducation center in Montana. Two years. Once I get out I won't be allowed to come back here to New England. I'll have to start my life all over."

"That's not so bad," said Dee Dee.

"Better than freezing," he agreed.

Nick said, "So you think this guy Kell is telling the truth?"

Another shrug. "From the looks of what he showed, he's either telling the truth or he's got damned better special graphics than I can do."

Carlos Otero was surprised by the call. He was in his office, going over the audience demographics of Kell's broadcast with his staff directors, when his phone announced that the chairwoman of the World Council wished to speak with him.

Otero blinked once, then immediately asked his staff people to leave his office.

"We'll continue this later," he said, unable to suppress a smile at the good news they had brought him. Kell's show had been a smashing success.

Once the office was cleared, he instructed the phone to put through the connection to Anita Halleck.

Without even a nod of greeting, Halleck's first words were, "I can see that it's futile to try to keep Kell from speaking out."

With a cautious smile, Otero said, "He has a right to speak his mind."

"No matter what the consequences."

"That was all decided almost five hundred years ago," Otero reminded her. "First amendment to our Constitution."

"The world has changed, Carlos."

"But not the right to freedom of expression."

For an instant Halleck looked as if she wanted to debate the idea, but then she composed a smile and said, "I suppose it's futile to restrict him and his wife to habitat *Gandhi.*"

Carefully, Otero replied, "It looks that way."

"Especially with you helping him," she snapped, almost angrily.

Otero spread his hands. "I'm just doing my job, Anita."

"No matter what the consequences."

Otero thought of a comeback, but buried it and simply smiled at her.

"Very well, then, Carlos. I'm going to allow Kell and his wife to return to Earth. If anything happens to them it will be on your head, not mine."

Otero nodded acceptance. But he thought, If anything happens to them it will be your doing, bitch.

As soon as Halleck cut the connection, Otero put in a call to the Unicorn agency. He wanted Kell's security team strengthened.

habitat gandhi

Chandra Natarajan's imposingly massive body seemed to fill the hotel room. He was beaming broadly at Jordan and Aditi, his strong white teeth contrasting sharply against his slate-dark skin.

Jordan gaped at the habitat's security chief. "You mean we're free to go?"

"You may leave whenever you wish," said Natarajan. "I received the call from Anita Halleck's new security director, and decided to bring you the good news in person."

"That's very kind of you," said Aditi.

Natarajan's smile diminished by a few watts. "Of course, we will be sorry to have such distinguished guests leave us. But please accept my personal invitation to return to *Gandhi* whenever you wish, and stay as long as you please."

"That's very gracious of you," Jordan said, switching to Hindi. "Thank you so much."

"It is my pleasure."

As soon as Natarajan left their room, Jordan phoned Hamilton Cree.

"Good news," he said to the security man's stolid holographic image. "We're leaving. We're going home."

Cree nodded impassively. "I just got a call from Chicago. We're already packing."

"Good."

"One more thing," Cree went on. "My boss tells me the Boston District Attorney's office wants you to testify at the trial of the kids who tried to shoot you."

Surprised, Jordan asked, "Do I have to?"

"There's a subpoena waiting for you when you land in Boston."

Vera Griffin sat disconsolately at her desk. Kell's latest broadcast had been a big success, but she had had practically nothing to do with it. The show was beamed to network headquarters and went out on the air while she merely sat in the control booth, watching it just like any other viewer.

It was good stuff, she realized, but Kell can produce shows like that without me. I'm sitting off to the sidelines, out in the cold. That's no way to get ahead. That's no way to impress Mr. Otero.

Her phone suddenly announced, "Mr. Otero calling."

Thinking he was probably going to reassign her back to "Neighbors and Friends," Griffin muttered, "Answer."

Otero looked excited. "Vera, Jordan Kell and his wife are returning to Earth!"

"Really? When?"

"They'll be landing at Logan tomorrow morning. You get a team together to cover their arrival."

"Right!"

Otero broke the connection, but Griffin sat there for several seconds, breathing hard. He's coming back! We can do shows from here in the studio.

I'm back in business!

Studying himself in his bathroom mirror, Rudolfo Castiglione decided that the stem cell therapy had indeed repaired his broken nose satisfactorily. I look as good as ever, he thought. Perhaps even a little bit better.

His phone announced, "Walter Edgerton, sir, returning your call."

Castiglione wrapped a bathrobe of royal blue about himself as he stepped into his sitting room. Through the windows of his condominium suite he could see row after row of Barcelona's high-rise office buildings and other condos. Off in the distance rose the fantastically sculptured towers of Gaudí's Cathedral of the Holy Family.

Edgerton was sitting relaxed in a recliner, a glass of amber liquid in one hand. He wore comfortable slacks and a velour pullover blouse. Even stretched out on the recliner he appeared very tall, long legs and arms, his dark face stubbled with two days' growth of beard.

"You called?" Walt asked, with a bemused half smile.

Castiglione wasted no words. "Jordan Kell is on his way back to Earth."

"Is he?"

"He lands at Boston in three hours."

"And?"

"And we must take steps."

"To do what?"

Castiglione realized that Edgerton was toying with him. *The man knows that my communications link is secure. No one is snooping on me. Yet he wants to hear me say specifically what he already knows I want of him.*

"He is to be silenced."

Edgerton's smile vanished. "That isn't something that can be arranged overnight. It takes time to recruit the appropriate, eh . . . volunteers."

"You won't need any volunteers. You and I should be able to handle this assignment without outside help."

Walt's face suddenly showed alarm, and Castiglione relished it.

"I don't do such things," the black man said.

"It's time you learned," said Castiglione.

LOVE YOUR ENEMIES

+++
++

There was a mob of newspeople at Boston's Logan Aerospaceport. Jordan was momentarily taken aback as he and Aditi stepped into the terminal to find themselves facing the urgent, impatient throng of reporters and their semiautonomous cameras.

Cree's security team had been beefed up with extra Unicorn people flown in from Chicago. Together with the regular Boston police they kept the nearly rabid news crews from actually grabbing Jordan, but no one could keep them silenced.

"Mr. Kell! Mr. Kell!"

"How does it feel to be back on Earth?"

"How do you feel about being reunited with your wife?"

"What are your plans now?"

"Will you campaign actively for the World Council seat?"

Jordan stopped and held up his hands. "This is rather overwhelming, you know," he said with a grin.

Another barrage of questions. Jordan rubbed his chin, then replied, "Aditi and I are delighted to be back on Earth. We intend to bend every effort toward getting the World Council to build and staff the starships we need to save the worlds that are endangered by the death wave."

"You've been nominated for a seat on the World Council," said a brittle-looking blond woman. "Do you expect to be elected?"

His smile widening, Jordan answered, "That's up to the people of North America and Europe. I won't be doing much campaigning. I intend to spend every available minute pushing to get those starships built."

In Barcelona, Rudolfo Castiglione unconsciously ran a finger along his nose as he watched Jordan's impromptu press conference.

Not campaigning for the World Council seat, he thought contemptuously. Every word he speaks is part of his campaign to win election. Anita is right to be frightened of him.

In Oakland, Walter Edgerton was also watching Jordan Kell's performance.

He's clever, Walt realized. Highly intelligent and extremely clever.

The cameras concentrated on Kell and his lovely wife. But Walt was able to pick out the security team that separated them from the demanding, unrelenting news reporters. There's only a handful of security guards, he said to himself. Shouldn't be too difficult to get through them. Or around them.

Jordan said to the reporters, "Thank you very much. That's all I have to say right now."

They grumbled and muttered but began to leave the terminal gate area, their cameras rolling along behind them.

Cree held out a cautionary hand as he watched them leave. At last he turned to Jordan and said, "Okay, let's go. There's a limo waiting for you outside. It'll take you to Mr. Otero's home. We'll be right behind you in a minivan."

Jordan nodded and they all started toward the terminal's central corridor.

But a nondescript man in a dark suit stepped toward them. He was portly, with a silly-looking tiny wing-tipped mustache under his bulbous nose. Cree stepped in front of him.

"I have to deliver this to Mr. Kell," the man said, pulling an envelope from his jacket. "I'm from the clerk of courts office."

Jordan asked, "Is that the subpoena?"

"Yes, sir, it is."

Jordan reached for the envelope. As he took it, the portly man said, in a mechanical tone that he must have used thousands of times before, "You are hereby served with this subpoena, commanding your presence at the trial of one Nicholas Motrenko and his accomplices, to be held—"

"I understand," Jordan interrupted, opening the envelope and swiftly scanning the legal document.

"Thank you," said the process server. His puffy face blossoming into a cherubic smile, he added, "I intend to vote for you next year, sir."

"Why, thank *you*," said Jordan.

Several minutes later, as he and Aditi sat in the rear of the limousine that was taking them to Concord, she asked, "Are you really going to appear at his trial?"

"I'm ordered to."

"Can't you get out of it? Millions of people saw him try to kill you. They don't really need your testimony."

"Perhaps not," Jordan said. "But I suspect that young Mr. Motrenko could use all the help he can get."

"Help? You're going to help him?"

Jordan patted her knee. "Aditi, dearest, there's another quote from the Bible: 'Love your enemies. Do good to those who hate you.'"

"'If someone strikes you on one cheek,'" Aditi recited, "'turn to him the other also.'"

"Yes," said Jordan. "That's what I'm going to try to do."

Aditi shook her head. "I think you're crazy."

the trial

Small though it was, the courtroom was almost empty. Hardly any onlookers at all, Jordan saw, and the news media's table was also nearly empty, although he recognized Vera Griffin sitting there, looking well dressed, as usual. Jordan nodded to her and she fluttered a hand in recognition.

A pair of uniformed court guards were checking the credentials of everyone trying to enter the courtroom. Jordan had shown them his subpoena as he noticed a half-dozen Massachusetts state troopers standing a few paces down the hall, heavy black pistols on their hips.

Is the state of Massachusetts deliberately downplaying this trial, he asked himself, or is its outcome such a foregone conclusion that not even the news media are much interested?

Sitting beside him on the hard wooden bench, Aditi nodded toward the three accused. "They look worried."

"They have good reason to be," Jordan muttered.

The judge entered the courtroom, a small, flinty-looking woman in a black robe. The bailiff cried, "All rise," and everyone stood up. Then the trial began.

The prosecutor spent his first few minutes confirming the identities and backgrounds of the three defendants. Then the judge—her face stern, with permanent frown marks between her eyebrows—asked for their plea.

The public defender rose with the trio and announced, "Not guilty, Your Honor, by reason of temporary insanity."

The judge's expression twitched with distaste, but she turned to the prosecutor and told him to proceed.

He showed the broadcast of Jordan's news conference. There was Motrenko, suddenly jumping to his feet and firing at Jordan.

The meager audience stirred as the prosecutor said, "What need do we have for further witnesses? Millions of people saw them try to assassinate Mr. Kell. The prosecution rests."

Jordan felt a twinge of surprise. Why did they subpoena me if he didn't plan to have me testify?

The judge nodded curtly, then turned to the defense attorney. "Your case, sir?"

Before the public defender could open his mouth, Jordan sprang to his feet. "May I speak, Your Honor?"

"Certainly, Mr. Kell. But the prosecution has already concluded its case against these three."

"I wish to speak on their behalf," Jordan said.

He could feel the courtroom stir. Voices muttered behind him. The handful of news reporters gaped. Motrenko and the two young women with him turned to stare at him.

"On their behalf?" the judge asked.

"Yes. It's my understanding that none of these three young persons has ever been involved in a crime before their attempt on my life. I ask the court to release them into my custody."

Out of the corner of his eye Jordan saw Aditi's questioning expression. The judge seemed stunned.

"Release the accused into your custody?" the judge asked, incredulous.

"Yes, if Your Honor pleases. I don't believe their lives should be ruined because of one mistake."

The judge rapped her gavel sharply. "Court recesses. Mr. Kell, counsels, in my chambers."

* * *

Sitting at the news media table, Vera Griffin's mouth dropped open at Jordan Kell's request. No live broadcast of the trial was permitted, of course. The courts maintained their dignity, they claimed. Griffin had inserted herself among the four news reporters merely to keep as close to Kell as she could.

Now she turned to the Otero reporter sitting beside her. "You got that all down?"

He shook his head. "No cameras allowed in court."

"But you've got a graphics synthesizer, don't you?"

The pouchy-eyed reporter nodded and tapped his lapel pin. "Sure. Everybody does," he answered, gesturing to the three other reporters at the desk.

"Then we can compose a re-creation of the scene."

"Yeah. Right."

"Get your footage to the office right away," Griffin commanded. "I want this on the evening news."

Jordan brought Aditi with him into the judge's chambers. The prosecutor and public defender came in right behind them.

The judge didn't bother to take off her black robe, but she poured herself a glass of iced tea from the jug behind her desk. At least, Jordan assumed it was iced tea.

"Now let me get this straight," she said, eyeing Jordan coldly. "You want me to release those three nut cases into your custody?"

Standing in front of the judge's heavy mahogany desk, Jordan said simply, "Yes."

The prosecuting attorney demanded, "What is this, a publicity stunt?"

Jordan felt surprised by the accusation. "No. Not at all. I've read the news reports about those three youngsters and I feel they shouldn't be put away for their first offense."

Sinking down into her high-backed desk chair, the judge asked, "How do you think we keep the peace in a world of twenty billion people? We catch criminals before they can do too much damage and we put them away where they can never threaten society again."

"You blight a lot of lives that way," Jordan said.

"But we keep the streets safe. We keep the peace."

"I'll take responsibility for their behavior," Jordan said.

"They'll murder you in your sleep," the prosecutor growled. Turning to Aditi, he added, "And your wife, too."

"We have a security team protecting us twenty-four hours a day."

The public defender spoke up. "If Mr. Kell accepts the responsibility, then we're off the hook. If those kids try anything, then we can put them away for good."

The judge shook her head. "If they kill him, the responsibility will blow back on me, for letting them go."

Trying to head off that line of reasoning, Jordan said, "From what I've read about them, those three young people believe that I'm working for the aliens from New Earth, helping them to take over our world."

"Alien invasion," muttered the prosecutor.

"Well, if they're with me day and night, they'll soon discover that there is no alien invasion. No takeover by the people of New Earth."

Aditi said, "They'll find out that all we want is to save Earth from the death wave. Earth, and the other intelligent civilizations that are also under its threat."

They went around and around the matter several more times until at last the judge said wearily, "All right. I may be crazy, but I'm going to allow you to take custody of the three accused."

"I object," snapped the prosecutor.

"Noted," the judge replied.

"Thank you," Jordan said, extending his hand toward her.

The judge took his hand, but said, "Before I sign off on this, though, I want to talk to your security chief. I want to make certain he's okay with this."

"Of course," Jordan agreed. "I'll call him and tell him about it right now."

babysitting

Hamilton Cree frowned with distaste.

"How are we supposed to protect you if you invite your assassins to live with you?" he asked Jordan.

They were still in the courthouse, sitting in a small conference room down the hall from the judge's chambers. Jordan had decided to talk to Cree in private before letting the security agent face the judge.

"They won't be living with us," Jordan replied. "The three of them will be quartered in an apartment or a condo unit, together with a team of your Unicorn people."

"But they'll be with you all day?"

"Yes, that's the plan."

Cree shook his head. "It's crazy."

"Hamilton, it's the only way I can see that will convince them I'm not part of an alien takeover of Earth."

"Freezing 'em is a lot simpler."

"Be reasonable, Hamilton," Jordan pleaded. "Let's give it a try, at least."

"Until they figure out a way to murder you."

Breaking into an almost rueful grin, Jordan said, "You'll be there to protect us."

Cree huffed. Then he asked, "Who's going to pay for this?"

Surprised, Jordan said, "Why, I will, I suppose. It's my idea, after all."

"You can afford a full-up security team, twenty-four/seven?"

"Yes."

"I don't like it."

"But you'll go along with it, won't you?"

Looking like a little boy facing a plate of broccoli, Cree murmured, "Yeah. I'll go along with it."

"Good! Let's go tell the judge." As they got up from their chairs, Jordan added, "Thank you, Hamilton. I appreciate this."

Cree nodded, but he was thinking, And if those three nuthatches assassinate him, who's going to catch the blame? Me, that's who.

Nick Motrenko looked suspicious as the judge explained Jordan's offer. Rachel seemed surprised and hopeful, Dee Dee downright delighted.

"Let me get this straight," Nick said to Jordan, his youthful brow furrowed with disbelief. "You want us to be with you all day, every day?"

"So that you can see for yourself what I'm doing. See that I'm not working for the New Earth people, and there's no alien invasion in the works."

Almost sullenly, Nick said, "You could be doing that while we're sleeping."

Rachel hissed, "Come on, Nick."

Dee Dee actually giggled. Nervously, Jordan thought.

Sitting behind her bulky desk, the judge fixed Nick with a stern gaze. "I don't think you realize what a favor Mr. Kell is willing to do for you. If you don't go along with it, you'll be found guilty of attempted murder and I'll have to sentence you to the freezers. All three of you."

"I guess it's better than freezing," Nick admitted, almost sullenly.

Jordan said, "I want you to see that my goal is to save Earth and those other worlds from the death wave. You can post a running commentary about what we're doing on your blog."

Jordan could see the surprise on Nick's face.

"You'd be willing to appear on my blog?"

"Every day. We can even work out an agreement with the Otero Network for global coverage."

Nick looked uncertain, wavering, but Dee Dee said, "We'll be helping you to get elected to the World Council, wouldn't we?"

With a nonchalant shrug, Jordan replied, "I'm not interested in being on the World Council. But if that's what it takes to save our world and the others, then I'll accept the responsibility."

A silence fell over the judge's chambers. Nick stood before her desk, looking somewhat hopeful despite himself, all eyes on him. Rachel looked pleading, Dee Dee buoyant. Off to one side, Cree's face was a noncommittal blank, but Jordan knew that the security agent thought the situation to be little short of murderously dangerous.

Aditi spoke up. "I agree with Jordan," she said to Motrenko. "The best way to show you that the people of New Earth are no threat to you is for you to work with us, day by day."

"For how long?" Nick asked.

"Until you are convinced."

Nick broke into a wary smile. "And when will you be convinced that I'm convinced?"

Jordan answered, "Quite frankly, I don't know. But I'm willing to give it a try. Are you?"

"You'll be on my blog every day?"

"Every day," Jordan promised.

Nick repeated, "It's better than the freezers."

The judge got to her feet and said to her phone, "Tell the bailiff that we will reconvene in ten minutes." Almost smiling, she said to Nick, "Mr. Kell is offering you your life. The least you could do is to show some appreciation."

"We appreciate it!" Rachel blurted.

With obvious reluctance, Nick extended his hand to Jordan, who took it in his own.

"He what?"

Anita Halleck was in her chauffeured sedan, heading through Barcelona's downtown traffic from the World Council headquarters to her home in the outlying hills.

In the car's holographic viewer, Castiglione's handsome face looked somewhere between amused and disgusted. "He's taken the would-be assassins under his wing. He's saved them from the freezers."

The view changed to show the Boston courtroom with the judge announcing that the three accused would be released into the custody of the man they had tried to murder. The cameras followed Kell and the trio of youngsters into the hallway outside the courtroom, where a phalanx of hastily assembled news reporters shouted questions at them.

Abruptly, Castiglione's face replaced the scene in Boston. "He's actually going to become their guardian." The Italian shook his head. "What madness."

"Madness, my foot," Halleck snapped. "It's a publicity stunt, pure and simple. And he claims he's not actively running for the Council seat."

"Ah. Politics," said Castiglione, as if that explained everything.

"He thinks he's so damnably clever," Halleck fumed.

"Perhaps too clever," Castiglione said. "I think he has outsmarted himself."

Walter Edgerton gave out a low whistle of admiration as he watched the scene outside the Boston courtroom.

He's saved my kids from the freezers, Walt said to himself. What a noble gesture. What a beautiful way to get the news media's attention.

Walt got up from his sofa and went to the glass sliders that opened onto his patio. His apartment was sixteen stories above the street, high enough so that he could see the Bay Bridge and, across the glittering water, San Francisco's high-rise towers.

The entire region had been rebuilt twice within the past two centuries. Devastating earthquakes had leveled the area, but despite the warnings of geologists and insurance adjusters, people and corporations had rebuilt along the same fault line. The triumph of hope over experience, Walt thought.

Well, I'm one of them, he admitted to himself.

There'd been some talk of using the same alien technology that produced the energy screens to make buildings truly invulnerable to earthquakes. But Walt knew that "invulnerable" was a relative term. If the quake is powerful enough, nothing is invulnerable.

As he stood gazing at the bay, he mentally counted off the seconds. Seventy-four one thousand, seventy-five one thousand . . .

At eighty-two seconds his phone announced, "Mr. Castiglione calling from Barcelona."

Walt nodded. "Put him on."

He turned to see Castiglione sitting in an easy chair, a stemmed wineglass in one hand.

"Good afternoon, Rudy," he said, stepping back toward his sofa.

"Good evening, Walter," said Castiglione. "I see you're letting your beard grow in."

With a dramatic sigh, Walt replied, "Yes. I'll be hitting the road again in a few days. Taking up my dingy old robe and mingling with the hoi polloi."

"Perhaps not," said Castiglione. "Have you seen the trial in Boston?"

"Yes. Kell's made a saintly gesture, hasn't he?"

"It could lead to his martyrdom, don't you think?"

Walt's brows rose perceptibly.

"I mean," Castiglione went one, "he's *inviting* the three who tried to assassinate him to live with him, travel with him, work with him."

"He's taking a big risk, isn't he?"

"Can you get in touch with your Mr. Motrenko?"

"I think so."

"Can you talk him into trying to destroy Jordan Kell once again?"

Walt rolled the idea around on his tongue for a few moments before answering, "Motrenko is an idealist, even though he doesn't realize it. Idealists make good assassins. They don't worry about the consequences."

Castiglione said, "Shave off the beard and find where Kell plans to go. Go there and give your idealist a chance to act on his fears."

LONDON

London had changed, Jordan saw.

It felt good to be back in England, even though the day was dark, dank, and drizzly. Yet the city was different from the London he had known two centuries ago. It was a vast forest of high-rise towers, some soaring more than a hundred stories high. They blotted out the older, earlier buildings. Or replaced them. It was difficult to make out the familiar landmarks he had known in his earlier life.

Still, as he stood at the window of his suite in the Hotel Savoy, Jordan could see the neo-Gothic stonework of Westminster Abbey and the Houses of Parliament through the dreary rain, with the tower that housed Big Ben rising against the gray clouds. At least that hasn't changed, he said to himself. Of course, it helped that they were alongside the Thames: the river protected them from being swallowed up by the newer buildings.

The dreary scene looks almost like Monet's painting, he thought. Or was it Whistler who did it?

Aditi came to his side. "What a miserable day," she said softly.

"It looks lovely to me," said Jordan with a happy smile. He turned to the holographic viewer on the wall opposite the bed. "Weather forecast, please."

A meteorological map sprang up, with isobars and a big red L hanging over London. As they watched, the low-pressure system slid away to the southeast and the synthesized voice of the forecast computer told them the next three days would be warm and sunny.

Jordan's smile widened. "We can go to Cornwall on Sunday. I'd like you to see where I was born and raised."

Aditi nodded agreement, but asked, "What about our three guests? And their, ah . . . escorts?"

"Nick and the ladies can stay here, there's plenty to see and do. Cree will keep watch over them."

"You mean we could be alone?"

"Yes. In the cottage that's been my home for as long as I can remember."

"Privacy," Aditi breathed. "We haven't had much of it."

Jordan suddenly realized that she was less than happy. "Dearest, I suppose this trip hasn't been easy for you."

They had crisscrossed much of North America over the past three weeks, visiting one city after another, meeting with local and national organizations, where Jordan spoke about the need to protect Earth from the coming death wave, and to save the other worlds that were in danger.

Everywhere they went, Nick Motrenko and his two young women accompanied them. Together with ten or twelve Unicorn security agents. Hamilton Cree was with them constantly, even though the people under his command changed with each city they visited.

In Chicago they dined with Mitchell Thornberry, who seemed strangely distant and aloof. Too busy making money, Jordan thought. It was Aditi who realized that Thornberry had been bought out by Anita Halleck, once Mitchell started enthusing about his development of faster-than-light communications.

"Do you really think he's sold out to Halleck?" Jordan had asked, incredulous, as they prepared for bed that night.

"He certainly seemed less than enthusiastic to see you," Aditi had replied. "Conflicted."

Sadly, Jordan nodded, agreeing with her. Mitch has made his choice, he thought. I hope he's happy with it.

Jordan insisted on making a side trip to the Native American reservation in North Dakota, to visit Paul Longyear. To his surprise and delight, Longyear treated them to a celebratory dinner that included hundreds of the reservation's family. For two days, Jordan was able to forget his responsibilities and enjoy their hospitality.

Even Nick Motrenko had been impressed. "They really like you," he'd said, with a tinge of awe in his voice, as they returned to Chicago and took the rocketplane for London.

Standing beside him in front of the rain-streaked hotel window, Aditi leaned her head on Jordan's shoulder. "I don't mind the traveling," she murmured. "I know that you're trying your best to save those other worlds."

"But?"

"But we don't have any privacy. Not really. Not with Nick and the girls with us every minute of the day. And Cree and his people. It's like traveling with a big family—a family of strangers, really."

Jordan looked down at her and lifted her chin gently. "It will be over soon. By Christmas, I promise you."

"Six weeks from now."

"We're booked to appear in Paris, Rome, Moscow, Stockholm, and Barcelona. After that it's home to Cornwall for a good old-fashioned Christmas."

She smiled wanly. "At least I'm seeing your world."

"And my world is seeing you. That's important, you know."

"I suppose so."

"It will all be over soon, I promise."

"The election is in January."

"Yes. Then we'll know if we've succeeded or not."

Aditi's smile warmed. "You'll succeed, Jordan. And I'll do everything I can to help you."

"Even putting up with our guests?"

"And a hundred more, if I have to."

He kissed her. "That's my beautiful wife," he whispered.

Someone knocked on the door to their suite.

Aditi sighed. "That must be Nick."

"Yes," Jordan said, heading into the sitting room. "I suppose it's time for today's interview."

Walt carefully followed Jordan's travels, recognizing the pattern of a political campaign. He's damned clever, Walt said to himself. He's bringing Nick over to his side.

Still in his apartment in Oakland, Walt had debated the possibility of contacting Nick, and decided to forego it—for the present. The security team that was protecting Kell would listen in on any phone call he made, and a personal contact seemed out of the question. So he bided his time.

Now Kell and his wife—together with their little entourage— had flown off to England. For the next few weeks he'd be campaigning in Europe, under the guise of pleading for help in sending expeditions out to the stars.

Leaning back in his favorite recliner, Walt pondered the situation. Life can be very strange, he thought. Since childhood he'd watched broadcasts about how someday the human race would go beyond the solar system and reach out for the stars. And now we're on the verge of doing it. Why? Not for science, and certainly not for profit. We're going to the stars on missions of mercy. Or so Kell says.

How can I get Nick back on the track? he asked himself. How can I convince him that Kell is actually selling us out to an insidious alien plan of conquest?

The kid was willing to murder Kell once. But that was when Kell was an abstraction, an idea, a concept of deceit and danger to the human race. Now he's seeing Kell every day, seeing a living human being, not an abstract concept.

How to convince him that he's being duped? How to show him that Kell is an evil that must be eradicated?

The buzz of his phone interrupted Walt's train of thought.

"Mr. Castiglione calling again."

Walt grunted. *Even the computerized phone seems fed up with Rudy. He's been calling every damned day.*

With a sigh, Walt told the phone to tell Castiglione he was unavailable and to take his message. He knew what the message would be: *When are you going to get your people to assassinate Kell?*

Walt thought wearily that his answer might have to be: *Never.*

"It's beautiful!" Aditi said.

"Rather small, actually," said Jordan.

"Quaint."

Smiling, he nodded. "Yes, I suppose that's the word for it. Quaint."

They were standing at the gate of the cottage that had been Jordan's childhood home. The trees were bare, the grass littered with dead leaves, the wind coming in from the nearby sea was sharp and cold.

But, as he looked at the old cottage for the first time in nearly two hundred years, he saw that Aditi was right. It certainly was lovely.

On an impulse, he leaned down and swooped Aditi up in his arms. She squealed with surprised delight.

"It's customary to carry the bride over the threshold," he said, happy that she felt so light in his arms.

In London, Nick, Rachel, and Dee Dee had found an amusement park.

The three of them were spending their Sunday exploring the city, and were drawn to the Eye, the huge cantilevered observation wheel that dominated the riverfront skyline. Cree was walking with them, sober-faced, intent, while his team of guards—Nick thought of them as guards—seemed to have blended into the crowd of fun-seekers thronging the park.

"Where's your people?" Nick asked Cree as they edged through the crowd closer to the giant wheel.

"They're around, don't worry. They can see you, even if you can't tell which ones of these people are Unicorn agents."

Dee Dee asked, "Are they supposed to be guarding us or protecting us?"

Cree's stolid face eased into a tight grin. "A little of both."

Rachel insisted that they had to ride the wheel. "Halfway to the stars," blared the recorded spiel that rang out above the hubbub of the crowd.

"It's just a big Ferris wheel," Cree said, squinting up through the bright morning sunshine.

"The oldest one in the world," said Dee Dee.

"You sure you want to try it?"

"Yes!"

Nick disliked heights, but he didn't want Rachel to see his fear. If she and Dee Dee went up and he stayed on the ground, he'd be humiliating himself.

So, trying to hide his reluctance, he climbed into one of the passenger-holding glass capsules with the two young women. Cree stayed on the ground, a sardonic, slightly bemused expression on his face.

Nick was stunned to see Walt sitting inside the capsule, clean-shaven, his hair clipped short, wearing an impeccable light gray suit and a beaming smile. He looked like a well-groomed British businessman.

"Hello, good people," said Walt as the three of them gaped at him.

"What're you doing here?" Nick asked as he took a seat facing the black man. Rachel sat beside him, Dee Dee beside Walt.

"Actually, I've come to see you." And the wheel started into motion, lifting their cage off the ground.

"All the way to London?" Dee Dee asked.

"All the way to London," Walt replied amiably. Looking into Nick's eyes, he asked, "How are you, friend? How is the star traveler treating you?"

Feeling a little confused and more than a little wary, Nick muttered, "Fine."

Rachel offered, "He's on Nick's blog just about every day. Nick has millions of followers, thanks to Jordan."

"Jordan?" Walt echoed. "He's not Mr. Kell anymore."

"He's been very good to us," Rachel said.

"Naturally."

"What do you mean by that?" Nick asked.

Walt shrugged his narrow shoulders. "Why shouldn't he be good to you? You're giving him worldwide publicity every day, you're showing everyone that he's a sweet, peaceable, trustworthy gentleman."

Nick heard that tinge of sarcasm in Walt's tone.

"Well, he is . . . kind of."

Walt nodded knowingly. "Of course he is, as long as he's running for election. But what happens after he gets himself onto the World Council—with your help?"

"He said we'd be free to go home."

"And the charge of attempted murder that's still hanging over you?"

Rachel said, "We'll be on probation."

"Probation. You'll have to report to a probation office. They'll tell you what you're allowed to do, where you're allowed to go. Like captive animals."

"It's better than being frozen," Rachel said.

With a philosophical tilt of his head, Walt admitted, "Yes, I suppose it is."

Nick saw that they were high above the ground now. But aside from the river threading through the city, there wasn't much to see aside from the clustered towers of Greater London that stretched out all around them, dwarfing them, making Nick feel like a guinea pig in a spinning cage.

We wouldn't be here if it wasn't for Jordan, Nick reminded himself. We'd be frozen bodies, in permanent storage.

"Jordan's treating us okay," he said to Walt. "Nobody else lifted a finger to help us."

Walt gave him a pitying smile. "I admit that Kell has played his little game expertly."

"Game?"

"He wants to convince the world that the aliens are no threat to us. Getting elected to the World Council is part of his plan."

"You think?" Dee Dee asked.

"What other reason does he have for treating you so magnanimously?" Walt hesitated barely a moment before adding, "Unless it's to get close to Rachel and Dee Dee?"

That stung Nick. He heard himself say, "He's got a wife, for cripe's sake."

"An alien, from another world."

Rachel said, "He's never come on to me. You, Dee?"

Dee Dee shook her head. "I wish."

With a cynical smile, Walt said to Nick, "And where is the saintly Mr. Kell now, may I ask?"

"He took the day off," Nick answered. Almost sullenly.

"He's showing his wife where he grew up," Rachel said.

"In Cornwall," Dee Dee added.

"Very romantic," said Walt. "If that's what he's actually doing."

"You don't think so?" Nick challenged.

"I have no way of knowing. Do you?" Walt's stare bored into Nick. "After all, you're the ones who are under guard, not him. He's free to go and do what he wants."

An icy silence filled the capsule. The wheel was swinging downward now. Slowly, slowly, they were returning to the ground. Walt sat silently, watching Nick intently. It made Nick uncomfortable, but he tried to hide it, tried to keep from squirming.

At last Walt spread his long arms and said, "Well, I really came to see if you were all right. You appear to be in good shape."

"Yeah," Nick muttered.

"Good. Enjoy yourselves. While it lasts."

The wheel stopped and a robot attendant opened the door to their capsule to let them out. Walt helped Dee Dee to her feet while Nick sat unmoving, the expression on his face a mixture of puzzlement and resentment.

As he stepped back onto terra firma, Walt turned and extended his hand to help Rachel step onto the platform. And he saw's Nick's face scowling at him.

The seed's been planted, Walt thought. Now to help it grow.

Aditi and Jordan stood at the edge of the cliff and watched the sun go down into the surging sea, turning the sky into a magnificent palette of violet streaked with glowing pink streamers of clouds.

"The ocean was much lower when I was a lad," Jordan said. "It's climbed halfway up the cliffs. No beach left at all."

"It's so beautiful," she murmured, leaning against him.

Jordan wrapped his arms around her waist. "I knew you would like it."

"How could I not?"

With a wry smile, he asked, "How would you like to spend the rest of your life here?"

"With you."

"Of course with me. Who else?" he mock growled.

"There's no one else in the world for me," Aditi said.

"No one else in two worlds for me," he replied.

Slowly, reluctantly, she disentangled from his embrace. "You've got a full day tomorrow, back in London."

Jordan nodded, but said, "Let's wait here a while. The stars will be out soon. I'd like to watch Sirius rising."

But he knew she was right. There was still so much to be done.

MOSCOW

++

++

"I had expected some snow," Jordan said as the sleek black sedan purred almost silently into the city along the special highway lane reserved for government vehicles.

"Snow will come," said Dmitri Kalnikov, their Russian host, in accentless English. "We will have a white Christmas, I assure you."

"But it's already December . . ."

"Global warming," said Kalnikov with a smile. "While you English worry about rising sea levels drowning you, we Russians enjoy a milder climate. Khrushchev's old idea of cultivating virgin lands in Siberia has come true. Russia is now the world's leading exporter of grains."

Jordan nodded understanding. "It's an ill wind that blows no good."

Kalnikov nodded back. He was a short, stocky man bundled into a black fur-trimmed overcoat. His glistening bald head was uncovered, though, and the coat was unbuttoned. His face was round, jowly, with a snub of a nose and thick lips that seemed curled into a perpetual smile. But his pale blue eyes were icy cold.

To Aditi, sitting beside Jordan, Kalnikov said, "We have arranged a suite for you in the best hotel in Moscow, right next to Red Square and the Kremlin."

"And the others?" she asked, meaning Motrenko and his two

female companions, plus Cree and the trio of Unicorn agents the Russians had allowed to enter their country.

"Same hotel, different floor. They will be quite comfortable, I assure you."

"That's good," said Jordan.

"Tomorrow you address the Duma," Kalnikov told Jordan, "but tonight you dine with the president of all the Russias, and a small group of his closest advisors. They are very eager to meet you."

Jordan understood the message behind his words. *The head of government wants to see me face-to-face and hear what I have to say.*

Vladimir Balakirev was the Russian president, a career bureaucrat who had slowly, patiently worked his way to the top of the government. Despite his years, he looked youthful, vigorous, thanks to rejuvenation therapies. His full head of hair was dark brown, his face lean and angular, his body trim. He wore lifts in his heels, though, and always sat in a chair that was a few centimeters higher than those around him. Driving his slow progress through the Kremlin was an insatiable ego.

"I know you have just arrived in Moscow," Balakirev said to Jordan, seated beside him at the big circular table. "You must stay long enough to allow me to show you and your lovely wife the city."

Jordan interpreted mentally, *He wants to be seen in public with us.*

"I'd be happy to," Jordan replied. "Aditi would especially appreciate a chance to see the ballet."

"Of course! Tomorrow night, after your address to the Duma."

One of the men halfway around the table moved his lips. *Making reservations for us,* Jordan realized.

There were several toasts before dinner was served. Toasts to interstellar friendship, to peace and understanding, to a glorious future. Jordan, aware of Russian drinking habits, had fortified himself with a thick slab of butter before starting out to the Kremlin.

"Coat the stomach," he told Aditi, remembering his old days as a diplomat. "Helps you from getting drunk."

After the vodka came the food. Caviar from the Caspian Sea, reclaimed from the pollution that had nearly poisoned the sturgeon into extinction; bloodred borscht, grilled caribou steaks.

As dessert was being served in delicate glass dishes, Balakirev asked, very casually, "So you want us to build starships and save alien civilizations?"

Jordan put down the gold spoon that had been halfway to his mouth. "I think it's important," he said. "It's a moral imperative."

"Let me tell you about moral imperatives," Balakirev said. "For more than a hundred years Russia fought a war against Islamic extremists, a war that we eventually won. Not because we slaughtered our enemies, but because we showed them that we would not allow them to change our way of life."

"Many were killed, on both sides," said one of the men across the table.

"But we persevered," Balakirev continued, waving a stumpy finger in the air. "Year after year, decade after decade. We showed the people of the Islamic states on our southern border that they could live as they wished, but they could never subdue the Russian people. *That* was a moral imperative."

Jordan dipped his chin in acknowledgment. "Yes, I suppose it was."

Balakirev's stern expression relaxed into a guarded smile. "Now you want to save alien races on distant worlds. As a moral imperative." His smile widening, the Russian president said, "That's the way the Jesuits felt about the Aztecs. And the Incas. And the Chinese. And so many other civilizations that the West emasculated."

"We've come a long way since then," Jordan countered. "We're going to these worlds to save them from extinction, not to colonize them."

Balakirev's dark eyebrows rose. "Still, the question remains, why should we go to the expense of trying to save people we know nothing about?"

"Because we know they exist," Jordan replied, "and that they will be wiped out unless we help them."

"But what's in it for us?" asked Kalnikov, sitting on the president's other side. "Why should we go to the expense—"

"The expense is trivial," Jordan snapped. "You spend more on vodka each year."

"Ah, but vodka is important," said one of the men halfway around the table. Everyone laughed.

Jordan made himself laugh, too. But then he said, "It would be criminal if we just sat by and let those other worlds die."

"Criminal?" Balakirev challenged. "You are a judge now?"

"I am a human being, and I believe it would be inhuman to allow whole civilizations to be wiped out when we have the means to help them."

Balakirev reached out and patted Jordan on the shoulder. "Yes, yes. Perhaps so."

He was testing me, Jordan realized. Taking in a calming breath, he added, "Besides, the starship building program could provide many jobs for your best and brightest scientists and engineers."

"So there is profit to be made for Russia?"

"I can't imagine the starship program going forward without Russian participation. After all, it was Russians who made humankind's first steps into space."

"That was long ago," said Balakirev.

"It's time for Russia to be great again. Time for Russia to reach for the stars."

Balakirev nodded, then turned to Kalnikov and said in Russian, "You can see why Halleck is so worried about this one."

Jordan understood every word.

"I miss walt," said Dee Dee.

She was sitting with Rachel and Nick in the corridor of a cheerless government building near Red Square. Hamilton Cree stood at the end of the corridor, with two Russian security guards, dour heavyset men who seemed incapable of smiling.

They had spent almost the entire morning seeking permission from the Russian government's communications bureaucracy to transmit Nick's daily blog from Moscow to the Otero network, as he had done in the other European cities they had visited. The stony reception he'd gotten from the bureaucrats sitting behind their formidable desks had not been encouraging.

The door across the hallway opened and a youngish blond woman came out, smiling brightly at them.

"I have good news for you," she said as Nick got to his feet. "The World Council has approved your request to broadcast your daily interviews with Mr. Kell from Moscow, and our communications department has endorsed their decision."

Breaking into a rare grin, Nick said, "That's great! Thank you."

"However," the blonde went on, her smile diminishing, "you will not be allowed to broadcast Mr. Kell's address to the Duma this afternoon. Tass will cover that event exclusively."

"But I can interview Mr. Kell afterward?"

The blonde nodded. "Along with all the other news representatives. A group interview."

*　*　*

Jordan stood before the members of the Russian legislature and pleaded his case for rescuing the worlds threatened by the death wave. Their response was polite, but hardly enthusiastic.

It wasn't until President Balakirev followed Jordan to the podium and pronounced, "It is time for Mother Russia to be great again. It is time for us to lead the way to the stars!" that the Duma rose to its feet as one person and cheered long and loud and lustily.

Sandwiched in with more than fifty other newspeople shouting questions at Jordan, Nick felt like a very small fish in a very large pond.

That's okay, he told himself. I'll interview him one-on-one when he gets back to the hotel, just him and me.

But Jordan was whisked away from the Kremlin by Russian security personnel, together with Aditi, Balakirev, and a handful of other Russian bigwigs.

To see the ballet, the same bright-eyed blonde explained when Nick complained to her. She shrugged. "I understand that Mrs. Kell wants to see our ballet."

Defeated, Nick returned to the hotel with Rachel and Dee Dee—and Cree and his cohorts.

Once in their suite, Nick tossed his minicam onto the desk and slumped on the long sectional sofa, dejected.

"This stinks," he grumbled. "Jordan shoulda told me he wouldn't be able to do the interview today."

Before either of the women could reply, the phone announced, "Incoming call from Mr. Edgerton."

Surprised, Nick said, "Put him on." The holographic viewer across the room lit up to show Walt sitting in what looked like a condo unit's living room in California.

"Hello, friends," said Walt, smiling warmly. He was dressed

casually in slacks and a pullover shirt, clean-shaven, as he had been when he'd appeared in London, rather than the seedy, unwashed guru he'd been when Nick had first met him.

Goggling at him, Rachel gasped, "You shouldn't be phoning us! They'll trace the call, find out where you are."

With a relaxed wave of his hand, Walt said, "Not to worry, sweet one. No one is monitoring my phone."

"How can you be sure?" Nick demanded.

"Friends in high places," said Walt. "And speaking of friends, I see that your starman was too busy to be interviewed by you today."

"He went to the ballet," Nick growled.

"Really?"

"Yeah."

"Makes a good cover story."

Rachel asked, "What do you mean by that?"

With a nonchalant shrug, Walt answered, "Suppose he's meeting with his Russian friends, in private?"

"You mean in secret," said Dee Dee.

"He's been with them all flickin' day," Nick said.

"All right, then," Walt rebutted, still smiling, "suppose he's meeting with some others?"

"Like who?"

"Like his friends on New Earth. I'm sure they want regular reports on how he's succeeding. And they'll want to give him his orders, of course."

"He hasn't been talking to anybody on New Earth," Rachel countered. "We're with him all the time, we'd know."

"All the time?" Walt challenged. "Like you're with him now?"

Nick frowned at Walt's image. "We can't be with him twenty-four/seven."

"That's that I mean."

"But we're with him enough to know that he's not a traitor."

"And you're sure about that? Absolutely positive? There's no way the man couldn't be fooling you? No way he couldn't be selling us out to the aliens?"

Nick snapped, "No way."

Walt's smile vanished. "That's an awfully big claim. Especially when the future of the human race depends on it."

Nick couldn't get to sleep that night. Even making love with Rachel didn't help: he felt tense, almost angry.

After an hour of tossing fitfully, he got out of the bed, pulled on the thin robe that the hotel supplied, and paced across their bedroom. Through the diaphanous curtains of the room's only window he could see the onion domes of the Kremlin across Red Square, brilliantly lighted against the gray, starless sky.

"What's the matter?" Rachel called drowsily from the bed.

Turning back toward her, Nick said apologetically, "I didn't mean to wake you up."

She sat up in the bed, blanket tucked under her armpits. "I wasn't sleeping anyway."

"I'm sorry."

"What's wrong?"

"Walt says Jordan's working for the aliens. How's he know that?"

Rachel shrugged her bare shoulders. Ordinarily the movement would have enticed Nick.

"I mean, how's he know that Jordan's working for the aliens? We've been with him for weeks now, and he seems to be just what he says he is."

"He's trying to get the government to save those other worlds from the death wave."

"Yeah. And us, too."

"But Walt doesn't believe him."

"But we know more about Jordan than Walt does. We're with him every day."

"Not all the time, though," Rachel pointed out. "He could be working with them when we're not with him. Like right now."

"You believe that?"

"I don't know. I guess not."

Nick sat on the edge of the bed. "I mean, I tried to *kill* the guy and he takes us under his wing. My blog's a big success, thanks to him."

"His wife is awful nice, too," said Rachel. "Not weird. She's just like us."

"Yeah."

For long moments neither of them said anything. Nick felt knotted up inside. He had believed Walt so completely that he had tried to kill the man. Now . . . now he just didn't know where he stood, who he should believe.

Finally Rachel asked, "So what do you want to do?"

"I don't know!"

In the shadows of the darkened room it was difficult to make out the expression on Rachel's face. But Nick could hear the anxiety in her voice.

"You know, Dee's asked about joining us."

"Huh?"

"She says she's tired of waiting for Walt. She thinks he's dumped her."

"Dee and Walt were making out?"

"Like mad. But she hasn't been to bed with him since we started all this traveling."

"And she wants to come to bed with us?"

"A threesome." Rachel hesitated a heartbeat, then, uncertainly, "Might be fun."

"No way," said Nick.

"Really?"

"You're my girl. I don't want anybody else and I'm not sharing you with anybody."

She threw her arms around his neck. "I'll tell Dee to talk to Walt next time he calls."

Nick kissed her warmly. But then he said, "That's another thing."

"What is?"

"Walt called us. Just like that. Like he's not afraid of the government tapping the phone or anything."

Remembering, Rachel said, "He said he's got friends in high places."

"Yeah. What's he mean by that?"

"You should ask him."

"I will," Nick said, clenching his fists in determination. "I will."

rise and strike

Rudolfo Castiglione peered unhappily through the rain-streaked window of the London hotel room.

"What a miserable climate," he said unhappily. "No wonder the British built themselves a worldwide empire. Anything to get away from this cold and rain."

Walter James Edgerton, sitting across the room relaxedly with his long legs crossed and his arms stretched across the back of the couch, took a more conciliatory attitude. "Oh, I don't know. The rain makes the flowers grow."

Castiglione turned and scowled at Walt. "We have plenty of flowers in Calabria. Flowers need sunshine, too."

Walt conceded the point with a nod. Then, "You didn't drag me here to London to discuss the weather."

"I didn't drag you anywhere," Castiglione replied. "I ordered you here."

"So here I am. Why?"

"We need to see some results about Jordan Kell."

"We? I presume you mean Anita Halleck."

"Precisely so. This would-be assassin of yours is a total failure."

Walt swung his arms down and sat up straighter on the couch. "I've got to admit, young Mr. Motrenko has disappointed me."

"He's useless," Castiglione complained.

Shaking his head, Walt countered, "No. He's an idealist. I told you that some time ago."

Before Castiglione could reply, Walt went on, "And we badly underestimated Kell. It was a stroke of genius, taking the lad under his wing. I'm afraid our boy Nick has been contaminated."

His face showing utter disdain, Castiglione headed for the minibar built into the wall below the room's holographic viewer.

Walt continued, "Kell has given Nick what the lad so desperately wanted: a place in the sun. His blog is watched worldwide, thanks to Kell's appearing on it almost every day."

"You sound as if you approve of what's happening."

"I admire talent wherever I find it," said Walt. "And Kell is a very talented man. He's made an adult out of Nick. And something more: he's given Nick someone to admire, someone to emulate, a father figure."

"Which means Motrenko is useless to us. He'll never assassinate Kell now."

Clasping his hands together almost prayerfully, Walt admitted, "I'm afraid you're right."

Castiglione opened the minibar, yanked out a split of red wine, frowned at the label, then kicked the bar closed again.

"Not to your liking?" Walt asked, barely suppressing a grin.

"None of this is to my liking. Halleck is on my neck night and day. She wants Kell removed! And your would-be assassin has failed us completely."

"Fortunes of war," said Walt philosophically.

"Kell's got to be put out of the way!"

"You've got the resources of the World Council behind you," Walt said. "Why not simply get a few military experts to stage a phony terrorist attack?"

The unopened wine bottle still clutched in his hand, Castiglione shook his head. "Too many people involved. Something that shocking would be investigated. Someone would crack."

Walt agreed. "There's always a weak link in every conspiracy. It's like old Ben Franklin said: three people can keep a secret—if two of them are dead."

Castiglione did not laugh. Instead, he said darkly, "The job has to be done by us."

"Us?" Walt felt a pang of alarm.

"You and me. No one else involved."

"I'm not an assassin."

"But you will be," Castiglione insisted.

Stunned, Walt watched the Italian go back to the minibar, grab a stemmed glass, and start to unscrew the wine bottle's cap.

And he realized that if he helped Castiglione murder Kell, his next victim would be Walter James Edgerton.

Dead men tell no tales.

Christmas Presents

"It's beautiful," said Aditi.

The christmas tree filled the cottage with the aroma of fresh pine. Its crown brushed the living room's low ceiling. The tree was decorated with sparkling bright ornaments and tiny winking lights. At its base lay a handful of colorfully wrapped gift boxes.

It was Christmas Eve. Jordan and Aditi had invited Nick, Rachel, and Dee Dee to spend the holiday evening with them. And Cree, of course. The cottage was too small for overnight guests, so they stayed at the inn in the nearby village.

Now they stood admiring the tree, smiling, warm, happy. Jordan had whipped up a bowl of frothy eggnog and even convinced Cree to have a cup. At Jordan's insistence, Cree had given the other security guards the holiday off.

"It's Christmas," he had told Cree. "Let them spend the holiday with their families."

Cree had nodded reluctantly. None of them in the cottage had family to be with. But he muttered, "The bad guys don't take Christmas off."

Jordan had conceded the point and phoned the local constabulary to ask them to block the road leading from the village to the cottage.

"Satisfied?" he had asked Cree, half teasing. "Cornwall's finest will protect us."

Cree's response was a guttural mumble.

As they crowded the cottage's tiny living room, sipping eggnog in front of the crackling fire that Jordan had built in the fireplace, Aditi said, "Remember to leave room for dinner."

"Dinner's not till seven o'clock," said Jordan, sitting next to her on the sofa. He glanced out the window and saw that it was already fully night outside. "The owner of the inn said his cook was making a special Christmas dinner for the six of us, with all the trimmings."

"And what are the trimmings?" Aditi asked.

Before Jordan could reply, the phone announced, "Professor Rudaki is calling."

"Rudaki?" Jordan responded, puzzled. "Put him through."

Janos Rudaki's image appeared in the viewer built over the fireplace. As usual, he appeared slightly rumpled, his thick mop of black hair askew, his face halfway between a frown and a tentative smile. He was wearing a festive red jacket instead of his usual dark suit.

"Professor," Jordan called cheerily. "Merry Christmas!"

"The same to you," Rudaki replied, "although it isn't Christmas Day as yet."

"Greetings of the season, then. It's good of you to call."

Rudaki's smile turned slightly warmer. "I have decided to give you a Christmas gift."

"You have? How thoughtful of you."

In the slight delay caused by relaying the message off a communications satellite in geosynchronous orbit, Jordan wondered what the crusty professor was up to. A Christmas present?

"Yes," Rudaki said. "You realize, of course, that you are campaigning for my seat on the World Council. I represent the European–North American bloc."

Suddenly alarmed, Jordan answered, "It's nothing personal, sir, I assure you."

"Yes, yes, I understand. Politics makes strange bedfellows and all that."

"I'm afraid so."

"Well, I have decided to retire from my seat on the Council. As of January first, you will be running unopposed."

Stunned, Jordan sank back into the sofa's cushions. "But I thought you said Halleck wouldn't allow you to retire."

Rudaki started to run a hand through his unruly hair, thought better of it. "She insisted I remain on the Council, but the time has come to stand on my own two feet once again. With you stepping in to replace me, I can retire gracefully—and even perhaps go to New Earth to join my daughter."

"Halleck won't like this," Jordan said.

With a careless shrug, Rudaki countered, "She'll live through it. She's a strong one."

Jordan realized that this meant his election to the Council was practically assured. "I . . . Professor, I don't know what to say, how to thank you."

With a knowing grin, Rudaki replied, "After sitting through a few Council meetings, you may not feel so grateful."

"I don't have a Christmas gift to give you in return."

"Get the next mission to New Earth started," Rudaki said. "And make certain that I am included on it."

"I will," said Jordan.

"Good. Now good-bye. And again, merry Christmas to you all." And his image winked off.

"You'll win the election!" Aditi said, radiating happiness.

"Congratulations," said Nick, offering his hand.

"I'd better tell headquarters about this," Cree said, reaching into his trousers pocket for his phone.

Rudolfo Castiglione stepped through the doorway from the dining room and said, "Put your phone away. No one is calling anyone."

Startled, Jordan saw a tall, gangling black man standing beside Castiglione. Both of them had guns in their hands.

conFrontation

++
++

Before Jordan or anyone else could utter a word, Castiglione smiled cynically and said, "I hope you don't mind our entering your cottage through the back door. I thought we should visit you on Christmas Eve."

"With guns leveled at us?" Jordan growled.

Nick stared at the black man. "Walt? What're you doing here?"

Walt looked tense, strained. "We didn't expect you three to be here. Thought you'd be back in the village, at the inn."

Castiglione nosed his pistol at Cree. "I presume you have a weapon."

Looking thoroughly disgusted, Cree jabbed a thumb toward his jacket, resting on the back of a chair by the fireplace. "In my coat."

"Fine. We'll leave it there."

Jordan asked, "How did you get past the police blockade?"

"One little car parked in the middle of the lane?" Castiglione replied, almost contemptuously. "Our satellite imagery showed it clearly, plus the country lanes that wove around it. Your policeman was probably asleep; he neither saw nor heard us."

"So why are you here?" Aditi asked, her voice brittle with tension.

Castiglione sighed dramatically. "I'm afraid there's going to be a fire. This cottage is going to burn to the ground—with all of you in it." He shook his head. "A great tragedy. The whole world will mourn your deaths."

"Walt!" Dee Dee screeched. "You can't—"

"He can and he will," Castiglione snapped. "He has no choice."

Nick took a step toward Walt. "Speak for yourself, man."

"Everybody dies," Walt said, barely above a whisper. "Sooner or later."

"In your case," said Castiglione, "it will be sooner. Within a few minutes."

"You can't expect to get away with this," Jordan said.

"With all the resources of the World Council behind me? Of course I will get away with it. Some faulty electrical connection in your tree's decorations will start a fire while you're asleep."

"You mean while we're unconscious," said Jordan. Pointing at the guns, he asked, "Neural tranquilizers, aren't they?"

"Yes. You will be blissfully unconscious. There will be no pain, I assure you."

Cree took a step and moved in front of Jordan. "You'll have to get past me first."

"No great trouble," said Castiglione, pointing his gun at Cree.

"And me," said Nick, stepping to Cree's side.

"What foolish bravado."

"Wait!" Aditi called. "You're overlooking something."

Castiglione frowned.

Aditi said, "Everything that I see and hear is transmitted back to New Earth automatically. My people are watching and listening to you."

"You're bluffing." But Castiglione's gun wavered ever so slightly.

That was all Cree needed. He slashed out with an edge-of-the-hand chop that knocked Castiglione's pistol skittering across the floor. Nick bellowed like a wild man and leaped at Walt, who fired at him point-blank.

Walt's gun cracked loudly and Nick's body spasmed even as he bowled into Walt. Jordan grabbed for the black man's gun and all three of them tumbled to the floor.

Dee Dee picked up Castiglione's gun while Jordan and Walt

struggled on the floor beside Nick's twitching body. The Italian stood frozen, wide-eyed, as Cree plucked the pistol from Dee Dee's hand, then stepped over and kicked Walt solidly on the side of his head. Walt's eyes rolled up and Jordan scrambled to his feet with the black man's gun in his hand.

Rachel knelt beside Nick's body. "He's dead!" she sobbed.

"No," said Cree, his eyes on Castiglione. "Just unconscious. He'll come around in a few minutes." To Jordan he asked, "What do you want to do with these two?"

Anger surging through him, Jordan snarled, "I'd like to toss them into the ocean, with anvils tied to their ankles."

"Jordan," Aditi said calmly.

"Call the constable's station," Jordan said through gritted teeth, "and tell them we've been attacked by a pair of would-be burglars."

They didn't get to the dinner the innkeeper's cook had prepared for them until hours later. Once the police showed up at the cottage, they were all taken to the station house, where Castiglione loudly claimed diplomatic immunity.

"For armed burglary?" the police sergeant practically spat at him. "Don't be daft."

Castiglione and Walt were locked into a cell. Nick—though still slightly woozy from the nerve jangler—broadcast a blow-by-blow description of the incident via the Otero network, and Cree asked his headquarters in Chicago for a beefed-up security team.

It was nearly midnight when the six of them finally got to the inn, where the cook happily reheated the entire meal he had painstakingly prepared. The innkeeper joined them at the table and listened to their story with grave concern.

"Nothing like this has happened here in living memory," he marveled.

Jordan said, "I'm sorry we weren't able to get here on time."

"Better late than never," said the cook as he deposited a steaming tray of mince pie on their table.

From outside the inn came voices singing, "Silent night, holy night . . ."

"The church choir," said the innkeeper, "starting the midnight service."

Jordan looked around the table at Cree, and Nick, Rachel, Dee Dee, and Aditi. "God bless us, every one," he breathed.

By the time Jordan and Aditi got back to the cottage, they were both tired and filled with Christmas dinner. And wine.

As he turned out the bedroom lights and slipped into bed next to her, Jordan asked, "Is what you told Castiglione really true? Are you sending everything you see and hear back to Adri on New Earth?"

In the darkness he could hear the amusement in her voice. "Almost everything."

"Ah. That's better," Jordan said as he reached for her.

ELECTION DAY

"Congratulations," said Anita Halleck. Her smile looked forced.

Jordan and Aditi were in Boston, where they were watching the election returns on the Otero Network from the comfort of the hotel suite that Carlos Otero had personally selected for them.

With less than half the votes counted, Halleck had called from her home in Barcelona. She sat alone in what appeared to be a comfortable study, dressed in a stylish ball gown and draped with sparkling jewelry. The room was decked with flowers. Yet she seemed far from pleased.

"Isn't this a bit premature?" Jordan asked her image. "The voting isn't completed yet."

"Oh, you've won," Halleck said, her voice flat and cold. "I should have insisted that you and your wife attend the party here at my home."

"A party?" Aditi asked.

"It's due to start in a few minutes. Champagne for the winners, beer for the losers."

Jordan asked, "And which will you be drinking?"

"Champagne," Halleck replied. "I always drink champagne."

"You always win."

The beginnings of a real smile touched the corners of her lips. "Yes. One way or the other."

With a glance at Aditi, Jordan said, "Douglas Stavenger called earlier. He told me that Selene has offered to build one of the starships we're going to be needing."

The tentative smile vanished. "Yes. He called me, too. A very generous offer."

"Too generous to refuse."

Her lips curving again, Halleck said, "I didn't refuse it. Not at all. In fact, I got him to increase his offer. Selene will refurbish the ship you went to New Earth in."

"For the follow-up mission!" Aditi exclaimed.

"Yes. You can return to your homeworld, if you wish."

"I do!" But then she turned to Jordan. "But that will have to wait, won't it?"

Patting her knee, he answered, "I'm afraid so."

"Too bad," said Halleck. "I had hoped to get rid of you for a while."

"Not so quickly."

Halleck sighed. "Ah well. One of the principles of politics is to recognize a bandwagon and get on it before it turns into a steamroller that flattens you. That's called leadership."

"You're not going to oppose sending rescue missions to the worlds threatened by the death wave?" Jordan asked.

"It doesn't seem like a practical course to take. You've become something of a Messiah to the voters."

"Hardly that."

"Close enough. You've created a bandwagon. As the leader of the World Council I have to climb onto it and guide it to success."

Aditi said, "You have the FTL communications technology."

"True enough. That should help us to weld the communities scattered through the solar system into a unified political system."

"With you at its head," Jordan said.

"With the World Council directing it. Don't forget, you'll be a member of that Council." She hesitated a heartbeat, then said, "I won't oppose your crusade to save the alien worlds."

"That's . . . very gracious of you," said Jordan.

"But in return, I need something from you."

"Something? What?"

"Your promise that you will be in favor of my reelection to the Council chair, when we reconvene next week."

"I have no interest in becoming chairman," said Jordan.

Her eyes locked on his, Halleck said icily, "That's not a promise."

Jordan felt his brows rise. "I mean it. You can keep your chair. I won't oppose you—as long as you don't oppose the starship program."

Halleck's smile turned genuine. "Ah. Now you're speaking like a politician."

"Quid pro quo," said Jordan.

"One hand washes the other."

And Jordan realized that he had taken on a whole galaxy of responsibilities.

Almost wearily, Halleck pushed herself to her feet. She looked resplendent, imposing—yet discontent, far from joyful.

"Well," she said, "I have guests waiting for me downstairs. And champagne."

"Wait," Jordan called. "What's happened to Castiglione? Apparently the British government turned him over the World Council's justice department."

"Rudy?" Halleck's expression saddened. "He's been sent to the penal colony in orbit around Saturn. We won't see him for a long time."

"Penal colony?" asked Aditi.

Jordan explained, "The habitat orbiting Saturn began as a place to send political misfits, troublemakers. But its people created their own stable government. They've been an independent nation now for more than two hundred years, much like Selene."

"Rudy won't be on bread and water, don't worry," Halleck said. "He should do quite well for himself out there."

"And the other one?" Jordan asked. "Walt something-or-other."

"Walter Edgerton," Halleck replied. "He's been an agent of our security organization for some years. He was released into our custody."

"And?"

"And given an early retirement. I understand he's writing a book. His autobiography. Perhaps your friend Motrenko will publish it digitally."

"Nick is working for the Otero Network now," said Aditi.

"Is he? How nice," Halleck said coolly. Then, "You really must excuse me. I have to play the hostess now."

And her image winked off.

Aditi stared at the darkened viewer for a moment, then turned to Jordan. "What a strange woman," she said.

"'Uneasy lies the head that wears a crown,'" he quoted.

Brightening, Aditi said, "But she's agreed to the rescue missions. Let's call Adri and give him the good news."

"By all means," said Jordan. But he was thinking, I'll have to work with Halleck, and watch my back every step of the way. Strange bedfellows, indeed.

Then he remembered an old Hungarian proverb: With a Hungarian for a friend, who needs an enemy?

EPILOGUE: Six Years Later

Mitchell Thornberry looked downright wistful as they watched the starship lift off.

There was no bellowing of rocket engines to disturb the scrubby desert landscape. No thunder of raw power. The lenticular-shaped craft, gleaming silver in the desert morning, rose slowly, almost silently, propelled by the same technology from New Earth that produced the almost ubiquitous energy shields.

The tremendous crowd that arced across the desert for miles around fell silent, awed at the majesty of the takeoff of this first mission to rescue an alien civilization from the death wave.

"Ah, if I were a younger man," Thornberry muttered, his eyes following the spacecraft's majestically slow trajectory into the sky.

He was standing high above the desert floor, on the VIP visitor's deck of the White Sands spaceport, beside Jordan, Aditi, the governor of New Mexico, and a small crowd of industrial magnates and politicians. Anita Halleck was conspicuously absent.

Down below them someone in the teeming crowd yelled, "Go!" More voices cheered the rising starship until the air rang with the chant. "Go! Go! Go!"

As if in answer to their plea, the starship arced across the clear morning sky, accelerating now, faster and faster until it was a barely discernible streak of coruscating color against the cloudless blue.

"Go!" Thornberry joined the chorus. "Go!"

"You want to go star-roving?" Jordan asked him, his expression cheerless. "So do I."

Thornberry replied, "Aye, I do, and that's the truth of it." With a shake of his head, "But I can't. Too many responsibilities. I'm pinned to Earth."

"I am, too," said Jordan. Glancing at the VIPs standing all around them, he added in a lower voice, "I hate to think what Halleck would do if I went traipsing off to one of the threatened worlds."

" 'Let us therefore brace ourselves to our duty,' " Thornberry quoted, sadly.

"At least Paul's on his way," said Aditi.

"Yes," Jordan replied wanly. "On his way to the stars."

Paul Longyear had leaped at the opportunity to be named chief biologist on the first rescue mission. Jordan had never seen the Native American smile so brightly as earlier that morning, when he boarded the minivan that took him and the rest of the expedition's biology team to the starship waiting out on the baking desert.

The dwindling dot of the starship finally became too small for the naked eye to see. The launch director's amplified voice boomed across the launch complex, "The launch of Star Mission One is complete. All aspects of the launch are well within design parameters. Godspeed, *Prometheus*."

The huge crowd below them started to slowly, almost grudgingly, disperse to the parking lots neatly spread across the desert floor. The notables on the observation deck began to head indoors to the air-conditioned visitors' center and the cocktail reception that awaited them.

Thornberry heaved a melancholic sigh. "Ah well, the news conference will be starting soon. I suppose we should go in and let ourselves be admired."

Hamilton Cree was surprised to see such a crowd at the Rio Grande Gorge. Cars were parked along the shoulders of the road on both sides of the bridge as far as the eye could see. Vendors had set up tables beneath the bright morning sunlight, offering all sorts of handmade jewelry and trinkets, including replicas of the starship carved from local New Mexico stones.

"It's like a holiday," said his wife. "A regular festival."

Cree nodded, impressed. "They've come to see the launch." And he clutched his five-year-old son's hand a little tighter.

"Do you think we'll see much from here?" his wife asked. "White Sands is a couple hundred miles from here, isn't it?"

Cree nodded at her. His superiors at the agency had given him his choice of Unicorn offices with his latest promotion. To his own surprise, he had picked Albuquerque. And even stranger, he had driven his tiny family to this spot, where he'd first seen Jordan Kell half a dozen years ago.

"We ought to get a good look at it." And he led his wife and child up past the picnic tables and the makeshift lot jammed with cars parked haphazardly, every which way.

"Where's the starship?" Hamilton Junior asked, squinting into the bright morning sky.

Cree glanced at his wristwatch. "Oughtta be coming up over the horizon right about—*look!*"

A streak of silver climbed above the horizon, carving an arch against the cloudless sky that quickly morphed into a thin line that shifted to red, yellow, and finally deepest blue.

"A rainbow!" Cree's wife shouted.

Cree dropped to one knee beside his son. "Look at it, Junior! That's the starship! It's going to another star!"

His eyes fixed on the man-made rainbow as it sped across the sky, Junior nodded solemnly. "I want to go to the stars, too."

Cree smiled and told his son, "You will, Junior. Someday you will."

Dee Dee tousled her boy's hair. "When you grow up, honey," she said. "When you grow up."

* * *

Jordan felt tired, and somehow disappointed. The day had been long and emotionally draining, with a crowded news conference following the starship's launch, then speeches by the assembled politicians—including Jordan, as the representative of the World Council—and finally a long, liquor-soaked luncheon hosted by the governor of New Mexico during which the politicians congratulated themselves on opening a new era of starflight for the human race. And finally a one-on-one interview with the Otero Network's Nick Motrenko.

He was close to exhaustion by the time he and Aditi reached their hotel suite. But as he sat on the bed and bent down to take off his shoes, Aditi touched his shoulder and said, "Adri is calling."

The leader of the New Earth people appeared in solid three dimensions in the viewer on the opposite bedroom wall.

"Friend Jordan," the old man said, "and Aditi, my dear one. I call to offer you my congratulations on your success."

Adri was standing, wearing a long robe of royal blue filigreed with silver threads. His bald, wrinkled face was beaming at them contentedly.

Without waiting for their response, Adri went on, "Perhaps you don't fully appreciate the high accomplishment that you have achieved. The first rescue mission is a significant step in itself, but it is symbolic of something far greater."

"Greater?" Jordan blurted, knowing his word would take an hour to reach New Earth.

With an almost guilty expression clouding his aged face, Adri explained, "You see, this crisis of the death wave has actually been a test of your people's vision and resolve."

Jordan felt his brows narrow and saw that Aditi looked equally puzzled.

"The death wave is a very real and very dangerous problem. Its threat to the less-advanced civilizations is acute, gravely serious. Entire species of intelligent creatures are under a sentence of death unless you people of Earth help them."

We know that, Jordan said to himself.

Adri continued, "But there is something else involved, as well. Something of even greater significance for the human race."

"Greater significance?" Jordan echoed.

"You have led your people to starflight. You have succeeded in one of the most significant steps that any intelligent species can take."

Aditi moved to the bed and sat beside Jordan. The two of them watched Adri's ancient, seamed face like a pair of schoolchildren listening to their tutor.

"A species that achieves spaceflight," Adri went on, "has separated its fate from the fate of the planet that gave them birth. Once a species has spaceflight, it can survive a catastrophe that destroys the world of its birth. No natural disaster on its home planet, no global war or environmental devastation, can drive that species into extinction, for it has created new homes for itself elsewhere in its solar system.

"But in the long term—the *very* long term—the species' eventual fate is tied to the fate of its birth star. If Earth's sun explodes, or merely throws off a supermassive coronal flare, life on Earth, life throughout the solar system, could be wiped out.

"Starflight gives your species a way to separate its fate from the fate of its home star. With starflight the human race can live for untold eons, spreading through the galaxy and giving rise to new intelligences, both biological and electronic. That is why starflight is so important. It guarantees the immortality of your species and its descendants."

Adri fell silent. Jordan started to reply, found his throat was dry.

Aditi said, "And the rescue missions we are undertaking are merely the first steps toward creating a true interstellar civilization."

Jordan found his voice. "We won't get his answer for another couple of hours, at least."

She nodded.

He grasped her wrist and led her to the glass sliders of their balcony. As they stepped into the dark, cloudless, desert night, Jordan murmured, "Astronomy began in the desert."

Gazing up at the thousands of bright pinpoints sparkling across the dark sky, Aditi said, "Yes, I'm sure that's right."

For long moments they stared upward. Jordan pointed out the Dippers, the fainter Dragon twining between them, the lopsided W of Cassiopeia, and, in the opposite direction, Orion climbing above the distant horizon.

"There's a story from the Old Testament," Jordan told her, his voice oddly low, "about God taking Abraham out into the desert night and telling him, 'I will make your descendants as numerous as the stars in the sky.'"

"That must have pleased Abraham."

"I'm sure it did. But I've always interpreted those words in a slightly different way. I think what they mean is that we will populate the stars in the sky. We will become a true interstellar civilization."

Aditi leaned her head on his shoulder. "And we're taking the first step, now."

"Yes, now," Jordan replied. "But it's only the first step."

Above them, the stars beckoned.